The Betting Game 3

By

Bella Dama

Printed in the United States of America

First Printing, 2023

ISBN 978-0-9859752-5-8 Paperback

Bella Dama, LLC
PO Box 480677
Charlotte, NC 28269
www.belladamabooks.com

The
Betting
Game
III

gage off my house for the money I just paid Zeke."

"Stop lying! You have over $200,000 in a private account funded by the father of the baby you're carrying. I guess you're fucking him, too…aren't you?"

"How do you know that? Stay the fuck out of my business, Bitch!"

Shana stormed out.

"Thank you, Angelica," said Matt.

"You're welcome."

"Yeah, thanks," said Thad. "And you too, Damian, for the easiest cash of life…dumb ass."

Matt and Thad hugged Angelica before leaving.

Damian thanked her for preventing him from making the biggest mistake of his life. He was excited to be rid of Shana, officially divorced and with no strings attached. Although, Damian admitted that the thought of a child excited him. Angelica assured him that he'd have his happy ending when the right woman came along. They hugged it out.

Angelica asked Zeke to stay.

"I guess your plan worked," said Zeke.

"It did."

"How did you know it would?"

"Because I knew she was only concentrating on my property."

"It worked like a charm."

"Thankfully."

Angelica knew Shana would be looking for specific information, like the property owner's details, the address of the property and the date of title transfer. So, Angelica tricked her by making sure the address she wanted to see stood out in big, bold lettering. That way, Shana wouldn't notice the additional verbiage stating that the property wasn't changing ownership. Instead, Shana's real property address was listed right below Angelica's in small letters as the real property to which she remained the owner. Angelica was never signing her house over to Zeke. She just made it look like she was so Zeke could collect his money. She also paid the supervisor at the county clerk's office five thousand dollars to confirm the transfer of title when the call came through. Angelica secretly texted her while Zeke was talking to Shana.

"How can I repay you?" asked Zeke.

"Stop betting against me. You'll lose every time."

"I see."

"Are you free later?" she asked him.

"Yes."

"Do you want to come over and talk?"

"Ok...I'll bring dinner."

"Fine by me."

Zeke left smiling.

Angelica invited Elizabeth into her office to go over her schedule for the remainder of the week, especially since she was off the following week for her birthday.

"Scandalous," said Elizabeth.

Angelica laughed at the way she said it.

They went over everything Angelica had on her plate. She assigned Elizabeth some tasks and then asked her to set up a meeting with Cherry, Damian and Zeke after she met with Austin, which she was late for.

Angelica knocked on the door. He motioned for her to come in as he was on the phone. She walked in, closed the door behind her and sat at the conference table, waiting for him to finish.

"Hey...sorry about that," he said, hanging up the phone.

"No worries. My apologies for being late."

"You're good. How are you?"

"Well, and you?"

"I'm ok."

"You look beautiful."

"Thank you," she said, smiling.

They met about the Christmas party, re-launch party, salary notifications and Paris.

"I need to get Asila in here to discuss ideas. The clock is ticking," said Austin.

Angelica called her to schedule a meeting.

"Done," said Angelica.

Afterward, they discussed the numbers for the Christmas bonuses and salary increases starting in January. They decided to increase the base pay incrementally to avoid using all their resources. All employees should reach their new pay rates around May if they stay on trajectory.

"I think a team, including Destiny and Elise, should go to Paris," said Angelica. "Destiny needs to do merchandising and store layouts while Elise can hire a PR team in that demographic and create a marketing strategy."

Austin agreed but wanted Angelica to go as well to oversee things. She could take everyone necessary to make it happen.

"What dates were you thinking?" she asked.

"I'll look and see when we can make it happen."

"Ok."

She reminded him that she'd be out the following week for her birthday and wanted Damian to be in charge in her absence. He had no problems with her decision.

"Big plans?" he asked regarding her birthday.

"Yes. I'll be in Miami."

Austin knew that meant she'd be with Falio.

"Have a great time."

"I will…thanks."

Before Angelica left, she handed Austin his Amex card.

"Thank you," he said, looking a little sad.

"You're welcome."

Angelica was going to say something sarcastic but didn't. Instead, she kissed him on the cheek and thanked him for everything. He hugged her tight and apologized one last time.

Angelica arrived at her office and saw her staff sitting at the conference table. First, she informed them that Damian would be in charge during her absence. He appreciated the opportunity. Next, she assigned projects for each of them to handle.

"Damian…if you need Mr. Zachery for approvals or to discuss any matter, please feel free to contact him."

"Ok."

Lastly, Angelica asked each one about their current projects and issues they were experiencing in their regions. She also wanted to know about any upcoming travel plans.

After the meeting, Angelica asked Cherry to stay behind. Angelica told her everything that had just happened. Cherry couldn't believe Shana was that fucked up.

"I understand why you wanted me to be careful," said Cherry.

"She's just a money-hungry bitch."

"Poor Damian."

"Yeah, I felt bad for him and Matt. She had them both on edge."

"And what about Zeke?"

"He's coming over later to fuck. I'll tell him about Falio then."

"You're nasty."

"I know."

"Does that mean it's over?"

"I don't know, but I can't be with him and Falio. And he has a lot going on himself."

"Just let him down easy."

Angelica just smiled.

"Are you and Q ready for the trip?"

"Yes. He's excited. He's flying out of Miami with the rest of your crew," said Cherry, giggling.

Angelica laughed. She never got tired of Cherry's attempts to sound cool.

Chapter 2
The Last Time

Angelica got home and pulled out a weed can. She turned on some music and began smoking to unwind. Angelica leaned back on the kitchen island and thought about Shana. She smiled as she beat her again at her own game. Then, she thought about her Ballantyne home, Shana's bets and her Tennessee property.

"I need to do something with that property," Angelica said out loud.

Zeke interrupted her thoughts when he texted that he was on the way. So, she hurried and showered. She couldn't wait to jump on that dick.

Angelica heard a knock at the door and opened it wearing a black tank top and bikini panties. He set the food down in the kitchen and pulled her towards him.

"I missed you," he whispered, kissing her neck.

"Show me."

They went upstairs to the bedroom and quickly came out of their clothes. He laid her down and sucked on her breasts. Then, he kissed downward on her stomach until he reached her spot. His hot tongue made her so wet that she grabbed the sheets when she came. Zeke wasted no time sliding inside to feel her pulsating. The feeling was so intense that she scratched him as he stroked deep and hard. He didn't care. She was wet, warm and moving her hips the way he liked. He whispered nasty things in her ear, turning her on even more. It made Angelica do more sexual things.

"Fuck! I don't want to cum yet," he said.

"Give it to me, Baby."

And he did.

Afterward, she said, "That was really good."

"It's always fuckin' good."

After a quick shower, they went into the kitchen. Angelica warmed up the fries in the air fryer and set the table.

"Pretty interesting day," said Zeke.

"It was."

"I didn't know Shana was like that. She's changed."

"No, she hasn't. She just figured out a way to be more trifling."

"I felt bad for Damian and Matt."

"Me too. Neither one deserved that."

Zeke bought a bunch of fried goodness, like fried fish, shrimp and chicken wings. It came with a bag of fries and hush puppies. Zeke also got a side of fried crab. Angelica set out all the condiments and placed the fries in a big bowl for them to share.

"This is good," she said, trying the fish.

"Yes, you are."

Angelica cracked a smile.

"How are things going with you?" she asked.

"Good. I'm finishing the restaurant. It should be open for Valentine's Day."

"That's in four months!"

"I know."

"That's great!"

"And I have a name."

"What?"

"Angelica's."

"Are you serious?!"

"Yes."

"Why?"

"Because you're the first person that didn't have an ulterior motive. Even after learning about my inheritance and the settlement from Diyani, you never asked me for anything or expected anything. Hell…you helped me get the money I needed to finish the restaurant."

"I was just trying to help you figure out what you want. I can't do that for you."

"I get it, but I've had people telling me what I need to do for a while now."

"Diyani?"

"Her, my family, friends…everyone has an opinion."

"And now?"

"Now…I still have to figure out some things, but I'm starting with the restaurant."

"Good. I'm glad you decided to open it."

"Me too."

"Speaking of Diyani, have you heard from her?"

"No…and I should be receiving my settlement money this weekend."

"In one lump sum?"

"All fifty million dollars of it."

"Good."

Then, he brought up Anthony and how he'd been partying like a rock star. He'd been with different women, drinking and smoking. The only time he focused was when he played football. However, the drinking was starting to affect that too. He was a mess.

"He's selling the house he bought for Claudia."

"Does she know?"

"Yes. She signed the papers and told him she wants nothing to do with him."

"Well…she wasn't in it for the money."

"He realized that after the fact and now regrets everything."

"He should've known that."

"He had some reservations."

"Why propose if he had doubts?"

"He loved her."

"Apparently, not enough."

Just then, Angelica received a call from Katrina.

"Hello."

"Angelica!"

"Yes."

"I need you to come to NY tomorrow."

"I can't."

Katrina explained what was happening and what she discovered about Victor's girlfriend, Lyness. She needed Angelica's help to resolve the matter.

"Ok…let me see what I can do."

"I booked the St. Regis suite for you through the weekend."

"But I'd only go for a day…two tops."

"Aren't you attending the ball on Saturday?"

"Yes, but I was going to fly back."

"Mmm-hmmm."

Katrina knew Angelica all too well. Once she arrived in the city, she knew Angelica would stay. So, she reserved her favorite suite at one of her favorite hotels.

Angelica excused herself to call Austin. Austin didn't mind her leaving but asked if she could visit a couple of New York stores and make it a work trip. Angelica agreed and called Katrina back. The jet would pick her up at 8:00 a.m.

"Sorry about all of that," she told Zeke.

"It's ok. Is everything alright?"

"Not really."

She didn't go into detail but just mentioned a friend needed her help.

They adjourned to the family room, where they smoked.

"I have something to tell you, and you may not like what I have to say," she said.

"Does it have anything to do with your date from the engagement party?"

"Yes."

Angelica talked about Falio and their history.

"Damn! That's fucked up!"

"I hear that a lot."

"Your own sister?"

"Yep."

"Oh…he's coming for you alright."

"I know he is, which is why I wanted to be honest with you."

She told him about their upcoming trip to Colorado. She assumed they were officially getting back together. Zeke understood.

"Is this our last rendezvous?" he asked.

"Maybe."

"Then, I'd better take advantage."

Zeke wasted no time getting Angelica back in bed.

Chapter 3
New York City

Angelica arrived at the airport by 7:30 a.m. She conducted business the entire way to New York. She had a conference call with Cherry, Damian and Zeke to assign additional duties since Angelica would be out of town. She also spoke with Elizabeth about rearranging her schedule if she wasn't back in a day or two.

Angelica went straight to Victor's office in Central Midtown. She walked in wearing a royal blue monochromatic outfit: a 2-piece suit with a lace corset top, McQueen heels and a wool trench coat. And she couldn't forget the royal blue Gucci handbag.

"Hello!" said Angelica, walking into Katrina's office.

"Hey, girl," said Katrina, hugging her.

Angelica saw some familiar faces and greeted them. It was Rick, Maggie and Roxy from the club.

"What up, Shorty?" Rick said to Angelica.

"Hey! How are you?"

"Good."

She hugged everyone and listened to what they had to say.

It seemed that Lyness was trying to take over. She increased drink prices and admission, changed the type of music played on the most popular nights and ordered uniforms for staff to wear. Lyness also had her hands in the cash registers every night and wasn't telling Victor what was happening. She lied and said employees were stealing, but the cameras caught her. And to top it off, Victor approved a corporate security team that walked around in designer suits and earbuds. Lyness was working towards replacing the security team he had.

"You know Grem from down the street?" Rick asked Angelica.

"Yeah."

"Well, she almost had him arrested for selling drugs."

"But Victor knows what he does and gets a cut."

"Right. So, I'm not sure what's going on."

"I do, and it's about to get handled."

"My girl."

After they left, Katrina told her everything she discovered about Lyness.

"You know she took you and Claudia off the list for Saturday," said Katrina.

"That bitch!"

"But we put you guys back on under aliases."

"And he doesn't see it?"

"Nope. You know how Victor gets."

"I know, but this is a bit much."

"That's why he has us…to watch his back."

They devised a plan but needed additional assistance from Victor's detective friend, DT Scott. So, Angelica reached out to DT and arranged to meet the next day.

"Well, I'll see you tomorrow," Angelica told Katrina. "I have to go shopping…on Victor."

"Have fun."

Katrina laughed because she knew she was telling the truth.

Angelica loved shopping near East Fifty-Seventh Street and

Madison Avenue. Her first stop was The Smoothie Palace. She ordered a mango papaya smoothie with a scoop of protein. Then, she went up and down Madison Avenue, buying some of her favorite name brands.

Angelica finally made her way to the hotel a few hours later.

"Angelica Zambrano," she told the woman behind the registration counter.

As the woman looked up her name, Angelica saw a familiar face approach the counter to check out. She almost didn't recognize him as he looked like a New Yorker in a black turtleneck, designer blue jeans, a tan wool coat and black Tims.

"Daammnn!" she said, messing with him.

The guy looked at her and laughed. It was Alex.

"Hey," said Alex, hugging her.

"What are you doing here?"

"A little business and a little pleasure. You?"

"Same."

Just then, the hotel attendant came in with all of her bags.

"Damn, girl! Did you buy everything in the stores?"

"No," she said, laughing. "I left some stuff for you to buy me."

They laughed as the woman handed Angelica her key.

"Don't you have people for that?" she asked him.

"What?"

"Return your key?"

"Yes, but I'm quite capable."

They talked a few more minutes before he asked, "What are you getting ready to do?"

"Grab some food. I'm starving."

"May I join you?"

"Sure. Just come upstairs with me so I can quickly change."

"Ok."

Katrina reserved the 3-bedroom Presidential Suite since she knew Claudia was flying in for Saturday's event. This suite was contemporary and classic mixed with chic and elegant. The room had bold, bright colors and had amenities like 24-hour gym access and exclusive spa services.

"Damn, girl...you ballin' like this?" asked Alex.

"Says the almost billionaire."

He laughed.

Angelica took some things out of her suitcase and realized she didn't know where they were going, to dress appropriately.

"Where are we going to eat?" she asked.

"Wherever you want."

She put on her light blue jeans with a long cream turtleneck sweater with a waist slit. She added her new cream-colored Chanel boots and jacket.

"Wow! You look amazing," he said.

"Thanks."

"Where do you want to go?"

"Where were you headed?"

"Check out my new spot. The renovations are finally complete."

"Let's go. We can order in."

He liked that idea.

Chapter 4
Alex's NYC Home

Alex and Angelica rode to Nolita in Lower Manhattan. The driver stopped in front of a red-brick building with green trim around the windows. The concierge greeted them before they entered the elevator. Alex swiped his fob and entered a code. It took them to the penthouse on the top floor with a grand gallery entrance.

"This is beautiful," said Angelica.

"Thank you."

Alex spared no expense in renovating his stunning 6-bedroom, 8-bath penthouse. It had double living rooms with fireplaces, a remarkable chef's kitchen with top-of-the-line appliances and an expansive terrace with lots of seating and a brick fireplace. He had custom finishes, 24-hour amenities, natural sunlight and oversized windows displaying New York's beautiful skyline.

They both decided on sushi from a nearby restaurant, Thai Leng. Alex ordered tons of sushi, soups and appetizers. Then, he showed her all of the upgrades he'd made to the unit.

They settled into the living room near the fireplace. He opened a bottle of wine as they got better acquainted.

"How have you been? How's business?" asked Angelica.

"Good."

Alex owned Newcomer Innovations Group. The company consisted of three businesses under one umbrella. The first business was AppMe, Inc. This business created hundreds of apps with three main streams of revenue. The first was client-based projects. Businesses hired Alex to design their apps. The second was creating apps and selling them to the highest bidder. And the third was creating apps and managing them in-house. Alex didn't sell everything he designed.

The second business was Prism Dev, Inc. This company developed software. Alex hired the best software engineers to develop products in different industries. Again, he made money through client-based referrals, selling to the highest bidder and managing in-house. Both AppMe, Inc. and Prism Dev, Inc. were based out of California.

The third business was Envision Play, Inc. It launched one of the most innovative, internet-enabled handheld gaming consoles on the market. It had a large screen with touchscreen controls, hi-def speakers, online gaming capabilities and screen sharing. These single-unit consoles were sleek, had a variety of accessories and came in multiple colors. However, Alex's company also developed the first complete Full-Dive Virtual Reality (VR) gaming system. In this system, players could fully immerse into the game world by using advanced motion sensors, hi-def audio and special VR headsets. Players could get lost in these alternative worlds and feel like the actual characters in fully interactive environments. The best part was that they could realistically interact with other players in a system set up for player versus player (PVP) play, depending on the game. This side of the business was based in Atlanta.

Alex told her about his current project, which was an interactive fashion app he was doing as a side project. He explained how it'd work, the cost and the estimated profit. Angelica was excited for him.

"You'll hit your billion-dollar mark in no time," she said.

"Actually…we just did."

"Congratulations!" she said, hugging him.

"Thanks."

His sister, Valentina, called him earlier to give him the good news.

"I didn't know you have a sister," said Angelica.

"Yes…she's older than me, married and lives in LA. She and her husband run the LA office."

"Nice."

Alex mentioned going to Japan in a few weeks for a software and gaming exclusivity deal. He stood to earn hundreds of millions of dollars.

"What about you? How's work?" he asked.

She mentioned Phil, the new investor and all the changes they were preparing for. She also told him about the new call center, other products coming to the stores and increasing salaries.

"You came up with all of this?" he asked.

"Some of it."

"And profit margins?"

She answered all of his questions.

"So why did the investment company give you a blank check, not your boss?"

"I don't know, but I researched the hell out of Zarvos Investment Group. I didn't find much except their corporate office is in South America, and the CEO does a lot of investing and donating to charities."

"Maybe you asked all of the right questions."

"Maybe…"

Just then, the food arrived. They took everything out of the bags and set it on the kitchen island. Angelica playfully kept bumping into Alex while serving herself. Alex didn't think she'd eat what was on her plate.

Out of the corner of her eye, Angelica noticed an envelope on the counter.

"Is that the invitation to the masquerade ball this weekend?" she asked.

"Yes. It's a fundraiser event I'm attending for the first time."

"You'll have fun."

"How do you know?"

"I go every year. My friend is hosting it."

"Victor Celani is your friend?"

"Yes. Why do you sound surprised?"

"No reason."

Alex was impressed with the company she kept.

"Now, tell me about this research paper you did on me. I never got a chance to ask you about it," said Alex.

Angelica's last finance class for her Master's Degree was Statistical Data Analytics. She had to find an up-and-coming entrepreneur and analyze their business strategies. Then, she had to outline why they were successful and predict their financial portfolio in ten years. Alex was all the buzz at the time with his Feed Me app. It was an app used to order food from local restaurants with delivery services. It also located different restaurants in the vicinity of a cell phone's GPS for dining in. And because he was a young Cuban entrepreneur, she felt he was the best fit.

"What did you predict?" he asked.

"That you'd be a billionaire by the age of thirty-three."

"I beat you by three years."

"You did."

They talked about his business strategy and a few of his apps that catapulted him into millionaire status. They also talked about the ball, her best friend, Claudia, and his best friend, Jordan.

After their bellies were satisfied, they adjourned back into the living room.

"I have something to tell you," he said.

Alex opened up about his on-again, off-again girlfriend, Kelly. They were off at the moment as he was given an ultimatum. He had until the end of the week to decide if they were off for good.

"What did you do?" she asked.

"Nothing."

"Mmm hmm."

"Why is the assumption that the man messed up?"

"You got the ultimatum."

"Maybe she did something to me and now I can't trust her."

"Did she?"

"Not that I know of."

They laughed as he told her why they were on and off so much.

Alex wanted a family but didn't have much availability. He was busy expanding his company and focusing on his side projects. That was the reason he and Kelly hadn't spent much time together lately. He also felt she deserved the kind of guy she was looking for…attentive, romantic and camera-ready. Alex was living his dream and meeting his financial goals at the moment. He didn't want to choose.

"That's tough because a woman wants to spend time with her man," said Angelica.

"I know but I love what I do."

"I understand."

"But that's not all."

Alex was a private person. He didn't like being in the limelight or being the center of attention. He made media appearances when necessary but preferred to be low-key. Kelly, on the other hand, always wanted to be seen. She was in PR and was regularly testing new theories. She was very good at her job, but he didn't want to be a part of it.

"I want to hold her hand without the click of a camera," he said. "Or kiss her without a flash in our faces."

Angelica laughed. She understood. Her sister, Ariana, was like that.

Alex was a romantic at heart. He didn't want to force it or constantly be reminded of what he needed to do. He wanted to do things on his own and surprise his woman the way his dad did with his mom. However, Kelly had certain expectations and always voiced her desire to be wooed. His sister didn't care for her.

"Why doesn't your sister like her?"

"She thinks she's pretentious."

"Were you with her when we kissed in Miami?"

"No."

"Labor Day when I went for dinner?"

"No."

"When we went to lunch?"

"No."

"Ok," she said smiling.

"I wouldn't do that."

"I had to ask."

Next, Angelica told Alex the whole story about Falio and how he got divorced. Alex responded the same way everyone else did. He couldn't believe her own sister did that to her. They talked about Falio's kids and how they may not be his. Angelica also mentioned how Falio put Alina through law school, helped Asila escape a bad relationship and was currently helping her parents financially.

"Our parents didn't raise us like that," said Angelica. "We were a typical Cuban family that struggled when I was young. I got a full ride to college and made the most of it. I met people along the way who nurtured me and exposed me to the finer things in life. Now, I'm on my journey to bigger and better and don't mind working for it."

"Wow! I never saw any of that coming."

"I know."

"I commend you for stepping up and striving to do better."

"Thank you. I saw my dad come home every night and have dinner with his family. He spent time with us and my mom. My dad still holds my mom's hand to this day. They dance even when there's no music. And he still buys her favorite flowers and snacks."

"That's sweet."

"It sounds corny, but they have a solid foundation. That's what I want."

"It doesn't sound corny. It just sounds impossible."

"How so?"

He pointed out that she was a busy woman. When would she make the time for a relationship? Then, he asked about public displays of affection. She loved PDA. She felt she, too, was a romantic. She liked doing nice things for her man, like buying gifts, candlelight dinners, trips and just loving on him. Her mom taught her how to build up a man so that he wanted to come home every night.

"Sounds nice," he said.

"I think I'll be great at it when I have the chance. And I will make time for my man when the time comes. Until then, I'm hard at work."

They talked and drank wine until the early morning. Angelica wound up staying the night. Nothing happened.

Chapter 5
Fun Day

Angelica woke up in his arms. It was nice. However, she had to leave and get ready for work.

"How long are you in town?" asked Alex.

"Not sure. I was supposed to go back tomorrow."

"Let's hang out today."

"Ok."

She texted Damian and then Cherry that she was staying the week.

Angelica made it to Victor's office by 9 a.m.

"I'm staying the week," Angelica told Katrina, walking through the door.

"I know," said Katrina, laughing.

DT Scott arrived shortly after. They filled him in on the plan. His team had to be ready to move once everything went down. They also looped in Victor's attorney, Arnold, and swore him to secrecy.

After the meeting, Angelica went to the Upper East Side store. She checked on staff and inspected the building to see if adding a bar would be beneficial. Just as she finished, Alex called. He decided to wrap up his work day early to spend time with her.

Angelica told him where she'd be and what time to pick her up.

Alex arrived at the store by noon. He didn't say a word as he watched Angelica work. However, when she saw him, she walked over and hugged him.

"Hi," she said.

"Hi."

"Let me grab my things."

"Ok."

She went to the back and quickly returned.

"Where to?" she asked.

"Wherever you want to go."

One of Angelica's favorite places was nearby, the Met Museum. She tried to visit a couple of times a year. She felt it was the perfect place to start their adventure.

They held hands while Alex listened to her talk about the museum's history in detail. He was pleasantly surprised that she was well-educated and well-versed with artists' names, backgrounds and fun facts. She was turning out to be full of surprises. They even took pictures to remember the moment.

As they were leaving, they stopped by the gift shop. Alex presented his VIP card at the register.

"You're a member?" she asked.

"Yes. Why?"

"You don't strike me as the type to be a member."

"My sister is the fan. She purchased the membership at a charity event."

"I'm starting to like your sister."

They grabbed their things and headed for the door.

"Where to next?" she asked.

"I don't know. I didn't plan anything. I just wanted to see you."

"Is there something you want to see or do?"

"Yes, but you have on too many articles of clothing," he said, laughing.

She laughed as she playfully hit his arm.

"Are you hungry?" she asked.

"I can eat."

"We can stop for pizza at Little Italy on Lexington Ave."

"Ok."

When they walked in, they stood in front of the menu. Alex ordered a medium pepperoni pizza with two house salads, cheese sticks and garlic bread.

"How do you know about this place?" he asked.

"Claudia and I discovered it one night."

She couldn't tell him they were high as hell and had the munchies when they found it.

Alex found an empty table and they sat down. They talked about family, traveling and why he bought the condo in New York.

"Where to now?" he asked after they ate.

"I've been coming up with ideas. Your turn."

"You're better at this…I'm not. I usually keep to a schedule."

"Really? You don't seem like that type."

"Well, I usually do but not today. Today, I'm just hanging out with no direction."

Alex didn't usually do random things. He intentionally planned all of his time. He was a very focused and work-driven individual who even scheduled his downtime and vacations.

"Well, today we're going to explore the city like tourists," she said.

"Ok."

They sat there and came up with a plan. Angelica looked up fun things to do in New York while Alex searched for a map of the city. Together, they decided to visit as many neighborhoods in Manhattan as possible. So, Alex typed the list of places on his phone.

"Since we started on the Upper East Side, we can work our way back to your place," suggested Angelica.

"Ok."

They stopped at The Penrose for an alcoholic beverage. Afterward, Angelica wanted to stop by Dylan's Candy Bar to buy Nina some candy and pick up a few things for herself. Their last stop on the Upper East Side was EarthWorks for a pottery class.

Next, they crossed Central Park on Seventy-Ninth Street and headed to the Upper West Side. Their first stop was The Juke Bar. They had a drink and a shot to warm up. After, they went to Levain's Bakery. Angelica heard great things and wanted to try it. She bought a bunch of baked goods and even walked out eating a chocolate chip cookie. As they rode back to the East Side, Angelica admired the old architectural buildings.

At about 6 p.m., they rode the tram to Roosevelt Island. They just wanted to ride across and return.

"I lost track of time," said Angelica.

"Me too."

"I forgot about rush hour."

"It's ok."

Alex and Angelica weren't in any rush, which meant time escaped them pretty easily.

Alex remembered Cornell Tech was on Roosevelt Island and wanted to check them out. But Angelica knew that was work-related, so they didn't go. Instead, they hopped on the next tram back.

Their next stop was St. Patrick's Cathedral. Angelica loved visiting. It always brought her peace.

"I wanted to get married here," she told him.

"You don't anymore?"

"I don't know."

"Why?"

"Haven't thought about marriage lately."

They sat there quietly, looking around. Angelica closed her eyes and prayed. She made the cross symbol with her hand before they left.

They decided to head towards Times Square. However, before taking in any more sites, they stopped to eat at a Cuban restaurant on West Forty-Sixth Street. They both ordered Cuban sandwiches and a couple of empanadas. While they waited for their food, they had to devise a new game plan. Some of the places on their list were closing soon.

"What are your top three things you still want to do?" she asked him.

"Let's see…"

He took out his phone and saw several missed calls from Kelly. She even texted him, confirming her attendance to the ball on Saturday. He just had a look on his face.

"Kelly?"

He nodded.

"It's ok."

He didn't want to think about Kelly.

They looked at the list and realized they'd done about half the things on it.

"What are you doing tomorrow evening?" he asked.

"Working and then shopping for my birthday."

"When is your birthday?"

"Next weekend."

"Ok. Big plans?"

She was even more honest and told him it was hers and Falio's birthday celebration. His birthday was the day after Angelica's, so they were going to Colorado to spend it together. She was sure they'd be getting back together. He didn't want to hear about them either.

Angelica looked up things to do in Times Square. They decided it would be their last stop for the evening. She found a paint and wine place nearby. So, they headed over before they closed.

After, they went drinking and stopped at Grand Central Station to people-watch.

"Where do you think she's going?" Angelica asked Alex.

"I don't know, but she's in a hurry."

"She's going to see her lover."

They laughed.

"He has to hurry home to cook," said Alex.

"He's late seeing his lover."

"She's running home to see the kids."

Angelica explained that he was supposed to make up out-of-the-box scenarios, not realistic ones.

"Do you ever feel like that's you?" she asked.

"What?"

"Always coming or going. Never pausing to take anything in."

He stared below, watching the people in silence. He thought about his life and her question. The more he thought about it, he couldn't remember when was the last time he stopped to enjoy anything. Then, he turned and looked at her. Without thinking, he kissed her. She didn't stop him.

On their way out, they stopped at Daisy's Flowers. She bought him a single white rose. He was pleasantly surprised and thanked her as they left holding hands.

The last stop for the night was Bowlero. They decided to play a few rounds of pool before she went back to the hotel.

"Did you have fun today?" she asked.

He kissed her.

They kissed until the driver pulled up to the hotel's entrance.

Alex grabbed her things and helped her upstairs, but Angelica rushed him off because of sexual temptation.

When he got back in the car, he called her. They talked until almost 4 a.m.

Chapter 6
The Fun Continued

The next morning, Angelica checked her emails and called the office. She had a conference call with Cherry, Damian and Zeke. She also called Austin as she prepared to head out to the SoHo store.

As she arrived at the store, Alex called her.

"Good morning, Beautiful. How did you sleep?"

"Good morning, Handsome. I napped just fine, and you?"

"Same," he said, chuckling.

They talked for about ten minutes before he rushed off. But not before reminding her that he'd pick her up from the store by four o'clock. They were finishing their fun day activities.

After a long day, Alex was ready to see Angelica.

"Wow, you look beautiful," he told her.

"Thank you."

Alex instructed the driver to take them to the pier. They boarded the helicopter for their 30-minute tour of the city. They each pointed out famous landmarks and places they'd never seen.

Next was a horse carriage ride around Central Park. And although it was pretty chilly, Angelica still wanted to go. So, they went to West Drive and West Fifty-Ninth Street for their one-hour tour around Central Park. They wrapped up in blankets and talked along the way.

"I've enjoyed myself these past couple of days," said Alex.

"Me too."

"I thought about you all day today."

"What did you think about?"

"I've done things with you that I've never done before."

"We just ran around New York like tourists."

"But I've never done that."

"Why?"

"I usually come for business and leave. I don't make a lot of time for fun."

"That's too bad. There's so much to do here."

"I've been so busy with work that I can't remember the last time I had real fun until yesterday."

"What do you and Kelly do for fun?"

Kelly's idea of fun was video blogging an entire workday. She loved being the center of attention and always pointed it out.

"That doesn't sound like much fun."

"It's not for me."

"Why are you with her?"

"It didn't start that way."

"What happened?"

"In the beginning, I thought it was cute that she recorded our first moments. As it continued, I grew uninterested. She wanted to record, blog and post everything. Everyone doesn't need to see every part of my life all the time. I guess I started distancing myself without realizing I was doing it."

"I understand. I feel the same way."

"And now she's coming to the ball on Saturday."

"Why do you sound like you don't want her to come?"

"Honestly…I don't."

"Why?"

"This is going to sound selfish, but I'm having a great time with you. I want to spend as much time with you as possible."

"Awwww…that's sweet."

Angelica changed the subject and talked about Asila's Christmas wedding. He turned around and asked Angelica about her dream wedding. She smiled as she told him some details, like her dress designer, the guest list, the type of flowers, her wedding colors and her wedding party. He didn't have as many details, but he described the feeling he wanted to experience on his big day.

After the horse carriage ride, they headed to A. Maison for dinner. He reserved the private room for a special candlelight dinner.

"For me?" she asked.

"Yes."

Alex ordered a bottle of wine and appetizers. He didn't want to do a pre-set menu not knowing what she liked. Besides, he knew she could eat.

"Tell me about your day," he said.

Angelica talked about some of the problems she was handling and setting up shop in Paris.

"What are your career goals?" he asked.

"I think I've reached it."

"You think?"

"I mean I've always wanted to be a Sr VP of HR before I turned thirty, making six figures. And I'm there."

"And that's all you want to do?"

"Funny story."

She told him about her land in Tennessee. She was uncertain what to do with it but wanted either residual income from it or make a large profit. She knew she wanted to build something important. She also wanted to retire her parents even though she didn't think her father would ever stop working. That was just the type of man he was.

"What did you have in mind for your property?"

"I was thinking of an adult luxury resort. But now, I'm thinking bigger, like million-dollar homes."

"I think you'll need more land than what you have."

"I know."

Angelica wanted to buy Victor's land that he purchased next to hers. Victor wanted to go into business with her, but she wasn't sure it would work out. Instead, Angelica wanted to buy his land piece by piece until it was all hers. Alex looked at land prices in Tennessee on his phone. He was surprised at how cheap it was.

"You're something else," he said.

"Why?"

"You're smart, beautiful, ambitious, fun…you seem like every man's dream."

"I don't know about every man but thank you."

"It's just that I couldn't talk to Kelly about these things."

"Why not?"

"She's not interested in my work."

"You better watch out for women like her. Hire a private investigator."

Angelica said it jokingly but was seriously suggesting it.

Alex talked about his financial goals for the future. He had big dreams. He excitedly talked about a few of his latest projects and what he stood to earn. Alex was also thinking about adding a communications business to his portfolio. Angelica challenged his ideas and gave a little advice. He was getting turned on by her interest.

"Do you want to go clubbing?" she asked after dinner.

"On a Thursday night?"

"Yes!"

"I don't usually do that, but ok."

"We need to stop by my room to get clothes."

When they arrived at her hotel, she started taking things out of the closet.

"What should I wear?" she asked.

"Nothing."

Alex couldn't take it anymore. He was feeling frisky and wanted to be with Angelica. He kissed her until she fell backward on the bed.

"I want you so bad," he whispered in her ear.

"I want you too."

They removed each other's clothes before Alex laid back on top of Angelica. He slowly slid inside of her as they kissed. Angelica started moving her hips when he began quivering. Alex came. Angelica wasn't sure what to say.

"I'm sorry. I have to go," said Alex, getting dressed.

"Wait, please."

But he took off.

Angelica was in shock. That had to be a record for a man ejaculating.

She decided to go to Victor's club by herself. She wanted to check on things with Lyness.

"Hey, Rick."

"Hey, Ange."

"How are things?"

"How do you think?"

"That bad?"

"Yes."

Rick hugged Angelica and then let her in. She went straight to the bar.

"Damn, girl! Don't hurt nobody," said Roxy.

"You know how I do," said Angelica, laughing.

Angelica hung out at the bar and watched Lyness, although she was thinking about Alex. She texted him to see if she could go over after the club, but he didn't respond. Angelica decided to go over anyway to check on him.

Angelica walked into his building wearing a full-length black fur. The concierge called Alex and then let her up. When the doors opened, Angelica slipped out of her fur coat. She walked up to him wearing a sleeveless, black shredded T-shirt dress with a nude bra and panties set underneath. The front was thigh-high while the back was long. She wore black strappy heels, diamond jewelry and wore her hair down.

"Damn!" said Alex when he saw her.

"Why haven't you replied to me?"

"Because that shit was embarrassing!"

"So what!"

"Well, I didn't want your pity."

"Good, 'cause you're not getting it."

Angelica jumped up on him and kissed him. He carried her to his bedroom.

"You're so beautiful," he said.

"So are you."

Alex sucked on her breasts as she rubbed on him. Angelica grew excited with every inch she felt. Alex got so turned on that he was stretched to capacity.

"Fuck me," she whispered in his ear.

This time, he was slightly assertive when sliding inside of her. Her moans and groans were louder with every stroke. He went harder and deeper as her hips moved. Angelica spoke Spanish as it was too good. Alex did the same fucking her intensely. She dug into his skin and constantly kissed him as he gently bit her while pulling her hair. They fucked soft and rough in different positions. However, Alex wasn't expecting her skills when he flipped her over so she could ride him. The gyration and bouncing drove him insane. He knew he was in for one hell of a night. This time, Alex was no short-timer.

Chapter 7
Claudia in NYC

Angelica woke up to Claudia's phone call.

"Hello."

"Bitch, get up!"

"I'm up. Where are you?"

"At the airport."

"What time does your flight get in?"

"I'll be there by ten."

"Ok. I'll meet you at the hotel."

"Get off the dick!"

"Shut up! Bye."

Angelica wasn't expecting her friend to say that, especially since she was lying beside Alex, who heard.

"Sorry about that," she told him.

"I like her."

Angelica asked to take a shower before leaving. He didn't mind and joined her. Angelica looked at his nakedness and fell into temptation. They were both back in the bedroom, indulging in sexual pleasure.

"Oh my God," said Alex.

"What?"

"Nothing."

"Good or bad?"

"Fucking great!"

He hadn't slept with Kelly in about a month, which explained his quickness at the hotel. She'd been busy while he was avoiding her. And Alex didn't think he'd be that nervous with Angelica, but he was. He described the way she moved and how it turned him on. He liked the passion between them.

"What are your plans for today?"

"Shopping!" she said, getting out of bed.

"You love to shop."

"Yes, I do."

"That's it?"

"No. We'll hang out and talk about you," laughed Angelica.

"What will you say about me?"

"I'll tell her about your sex game."

"What about it?" he asked, kissing her neck and rubbing her nipples from behind.

"Will you stop that?"

"No."

He kissed the other side of her neck and slid his fingers between her panties. Angelica was leaning forward against the counter, trying to apply mascara. Alex made it difficult as he began rubbing faster. She quickly set the mascara down as it felt too good.

"Right there," she whispered. "Oh my God…right there."

Angelica couldn't hold on and came. He slid her panties off and fucked her from behind. He pulled her hair as they were both going hard until they came.

"Oh my God…"

"I know."

Angelica got dressed and headed for the door. She had to

leave or they'd be fucking all day.

"Hey," he said before she headed out.

"Yeah."

"Is it ok if I take you both to dinner tonight?"

"Yes…that would be nice."

"Ok."

She went to kiss him, but he grabbed her instead.

"I like you," he said with a sparkle in his eyes.

"I like you too."

She kissed him goodbye and left.

When she got to the hotel, Claudia was at the door trying to open it. The ladies screamed and hugged. Angelica was excited to see her best friend. She had lots to tell her. Claudia also had some stuff to share.

While Claudia got settled, Angelica lit a blunt. She told Claudia all about Alex and how much fun they'd had the past couple of days. She never thought he'd be so down to Earth and fun for a tech guy. He was also humble and innocent of a lot of things.

"And the sex…Amazing!"

Angelica seemed smitten by Alex. Claudia listened to her talk and talk about him. Then, she asked about Falio. She told Angelica that he was planning something big, according to Nico. Angelica assumed a proposal.

"And if he does, what will you say?" asked Claudia.

"Yes."

"And Alex? Does he know about Falio?"

"Yes. And he has someone, too."

It was like their last fling before he reconciled with Kelly and she made up with Falio.

"What are you going to do, Ange?"

"Enjoy him today because his girlfriend will be here tomorrow. She's going to the ball with him."

"That should be interesting."

"I know."

Then, they talked about Claudia and Nico. They'd gotten closer since everything happened with Anthony.

"I've been thinking about marriage and kids a lot more lately," said Claudia.

"With Nico?"

"No! Maybe. I don't know!"

"Damn! Why not? You said you two are good."

"We are but not sure I want his lifestyle for the rest of my life."

"Claude! This is Nico we're talking about. This is what you've always wanted."

"I know…I know. And he's faithful now."

"You spoke about him with such passion last month. What happened?"

Claudia loved Nico but wasn't sure if it was enough. She wanted the high-profile lifestyle that she experienced with Anthony. She missed the social gatherings and exclusive events that she and Anthony attended. She wasn't interested in clubbing and Nico conducting drug deals all the time. And she damn sure didn't want to worry about people coming after him or her. She wanted a different type of life. She knew what street life came with. Besides, her family disapproved of him.

"Wow, Claude. I didn't know you felt that way."

"This is going to sound really messed up, but I think I only want Nico for sex."

Claudia loved Nico but hadn't realized how crazy his life was until they started spending more time together. It was good when she was younger or when they hooked up, but now she wanted stability, safety and financial security.

"You know how Nico is…he won't go around new people. He never wants to take pictures and post them on social media. It's like he wants to be in the background."

"You know he can't be out there like that," said Angelica, making a face.

"I know."

"Have you told him how you feel?"

"No."

"Why?"

"Because I'm afraid I'll lose him."

"But if he isn't who you want, let him go."

"I'm afraid to do that."

"No! You're just waiting for someone else to come along and sweep you off your feet. You don't fool me."

Angelica knew that Claudia didn't want to be alone. Nico was her "just in case" guy, and she didn't want to give him up until the "for sure" guy came along.

Angelica understood Claudia wanting stability. Alex was the first guy she'd been honest with in a while. He was easy to talk to and came from the same family background. He understood her culture, and she liked that.

"I think turning thirty scares me a little," said Angelica.

"I know what you mean. It's like we can't keep partying forever."

"And I do want that one guy…that special guy."

"And a family, a home, a business…"

"So, when do we start? How does it work?"

"I don't know, but I think about my future more and more every day. I see what it looks like. I just don't know how to get there."

"And Nico's not in it? Be honest."

"I don't think so."

"What if he changes?"

"Why hasn't he already if he's capable?

The ladies lay on the floor smoking and thinking about their conversation. Angelica didn't know what to say about Nico. She hadn't realized that Claudia felt the same way about wanting more and settling down.

"I heard Anthony was selling the house. How's that going?" asked Angelica.

"Fine. I signed the papers so he could sell it and told him I didn't want any parts of the money."

"That's cool."

"And Zeke? You haven't mentioned him at all."

"I fucked him before I came and sent him on his way. I told him about Falio and how I was going back to him."

"But you work with him."

"So."

"Girl, I don't know how you do it."

"What?"

"Work with your exes."

"Because I'm no longer interested, so it doesn't bother me."

Chapter 8
Claudia meets Alex

The ladies finished smoking and took a few silly pictures to post on social media. Afterward, they got dressed and left for their shopping excursion.

Their first stop was Harry Winston. The ladies splurged and treated themselves to beautiful jewelry sets, rings and watches. Next, they went up and down Fifth Avenue, shopping at H&M, Victoria's Secret and Zara. But they also visited Louis Vuitton, Gucci and Dolce and Gabbana.

Alex texted Angelica, but she called him.

"Hey, Handsome."

"Hello, Beautiful. How's it going?"

"Good. We've done some damage," said Angelica, laughing.

"Well, I've seen what you can do."

"Not really."

"Are you trying to scare me off?"

"A little shopping never hurt anybody."

Alex laughed at her definition of "a little".

"Where would you like to go to dinner?" he asked.

"I was thinking Serendipity."

"Are you sure?"

"Yes. We don't want anything fancy. We both want a good burger."

"Ok. What time?"

"Seven?"

"I'll be there."

"Ok."

The ladies arrived at the hotel shortly before Alex.

"Well, hello," said Claudia when she saw him.

"Hi," he said, smiling.

"I see what you mean, girl."

Claudia gave him a big hug before they headed out.

Alex listened to them talk about their day as they rode to the restaurant. However, he became engaged when Claudia began grilling him. Alex thought Claudia was funny.

Angelica got excited when she saw the menu. She ordered a double bacon BBQ cheeseburger with fries and a soda. Claudia ordered the same. Alex ordered a bunch of appetizers to share, like mozzarella sticks, wagyu sliders, spicy shrimp and loaded potato skins. He also ordered a truffle burger with double bacon, fries and a soda. They all ordered frozen hot chocolates.

"Damn! You're ordering like you're high," Claudia told Alex.

"A little."

"You smoke?" asked Angelica shocked.

"Sometimes, but I mostly do edibles."

"You didn't know he smoked?" Claudia asked Angelica.

"No."

"And you didn't know she smoked?" Claudia asked Alex.

"No."

"You're welcome."

Angelica couldn't believe Alex dabbled. She was relieved like he was. Smoking was another one of the things Kelly didn't like about him. Alex explained it helped take the edge off when he had to attend important events. He frequently got nervous, so it helped him loosen up.

After dinner, they went back to the hotel to hang out. Claudia asked Alex more questions about Kelly. Then, they talked about relationships in general. Alex was slightly green in that department. He'd only experienced love a couple of times in his life. Most of the women he dated, he strongly liked.

Just then, Nico called Claudia. So, Angelica took Alex to her room to give Claudia some privacy.

"Were you high on our fun adventure?" she asked him.

"Yes."

"Why?"

"I was nervous as hell about hanging out with you."

"Why?"

"Because you're you, and I'm me."

"What does that mean?"

"You're free-spirited and fun. I'm not. But I felt this connection between us and wanted to see if I could have a good time with you."

"Well, you could've said something. We could've been high together."

"I was afraid you'd run off."

"Have you ever not been high around me?"

"Yes. When I was checking out of the hotel and our first time having sex."

"Awww…that makes sense, especially if you hadn't had sex in so long."

"Exactly!"

"Well, I think you're amazing."

Alex playfully pushed Angelica onto the bed and laid on top of her. Things were getting hot and heavy. Angelica unbuttoned his pants and began sliding his pants down with her feet. However,

Claudia busted open the door.

"No fucking right now. Get up!" said Claudia, looking at Alex's exposed butt. "Nice ass!"

They laughed as she left the door open.

"I want to fuck you so bad," he whispered in her ear.

"I like it when you talk dirty to me."

"I do when I'm around you."

They fixed themselves and went back into the living room. Alex stayed for about another hour before he decided to leave.

"It was a pleasure meeting you, Claudia."

"You too, Alex. And I'll be seeing you around."

"I hope so."

Angelica went to walk Alex downstairs but stopped in the gym first. She was horny and had to fuck him. So, they went into the ladies' locker room.

"What are we doing…"

Angelica sat him down on the bench and got on top. Her hips moved in a slow circular motion while they kissed. Alex took off her shirt and sucked on her breasts. Her head fell back as she was getting turned on.

"Fuck me," she whispered in his ear.

Alex stood up and dropped his pants. Angelica took off her panties, turned around and bent over.

"Is this what you want?"

"Yes!"

Alex slowly slid in and out of her wetness. She lifted her leg to feel him deep inside. Alex was so aroused by her body movements that he fucked her harder. That was when she decided not to play fair and threw some tricks into the mix.

"You're amazing."

"I know."

He laughed as they got dressed and left.

Angelica and Claudia got dressed and went clubbing. She sent Alex a picture of her outfit. He replied with an eggplant emoji.

Chapter 9
Masquerade Ball

Every year for Halloween, Victor threw his annual masquerade ball at Club Savvy. His club was always filled with the most elite ready to drop loads of cash for this charity event.

Outside were roaming searchlights, giant masks and tons of balloons as guests received the "red carpet" treatment. Inside was always grand and luxurious, with large crystal chandeliers, a draped ceiling and enormous masks along the walls. This year, the colors were red, white and gold. That meant red and gold lighting everywhere, large centerpieces with florals and feathers and smoke on the dance floor for that mysterious illusion.

Angelica and Claudia had gone the past few years. This year wouldn't be any different.

"Hey, Rick. You look good in your suit."

"Thanks, Ange. How are you doing, Ms. Claudia?"

"I'm good, Rick. Thanks for asking. How are you?"

"I'm good." Then, he turned to Angelica and said, "Yo' boy is in rare form tonight. Be careful."

"Everything ready?" asked Angelica.

"Yep."

"Ok. Here we go."

Rick hugged her and let them in.

Angelica and Claudia received several looks as they entered. Angelica wore a stunning red 3D floral appliqué gown with a thigh-high split. The top was fitting with a plunging V sweetheart neckline. The skirt had multiple layers of red tulle, adding a dramatic flair with a chapel train. She wore a quarter-length red fur coat, Alaïa's red satin heels and her hair was down. Her mask matched her dress.

Claudia wore a nude-colored dress with bronze sequin appliqués throughout. It had spaghetti straps, a plunging V-neckline and no back. It fit her body in all the right places and had a chapel train. She wore it with a black fur coat, TF bronze heels and wore her hair down. Her mask matched her dress.

"I'm going to find Victor," Angelica told Claudia.

"Are you sure that's a good idea?"

"Yep."

"Good luck. I'm going to get a drink. Let me know if you need me."

"I will."

Angelica walked around the club. She stopped by the bar to speak to Roxy and Maggie. They hugged and informed Angelica of what was happening.

"Damn girl...you look hot," Roxy told Angelica.

"Thanks. Have you seen Victor?"

"No. But we've seen Lyness. She stuffed her bra twice with $5000 each time."

"That's ok. It all ends tonight."

Roxy handed Angelica an earbud so that DT Scott could record everything when it was show time.

Claudia approached the bar on the opposite side of the room. Just as she ordered a drink, a remarkably handsome man approached her. He was tall with sultry brown eyes, soft brown hair slicked back, a well-groomed goatee and kissable lips.

"Hello," said the stranger to Claudia.

"Hello."

"I'm Bronson."

"Claudia."

"Nice to meet you, Claudia."

"Likewise."

"May I have this dance?"

"Sure."

He spun her around the dance floor a few times before wrapping his arms around her.

"So, Claudia…what is a beautiful woman like yourself doing here alone?"

"Who said I'm alone?"

"Well, I'm dancing with you, not him. Why is that?"

"Because he is a she. I'm here with my best friend, Angelica."

"Even better. I get you all to myself."

Bronson laid it on pretty thick. Both of them flirted, talked and laughed as they danced.

Angelica finally spotted Victor and went to him.

"Victor."

"Angelica."

"How are you?" she said, hugging him.

"Well, thank you. And you?"

"I'm good. Is there somewhere we can talk?"

Before he could say anything, Lyness said, "No. And how did you get in here? I took your name off the list."

"You don't run shit."

"Rick and his whole team are fired! They're just a bunch of thugs anyway."

"Victor! Aren't you going to say anything? Those thugs, as she called them, are your friends."

"She's joking," he said being nonchalant. "No one is getting fired. Please stay and enjoy the party."

Angelica went to say something, but Lyness kissed him, distracting him. She looked at Angelica while doing it.

"Oh, hell no! This bitch has to go!" Angelica said to herself.

She stormed off to look for Claudia. As she passed by the dance floor, a man with a full-face gold mask stopped her.

"Hello, Beautiful."

"Hello."

"What's wrong?"

"I'm agitated."

She tried to leave, but the man wouldn't let her. Instead, he escorted her onto the dance floor and held her close.

"I could have you sent to the dungeon for doing that," said Angelica.

"I'll take that chance."

"And what shall I call you?"

"Adventurous."

"Well, Mr. Adventurous…I have to go find my friend."

"No, you don't. You have to dance with me."

Angelica's mystery man held her close as they danced, staring into each other's eyes. He twirled her around and dipped her. It was sexy and slow…intense and passionate…very mysterious since he had on the mask.

"Thank you for the dance," he said, kissing her hand before walking away.

Claudia found Angelica and snapped her out of the moment.

"Girl…you'll never guess who I met."

"Who?"

"Bronson Wells."

"Really?"

"Yes. And Alex is here."

"Where?"

"Come on."

Angelica saw Alex standing alone.

"Hey, Handsome. You're here alone?"

"Yes."

"What happened to…"

"She had another engagement."

"Good."

Alex saw Bronson and greeted him. Then, the four of them went dancing. All the while, Angelica's mystery man was watching her.

As they were dancing, Lyness and Victor asked to speak to Angelica. She texted Katrina that it was time.

"Excuse me for a moment. I'll be back," Angelica told them.

As she followed them to Victor's office, she discreetly placed the earbud in her ear for Katrina and DT to hear and record.

Chapter 10
Victor's Office

Walking through the door, Lyness started with her antics.

"Tell her, Victor!"

"Tell me what, Victor?"

"Angelica, I'm gonna need my black card back."

"Ok."

"And I'm going to need all of my money back.

"What money?"

"You know…the money I gave you."

"No, Victor…I don't know what you're talking about."

"Are you listening to him?" asked Lyness.

"Sure."

Victor didn't like her ignoring him.

"Angelica! Did you hear me?"

"Yes!"

"Well, then…what are you waiting for?"

"For you to finish."

"Finish what?"

"Yelling and screaming."

Victor kept yelling while Angelica just agreed. She wasn't engaging in the conversation or answering any of his questions.

She was on her phone texting Katrina. She wanted to be sure all of Victor's assets were frozen. She didn't want any transactions in or out. She was getting ready to push Lyness to her demise.

"Ok. Well, thanks for the talk. I'll see you tomorrow," said Angelica, ready to walk out.

"Oh no! You aren't going anywhere," said Lyness, blocking her.

"Move bitch! Get out the way!"

"Make me!"

Angelica obliged and pushed her out of the way. Victor didn't like that.

"Angelica!"

"What, Victor?"

"I'll cancel my card!"

"Ok."

"As for the houses, I'll get the money back. Lyness found a way out of the contracts."

"Do you even hear yourself right now? Do you recognize who you are anymore? Why is she looking at your financials?"

"Because I trust her."

"Like the others?"

"Others? What others?" asked Lyness.

"Angelica!"

"Victor!"

"You're just mad because I don't want you. And I don't want you to be a part of my life anymore!"

"I'm ok with it. Because at the end of the day, I get your billions. And as for your money, it's frozen. You can't buy shit, cancel shit or anything else with your money. So, bye."

"Wait a minute!" said Lyness. "You aren't walking out of here with his money! Those billions belong to me!"

"And how so? Did you work for them? Did you put in the

time, blood, sweat, tears…or energy? No! You just fucked him and think you're entitled because you opened your legs," said Angelica. "I beg to differ."

"Well, isn't that what you did?"

"Yes, but I'm much better at it than you," said Angelica, winking.

Lyness explained that she was working with an international corporation with tremendous financial backing in which she could purchase the homes.

"So, there won't be any breach of contract," said Lyness.

"That's fine as long as you understand you'd be purchasing at the retail price, not the purchase price. And he still wouldn't get his money."

"Why not?"

"I still have to release the funds after the purchase. Didn't you read the contract?

"Yes, but you will since you're keeping the biggest house."

"Oh, but I won't. And what's the name of the international corporation?"

"I don't have to answer you."

Just then, his attorney, Arnold, walked in.

"I invited Arnold to join us so he can explain everything," said Victor.

"Tell me the name of the corporation, or I won't release his money," said Angelica.

"You don't have the authority to do that," said Victor. "Right, Arnold?"

"Well, actually…she does."

Angelica asked Arnold to read the addendum Victor wrote for himself that stated Angelica approved or rejected all transactions made once the agreement went into effect.

Lyness became livid. She told Victor a few choice words and

then told Angelica the name of the corporation. Angelica repeated the name so Katrina could find out more about that company.

"Don't bother because I won't approve or release the funds," said Angelica.

Lyness got angry with Victor, who in turn got angrier with Angelica.

"Give me my money!"

"No!"

"I don't need you!"

"Good!"

"Angelica!"

"Victor!"

"Arnold, I want her off of everything!" said Victor.

"I'm afraid I can't, sir."

"Why?"

"We wrote an iron-clad contract. You will lose everything if Angelica releases anything."

"How stupid could you be to sign that contract?" Lyness asked Victor.

"Do not use that tone with me!"

"Arnold, what can I do?" asked Victor.

"Nothing, sir."

"I need to release her from being my guardian over MY money."

"Well, if you need more money…"

"NO!" yelled Angelica, not letting him finish.

Katrina warned Angelica that she wouldn't like what Arnold was about to say.

"Unfortunately, Angelica…this one you can't stop," said Arnold with a check in his hand.

"What are you talking about?"

Arnold received a call to sell the 10,000 acres he purchased in

Tennessee. He forgot to include it in the contract because it was in the process of being purchased.

"But Arnold...I didn't call you to make that sale," said Victor.

"Oh...that was me, Dear," said Lyness, smiling.

"How the fuck did you know about it?" asked Angelica.

"Victor told me."

"Well, technically, you committed fraud," said Arnold. "And Angelica can press charges."

"Angelica...you can't do that!" said Victor.

"I can and will unless that land is returned immediately and she leaves. She's stealing from you, Victor. Why can't you see that?"

"I'm not going anywhere. He's my nest egg," said Lyness.

"Nest egg?" asked Angelica. "Do you hear her, Victor?"

"I made the call," said Victor.

"If you do that, I'm done with you."

Angelica looked him in the face and began talking to him. She pointed out several things about Lyness that made sense. Lyness saw that Victor was contemplating things and got right back in his head.

"Baby, don't listen to her. She's poison. Please sign the paper so I won't go to jail."

"Arnold, where do I sign?"

Angelica looked disgusted.

"Ten million! That's what you sold the land for?" Victor asked Lyness.

"What!" yelled Angelica.

"Honey, we discussed this. It was for that thing you said you were buying me...remember?"

"Yeah, but you sold it for less than half the purchase price. I lost a lot of money."

Victor was mad, but he still didn't say anything to her. Lyness took the check from Victor and endorsed it.

"You're just going to let her do that?" asked Angelica.

Katrina chimed in and told Angelica everything about the international corporation that Lyness supposedly worked with.

It turned out that Lyness was actually married to a European man named Edgar. They went around scamming money from the rich. They pretended to fall in love with their victims while siphoning money into shell accounts in the Cayman Islands. They were in the States doing a job before heading to another country. Katrina and her computer friend were able to access several accounts, totaling over $650 million. They also found receipts for two plane tickets to South America.

Angelica told her to take it all and send it to a dummy corporation. However, they couldn't because the accounts would alert Edgar and Lyness when any activity occurred. So, Angelica had to stall until the police arrived at Edgar's location. They were both going down.

"Ok, Victor…I'll release your money as long as Arnold deposits that check into your account," said Angelica.

"But Angelica…you can't or he'll lose everything."

"I understand, Arnold, but trust me. This is what Victor wants."

"Yes, it is," said Lyness. "But what guarantee do we have that you'll do it once I give him the check?"

"You don't."

"Give them the check," said Victor. "I trust them."

As Arnold scanned the check and sent it to Katrina, Angelica went over her terms and conditions for releasing his money. She hoped it gave Katrina the time she needed to work her magic.

About fifteen minutes later, Victor received a bank alert regarding the ten million dollars. He received another alert for $650 million. Lyness's eyes lit up. That was until she received an alert that her money was gone. She yelled really loud. DT Scott, along with other law enforcement agencies, busted through the door to take her into custody. Before leaving, Angelica reached into her bra and took the $10,000 back.

"I can't believe this," said Victor.

Angelica told Victor everything about Lyness and her husband scamming people. She told him what Lyness was doing in the club, including taking cash from the register. Victor couldn't believe how oblivious he'd been. Lastly, Angelica told him to return the $650 million to their victims. He agreed.

"Victor, can I speak to you alone, please?" asked Angelica.

DT agreed to come back in the morning for their statements and everyone left the room.

"They picked up her husband in Texas," said Angelica.

"I can't believe it," said Victor. "Thank you."

"You're welcome."

Victor sat in silence.

"I feel like such a fool."

"Victor, stop! You just believe in love."

"But my actions were foolish."

"Yes, but you have a big heart when you love someone."

"Why do you put up with me?"

"Because you're my friend."

"Would you put up with me if I was poor?"

Angelica started to walk out, but he stopped her.

"I'm sorry. I know you did everything you were supposed to do. You stayed through the humiliation, shit talking and my nastiness. Thank you."

"You're welcome."

Victor gave her a big hug. He went to kiss her, but she pulled back.

"I'll see you tomorrow," she said.

She heard glass smashing as she closed the door. She knew he was pissed.

Chapter 11
After the Ball

Angelica was headed back to the party when she got pulled into a dark corner. She saw the half-masked man and wasn't afraid. He backed her up against the wall and got really close. He held her hands as he softly kissed her neck. The touch of his lips sent chills throughout Angelica's body. She couldn't resist him as he moved from her neck to her lips. They kissed with such intensity. Angelica was getting turned on as his hand slowly slid up her thigh to her butt. It was electrifying.

"I can't wait to fuck you," she said.

However, the man didn't reply. Instead, he left. Angelica wasn't sure why Alex ran away but figured he was trying to be mysterious. So, she fixed herself and found Claudia.

"Is everything ok?" asked Claudia.

"Yes."

She told her what just happened.

"It wasn't Alex," said Claudia. "He's been here with us."

"Damn! Then who was that wearing the same mask."

"I don't know."

Angelica wasn't overly concerned and returned to the dance floor with Alex.

Bronson invited them to Club Amnesty. Claudia was in, but Alex and Angelica wanted to go back to his place. However, before they left, Angelica pulled Bronson aside and gave him "the talk" about caring for her friend. She warned him of the consequences if something happened to her. He promised that she was in good hands.

Alex and Angelica were riding in the back seat when she slid her hand down his pants. She rubbed on him, hoping to wake him up. He tried opening her legs, but Angelica kept them closed. She wanted to please him. Thankfully, it was a very short ride. Alex was horny as hell.

When the penthouse doors opened, they began removing his clothes. They made it to the living room, where Alex unzipped Angelica's dress and watched it fall to the floor. He bit his bottom lip when he saw her in a lace lingerie set. She slowly unsnapped her bra, walking towards him. She took off her panties and sat on top of him.

"I've been waiting for this all night," he said.

"Fuck me."

Angelica slowly moved her hips as they became one. He grabbed her by the waist and started talking in Spanish. His breathing became faint as she held onto the back of the sofa, rocking back and forth. He was so turned on that he eventually came.

"Do you want to smoke?" she asked him.

"Sure."

They changed into some of Alex's clothes and went outside onto the balcony. He turned on the heat lamps along with the fireplace.

"I have something to tell you," he said.

"I'm listening."

Alex had been talking to his parents and sister about his relationship. His parents felt he should give it one last chance to see if Kelly was who he wanted.

"Let me ask you something and be honest," she said.

"Ok."

"Would you have gone back to her if you didn't run into me this week?"

"Honestly…probably."

"Why?"

"Out of habit, to be honest."

Alex told her about the ultimatum. Kelly wanted to get married and start a family. He just wasn't sure he wanted to do it with her. Alex didn't want to be rushed or forced into a decision. So, he took a sabbatical to clear his head. He decided to finish his New York penthouse to get away and figure some things out.

"My father said that sometimes we have to do what is right regardless of our happiness," said Alex.

"I get that, but this is the second time you've said you want the same things she does but not with her."

"I know…and I know it sounds crazy."

"No. It just sounds like Kelly's not the one, and you deserve to be happy with the right one."

"What does that really even look like?"

"Well…your meaning is different from everyone else's."

They talked about love and what his ideal life looked like. He told her what he'd always dreamt of.

"Don't lose sight of that," she told him. "Your family is forever and will be there for you regardless of your decision. Don't compromise your dreams and happiness, especially if it means losing who you are."

"I don't want to."

"Don't."

Alex momentarily got quiet and then said, "You know…I've

talked to you more about my problems than anyone else. And I've been honest with you."

"Well, you don't have to lie to me. And you say it like it's a bad thing."

"No…it's just most women wouldn't stick around. But not you."

"I'm not most women."

Angelica, in turn, was honest about Falio possibly proposing, according to Claudia.

"Will you marry him?"

"Yes. He's been there for me my whole adult life."

"Does that make you obligated?"

"No, I love him."

"Yet you're here with me."

"I am."

"How do you do that? How do you marry someone after our time together? Because I know you feel what I feel."

Angelica did like Alex. He turned out to be different than she anticipated. However, they both had situations and she wouldn't leave Falio for the unknown.

"Do you love Kelly less because you're with me?" she asked him.

"No."

"And are you still thinking about going back to her?"

"Yes."

"Then, it sounds like we're both doing it. Not just me."

"But you're talking about marriage."

"And I've known him longer."

Alex got up and quietly looked over the balcony. He knew she was right, but a shift had taken place within him. Angelica opened him up to a whole new way of feeling, thinking and speaking.

"This is perfect to me," he said high as hell. "This! Us! It makes sense. This is how I want to be with my wife...honest, respectful and trusting. I want to be excited to discuss new projects and she gives me input. I want her to be my best friend and lover at the same time. I want to wrap my arms around her sexy ass every night. I want to try new things, like having sex in a ladies' locker room at a hotel gym. I want us to travel together, make money together and I want to think about her all day long when she's not in my presence."

"I understand and it sounds wonderful, but we have to be realistic. Falio is sure about me whereas you aren't sure about anything. And I'm second to no one."

"But I'm sure about you."

"And what does that look like? Where do I fit?"

The discussion was short as their feelings were way too premature. She felt his newfound awakening was genuine and sexual.

"You know...I didn't know what my wife looked like. I didn't know that I could have these feelings. But I do now. You changed that."

She caressed his face and kissed him.

Alex didn't want to waste any more time. He led her to the shower where he wrapped his arms around her and stared into her eyes. He just kept thinking it was their last night together as the water rained down on them.

"Stick your tongue out," she told him.

Angelica wrapped her lips around his tongue and slid back and forth while gently sucking. His fingers dug into her back as she imitated sucking dick. Then, she opened her mouth and kissed him. Alex couldn't control himself and slid his finger between her legs gently rubbing her clit. She tried massaging him but the more he rubbed the more she wanted to come.

"Damn, baby...you're gonna make me cum."

They got out and went to his bed. Alex threw caution to the wind as he was feeling courageous. He kissed her body until his tongue spread her lips apart to taste her.

"Shit!"

Alex loved how her body reacted to his tongue. She grabbed the sheets as her back arched up the more he sucked. The nastier she talked the harder he went.

"Baby…" she said as she came again.

He held her down as she moved intensely. He made sure to taste all of her goodness. Then, he took his time with Angelica. Their sex was passionate and intense. And he became so comfortable with her that he tried new things. She wasn't sure what happened but loved this version of him.

Chapter 12
He's Back

The next morning, Alex held Angelica in his arms. He didn't want to let her go.

"Thank you," he told her.

"For what?"

"Opening my eyes, having fun and going on this great adventure."

"You're welcome."

Around ten, Angelica left and went to the hotel. She had to check on Claudia and change to go see Victor.

Angelica went straight to Claudia's room. She jumped in the bed, but to her surprise, Bronson was there.

"Hi, Bronson."

"Hey, Angelica."

"Damn, Biatch! You look like you haven't slept all night," laughed Claudia.

"Girl…"

"I'll be right back," Claudia told Bronson.

Claudia and Angelica went to Angelica's room to hear about her night.

"Damn, Ange…it sounds like he fell for you already."

"I know, but what am I supposed to do?"

"I don't know, but that's tough."

"Well, he's going back to Kelly. So…"

"Yeah, but you know she ain't you."

"I know."

"I'm just saying…you both are feelin' each other."

"I know, but I can't tell Falio I'm not going to be with him because I had fucking amazing sex with Alex. You know our history."

"I know, but you can't act like you don't feel something for Alex."

"How's Bronson?" asked Angelica, changing the subject.

"Mmm hmmm."

Claudia recapped her evening and why he was still there.

"So, wait! You didn't sleep with him?"

"No."

"Shocking!"

"I know!"

"What does that mean?"

"I don't know, but I'm hanging out with him again today. We're going to see his sister's new place and then have lunch."

"Meeting the sister?"

"Yes!"

"Are you going to sleep with him?"

"I don't know. We'll see how the date goes."

"Well, I'm going to see Victor."

"Is he ok after everything that happened?"

"No, but he will be."

"Ok."

Angelica showered and left. She arrived at Victor's office an hour later.

"How is he?" Angelica asked Katrina.

"Better but not completely ok."

She nodded.

"And DT Scott is on his way."

"Ok."

Angelica walked into his office and saw him sitting at his desk.

"Victor...how are you?"

"I'm pissed, but I'm back. Update me on things."

Angelica sold all of the properties in Charlotte, tripling his money. She asked Katrina to transfer everything back to him.

"I taught you well," he said.

"Yes, you did."

She updated him on the Paris properties. She sold all but one.

"I think I'll keep that one," he said.

"Why? You already have two."

"I just sold one for five times what I paid. So, I'll keep the other to entertain."

He thanked her for being there and dealing with his crap.

Just then, DT Scott arrived. He got their statements and updated them on the case.

"How did you find Edgar?" Victor asked DT.

Texas authorities got a tip about Edgar and started investigating him months ago. They had no real leads until DT ran Lyness's name. She came back as a known associate of Edgar's. So, DT spoke with the leading officer in Texas and coordinated his takedown since they were on the clock.

"You guys did an amazing job," said Angelica.

"Thanks."

Victor asked for the names of the victims and the amounts they were owed. He wanted to personally return their money to each victim. DT assured him he'd have what he needed by the following week.

After he left, Angelica wanted an update on the Tennessee

property.

"What's happening with the land Lyness sold?"

"I have Arnold looking into it."

Victor wanted to know who purchased it so he could buy it back.

"What if they don't want to sell?"

"Everyone has a price."

"What should I do in the meantime? Does that mean I need to find land elsewhere?"

"Not yet. Let me get back to you."

Angelica became furious. She hadn't realized how much she wanted it until that very second. Victor saw her face and reassured her that it would be hers.

Next, they discussed Angelica's financial portfolio. It was coming up on her third year of investing with Victor and he wanted to know her next steps.

"You've done well for yourself," he said.

"Thanks to you for taking a chance on me, but I still can't believe it's mine."

"Why?"

"I've handled millions of dollars for others but never for myself. My account has never had that many zeros."

"Well…technically, you've had it. You just couldn't touch it for the first three years. Now, you can actually withdraw some money and put it into your bank account."

"Thank you for everything," she said, hugging him.

"You're welcome."

Angelica got emotional because her finances were starting to fall into place, just like Victor said they would. And she never told a soul.

When Angelica agreed to start a real estate management company for Victor, she had no clue what she was getting herself into.

She thought she was just helping a friend by simply putting the company in her name while he provided all of the staff and resources. However, she quickly learned it was also a way to create wealth for herself.

Victor invested in extravagant real estate all over the world. He'd acquire luxurious mansions, chateaus and villas in clusters of fifteen or more for a deep discount. Then, teams of real estate agents, brokers, attorneys and administrative staff created listings for each cluster purchased. Different teams worked on different listings, according to the demographics. And as a thank you, Victor allowed Angelica to keep one property from each listing.

In her first year, Angelica wasn't sure how to make lots of money. She'd select cheaper homes because she didn't want to seem greedy. But by the second year, Angelica got smart and took Victor's advice. Each time Victor was on one of his escapades, Angelica kept the most expensive properties. She sold them for a premium, earning a hefty profit. After three year of selling and investing, Angelica was worth fifty million dollars.

The other thing Victor did for Angelica was invest three million dollars into stocks, bonds and start-up companies. He showed her how to select potentially high-money makers. Again, the catch was that Angelica couldn't withdraw any of the money she'd made. She had to keep reinvesting for the first three years to prevent prematurely losing money. Three years was a sufficient amount of time to see if the companies would be successful or not.

"Your birthday makes three years," said Victor. "What would you like to do? You can cash out, stay on your path or leave some and take some."

Angelica wanted cash easily accessible to purchase the Tennessee land when it became available.

"I don't want to cash everything out. I just need enough for Tennessee."

"Ok. You're up to twelve million from your start-up companies. You can pull out nine and keep three to reinvest," said Victor.

"Ok, but I still need six."

"Why fifteen if the land sold for ten?"

"To account for extra cost and taxes."

Victor promised to show her a few tax tricks.

Angelica decided to look at her investment properties for the additional cash. She wasn't touching her stocks, bonds and mutual funds. And she agreed to reinvest three million dollars in five new start-up companies.

As a rule of thumb, Angelica didn't have more than five investment properties at a time. She currently had two homes in California, one in Florida, one in the Caymans and one in Vegas. However, the properties Angelica decided to keep were growing as well. She currently had the Ballantyne home in Charlotte that she was slowly moving into, a home in Canada, one in Massachusetts and her Paris home. She was leaning towards keeping the two homes in California and the one in Vegas. Not to mention, she had her condo in Miami and the house Austin bought her.

"I've decided to sell the house in the Caymans."

"What about one of the homes in California?"

"Not right now."

"Ok. You'll earn five million after selling the house in the Caymans."

"That's great!"

"And it's just enough for what you need."

"When will it be deposited?"

"The business day following your birthday."

"Ok."

Victor showed her a list of new start-up companies to invest the three million dollars. After calculating the financial risks of her top five picks, Angelica selected the three companies where Victor could reinvest the money.

Then, they discussed the ball.

"Someone really likes you."

"Who?"

"I need you to meet with someone," he said, smiling.

"Who?"

"A colleague."

"Who is it, Victor?"

"Someone who can take you to the next level. Is that still what you want?"

"Yes."

"He can help you develop the Tennessee property and turn it into hundreds of millions of dollars."

"But I don't have the land anymore."

"But you will. And don't tell him that when you see him at six."

"Today?"

"Yes…today."

"But I had…"

"What do you want, Angelica?"

"Ok…six o'clock."

"But be careful."

"You can't tell me to go and then say be careful."

"I didn't mean it in a bad way. I meant he is smitten by you. I don't know what you did, but he has it bad."

Just then, her phone rang. It was Alex. She stepped away for a moment to speak to him.

"Hey."

"Hi. Am I interrupting anything?"

"I'm still in my meeting. How was your flight?"

"I didn't leave."

"Why?"

"I wanted to spend one last night with you. I figured I could drop you off in Charlotte in the morning."

"Ok…but I have a meeting at six. After that?"

"I look forward to it."

Angelica was smiling when she approached Victor.

"I would cancel that date if I were you," said Victor. "I don't think you'll be seeing whoever that was on the phone."

"What is that supposed to mean? Is this really a business meeting?"

"Yes, and like I said, he can take you where you want to go and beyond. But you have to be ready. He won't waste his time. It's just he can be a little complicated."

"Complicated?"

"Yes."

"Who is it, Victor?"

"He saw you last night at the ball. He danced with you."

"Oh yes…Mr. Adventurous."

"Well, he has it bad. And he's not the type of man that takes no for an answer."

Angelica questioned Victor, but he was being a little vague. Victor explained that her mystery man went to see him after all the chaos. And although Victor spoke highly of Angelica, the mystery man wanted to check her out for himself. So, he scheduled the meeting. Angelica decided to go and see what it was all about. She trusted Victor enough that he wouldn't put her in harm's way. Victor reminded her to be confident no matter how much money he has.

Chapter 13
Mr. Adventurous

Angelica returned to the hotel to smoke, shower and change her clothes. She thought about her conversation with Victor, but she thought about Alex's dick more. She was going to fuck him so good that she was the only person he thought about.

She searched for the perfect outfit to entice Alex and decided on a short, black mini-dress. It was spandex, had long sleeves and hugged all the right places. She also wore black thigh-high boots, diamonds and a black mink coat.

Promptly at six, a Maybach arrived to pick up Angelica. The driver stopped in front of a tan brick building on the Upper East Side. She knew she was dealing with big money once she entered the gorgeous lobby. She figured the meeting would take an hour, two tops.

She rode the elevator up to his Contemporary 2-story penthouse, which occupied the entire top floor. When the elevator doors opened, he was standing there waiting for her.

"Hello," she said, smiling.

"Hello."

Angelica immediately got butterflies in her stomach when she saw his face. She even stopped breathing for a second as he walked towards her.

"The man behind the mask," she said, keeping her cool.

"What do you think?"

"Very handsome."

"Thank you."

"What shall I call you?"

"Chad…Chad Matthews," he said, kissing her on the cheek.

Chad was hot for a white man in his late thirties. He stood about six feet tall with blue eyes and sandy blonde hair worn slicked back. He was dressed casually in a white button-up shirt and jeans. And he smelled intoxicating.

He walked behind her and got really close to her ear.

"May I take your coat?"

"Yes. Thank you."

Angelica let it slide off. Then, she turned and faced him.

"Wow! You are beautiful."

"Thank you. And you have blue eyes?"

"Yes. The brown contacts were part of the mystery."

Chad hung up her coat and then hugged her. Angelica hugged him back, gently placing one hand on the nape of his neck and the other on his back. Subtly, he smelled her neck and softly kissed it. His lips were so soft.

"May I get you something to drink?"

"What do you have?"

He took her by the hand and led her into his massive double living room with two fireplaces, a grand piano and enormous doors to the wrap-around balcony. His place was the largest in the building with over 8,000 square feet, seven bedrooms, eight bathrooms and all of the luxuries, like stone floors, marble walls, lots of openness and spectacular views of Central Park and New York's skyline.

Angelica went onto the balcony as he poured her a glass of

Chardonnay.

"This is beautiful," she said.

"So are you."

He handed her a single red rose with her glass of wine.

"Thank you."

"You're welcome," he said, wrapping his arms around her.

"What are you doing?"

He leaned in and whispered, "I can't wait to fuck you too."

Angelica laughed because she knew it was him that she kissed at the ball.

"That wasn't meant for you," she said.

He gazed into her eyes in silence. Then, he softly kissed each side of her neck. He stopped in front of her lips and said, "Yes, it was."

"I thought you were someone else."

"Well, I'm taking you up on your offer."

Angelica looked at him in disbelief.

Chad stood there staring at Angelica. She stared back. However, she felt he was piercing her soul with an intense yet calming and comforting look. All she thought about was his suave mannerism that made him irresistible. He was charming, attentive and made her smile. This alluring man had Angelica's attention.

"I was told you were trouble," said Angelica.

"And I was told you were worth it."

Chad got close to her face and asked, "Are you hungry?"

"I can eat. I had a light lunch."

Out of the blue, he did something she wasn't expecting. He pinched her nipple. So, she pinched his back. He smiled and nodded.

He took her by the hand and led her to the open dining terrace with stone columns, an arched stone wall, beautiful shrubbery and a retractable roof.

Angelica's eyes lit up when she saw an incredibly romantic candlelight dinner for two. Large bouquets of roses, multiple-sized candles and red rose petals covered the floor.

"All of this for me?" she asked as he pulled out her chair.

"Yes. I wanted to impress you."

"You did ok," she said, smiling.

He leaned in and whispered, "I'll do better next time."

Angelica felt all kinds of emotions. She constantly got butterflies in her stomach when he looked at her. She held her breath in anticipation of what he'd say or do next. Angelica was on edge but not in a bad way. The idea of being seduced excited her.

"What do you want, Angelica?"

"Are we talking business?"

"Isn't that why you're here?"

"It was a vague question. There's a lot I want out of life."

"Enlighten me."

Just then, Alex texted her.

"Please excuse me," she said, walking away to call him.

She apologized as she wasn't sure when she'd be free. He was disappointed but understood. He wished her luck.

"My apologies," she said.

"No problem."

Chad grilled her on business topics. He wanted to get a feel for what she knew. Angelica was prepared and answered every question intelligently. Then, he talked about the wine she was drinking. Chad acquired the winery, revamped it and made it one of the most successful brands. He mentioned a few other businesses he'd done that with.

"So, I'll ask you again. What do you want, Angelica?"

She told him her ideas for the Tennessee property but confessed she was a virgin when it came to real estate development and building her empire. He offered to pop her cherry. She just laughed.

"Smart and beautiful," he said.

"Yes."

"And confident…I like it."

"Thank you. May I use your restroom?"

He showed her the way and closed the door behind her.

Angelica had to breathe. She was losing her footing with this man. Although she held her own, he was enticing, cunning and drew her in. She wasn't supposed to be undressing him in her mind. She wasn't supposed to be wanting to kiss his soft lips. And she definitely wasn't supposed to be thinking about his dick inside of her. She had to calm down.

She took a deep breath and opened the door. Angelica screamed as Chad startled her. He stood against the wall next to the door, waiting for her.

"Stalker," she said, teasing.

Chad walked up to her as though he was going to kiss her. Instead, he asked if she found everything ok.

"If you're not going to kiss me, stop getting in my face," she told him, walking away.

But she didn't get very far as he grabbed her and kissed her. Angelica melted when his hands touched her face. Then, Chad grabbed her hair and pushed her closer to his mouth, if it were possible.

"Is that what you wanted?"

She touched his penis and said, "Yes."

"Well since we're touching," he said, reaching under her dress.

Angelica didn't have on underwear. So, he licked his finger and slid it between her lips. He tickled her clit, making her wet.

"You're not fucking him tonight," he whispered in her ear.

"Clearly."

Angelica knew she was a goner. His smile, his look, his

eyes…he made her want him. And she didn't know how to control the sensations throughout her body when he focused on her.

He took off her dress and sucked on her breasts. Angelica grabbed his hair and told him how she liked it. Her assertiveness turned Chad on. So, he felt she could handle what was coming next.

He led her to his bedroom and gently threw her on the bed. After removing each boot, he kissed upward on her thighs. Her stomach sank in when she felt a hot tongue play with her pearl. She grabbed the sheets as he insanely sucked and tasted her. Her body movements and sex talk turned him on. So, he did a trick that made her quiver uncontrollably.

He crawled up and slid inside of her. Angelica let out a scream. He slid so deep that he felt her pulsating.

"That's what I wanted," he said.

He made a move that made her squirt everywhere. After her release, he went into beast mode. His animalistic mannerisms came out with every stroke. Then, he flipped her over so she could ride him. He grabbed her by the waist as she went to work. Her hips moved in slow, circular motions. In an instant, Chad sat up. He wasn't expecting that feeling. He began breathing heavily and talking nasty. It made Angelica go even harder. Chad immediately stood up and backed away. He didn't want to cum yet. But Angelica didn't care. She hiked her ass up doggie style right in front of him. He obliged, and they were back at it.

Chapter 14
First Bet

Angelica and Claudia took an early flight to Charlotte. Claudia decided to spend the day with Angelica before heading back to Miami. They had a lot to catch up on.

Angelica took out three cans of weed. Claudia picked one and they smoked.

"Claude, what am I going to do?"

"About?"

"These men."

"I thought you were ready to settle down with Falio."

"I was...I am."

"So, what's the problem?"

"I didn't expect Alex and Chad."

"You like him, don't you?"

"Who?"

"Alex."

"Yes!"

Aside from being very handsome, Alex was funny, charming and humble. It didn't hurt that he was smart, Hispanic and wealthy. However, Angelica liked his small gestures, like cuddling in bed, holding her hand in public and his smile. She felt like the only woman in his life, and they spoke with honesty. He wasn't as outgoing as Angelica but was willing to try new things.

"Girl…that dick was so good. I want to know what else he can do," said Angelica, laughing.

"He might turn you out."

"He might. He has the potential. I just don't think anyone has pulled it out of him…not fully."

"And you're going to do it?"

"What?"

"Turn him into your sex slave?"

"No! I'm supposed to be with Falio, remember?"

"I remember. Do you?"

"I wouldn't mind jumping on his dick every day," said Angelica, making sexual gestures with her tongue out.

"You nasty," said Claudia, laughing.

"So."

After they laughed, Claudia asked about Chad.

"I don't know, Claude. He's dangerous for me."

"What do you mean?"

"I mean he was mind-blowing."

"What do you mean?"

Chad was not only smart, rich and good-looking but also very confident. He had this take-charge mannerism and knew what he wanted. He was aggressive but gentle, coy but mysterious and phenomenal in bed. Not to mention, his eyes captivated her and turned her to mush. Angelica didn't know what it was about that man, but the attraction was off the charts sexually. Infatuation was an understatement.

"Damn, Biatch!"

"I know!"

"You better be careful, Ange. Those types of men can be narcissistic and mind fuck you."

"I know, but it was electrifying."

"I don't even know what to say to that."

They talked about him a little more before Angelica asked about Bronson. Claudia smiled.

Bronson was thirty-four years old, had a sexy body and recently single. His family was very wealthy and he was the second oldest of four children.

"Are the rumors true about Mr. Wells?"

"What?"

"Snobbish, rude and talks about money?"

"No. I didn't get any of that."

"What's he like?"

The media loved gossiping about the Wells family. They were old money and one of the most prominent families in New York. They owned a multinational conglomerate corporation that primarily operated in oil, technology and banking. However, they also had their hands in commodities, investing and commercial fishery.

Bronson and his older brother, Blaine, were big-time corporate attorneys for the family business. His younger sibling and only sister, Bethany, was into fashion. And the youngest sibling, Baylor, was deciding what to be. So whenever Bronson or one of his siblings did something, it made news headlines. However, Bronson was the opposite of what they portrayed him to be. He was ambitious, well-rounded and could talk about anything.

"I can see why people might think he's arrogant, but it's confidence. He knows what he wants and doesn't waste a woman's time."

"He sounds like Chad."

"Sort of. I didn't have that same experience but yes…very confident. And Bronson does draw you in with his looks," said Claudia, smiling.

"Did you fuck him?"

"No."

"Why?"

After they went to see Bethany's new house, Bronson and Claudia spent most of the day on his yacht. Bethany and Baylor joined them. So, they drank, danced and got to know one another better. They had fun with no pressure. However, they were undeniably attracted to one another.

"Did he tell you what happened to his ex?" asked Angelica.

Bronson recently dated a woman named Chasity Martin for about a year. Things were going well until she began demanding marriage. Bronson didn't like that and called off the relationship. He later discovered that her family didn't have as much money as she claimed. Her parents were counting on their union to save the family business.

"He doesn't sound like the whore media portrays him to be," said Angelica.

"He's not. He's really sweet. Chasity is the one making him sound horrible to the public."

Chasity had been smearing Bronson's name through the mud since their breakup a couple of weeks ago.

"She took his credit card and spent ten thousand dollars without permission. Then, she took pictures of everything she bought and posted them on social media with the caption "Shopping on him," said Claudia.

"Wow! That's bold."

"Yeah…she's starting to cause problems. Bronson's family is upset."

"I can imagine."

Angelica didn't like women like Chasity.

"So now what?" asked Angelica.

"Now nothing."

"I mean, where does he fit in your life? Are you going to settle down with Nico?"

"I don't know, but I'm not letting him go."

Claudia knew she'd have the life she wanted with Bronson if it got serious. And not just financially. They had unexplainable chemistry.

Then, Claudia changed the subject.

"My parents are hounding me about settling down with Seth."

"Still?"

"Yes! Especially my mom. It's like she's obsessed."

"Have you seen him lately?"

"On social media."

Claudia grabbed her phone and showed Angelica a picture.

"Damn! He's gorgeous! Why don't you want to date him again?"

"I don't want someone that my parents want."

"Claude…you know how your parents are."

"I know, but I refuse to be with someone like him. Besides, I think they just want me off their payroll."

"Probably, and what do you mean "someone like him"?"

"He's not the settling down type. Too many girlfriends."

Claudia's family was extremely wealthy, although she didn't always act like it. She didn't follow in her brother's footsteps by getting married early and joining the family business. She wanted to live life and test the waters before settling down. Her father allowed her some freedom and gave her whatever she asked for, including a monthly stipend. However, she had until her thirty-first birthday to be married or work for the family business. Otherwise, her father would decide for her.

"Maybe you should go out with Seth and see what happens," said Angelica.

"Hell no!"

"Why?"

"Because he's attached to my parents."

"Well, at least you wouldn't have to worry about them liking him," said Angelica, laughing.

"Not funny," said Claudia, chuckling. "But seriously, I have to decide if I'm keeping my job, going to work for my father or starting my own company," said Claudia.

"What kind of business would you own?"

Claudia thought about a financial investment firm. She also thought about consulting. She wasn't sure what she wanted to do. She just knew that she had to decide soon.

"My father always tells me to put away my childish ways," said Claudia.

"What does he mean?"

"The partying, men, shopping sprees, vacations…"

"Yeah, my parents are on me as well. They keep saying I'm not in college anymore. I need to start thinking about my future and starting a family. I'll be thirty soon.

They each took a hit of the blunt.

"What do your thirties look like?" asked Claudia.

"I'll get married to my best friend, have three kids and make money."

"Same, but two kids. Who do you see as your husband?"

"Honestly…I always imagined I'd be married to Falio. He knows me and loves me."

"Don't you get scared about his lifestyle, though?"

"Yes, but he has always protected me."

"Nico too, but still…"

"But now…I don't know."

"Alex?"

"Yes. I can actually see a future with him. Hopefully, he's the same man I'm getting to know."

"I think he is. He seems pretty genuine."

Just then, Alex called Angelica. Immediately after, Bronson called Claudia. They each went into different rooms to talk. When they came back, they were both smiling. But before they could talk about their men, Chad called Angelica. He wanted to spend a few days with her in Tennessee and "discuss business". She agreed and hung up.

"What are you going to do?" asked Claudia.

"Go see Chad tomorrow since I'm off the rest of the week," laughed Angelica.

"Bronson will be in Miami Wednesday. I can't wait to see him."

"I think you should go out with Seth."

"No!"

"Why? And stop saying he's your parents' choice!"

"But he is!"

"Let's bet."

"Oh no!"

"I bet you will enjoy your date with Seth if you give him a chance. And I mean, give him a fair shot. You have to treat him like he doesn't know your parents and no negativity."

"And when is this supposed to happen if Bronson is coming and we leave Friday for Colorado?"

"Thursday night."

"Ok. You have to fuck Alex before our trip on Friday."

"How...if I'm going with Chad until Thursday night?"

"Not my problem."

"Ok, Biatch! You're on, but not money. I want the new Gucci."

"Ok...and I want the new Chanel."

They shook on it.

"You do realize that we just talked about settling down and

getting married."

"I know, but we can play a little longer. I feel like when it happens, we'll know," said Claudia.

The ladies laughed at themselves as they got dressed and went to the grocery store.

Chapter 15
Tennessee

Angelica left for the airport at 8 a.m. to catch her flight to Tennessee. Chad sent a private jet to pick her up. He told her not to pack, but Angelica never traveled without at least an overnight bag.

On the way to the airport, she called Alex.

"Hey, Handsome."

"Hey, Beautiful."

"You busy?"

"A little."

"Did you work out this morning?"

"Yes."

Alex was an early riser. His routine consisted of a 5 a.m. workout, watching the world news and a light breakfast with a protein shake. Then, he'd head to the office to begin his work day.

"So, what are you up to? How's vacation life?" he asked.

"Not much of a vacation. I'm traveling for business."

"Tennessee?"

"Yes."

She didn't know what Chad had planned but had to figure out the next steps.

"So, I take it the meeting went well?" he asked.

"Yes, it did."

"That's great."

"Thanks."

"What did you decide to build?"

Angelica was honest and told him about Victor's land being sold. She was concerned because the meeting was about developing all that land, yet she didn't have it anymore. Victor advised her to attend the meeting anyway and continue with her plans. He was working on acquiring it back. Alex agreed and reassured her that she'd have it.

"How are you and Kelly?" she asked, changing the subject.

"We're good."

"Are you officially back together?"

"Not quite. She's out of town right now but gets back on Friday. We will talk then."

"Can I steal a kiss from you on Thursday?"

"You can do whatever you want!"

Angelica laughed and then said, "I want to see you before my big trip to Colorado."

"I'll see you Thursday."

"See you then."

Angelica texted Claudia about her date with Alex on Thursday. Claudia replied with similar news. She had a date with Seth on Thursday. She planned to use the trip to Colorado to end the evening early.

Although the flight into McGhee Tyson Airport was short, Angelica brushed up on tax laws and credits, business law and negotiation skills as instructed by Victor. She needed to be ready.

Chad smiled when he saw her exit the plane.

"Hi," she said, smiling back.

"Hello," he said, kissing her.

He handed her a white rose as they walked towards a helicopter.

"Where are we going?" she asked.

"You'll see."

They rode around a vast area of land near Sevierville.

"Does this look familiar?" he asked her.

"No."

"Well, it should. This is yours."

"I've only seen it in pictures."

Angelica was amazed at how much land there was.

The helicopter landed on a patch of grass. Chad helped her out and told her to look around. There was nothing but greenery for miles. Angelica closed her eyes and imagined what could be. She vividly saw million-dollar homes with beautiful mountain views. She also pictured a health food store, high-end shopping and something for the kids. A world-class golf course came to mind as well. She became flooded with ideas.

"Tell me what you see," said Chad.

She described everything.

"Smart. And it can all be developed."

The more Angelica talked, the more dollar signs Chad saw. He added a few ideas and estimated the cost of more land and construction.

Just then, another helicopter landed. Four people got out, but Angelica's eyes focused on one fine specimen of a man. He was tall, tanned and tantalizing. He had beautiful eyes, dark hair slicked back, looked damn good in his suit and looked like he should be on the cover of GQ.

"Tom…good to see you," said Chad as they shook hands. "This is the young lady I was telling you about."

"Hi…Angelica."

"Nice to meet you."

Tom introduced the rest of his team as they got down to business.

Tom Hoffner was not only Chad's business partner but a well-known real estate developer. Chad set up the meeting to give Angelica some perspective regarding her ideas. No one knew how to build communities like Tom. And Chad wanted Angelica to have the best.

Tom asked Angelica lots of questions. She threw out some ideas along with Chad. Chad was impressed with her professionalism and ability to discuss preliminary numbers. So, Chad invited Tom back to his place to further discuss the plans in private. He accepted and sent his team off while he rode with Chad and Angelica.

Angelica looked out of the window and became emotional. She was nervous, excited and scared. It was a huge project and a huge undertaking. Did she have time, considering her job? Was she ready for this? How was she going to get the land back that Victor lost? She needed that land to build on. Then, Angelica stopped trying to talk her way out of it. She was self-sabotaging and running a little scared. She deserved to be a part of the millionaire's club. So, she instantly smiled. Chad saw that and kissed her.

The helicopter landed on Chad's property near Nashville in Franklin. His palatial estate had three floors and sat on over four acres of land. The exterior was a cream-colored brick with grand Roman columns and wrought iron doors covering the openings. The interior boasted thirty-foot ceilings, a fireplace in every room, three kitchens, a spacious wine cellar and was an entertainer's paradise.

"This is beautiful," Angelica told Chad.

"Thank you."

Chad invited everyone out back as staff brought out food and drinks.

Tom took out his tablet and showed Angelica how he could split up the 10,000 acres of land.

"Do you want something like this with lots of land?" asked Tom, referring to Chad's home. "Or less acreage and more house?"

"Let's look at all of my options," said Angelica.

When developing new homes, there was so much to consider. It wasn't just the materials for the homes but things like infrastructure, water, sewage, etc. Angelica began questioning everything. She needed to know the how, the timeframe and what actually had to be paid out. She also needed to know how much money she'd make.

"Another question. Do you want the land for million-dollar homes or mixed-use?" asked Tom.

"Mixed-use."

Tom prepared a quick layout plan to plot each section intended for residential homes and commercial properties. They went back and forth readjusting the layout according to Angelica's vision. Chad questioned her every design choice and made her explain plot changes. She became irritated by Chad's tone but knew she couldn't take it personally. It was business. But even Tom gave Chad a look.

Once Angelica saw the plans to develop multiple residential communities, she allocated between one and four acres of land per million-dollar estate. Tom then showed her design aspects while explaining options for high-end materials and name-brand appliances. He included bonus features in each design package. Angelica threw out some tax credit information and ways to save on costs while earning a higher profit. They were impressed since one of the ideas could save them millions. Tom stepped away to call his assistant to run the numbers.

"That was so sexy," whispered Chad.

"You're an asshole."

"But you like it. It challenges you."

"You're rude as fuck."

"Do you think people will be nice when they give you hundreds of millions of dollars to build your dreams? There is no emotion when it comes to money. There are only smart decisions."

Angelica knew he was right and stayed quiet. She really needed a blunt to calm her nerves.

"I want to fuck you," he whispered.

"I bet you do," she said, fake smiling.

Tom came back and hugged Angelica.

"You are brilliant!" said Tom excitedly.

"I know, but why this time?" she said, making them laugh.

Angelica's tax tips were going to save his company millions in fees. He asked his assistant to review his current projects to see if the tax credits applied.

"I should get a consulting fee," she told Tom jokingly.

"How about five percent of what I recoup?"

"How about twenty," said Chad.

"Ten."

"How about fifteen percent, and you design a home for yourself from my project?" said Angelica.

Tom shook on it, but Angelica wanted it in writing before he left. He sent his attorney a message with details for the contract.

"You need a name for your new consulting business," Chad told Angelica.

"How about…Zambrano Consulting?"

"Sounds great. I'll get it set up for you."

"Thanks."

Tom advised Angelica that he couldn't begin until February of

the following year. He had several major projects he was finishing up and needed until January to complete. She hugged and
thanked him.

"I'm going to have to hire an assistant," said Angelica.

"Every billionaire has one," said Chad, winking.

Chad elevated her with just one word.

Chapter 16
What A Party

Tom called for his helicopter and left. Shortly after, Chad received a call and excused himself. Angelica stood up and stared out onto the acreages of greenery. It hit her! She could potentially earn nine figures or more at the end of it. She immediately texted Alex the good news. After, she went to the restroom to collect herself.

"Holy shit! This is really happening," she whispered.

She paced back and forth. Then, she stopped and looked at herself in the mirror. She thought about the money she earned from investing with Victor. She thought about her conversation with Claudia. She also thought about retiring her parents and helping her sisters. Angelica could be her own boss and set her family up for life. She could do anything. And although there were still a lot of details to work out, Angelica finally imagined financial freedom. It was like a shift took place within her.

Angelica got herself together and opened the door to leave. She screamed as Chad startled her.

"Oh my God… you scared…"

His tongue was down her throat as he pushed her back inside. He rubbed on her nipples while she rubbed on his dick. Angelica wanted to feel him, so she unfastened his pants and stroked his dick. Chad wanted to taste her, so he ripped open her blouse and sucked on her breasts. They were hot and heavy when Chad turned her around and fucked her from behind. He fucked her good and hard. It was intense.

"I've wanted to do this all day," he said.

"Give it to me, Baby."

Afterward, they showered and adjourned to his bedroom.

"You owe me a shirt," she told him.

"I was very impressed with you."

"Why? You thought I was some young, dumb chick who didn't know anything?"

"Yes."

"Gotta love your honesty."

"Most don't appreciate it."

"Can't ever imagine why," she said, sarcastically.

He went into his closet and brought out a big box.

"This is for you," he said.

Angelica smiled. Inside was a stunning red strapless corset dress with a gathered waist and split on one side.

"This is gorgeous. Thank you."

"You're welcome."

He brought out another box. It was the shoes to match. Then, he brought out four more boxes with jewelry inside each one.

"May I take you to dinner?" he asked.

"Yes, I'd like that."

After getting dressed, Chad escorted Angelica to the formal dining room. He arranged for a romantic dinner with flowers, candles and music in the background.

He pulled out her chair and sat down.

"You did all of this for me?" she asked.

"Yes. I like you."

"So, when are you going to stop acting like an asshole?"

"There's one more test."

"Ok."

Angelica knew he'd been testing her but didn't think it'd be so extreme.

At dinner, Chad opened up about some of his businesses, all of the traveling he does and some of the things he likes to do. Angelica mostly talked about her family, big dreams and why she pushes herself as hard as she does.

After a delicious meal, they went back to Chad's bedroom. Angelica changed into a silver mesh mini-dress. It had a halter neckline, no back and side splits. She wore silver heels, diamond jewelry and a thong to go with it.

"Where are we going? A strip club?" she asked.

"We're going to a party."

Angelica wasn't sure what kind of party it was, but the dress left nothing to the imagination.

"And under no circumstances are you to fraternize with Tom this evening," said Chad.

"Why?"

"Because you're mine, and I don't like to share," he said close to her face.

Angelica wasn't sure what that meant but said, "Ok."

They rode a short distance to a luxury mansion in a neighboring community. Angelica didn't take a purse or phone as it was not permitted. When they walked inside, she instantly smelled weed.

"I need some of that," she said.

A topless woman brought over a tray with mini gold pipes and baggies with different strains of marijuana. Angelica grabbed a pipe and a baggie with OG Kush on it. Chad did the same thing. She let the day go as she inhaled and exhaled.

Angelica looked around and saw a sexual paradise. It was a smaller version of London, which she didn't mention.

"Do you see something you like?" he asked.

"Yes...you."

Angelica kissed him.

"No, I mean something else."

"No."

Angelica got high as a kite and became quiet and very observant. She watched Chad as he greeted women by pinching their nipples, smacking them on the butt and he even took a pill from one of their mouths. Angelica watched him trying to be cool and laughed as she was not impressed. All day, she felt intimidated by him. He even turned on the charm at dinner. Yet, at that very moment, she saw him as a grown-ass child in an adult candy store. Being that high changed her perspective of him.

Chad told Angelica to roam and see if she liked something. Instead, she ran into a familiar face.

"Angelica?"

"Tom?"

"Hey, how are you?"

"Good, and you?" asked Angelica, hugging him.

"Not sure."

"First time at one of these?"

"Yes."

Neither one of them really wanted to be there. So, they smoked and mostly talked about work. However, when Chad found her, he whisked her away.

"I told you not to talk to him."

She just laughed.

He grabbed her by the hair and said, "I mean it. You're mine."

Angelica laughed again.

He took her into a room where other people were having sex.

One lady, in particular, was sitting on a chair and stood up when she saw Chad. She pushed him against the wall and pulled down his pants. She began pleasuring him as Angelica watched. He thought it would get her horny for him. Instead, she walked away. She looked for Tom and waited for Chad to exit the room. Once she saw Chad, she hugged Tom and kissed him on the cheek. Chad immediately grabbed her and left.

"What the fuck is wrong with you?" he yelled once they got into his house.

"Nothing!"

"I told you not him!"

"Nothing happened!"

"What part of not him don't you understand?"

"We were just talking!"

"I don't care!"

"Why did you take me there? To fuck someone else?"

"No! I wanted us to have a good time."

"Oh…because we weren't having one before that?"

"I thought you liked that kind of stuff."

"Whatever gave you that impression?"

"You're young! All young people are into that!"

"No…not all of us!"

Angelica dropped her dress to change. Chad stared at her in a thong and heels.

"I'm sorry," he said, wrapping his arms around her.

"You should be."

"I was trying to show you a good time."

"You were up until that point."

"Dance with me."

"Let me put something on."

"No. Just like that."

"Ok."

Chad turned on the music and removed his clothes. He made her laugh. They danced close, feeling every inch of one another's bodies. Sexual desires quickly grew. Angelica knew what he wanted and gave in.

Chapter 17
Forgiveness

Angelica woke up and packer her bag. She was ready to go.

"Can you take me to the airport?" she asked him.

"Please don't leave."

"Chad, I didn't like who I saw last night. And if that's your lifestyle, then you can have it."

"It's not."

"So, again…why did you take me there?"

"Because I honestly thought you were into that stuff."

"Again…what gave you that impression?"

Chad explained that the younger women he'd dated in the past seemed to like that scene. Then, he talked about her friendly mannerisms, like kissing him at the ball and fucking him on their first encounter.

"I'm done!"

"No…wait, please."

"You basically called me a friendly, free-spirited hoe."

"I didn't mean it like that."

"I thought you were someone else when I kissed you! You know that!"

"That guy you left with?"

"Yes! I don't just go around kissing random strangers. And I fucked you the first time I met you because I found you to be charming and intriguing. Your eyes and the way you looked at me...I got butterflies. You made me feel safe to be with you. So, I took a chance. But this..."

"I'm sorry, Angelica. Please don't leave."

Chad ran and grabbed their pipes along with more weed. He could explain himself better high. They talked and smoked, even though he had an ulterior motive.

"Can I be honest with you?" asked Angelica high and calm.

"Sure."

"The night we actually met...at your house...you were magic. You were absolutely gorgeous when I first saw you. You were charming but mysterious. You were aggressive but gentle. And your body...oh my goodness. And the entire time I was with you, I thought you were smart, business savvy and could teach me a thing or two. But after last night..."

Chad didn't let her finish. He pulled her out of her seat and onto his lap.

"Don't leave me. Let me make it up to you," he said.

"Why did you get me excited about you if you were just going to behave that way?"

Chad opened up about previous relationships. The money, cars and lifestyle changed women once they experienced his way of living. They always had an ulterior motive, like wanting to be kept or using him to start some kind of business endeavor. Yet when he asked the hard questions about finances, they didn't know how to run a business or make a profit.

"But then you happened," he said. "You knocked it out of the park yesterday. You talked the talk and walked the walk. You weren't afraid to speak up. You threw your ideas out there. Hell, you even negotiated a consultant's fee, which landed you a new business. You handled yourself professionally even when I pushed you. That's what I was truly testing."

"Why though?"

"Angelica, no one ever gives you anything like I told you. You have to work hard for what you want. And I'm not saying money is everything but it is. It offers the freedom you otherwise don't have. And people want that. They want what you have without working for it. So, I challenged you."

"You most certainly did."

"I heard everything you said on our first night. You knew what you really wanted but the thought of having it made you afraid. I made it real."

"It's gonna be a great project."

"When I spoke to Victor, he praised you. But I didn't think anyone could be that awesome…besides me of course."

They both laughed, and she hugged him.

"This is the man I like…sweet and sincere. Not that ratchet ass man I experienced last night."

He kissed her again.

"Thank you for trusting me," he said.

"You're welcome."

"And I don't think you're a free-spirited hoe."

She hit him on his arm as they laughed.

"Come home with me," he said.

"New York?"

"Yes."

"I have to be back in Charlotte tomorrow."

"Why?"

"I'm doing a girl's trip for my birthday."

"When is your birthday?"

"Saturday."

Chad called his pilot and asked him to fuel up the jet. Then, he made a few more phone calls in preparation for what was to come. He kept smiling as he planned a huge surprise for Angelica.

They grabbed breakfast before heading out. During their plane ride, Chad made her cum multiple times.

Chapter 18
The "Chad" Treatment

They made it to New York in no time. Their first stop was his place.

"This is for you," he said, handing Angelica a red rose.

"Thank you."

"Now we have a busy day ahead of us."

"We do?"

"Yes. You are getting the Chad Matthews birthday treatment for the day."

"And what does that entail?"

He hugged her and said, "I want to spoil you like the queen you are."

"Ok. Let's see how good you are."

"Baby, you know how good I am."

"I do."

As they were leaving, the chef was arriving. Angelica pulled him aside and asked for a favor. She knew Chad had plans but wanted to include some of her own.

Their first stop was on Washington Avenue near Watts Street. The light brick building had a black facade storefront with gold doors and no name on the front. Chad held her hand as they walked inside. Immediately, they were each handed a glass of champagne as an attendant took Angelica's measurements. Then, Chad and Angelica were escorted to the second floor and seated. Several store attendants brought out high-end designer clothing, shoes and accessories that weren't available to the public yet. Angelica would be the first to own them since they weren't coming out for months.

"You can have whatever you want," he whispered in her ear.

Her eyes lit up with joy.

Chad was very affectionate towards Angelica. He constantly kissed her hand and did little things to play with her. He even kept opening the dressing room door to kiss her. Angelica saw some things she liked for Chad and made him try them on. They wound up leaving in new clothes. The manager reassured Chad that everything would be immediately sent to his penthouse by courier. Chad bought Angelica everything she wanted.

"Oh my God! That was exciting!" she said. "Thank you."

"You're welcome. I'm glad you had fun."

"I did."

Angelica worked up an appetite after all of that shopping. He suggested they stop at this little restaurant a few blocks down West Broadway near Grand Street. Again, Chad held her hand as they walked inside. A middle-aged gentleman with jet black hair, clean-shaven and a slight Italian accent welcomed them. Chad and Angelica were immediately seated.

"Is this Palacio's?" whispered Angelica.

"Yes."

"That was Chef Jacques."

"I know."

"You can't get in here ever."

"You can when you own it."

Angelica looked at him like he had two heads.

"What?" he asked, chuckling.

"Nothing."

Chad sat close to Angelica and fed her while sharing three new dishes: mini BBQ salmon burgers with savory sweet potato fries, garlic butter scallops on a bed of zucchini pasta and lobster-filled steak with a veggie medley.

"That was so good," she said.

"I'm glad you liked it."

Chad had another surprise for Angelica. They stopped in front of a red brick building on Broadway near Prince Street. When they walked inside, it smelled heavenly.

"Hi. I'm Roshi."

"Angelica…nice to meet you."

"Likewise."

They shook hands as Roshi greeted Chad. Roshi then began discussing the store and the perfume-making process. He further explained on the elevator ride up to the third floor. As they stepped out, Angelica saw several tables arranged with various items on them, like oils, spices, flowers, bottles and droppers.

"What are we doing here?" she asked Chad.

"You, Angelica, are going to create your own perfume collection."

"What?"

"These fine people have created designer fragrances for decades. They are knowledgeable about scents, bottle designs and packaging. They will help you create a few scents of your own."

She kissed him and thanked him. She thought it was sweet of him to do that.

Angelica began with the carrier oils before moving on to the scented oils. She carefully mixed various ingredients until she created three scents she liked. Chad also made a few good suggestions that Angelica incorporated.

"You have great taste," said Chad. "What are you going to call it?"

"Angelica," she said jokingly.

"I like it."

"It was a joke."

"Why?"

"It was the first thing that came to mind, so I yelled it out."

"And it's good. Who better than you to represent your perfume?"

"What about a different name?"

"Like what?"

"Like…"

Angelica came up with other names, but Chad didn't like any of them. Instead, he asked her to think of three adjectives that best described her.

"Amor…Dulce…Rebelde," said Angelica.

"What's rebelde?"

"Rebel in Spanish."

"I like it. And dulce means sweet. And, of course, amor is love."

"Yes."

Next, Roshi showed them various bottle designs and packaging materials on his tablet. Angelica selected a few bottles that best matched her style. Chad asked Roshi to digitally add Angelica's name to one of the bottles. Then, in smaller letters beneath it, he added the word Amoré.

"It's beautiful," said Angelica.

Chad asked Roshi to do the same with the remaining two bottles. Each had her name at the top with the words Dulcé and Rebeldé in smaller letters underneath. Angelica loved it.

"You should receive samples within the next couple of weeks," said Roshi.

"Thank you."

They left and headed to a cafe on East Twentieth Street.

"This cafe has the best coffee," he said.

"Wow. This crowd is insane."

A young woman saw Chad and rushed over. Chad ordered a chocolate croissant and French coffee. Angelica got an eclair and macaroons with a cappuccino. After placing their order, they went upstairs to a beautiful loft on the seventh floor. Moments later, the same young lady brought up a tray of food and drinks along with a black book.

"You own the place, don't you?" asked Angelica.

"I do."

"Do you bring all your women here?"

"You're the first, but maybe I will."

She gave him a look.

Angelica drank her cappuccino while staring out of the window. She thought about her day and was beginning to understand his wealth.

"I know what you're doing," she said as he walked up behind her.

"What am I doing?"

"You're showing me how to build wealth through multiple streams of income."

"You're right."

"The shopping, the restaurant and this cafe…"

"It's all mine."

"And the perfume…is it a business endeavor?"

"Yes."

"So, it wasn't just a personal creation? It will be mass-produced?

"Correct."

"And those names…Amoré, Dulcé and Rebeldé?"

"The three fragrances in your first collection."

"First collection? As in more than one?"

"Yes."

"And you expect to make money from this?"

"With my help. And each fragrance will have the matching lotion."

"Is it always business with you?"

"Not always, but mostly…yes."

"Why?"

"Make money by investing in the things you like. You like to shop? Have retail establishments. You like to eat? Own eating establishments. You like to drink coffee? Own cafes. You like to smell good? Own your own fragrances. Don't keep paying other people for what you like. Own it and make it available to others."

Angelica never really looked at life that way. She never worried about it because she usually spent other people's money. But now that she was about to have her own, he had a point.

"So, the boutique on Washington Ave?" she asked.

"People pay me a fee for high-end merchandise unavailable to the public. And the designers can charge a higher price, which I get a percentage of, because of the exclusivity."

Angelica was amazed.

"The coffee is delicious. You should franchise," she said.

He just smiled.

It was getting late, but Angelica asked Chad to make a stop. She wanted to go to FAO Schwartz to buy Nina, Ricky and Angelo some toys for Christmas. She always started early and wasn't sure when she'd be back. Chad didn't mind and made a phone call.

A brown-skinned woman with black hair and a big smile greeted Chad and Angelica as they walked in. Chad asked to speak with her privately. When they returned, the woman gave Angelica a scanner gun and asked her to scan all the items she wanted. She thanked the woman and kissed Chad.

They went throughout the store, playing with different things and remembering childhood toys. Angelica saw that Chad was having a great time. He laughed and played with all kinds of stuff. Angelica hadn't realized how much she scanned. But it didn't matter because Chad took care of the bill.

Chad had one more surprise for her. They went into a nearby jewelry store. The manager greeted Chad and accompanied them to the third floor. He went into a safe and brought out some exclusive pieces. Chad saw matching his and hers gold and diamond Rolexes. He placed hers on her wrist. Then, she put his on him. Chad picked up a Patek Philippe rose gold diamond watch and placed it on her other wrist. He also selected a stunning diamond necklace with a large diamond pendant and placed it around her neck. Chad added several diamond bracelets to her wrists and bought her a pair of diamond studs and droplet earrings.

They finally made it back to his place. The aroma of food permeated throughout his home. Angelica couldn't wait to sit down and eat.

Chad was ready to relax. So, they changed into something more casual.

"I have a surprise for you now," she said.

"Ok."

She blindfolded him and led him into the living room. Chad was pleasantly surprised when she removed the blindfold. The chef set up a romantic picnic on a chabudai table. Flowers and candles added to the ambiance while large throw pillows sat on the floor. Soft music played in the background, and the chef stood nearby, waiting to serve.

"You did this?" he asked.

"Yes."

He kissed and thanked her.

The chef served them a glass of champagne and brought out the appetizers. It was the perfect way to end the day.

Over the next couple of hours, they enjoyed dinner, talked and laughed. Chad opened up about his family, and they talked a little business.

"Thank you for today," he said. "It was fun."

"You're welcome. And thank you for all of my gifts."

"You're welcome. Happy birthday."

"Thanks."

Angelica was happy. She was drunk, high and in great company. Chad, however, was ready for dessert. He made love to Angelica and took his time. He did more things to her body that only he knew how to do.

Chapter 19
Atlanta Bound

The next morning, Chad brought her breakfast in bed.

"This is a pleasant surprise. Thank you."

"You're welcome. Enjoy."

Chad left Angelica alone to eat while he went into his office. After she finished, she got dressed and went looking for him. She stopped at a bookshelf and read some of the titles. They were all fabulous books.

"You like to read as well?" he asked from behind.

"Yes. And you have great taste in books."

"I know. I have great taste in everything."

"A little cocky?"

"Honest."

Angelica got the feeling that sweet Chad was gone and the all-business Chad was back.

"I have to catch a flight to Mexico in a couple of hours," he said.

"Ok. I'll get my things."

Angelica was ecstatic because she didn't have to make up a lie about leaving for Atlanta. Chad was under the impression she was going back to Charlotte. So, it worked out perfectly.

"Can I take a quick shower?" she asked.

"Sure."

Angelica was in the shower, wondering what was up with Chad. He was distant and different. She wasn't sure if something happened while she was asleep.

A few minutes later, Chad joined her. He looked at Angelica practically obsessively. Chad gently touched her face, eyes and lips. Then, he grabbed her by the hair.

"Are you real?" he asked.

"I'll show you if you don't let go of my hair."

"You didn't say that last night."

"That was different."

"I don't want to share you."

"Let go of my hair."

"Did you hear me?"

Angelica pulled his pubic hair and asked, "Did you hear me?"

Chad was rattled but not enough to let go. It was almost like he liked it.

He finally let go and kissed her.

"What's wrong?" she asked.

"You."

"What did I do?"

Chad turned off the water and went back into the bedroom. Their sex was passion-fueled and off the charts. Angelica didn't know what got into him but loved it.

"Stay with me. Live with me," he said afterward.

"Like move in?"

"Like be my girlfriend, and I'll be your boyfriend."

"And what does being my boyfriend look like to you?"

Chad explained that exclusivity was a must on her behalf. She couldn't sleep with anyone else. He wanted her just for himself and was willing to pay the price for it. He offered to buy her a condo if she didn't want to live with him, take her on shopping sprees and buy her whatever she wanted as long as she answered when he called.

Angelica looked at him in amazement. This man…who she'd had the most magical night and morning with…just insulted her in a way no man had ever done. And she knew he was serious, which was the worst part.

"Did you just Pretty Woman me?" she asked.

"What's that?"

She looked at him strangely and then asked, "Are you married?"

"No."

Angelica got dressed and gathered her things. She texted Alex that she'd be there soon. Afterward, Angelica called Victor and asked him to use his jet. Last, she called for a car to pick her up.

"What are you doing? Wait! Did I say something?" he asked.

"Thank you for a lovely time."

"Angelica…wait!!!"

"I'm not a hoe or a piece of property."

"I wasn't asking you to do something I'm unwilling to do myself."

"What does that mean?"

"I'll be available for you."

"It sounds like a business transaction. What happened to love?"

"Overrated."

"Then, I'm definitely not your girl. I still believe in it."

Angelica went to walk out, and he stopped her.

"Where are you going?"

"To mind my business. Now move!"

Chad moved out of her way.

Angelica made it to the airport within an hour. She boarded

the plane and thought about his offer. She felt like Julia Roberts in Pretty Woman.

Once she landed, she saw Alex waiting for her. She buried her feelings for Chad and smiled. She didn't want to take something out on Alex that was meant for Chad.

Angelica ran and jumped on him. He kissed her like he missed her.

"Hi," he said, smiling.

"Hi."

"I missed you."

"You'll have to show me later," she whispered.

"Definitely."

They drove off in Alex's Bentley Continental GT convertible. It was black with a red leather interior and monogrammed floor mats.

"This is beautiful," she told him.

"Thanks. Where's your luggage?"

"This is all I have."

"Not you...Miss Shopping Queen."

"I'll make up for it while I'm here," she said, winking.

She didn't want to bring up her shopping excursion with Chad.

"I hope you don't mind, but I have a few errands to run before we go to the house."

"No problem. Can we stop by Phipps Plaza? I want to check in on Sasha and buy a few things."

"Yes."

Alex kissed her again.

They went to look at a few condos for Alex's sister, Val. Although her main home was in California, she frequently visited Alex and wanted her own space.

The next stop was Phipps Plaza. Angelica went straight to Sasha's shop. She saw Sasha and Nicole from outside the window.

The ladies screamed and hugged when they saw each other. The ladies also greeted Alex. Nicole was happy to see them together.

Angelica looked around the store and saw so many things she wanted. She even tried on a few dresses. Alex thought she looked good in everything. So, Angelica went a little overboard buying stuff, primarily to support Sasha. Alex handed Sasha his credit card. Angelica didn't expect him to pay.

"Thank you."

"You're welcome."

The ladies packed everything up and said their goodbyes. Alex and Angelica were off to other stores.

"Why did you do that," asked Angelica outside Sasha's store.

"I wanted to buy you something for your birthday but didn't know what to get you. This way, you get what you want and I can't mess it up. Besides, you needed clothes. So, get whatever you want. It's on me."

"Are you sure?"

"Yes."

Angelica was sad she left most of the things Chad bought in New York. But Alex made up for it as they went in and out of stores. He picked out things he wanted her to have, like an 18-carat blue topaz cocktail ring from Tiffany's. They stopped in the fur store, and Alex purchased the one he wanted to see her in after dinner. Lastly, they stopped in Chanel. She got a few things, including Claudia's bag.

When they got to Alex's house, his best friend, Jordan, was there with his girlfriend, Siya. Alex made the introductions, and Angelica gave them a big hug. Then, Angelica asked Alex to order wings and fries from the best place in town. Alex placed a large order at Chicken King and then went to smoke and chill with everyone on the back patio.

"Miss Angelica…I've heard a lot about you," said Jordan.

"All good, I hope."

"All wonderful."

"I've heard some things about you as well."

"Oh no! What did this fool say about me?"

"All good things."

Jordan Jimenez was Cuban-Dominican and played professional football for New York. This six-foot-tall running back was beautiful with short black hair, bronzy skin, ravishing brown eyes and an inviting smile. Siya was equally beautiful with long brown hair, glowing green eyes and a petite frame.

Jordan mentioned New York and couldn't believe she got Alex to have fun. He was such a workaholic. Then, they talked about football. They discussed his previous games and what he could do better.

"Man…I like her. She knows football," said Jordan.

"She never ceases to amaze me."

Alex got a text about the food. So, everyone went inside. As Angelica took everything out of the bags, Alex walked up behind her and hugged her. She turned around and kissed him.

"Y'all cut that out!" yelled Jordan.

They laughed and served themselves.

Alex couldn't keep his hands off her. He'd caress her face or hold her hand, but he had to touch her. Jordan smiled because he saw his friend evolving. He'd never seen Alex and Kelly interact the way he did with Angelica. Jordan was happy for his friend.

Jordan and Siya left a few hours later. Alex and Angelica were finally alone.

"I want you so bad," said Alex, kissing her.

"You'll have to show me after I shower."

Alex turned on the water and showered with Angelica. Afterward, they went to his bedroom. He sat on the bed and pulled Angelica on top of him. She hissed as his hot tongue tickled her nipples. She pressed his head in and moved her hips as it felt good.

Alex wanted her wet, so he slid his finger between her lips. Angelica moved like she was having sex. He made her cum.

"I want to feel him," she whispered.

Alex obliged and slid inside. The moans, groans and dirty sex talk made it hotter. She drove him crazy with the hip gyration. There was hair pulling, booty popping and deep stroking, which made him cum.

"You did good, Mr. Mendoza."

"I aim to please, Ms. Zambrano."

Alex made her wear the fur coat on their next round.

Chapter 20
Claudia's Date

Claudia scheduled an early dinner with Seth. She just wanted to get it over with and spend the evening with Nico.

Angelica texted Claudia several pictures of her and Alex. Claudia laughed and then replied.

"I'm not in the mood for this date," said Claudia out loud.

She was reluctant to go on the date, but a deal was a deal. So, Claudia had to go.

Claudia lit a blunt and turned on some music while she went in and out of her closet. She couldn't decide what to wear but knew they were having dinner. She prayed that was it.

As she applied her lipstick, she heard a knock at the door.

"Coming!"

When she opened the door, Seth was even more gorgeous in person. He appeared rugged but well-groomed with slicked-back black hair and clear blue eyes. He was also impeccably dressed.

"Seth."

"Claudia."

She hugged him and then invited him in. And like a true gentleman, he brought flowers.

"You look beautiful," he told her.

"Thank you."

Claudia wore a black sequin dress with a high neck, no sleeves and a thigh-high split on the side. She paired it with Louboutin heels, Chanel red lipstick and an updo with sweeping bangs.

"Shall we?" he asked, holding out his arm.

"Yes."

Seth opened the passenger door to his black Lamborghini Aventador and helped her inside. They drove down the street to Miami Towers on South Biscayne Blvd.

"Oh my God. I didn't know you lived this close to me," she said.

"I know. I thought the same thing when I looked up your address."

They stopped by his place to pick up a few things. It was elegant with large decorative pieces.

"This is beautiful," she said.

"Thank you."

Seth had three units converted into one, giving him over 7,000 square feet, five bedrooms and lots of space for entertaining.

Seth grabbed her hand and led her onto the balcony. He pointed at a 150' yacht docked below.

"Do you get seasick?"

"No."

"Great."

Seth escorted her down to the yacht. The staff greeted them as they boarded the vessel. Claudia followed Seth to the lower deck, which doubled as a large entertainment area.

"Can I get you something to drink?" he asked.

"I'll have what you're having."

He made her a peach mint watermelon margarita with an extra shot of tequila on the side. He made himself a Tequila Soda with an extra shot on the side.

"To tonight," he said, raising the shot glass.

"To tonight."

They drank the shots and then sipped on their drinks.

"Wow! This is tasty," she told him.

"Thanks."

Seth broke up the awkwardness.

"Claudia…I need to say something."

"Ok."

"I didn't want to come tonight."

"Me either," said Claudia, relieved.

"And maybe I still don't want to be here…on this date…with you. But I promised my father I'd be the perfect gentleman and give this a try."

"Me too! My mother is obsessed with you."

"Since we both have to be here, what do you say we just be ourselves?"

"Ok."

Claudia was able to relax as they talked.

She noticed that Seth wasn't as uptight as she thought. He was actually pretty funny. They told stories about their parents, talked about his reputation and evaluated past relationships.

"I knew he was cheating," said Seth.

"Who?"

"Anthony."

"How?"

"Well, first off, I'm a man. Second, the way he eyed women behind your back. It was utter disrespect."

"Yeah, everyone told me things after we broke up."

"What did you see in that guy?"

"For the most part, he treated me well, and I thought I loved him."

"What does love look like to you?"

"I never thought about it in words. I believe it's a feeling invoked by actions."

"You don't like words?"

"Yes, but ultimately actions give words their validity."

"I get that."

"What about you and all of your girlfriends or boyfriends? What does love look like for you?"

"Well…my current girlfriend is in Dubai with my current boyfriend. So, I'm not big on love."

"Not big on love? She must've broken your heart?"

"Can a heart truly be broken? Or is it just disappointment that your investment didn't work out?"

"Investment?"

"Everyone and everything are investments. We invest in businesses to earn a profit. We invest in employees because they're an asset. We invest in homes to live in. We invest time, money and headspace into learning a person. You find out what makes them happy, sad, angry and scared. You find out all of their favorites, like flowers, colors and food. You spend time together, make plans together and buy them nice gifts to show your appreciation."

"Investment," said Claudia, understanding his interpretation.

"Yes."

"I see your point."

"So, what's your favorite flower?"

Claudia laughed as they talked about some of their favorites.

A staff member invited them to the dining area. The setting was beautifully adorned with a romantic touch. He pulled out her chair and handed her a napkin.

They discussed several topics, including finances, business ideas and politics. Claudia was pleasantly surprised at his level-headedness. They could agree to disagree.

After dinner, they adjourned to the top deck. Seth took off his tie and unbuttoned a few buttons on his shirt. He laid back on one of the lounge chairs to relax. Claudia took off her heels and lay next to him in her chair.

"I didn't think I'd like you very much," he told her.

"Well damn…honest much."

"Always honest."

"Truth be told, I didn't think I'd like you either."

"And now?"

"You're not too bad. I can deal with you."

Seth pulled out a little black box from his pocket. It was his mini pipe and weed stash.

"You smoke?" she asked loudly.

"You sound surprised."

"I am."

They smoked and talked about more relationship topics.

"Do you dance?" he asked.

"Yes."

"What's your favorite sex song?"

"Why? I'm not sleeping with you."

"I just want us to dance to your favorite sex song."

"Mmmm hmmm."

He stood up and took her by the hand. He gently wrapped one arm around her waist, while she softly caressed the nape of his neck.

"I should take my shirt off so it can be sexier?" he said jokingly.

"Sure, why not," she said, chuckling.

Seth stepped back and unbuttoned his shirt. As he slid it off, Claudia bit her bottom lip. His body was gorgeous with a serious V.

"Don't hurt that lip," he said, walking up to her and kissing it. "It's too beautiful."

Claudia was speechless.

This time, as they danced, he slowly lifted her dress, pulling her closer by her thigh. Their eyes locked, and they simply stared into each other, lost in the moment.

"You're beautiful," he told her.

"You too."

Seth started touching upwards on her thigh, Claudia couldn't resist and kissed him. It became a very passionate moment.

They made it to Alarie Island two hours later.

"You have your own island?"

"Yes."

The island lay between the main islands of North and South Bimini. They disembarked from the yacht and boarded a helicopter. Within minutes, they arrived at his beachfront estate.

Claudia knew she was not going to make her date with Nico. So, she texted him that they'd meet at the airport in the morning.

"Do you swim?" he asked.

"Yes, but I didn't bring my bathing suit."

"No worries."

They went into one of the bedrooms.

"Pick one," he told her.

"I'm not wearing any of these."

"They're brand new...I promise."

"Won't your girlfriend get mad?"

"I don't see her here. Besides, these swimsuits are merchandise for a shop I'm opening."

Claudia picked the one she liked and changed. When she walked out, he was in awe.

"Quit staring," she said jokingly.

"Can't help it."

He walked up to her and kissed her. Then, he went into his closet and changed into a pair of swimming shorts.

"Damn!" she said out loud.

"You like?"

She just nodded as they were short and hugged his body parts in all the right places.

Seth asked the staff to take robes, slippers and champagne with strawberries to the pool area.

"What kind of shop are you opening?" asked Claudia.

"I'm starting a luxe swimwear brand apart from the family business. It will be my own side business."

"Well, they're beautiful. You have good taste."

"Thank you," he said, swimming to her.

Seth Alarie was tremendously wealthy. His family owned a luxe brand empire. They had a 9-figure fashion brand along with a 9-figure liquor brand. So, he wasn't concerned with money. However, he wanted to try something on his own.

"I have a confession to make," he said.

"Uh oh. It's too soon for that."

The truth was that his girlfriend ran off with his best friend.

"So, you're not really gay?"

"No."

"And your boyfriend was actually your best friend?"

"Yes."

"I'm so sorry to hear that. What happened?"

"She was jealous of me hanging out with models."

"I can understand. You're around beautiful women all day."

"Yes, but nothing was going on. It was all business. Photo shoots, interviews, product branding meetings…"

"Then, she wasn't confident in herself or your relationship."

"I guess. But at this point, I don't care. She lied to me and I'm not a forgiving person. You have one time to lie to me."

"Good to know."

He grabbed a strawberry and fed it to her. Then, she put one in her mouth and fed it to him. They locked lips as they shared the strawberry.

"I want to fuck you," she whispered in his ear.

"No. We aren't doing that remember?"

"Ok."

She tried to get away, but Seth grabbed her.

"I want to fuck you too."

They adjourned to his bedroom, where he removed his robe and shorts. Claudia did backflips in her mind when she saw his penis. She understood why he had a reputation.

He removed her robe and untied the bikini. He stared at her body as the swimsuit fell to the floor. He laid her down on the bed and got on top of her.

"You are beautiful," he said in her ear.

"You too."

Seth took a rose from the vase on his nightstand and softly feathered one nipple while licking the other. She let out a moan as her stomach sank in. He smiled and did tongue twirls, making her hips slowly gyrate. The way her body moved turned Seth on. He slid the rose further down to her stomach.

"Oh my God!" she quietly said.

His tongue followed the path of the rose. He feathered her clit with the rose while his tongue slowly continued down her body. Right before Seth's tongue tasted her, he slid inside of her. Claudia gasped for air as she grabbed the sheets. Seth kissed her as he went slow and deep. Claudia let out moans and groans as he began fucking her. Then, Seth flipped her over so she could ride him. He pulled her hair as he became the loud one. It was a back-and-forth session of pleasuring one another.

Around 2 a.m., they headed back to Miami. They fucked and had a good time back.

Chapter 21
Plane Ride to Denver

It was the most anticipated weekend of the year...Angelica and Falio's birthday weekend. Falio had been planning something special with their family and friends in Denver, Colorado. The plan was for Angelica and Cherry to fly out of Charlotte while the others flew out of Miami, including Thad and Asila. They dropped Nina off with Asila's parents. But Angelica never made it home.

"Morning, sleepy head," said Angelica.

"Good morning," said Alex, hugging her tight.

Angelica was lying in Alex's arms when Claudia called. They were about to take off and wanted her to know that her sister, Jazmina, was going. Angelica didn't care but advised her to tell Falio. She wasn't sure what he had planned.

"Angelica...I want to talk to you before you leave."

"Ok."

Alex knew that everything would change once she left.

"Kelly flies in this evening," he said.

"Are you guys getting back together?"

"Yes, but my feelings for her have changed."

"What do you mean?"

"I can't feel for her what I feel for you. I really like you, and I'd love to see where this goes between us."

"But you know I can't. I'm almost certain Falio is going to propose."

"And you're going to accept?"

"Yes."

Alex lay on his back, looking up at the ceiling.

"This isn't easy for me if that's what you're wondering," she told him. "If things were different, you'd be mine."

"Then don't do it."

"But what about him? What if you finally had a chance to get the girl of your dreams? What would you do?"

"The same thing."

"So, what do you expect me to do? I've been honest with you this entire time."

"I know. I just don't like this situation."

"Me either. But you're getting back with Kelly, too. So, it's not just on me."

Alex was bummed but got up to take her to the airport. Angelica's plane arrived at 8:30 a.m. She saw Cherry waving from inside the plane.

"Well…my ride is here," she said.

"Do you have to leave?"

"Yes, and this isn't goodbye. We're still friends."

He made a face.

"Besides, I have to come back for my stuff. Are you sure it's ok in your closet?"

"Yes. No one will touch it."

She went to hug him, but he stuck his tongue in her mouth. So, she jumped up on him and kissed him some more.

"I'll let you know I made it safely."

"Ok."

The luggage attendant helped Angelica with her luggage as she approached the plane. She looked back and waved as she climbed the stairs. Alex waved back.

When Angelica boarded the plane, Cherry asked, "Are you ok?"

"I have so much to tell you."

First, Angelica asked about work. She felt out of the loop and in a different world since she'd been away. Cherry mentioned some issues Damian stepped up to handle.

"You know Damian and Shana aren't speaking," said Cherry.

"I'm sure. Shana didn't like that bomb I dropped."

"Zeke looks pitiful since you dropped him," said Cherry, trying to sound cool.

"He'll be fine."

"And Austin has been working non-stop getting ready for the relaunch party in January."

"How's Asila working out?"

"It sounds like Austin and Elise are happy with her work."

"Ok, cool."

Then, Cherry asked, "What was the big emergency that you had to leave?"

"My friend, Victor, was in trouble."

Angelica gave Cherry a little background on her and Victor's relationship.

"Why did you guys break up?" asked Cherry.

"Several reasons. I felt Victor was too flirtatious. He didn't like me talking to Falio, even though I never cheated on him with Falio."

"Do you regret it?"

"No. Victor and I are better as friends."

Next, she told her about running into Alex in New York.

"Yes, please explain how he went from barely being in your

life to picking you up in Atlanta," said Cherry, giggling.

Angelica told her everything about them hanging out, talking about their relationships, their fun days and all the sex.

"Of course, you had sex with him," said Cherry.

"And I never expected Alex to become as relevant as he is in my life."

"Is he getting back together with Kelly?"

"Yes."

"Will you see him again?"

"I will. The clothes he bought me are at his house. But we both understood what last night was about."

"It still doesn't mean he didn't fall for you."

"I know. And to be honest, I kinda fell for Alex too, but Falio deserves his chance now."

"Was last night goodbye sex?"

"Yes."

Cherry just shook her head.

Angelica talked about the ball, Claudia meeting Bronson and the mix-up kiss with Chad.

"How did you confuse Chad for Alex?" asked Cherry. "Aren't there physical differences?"

"Yes, but it was dark, everyone wore masks and Claudia and I had been drinking and smoking. But still…I could've sworn it was Alex's mask I saw.

"What do you mean?"

"It looked exactly like his."

Alex wasn't an audacious person. He was more reserved, stayed in his comfort zone and played it safe. So, she thought he was trying to step his game up by being bold and daring.

"Ahhh…so you thought it was Alex who kissed you in the corner?"

"Yes!"

They laughed.

Next, Angelica spoke about Chad with excitement in her voice. She mentioned Victor setting up the meeting between them. She described his physical features, his penthouse, how she wore no underwear to their first meeting and their first time together.

"You're nasty," said Cherry, laughing.

"I know, but I thought I was seeing Alex afterward."

"Chad sounds dreamy."

"He is."

Angelica told her about Tennessee and all of his shenanigans. She also told her how he made up for it when they got to New York.

"It was the way he did things," said Angelica.

"What do you mean?"

She loved the exclusivity that came with him. She explained the shopping, the perfume, the restaurant and the jewelry store.

"No one asked questions. No mishaps. We showed up and received VIP treatment everywhere we went."

"Wow, that sounds nice."

"It was next level."

She even told her about the toy store. After one call, they bought thousands of dollars in toys for her niece and nephews. The feeling was compared to royalty.

"And the sex…"

Angelica described his smell, his lips and the way his hands touched her body. Angelica got goosebumps describing his eyes looking into hers. Cherry listened on the edge of her seat.

"But if you were with Chad, how did you end up in Atlanta?" asked Cherry. "And does Chad know about Falio?"

"No! He doesn't know about Falio and he had to leave for Mexico yesterday afternoon. So, I came to Atlanta to fuck Alex one last time."

"Angelica!"

"What!"

Cherry shook her head.

"What are you going to do? It sounds like you really like Chad."

"Chad is almost unreal. He's smart as hell, very handsome and very sexual. I feel like he's dangerous for me."

"How so?"

"Like I'm infatuated with him, and I could easily get addicted to his sex and his lifestyle."

"I understand."

"He asked me to be his girlfriend."

"What did you say?"

"I asked if he was married because of the way he said it."

"Is he?"

"He said no, but I get this weird feeling there's more to him than he leads on."

"Like what?"

"The day I left, it felt like he didn't know if he should be an ass or love on me. It's like he'd say stupid shit to get under my skin, but then wants me at his beck and call."

"That's weird."

"Yeah…I don't know. He just kept holding me close to him before I left. And then he'd say something smart to piss me off."

"It sounds like he likes you but is afraid to fall."

"I don't know."

"So, Chad and Alex?"

"Yes, but you know what…Alex was like a breath of fresh air. We come from similar backgrounds, we can talk about anything and his sex game is ridiculous. I want to pull out that inner freak," said Angelica, laughing.

"Poor Alex."

"He's a close second to Falio."

"What does that mean?"

"It means I'd be with him if Falio wasn't in the picture."

Cherry was surprised.

Chapter 22
Friday Night

Angelica and Cherry arrived in Denver around noon. Falio was there as soon as Angelica got off the plane. He picked her up and swung her around before kissing her.

"You remember Cherry?"

"Yes."

Falio hugged Cherry.

"Where's everyone else?" Angelica asked him.

"They should be here any minute."

"What do you mean? Didn't you fly in with them?"

"No."

"When did you get here?"

"Yesterday."

"You're up to something."

"Yes, I am."

Soon after, the Miami gang arrived. It gave Angelica a second to text Alex.

All that attended: Falio and Angelica, Claudia and Nico, John and Paula, Jessica and Julio, Thad and Asila, Cherry and Q, Nico's brother, Sal, and Claudia's sister, Jazmina.

When Angelica saw Sal, she asked Falio, "What is he doing

here?"

"Damn! You don't want him here?"

"No…not like that. It's just Sal never comes to any of our functions."

"Nico wanted him to get away for the weekend and clear his head. Girl troubles."

"Oh ok. Cool."

Angelica liked Sal. She thought he had a good head on his shoulders but needed the right opportunity to get ahead. He wanted to be a model and had potential. But he needed to get serious about his career.

"It's good to see Julio and Jessica."

"Yeah…you know she and Paula are inseparable like you and Claudia."

Julio was Falio's attorney, but more importantly, his friend. And Jessica was not only Julio's wife but Paula's best friend. They often hung out together.

Angelica screamed with excitement as she hugged everyone. Asila hugged Angelica tight and thanked her for everything.

"You are looking at the official event coordinator for Sportie Fans," said Asila.

"Congrats, sis!"

"Thanks. I even got a five-thousand-dollar sign-on bonus."

"I'm so happy for you!"

"I couldn't have done it without you," said Asila, hugging her.

They walked and talked until they exited the terminal and boarded their private luxury bus.

"Fuck, it's cold," said Angelica.

"For real," said Asila.

It was cold and overcast, with a high of thirty-nine degrees.

"Take us to the best cannabis dispensaries," Falio told the driver, Ben.

He gave him five hundred dollars for the favor.

They stopped at a few spots and got edibles, oils and weed. Falio bought edibles for everyone to try. Angelica tried to warn Cherry, but it was too late. She'd already eaten half of a chocolate chip cookie.

Ben stopped in front of a 2-story, contemporary mountain home with a light-colored stone exterior on Sandy Lake Road. Six stone columns and plenty of plush trees surrounded the elongated entryway.

"Whose house is this?" Angelica asked Falio.

"It's ours, Mi Angel. Happy Birthday."

"Falio, I can't believe you did this," she said, hugging and kissing him.

Their 9-bedroom, 15-bath mansion spanned over 23,000 square feet and sat on three acres. It had a 25-foot ceiling in the foyer, open concept and marble and hardwood flooring throughout. There were huge windows all around and a double floor-to-ceiling stone fireplace between the formal living room and dining room. The kitchen had two rectangular islands with plenty of pantry space. And for fun, it came with a craft room, a theater and a game room with bowling, billiards and darts.

Falio and Angelica sat with the realtor to sign the paperwork while everyone else toured the home.

"Congratulations," said the realtor to Falio and Angelica, shaking their hands.

They both thanked her as she handed over the keys.

"I love you, Mi Angel."

"I love you, too, Papi."

Angelica noticed that the house was fully furnished.

"This is beautiful, Babe," Angelica told Falio.

"I'm glad you like it."

The chef arrived just as the realtor was leaving. Falio escorted him and his two staff members to the 4-bedroom guest house on the side of the main house. They were staying the entire weekend to prepare all the meals. Then, Falio showed him the kitchen and gave him the CBD and THC oils for him to use in their meals.

Julio and John asked to speak to Falio alone. So, Claudia discreetly grabbed Angelica and went up to the master bedroom.

"I can't stop thinking about him."

"Who?"

"Seth."

"What happened?" asked Angelica.

She told her everything, including the boat ride back to Miami.

"I thought you weren't going to like him."

"He wasn't at all what I thought. He didn't want to go on the date either but obliged his parents."

"They're after him, too?"

"Yes! They want him to settle down and get married."

Then, Claudia told her about his ex and best friend.

"What are you going to do, Claude?"

"I don't know, but Nico thinks I'm acting a little funny since I slept over at my parent's house last night," she said, winking.

Angelica laughed.

"Well, you better try harder with Nico because he's gonna know something's up."

"I know…I know."

Claudia changed the subject and asked about Chad and Alex. Angelica told her all about Chad in Tennessee, the freak party and the "Chad" treatment in New York. But she didn't provide details about the Tennessee project or the perfume collection.

"He asked me to be his girlfriend."

"What did you say?"

"No."

"Why?"

"Hello! Falio! And it was the way he asked."

She explained what she meant and then told her about Alex.

"Awwww!" said Claudia.

"Yeah...I like him, Claude."

"But didn't you say he had a girlfriend?"

"He does, and I'm with Falio."

Just then, Falio walked into the room and politely kicked Claudia out.

"I love you, Angelica."

"I love you, too, Falio."

Falio kissed her until she fell back on the bed. He took off her clothes and removed his. He laid on top of her.

"You're finally mine."

"Yes, Papi...I am."

After their afternoon quickie, Falio suggested everyone go sightseeing and do a little shopping while the chef prepared a special dinner. So, they got back on the bus and headed out.

Cherry couldn't stop giggling, which made everyone laugh. Angelica knew she was high. So, they decided to stop and get food. Ben took them to a nearby pizza place, off South University Blvd and Girard Place East.

They walked in and found a place to sit. A young white girl approached them with menus.

"Hi. My name is Katy. I'll be your server."

Everyone greeted her and then ordered drinks. They looked at the menus and figured out what they wanted. Falio ordered four x-large pizzas with five orders of wings, garlic bread and cheese sticks for everyone, including Ben.

After about an hour, they all got up to leave.

"Thank you!" said Katy, receiving a five hundred dollar tip.

"Thanks for putting up with us," said Falio, winking.

Afterward, they went next door to get gelato. Even though it was cold as hell, they wanted to try it.

Falio told Ben to take them to the nearest fur coat store. They rode up South University Blvd until they reached ML Furs. Everyone came out with a coat.

Next, they drove down East Third Avenue and stopped at several shops to support the local businesses. However, they saw a sign for Cherry Creek shopping mall.

"Ben…to the mall," said Angelica.

Angelica handed Cherry the black Amex from Falio, Falio gave Thad $25K in cash, Nico took care of Sal and Jazmina had her own card.

Everyone started together but split up. Falio spoiled Angelica, as did Thad with Asila and Nina. Cherry and Q bought more than anticipated. And the shocker was Sal and Jazmina holding hands.

They made it back to the house about 7 p.m. Claudia asked everyone to get off the bus except Angelica and Cherry. She had a gift for her best friend.

"What did you get me, Claude?"

"Nothing. I needed everyone gone."

"Why?"

"Ange…I have to show you something, but you're not gonna like it."

"What?"

Claudia showed her the latest news on all social media feeds. It was about Chad getting engaged to Delilah Sutton of Sutton Oil in Mexico.

"That mutha fucker!" screamed Angelica.

Claudia lit a blunt as Cherry read the article.

"I can't believe it. I knew something was up with him," said Angelica, pacing.

"What do you need?" asked Claudia.

Angelica was quiet. At that moment, Chad called her.

"Is it true?"

Chad tried explaining, but Angelica kept asking for a simple yes or no answer. Chad finally admitted it was true. She hung up.

"Ange…say something."

"I'm fuckin' mad right now!"

The ladies didn't say much as Angelica paced while processing everything.

"I knew something was up with him," repeated Angelica.

"Well, it sounds like they've been together a while," said Cherry, reading the article. "But why did he play with you like that?"

"Because he's an Asshole!"

"What are you going to do?" asked Claudia.

She sat down and closed her eyes. She imagined Chad's body against hers. She imagined his smell, touch and look in his eyes. When she opened her eyes, she was calm.

"The part that sucks is that he drew me in," said Angelica, smoking. "I know it's wrong, but I liked him."

"What will you do now?" asked Cherry.

She paused and said, "Nothing. It's next week's problem. I have to put it all aside this weekend. I can't do that to Falio."

Angelica thought about the men in her life.

"Victor warned me, but I thought I had it all under control."

"Push it down, Ange."

Angelica closed her eyes one last time. Her eyes watered, but she would not let a tear fall. She thought about their physical attraction and realized feelings had crept in. Angelica opened her eyes and hit the blunt a few more times.

"You pushed it down?" asked Claudia.

"Yep."

"You ready?"

"Yep."

Cherry wasn't sure what just happened but assumed Claudia hyped Angelica into pushing her emotions to the side. Falio couldn't know anything was wrong.

Angelica went upstairs and ran a hot shower. Falio joined her. She hugged him tight as tears fell, but he couldn't see them under the water. Then, she did what she'd never done before. She thought about Chad while being with Falio. She kissed his neck while massaging his dick. He rubbed her back as she was turning him on. She went down and pleasured Falio real good. He didn't know what got into her, but he couldn't handle it. He came.

"Damn, Baby," said Falio breathing heavily.

She didn't say anything. She finished her shower and got out. Falio didn't let her get dressed. He spread her legs apart and tasted her goodness. She couldn't stay still as he was pleasuring her insanely good. She came.

"Damn, mami…you taste so good."

She didn't say anything as she was trying to catch her breath.

Around nine, everyone adjourned to the dinner table. The chef brought several bottles of wine along with various appetizers, including spicy shrimp in a warm cannabis butter sauce.

"Cherry…wait!" said Angelica, but again, it was too late.

Cherry had eaten several shrimp and other appetizers.

"This was good."

"Just know you'll be high," Angelica told her.

"I'll be fine."

Cherry didn't care. She just wanted to eat.

Next, the chef served a spinach and kale salad with a cranberry vinaigrette. He also brought hot dinner rolls with warm garlic cannabis butter.

"I don't want to wait anymore," said Falio.

He got up and kneeled in front of Angelica. He opened a ring box with a custom-made 15-carat diamond ring inside.

"Will you marry me?"

"Yes," she said, kissing him.

The center stone was a 10-carat Radiant solitaire with a micro-pave diamond halo. The three-row band had a single row of baguettes in the center with rows of micro pavé diamonds on each side.

He slid it on her finger and then kissed her. Everyone clapped and cheered as the chef served grilled salmon drizzled in cannabis olive oil with creamy butter risotto and green beans with thinly sliced almonds.

Chapter 23
Birthdays

Angelica woke up to Falio staring at her.

"What are you doing?"

"Looking at my future wife. Happy birthday, Baby."

She smiled as he wrapped his arm around her.

"Happy almost birthday, future husband."

Falio loved the sound of that.

"What are we doing today?" she asked.

"Having fun."

"Baby, all of your gifts are at my house."

"You've given me the best gift I could ever ask for."

Falio got up and lit a blunt. He went to get the others up while Angelica jumped in bed with Claudia and Nico. Nico was used to them doing that, so he got up and went to smoke with Falio, leaving them alone to talk.

"How are you today?" Claudia asked her.

"I'm good."

"The truth."

Angelica still felt some kind of way about Chad but pushed it down. Her feelings didn't matter since she was engaged.

"He wasn't mine, Claude. We weren't dating or exclusive. He

just blew my mind and that's on me."

"Is that what you're telling yourself to get through it?"

"It's the truth."

"I know you. And I know it's hard, but I understand. Seth completely rocked my world. I never saw that coming."

"Has he called?"

"No. I told him I was going to be on a girls' trip this weekend."

"And how are things with you and Nico?"

"We're good but he keeps hinting at marriage and our dream home."

"Claude! What are you going to do?"

"I don't know but Bronson texted yesterday. I told him I was celebrating your birthday and that I'd reach out when I got back."

"Does he know about Nico?"

"No!"

"How are things with him?"

"They were good until a couple of days ago."

"What happened?"

"Seth!"

"Dang…he must've fucked you real good."

"He did and I'm scared, Ange."

"You like him?"

"I can get used to the sex."

"I know what you mean."

"Ange…it's like we have a lot in common, and we both think outside the box."

Then, Angelica made a face and said, "I did something I shouldn't have done last night."

"What?"

"Thought about Chad when I was with Falio."

"Ange!"

"I know, but I didn't mean to. It just happened. I was high as hell and just kept thinking about his engagement. I pretended it was our last time and pulled some tricks out of the vault."

The ladies laughed as Angelica demonstrated.

"I can't say anything. I did the same."

"Claude!"

The ladies laughed at themselves but knew they were wrong.

"Nico asked for the ring back."

"What ring?"

"The diamond ring he gave me when I was with Anthony. This one," said Claudia showing her the picture.

"Oh...that one! Did he say why?"

"No. He just said not to worry."

"Then, he's probably getting you a better one."

"I don't know."

Then, Claudia changed the subject.

"Do you see my sister with Sal?"

"Yes! They are quite cozy."

"I don't need them being a couple."

"Why?"

"What if I don't end up with Nico?"

Angelica just made a face.

Everyone got up for breakfast. They were high and hungry from all of the smoking. Excitement hit their stomachs when they saw all of the food. There was every kind of breakfast food, including chocolate chip waffles, mini frittatas, fresh fruit and freshly squeezed orange juice.

"Everyone needs to dress warm," said Falio.

"Why?" asked Angelica.

"I reserved the entire ice arena for a few hours to go ice skating."

Angelica screamed and kissed him.

After breakfast, everyone got dressed and headed to their

winter land destination. Upon their arrival, they were loud and ready to have fun, even though not everyone knew how to skate. Thad and Cherry glided all over the ice like pros. Asila, Paula and Jessica were on the side learning to skate with trainers. John and Sal joined them as they hadn't skated before. Surprisingly, Julio, Jazmina and Angelica weren't too bad. Falio, Nico and Claudia weren't feeling it at all, but Falio had to participate. After a while, everyone was out there. The biggest surprise was when the professional hockey team showed up to play a friendly game of hockey. The coach and a few players were really impressed with Thad and felt he missed his calling. He was so good that he gave the star player a run for his money. They took lots of pictures and posted them on social media. It was a wonderful time.

Falio left the rest of the day open. He wanted Angelica to choose other things to do. So, everyone got on their phones and looked up events occurring nearby. Claudia suggested the wine festival. Then, Angelica found the Christmas craft festival at the convention center. They attended both events. Afterward, everyone went back to the house to relax and have dinner. They were all traveling back home the next day.

Julio excused himself as he took a call. Afterward, he pulled John, Falio and Jessica aside. After a few minutes, Falio let out a loud yell of excitement. When he returned, he picked up Angelica and swung her around.

"What happened?"

"I did it, Mi Angel!"

Falio took her to their room.

"I officially own a bank."

"What!"

"Yes!"

Jessica's father owned several banks in Colombia. He branched into the U.S. with the understanding that Jessica and

John were purchasing it from him. They needed one hundred million to take ownership. They each had their half but John thought about Falio. He could use the bank to stash his illegal money, and a third investor meant less money upfront for Jessica and John. So Jessica agreed, and Julio worked the legal side of it.

"Mila just called Julio and told him we got it. It's officially ours! We have to sign the paperwork when we get back."

"Mila?"

"Julio's new attorney."

"Congrats, Baby. I'm proud of you," she said, hugging him.

"Thank you, Mi Angel, but you know I did this for us?"

"I know, Papi."

"John has been helping me with investments."

"That's good."

"And Paula will come to work for the bank along with John and Jessica."

"That's good."

"This feels right. Only bigger and better is coming."

"I know and I'm happy for you."

"Zarvos-Salis International Bank."

"Zarvos?"

"Yes. Why?"

"Who owns Zarvos?"

"Not sure, but Jessica's father deals with that investment group. And check this out. They agreed to front half the required amount for an equal twenty-five percent and name the bank after them."

"Makes sense. The Zarvos name is huge."

"Exactly! And since this was John's project, he agreed to pay a little more to have his name added. Instead of contributing thirty-five million dollars, I only have to pay fifteen."

She hugged him.

"Do you know the kind of business we're going to get guaranteed? It will bring in prestigious clientele with their names attached."

"Did you give John the rest of the money for the other investments?"

"Yes. We're using the surplus for loan programs and other investments."

"Nice."

"I'm also investing with Nico. He has big plans for him and Claudia."

"Like what?"

"Can't tell you yet, but it's big. Nico wants to give Claudia the life she deserves."

Angelica was immensely proud of him.

Falio removed all of her clothes while backing her up to the wall. He sucked on her breast while she played with him. Once he was hard, he stuck his dick inside of her. She let out a loud groan. Angelica unintentionally scratched his back. Falio was emotionally-driven while having sex.

They went back into the living room after their rendezvous. John, Paula, Jessica and Julio were drinking and talking. Sal and Jazmina were down in the game room bowling with Cherry and Q. Thad and Asila were playing table tennis. And Nico and Claudia were somewhere, probably having sex.

Everyone spent the rest of the evening socializing, eating good food and getting fucked up. There was plenty of weed and liquor.

Chapter 24
Monday Morning

Angelica walked into work looking fabulous. She wore a crisp white designer suit with a white lace bustier top, a white Prada bag and Prada slingback heels. Her hair was flowing, her makeup was flawless, she accessorized in diamonds and she wore a designer wool trench coat.

"Good morning, Elizabeth."

"Wow! Good morning, Angelica. You look fantastic!"

"Thank you. Did a little shopping while I was away."

"I'd say."

"How are things around here?"

"I have so much to tell you, but…"

Elizabeth tried to warn Angelica before she walked into her office. She wasn't ready for what she was about to see.

"What the hell…" said Angelica.

"I was trying to catch you before you walked in."

Large and small floral arrangements in all colors, shapes and sizes filled her office. The conference table had several gift bags from her favorite stores and near the window were beautiful LV trunks filled with all of the stuff Chad bought her while in New York. Last, she had a beautiful gold box with a satin black bow sitting on her desk. It was expensive truffles.

"Do you know who did this?" Elizabeth asked Angelica.

"I have an idea."

Angelica's phone rang with a familiar number. She asked Elizabeth for some privacy.

"Hello."

"Please don't hang up."

"What do you want?"

"I want to apologize."

"For what?"

"Not being truthful with you about my engagement."

"We're even. I didn't tell you about mine."

"What!"

"Thanks for the gifts, but please stop sending me things. I don't want anything to do with you, Chad. And I will deal with Tom regarding my project. Goodbye."

Angelica hung up and blocked him. She didn't want to hear anything he had to say. They were both engaged. That meant keeping communication to the very minimum. She'd deal with him once the Tennessee project got started.

After she hung up, Angelica received a bank transfer notification for fourteen million dollars. She did a happy dance as she couldn't contain her excitement. Angelica texted Victor and thanked him. She also inquired about the property. She was ready to purchase. Victor hadn't heard anything yet.

Angelica called Elizabeth back into her office. They discussed Angelica's calendar and the meetings Damian set up for her. Elizabeth updated her on events in her absence. They also discussed pending issues and Angelica's travel plans for the rest of the year.

"And congratulations."

"On what?"

"You're engagement. It's hard to miss that rock."

"Thank you."

She hugged Angelica and left.

Angelica's first meeting of the day was with Austin. She hurried to his office.

"Hi," she said, knocking on the door.

"Come in."

Austin stared at her as she walked into his office. And she couldn't help but notice how good he looked in his black Armani suit.

"Good morning," she said, breaking up the awkwardness.

"Good morning. You look amazing."

"Thank you. You as well."

"Thank you." Then, he looked at her ring finger and said, "I see congratulations are in order."

"Yes…thank you."

Angelica updated him on the New York stores. She wanted Zeke to meet with managers at two stores since it was his region. She started the preliminary work but needed him to follow up. Angelica also told him which store should include the sports bar.

Next, they discussed Paris. Austin needed Angelica and her team there as soon as possible. With their flagship store opening in time for the holidays, Austin wanted everything perfect. That meant Destiny had to go for merchandising, Elise needed to hire a PR team for marketing and Angelica could take whoever else she needed to assist. She suggested her senior directors, except for Zeke, since he'd be in New York.

"I'm thinking next week you're in Paris. What do you think?" asked Austin.

Angelica looked at her calendar.

"I think we're pushing it. It's the week before Thanksgiving."

"I know, but if we don't go now, we can't go until December. And I want to be open for Black Friday."

"You know they don't celebrate the same holidays as the U.S."

"But we're a U.S.-based company."

"Ok. We'll need to leave Sunday to be there Monday."

"Ok."

Austin wanted Destiny and Elise to visit the other stores to make sure they were getting the proper exposure. Angelica agreed. So, Austin called them into his office.

"Destiny, I need everything to look perfect," said Austin.

"Ok."

"And make sure we have plenty of inventory, staging equipment, mannequins…"

"I got it," she reassured him.

She showed them some design plans she'd been working on. Austin liked the layout she came up with. He was hoping it would attract more people.

"Elise…find the best PR firm on that side of the hemisphere within budget."

"I've already gotten quotes. I was waiting to schedule a meet and greet. But I'll schedule now since we'll be there next week."

"Great! And I need them to handle our branding for our European stores. I want to saturate the market with exposure."

"Ok."

"And I'll handle our travel requests," said Angelica.

"Thank you," said Austin.

Angelica went back to her office and asked Elizabeth to call Damian to her office. Fifteen minutes later, he arrived.

"Well, Damn!"

"Shut up. Come in."

They went through all of the issues Damian resolved and discussed the meetings he scheduled.

"Great job!"

"Thanks. Great teacher."

Afterward, Angelica called for Zeke and Cherry to join them.

"Damn!" said Zeke.

"Come in, come in."

Cherry just mouthed, "Falio?"

Angelica shook her head no and mouthed, "Chad."

Cherry just shook her head.

Angelica asked Zeke to travel to New York the following week to finish what she'd started. Then, she invited the others to Paris. Zeke was a little disappointed he couldn't go, but Angelica assured him he'd go on the next trip. She mentioned the other senior directors being invited to Paris as well.

Just as they were all leaving, Asila and Thad knocked on her door.

"Damn! Who messed up?" asked Thad.

"Damn, girl. Who did this? And you look fabulous!" said Asila.

Angelica hugged her sister and said, "Thank you. What are you doing here?"

"Had a meeting with Austin to discuss the Christmas party."

"How's that going?"

"Good. Now, stop avoiding the question. Who sent all of this?"

"Long story."

"Well, come over later for dinner. I'll cook," said Thad.

"Ok, thanks."

"Was it Falio?" asked Asila.

"No."

"Angelica!"

"I didn't expect this. It isn't my fault."

"It's always your fault," said Thad, laughing.

"Shut up!"

"Please don't fuck it up!" exclaimed Asila.

"I'm not!"

Asila saw the fancy box on her desk.

"And the good chocolates," said Asila.

"Take them if you want."

Asila unwrapped the box and grabbed one. She saw a black velvet box underneath. Asila opened it and found a pair of 8-carat diamond stud earrings.

"Can I have these as well?"

"What?"

Angelica didn't realize there were more gifts underneath the truffles.

"Umm…no. I'm keeping those."

They laughed as they removed the candy and saw all the gift boxes.

"Damn, girl. Someone either fucked up or wants you bad," said Thad.

"Both."

They laughed.

By 1:00 p.m., Angelica was starving. She'd been working and forgot to order lunch. Just as she was going to ask Elizabeth to order food, Elizabeth called her.

"You have a visitor."

"Who is it?"

"Alex Mendoza."

"Send him in."

Alex surprised her.

"Hey, Handsome," she said, giving him the biggest hug.

"Well, hello, Beautiful. You look amazing!"

"Thank you. You, too. And you smell delicious."

"Thank you," he said, smiling.

"So, what are you doing here?"

"I came to talk and take you to lunch."

"That was sweet."

"Well, I think this is sweet," he said, referring to all the flowers around her office.

"It is."

"He really does love you."

"He does."

Alex assumed Falio sent all the flowers, and she didn't correct him. She wasn't sure how to explain Chad, considering she was also with Alex.

"Let's go get that lunch," she suggested.

"Let's go."

Chapter 25
Lunch Date

Angelica suggested Firebirds near the mall. When they walked in, the hostess immediately seated them. They ordered drinks and appetizers. Alex wasted no time asking the question.

"Are you happy?"

"Yes."

"He has good taste," said Alex, referring to her ring.

"Thanks. What about you? What happened with Kelly?"

"She's back."

"Don't sound like that. It makes me sad."

"I can't help it."

Alex had the conversation with Kelly on Friday as planned. They both agreed to work on the things that bothered the other.

"If it doesn't work, I'm not trying with her anymore."

"Why?"

"Because it'd be a waste of my time."

"Does she know?"

"Yes. I was very honest with her."

"How did she take it?"

"She said she understood, and she didn't want to waste any more time either."

"It's good that you both agreed."

"Yeah, but honestly… I don't feel like I need to change."

"Why?"

"The things that bothered her can't be helped."

Kelly wanted the same things she'd been complaining about. She wanted Alex to work a nine-to-five schedule, which was impossible. She wanted more vacations, more gifts and more participation in her blogs.

"I'm not doing the blogs. Out of the question."

"I knew that one."

"I'm not working that schedule, and I can't go on a vacation right now. I'm leaving for Japan next week. I have a good feeling about this business deal."

She inquired about the app's progress.

"Yeah…I don't think Kelly will get what she wants," said Angelica.

"Exactly. And while I can get her gifts, I still feel pressured to do it. I don't like that feeling."

"I understand."

"I want to give freely, as I did with you."

"I understand, but you have to think of something if you want it to work," she said, touching his hand.

He touched hers back and said, "I'm not sure I want it to."

Angelica pulled back and said, "Alex…"

"Angelica…"

"Don't do that. Don't compare her to me."

"It's hard not to."

Alex was very honest and admitted that he'd thought about her every day. He imagined her smile, them playing, their New York fun days and his best friend finally liked someone.

"He loves you," said Alex.

"Who?"

"Jordan."

"Awww, that's sweet. I think he's great."

The waitress came and took their order. Angelica got the honey garlic chicken with a loaded baked potato and a side salad. Alex ordered lobster stuffed salmon with the same sides as Angelica.

Alex brought up Jordan. He loved the idea of Alex and Angelica together. She got him out of his shell and experienced real feelings. Jordan hadn't seen Alex that happy or affectionate with anyone.

"He likes your confidence and the fact that you like football," said Alex, laughing.

"Love football."

"You should come to one of the games. You know Nicole will hook you up."

"Great idea."

Then, he told her about his conversation with his sister. She helped him understand what he lacked with Kelly and what he'd found in Angelica.

"I like your sister. She's a smart woman."

"She is. She told me to step my game up."

"You should."

"With you."

"Oh no! You can't!"

Alex laughed. He assured her that he wouldn't interfere in her love life. But if he had the chance, he'd fight for her.

"So, how was your birthday?" he asked. "It looked like you had a great time."

She knew he'd seen her social media stories.

Angelica told him about the dispensaries, different edibles and shopping. She shared her excitement about meeting the professional hockey team and Falio renting out the ice arena to ice skate.

Last, they talked about the festivals and her new home in Denver.

"Damn! He bought you a house?"

"Yes…a beautiful one," she said, showing him pictures.

"Wow! Just like that…he bought it?"

"Yes. Why did you say it like that?"

"That's a large investment."

"It is, but he doesn't see it that way. He bought it to make me happy. We've talked about owning properties in several states and using them as vacation homes. This is our first vacation home."

"He loves you."

"Unconditionally. And now he owns a bank, so he can get me whatever I want."

"A bank?"

"Yes. Falio owns a bank."

"Wow. That's impressive."

Angelica told him about renting out the vacation home to earn a profit while it wasn't being used. And they'd do the same with other properties purchased.

"You never cease to amaze me."

"Why?"

"You're smart, sexy and savvy."

"Thank you."

"I am a little jealous, though."

"Why?"

"To think about that kind of love…"

"Love isn't something you think about. You feel it. It's overwhelming, uncontrollable and wonderful at the same time. Love fires you up and grabs hold of you. There's passion, intensity and togetherness in love."

Alex knew what she meant. He'd never met a woman like Angelica. She was genuinely interested in him and not his money. She took him out of his comfort zone. Angelica made him feel rather than think about things. And he loved her tenacity and fearlessness.

"I really want those things with you," he said.

"Just out of curiosity, what would our life look like?"

"The same but with me."

They laughed, and then he told her.

He knew about women and shopping because of his mom and sister. But after seeing her shop, he really understood it. He, too, wanted to purchase vacation homes but in other countries. He envisioned them doing projects together that would boost their financial portfolio. They'd be involved in several charities. He'd support her in all of her business endeavors like she would him. And he'd do things, like send her flowers, surprise her with lunch, whisk her away on trips, buy her jewelry, try new things and have as many babies as she wanted.

"How many kids do you want?" she asked.

"Three...two boys and a girl."

"Me too!"

She smiled as she just looked at him.

"Can I ask you something?" asked Angelica.

"Sure."

"How is it that you can describe us, but can't do the same with Kelly?"

Alex made a face.

"We were never like you and I. Kelly and I never had the spark that we have. And she doesn't fuck like you...my God."

"Stop!"

Alex described their sex in detail. She was getting turned on, so she changed the subject.

"I have to tell you about Tennessee."

"I know what you're doing."

"Me too."

Angelica mentioned meeting the real estate developers to plot out the land.

"It's going to be an amazing project."

"Did you decide what to do with it?"

"Yes."

Angelica planned to build house million-dollar homes, a prestigious golf course, an upscale mall, entertainment venues for kids and commercial properties, like business offices. She wanted to build a resort but didn't think she had enough land. Alex made some suggestions and told her to get her own attorney. She should never have all businesses under one company.

Chapter 26
Asila's House

Angelica left work around six o'clock. She called Claudia as she drove to Asila's. They talked until she arrived.

Thad, Asila and Nina stood at the door as Angelica drove up.

"Hello," said Angelica, hugging the adults. Then, she picked up Nina and said, "Oh my God! Titi missed you. How are you?"

"Good."

Angelica hugged her and said, "I love you."

"I love you."

They went into the kitchen. Angelica saw chips, salsa and fresh guacamole sitting on the island. Thad whipped up some strawberry margaritas with fresh limes as he cooked.

"So, do tell," said Asila.

Angelica caught them up on her life since the Shana incident. She began with Zeke and their last rendezvous. Then, Angelica talked about New York and Victor. While there, she ran into Alex. Angelica told them everything about her time with Alex. Lastly, she mentioned the masquerade ball, meeting Chad and everything dealing with him, including new business endeavors and his engagement to Delilah.

"Damn! That's crazy," Thad told Angelica.

"I know."

"So, he sent the flowers and gifts to make up for leading you on?" asked Asila.

"Pretty much."

"I knew something was wrong with you on Friday."

"Yep. That's when I found out but couldn't say anything because I was with Falio."

"I just don't get why he'd ask you to be his girlfriend knowing he was getting married?"

"Because he has it bad," said Thad, laughing.

"What about Alex? He sounds sweet," said Asila.

"He is. Like today…he just showed up to take me to lunch." Angelica told them about her lunch date.

"He came to see if it was real," said Thad.

"What do you mean?"

"He wanted to see if you were available or not. There's no doubt that he's into you."

"I know, but he got back with Kelly."

"Only because you aren't available. You're the one Alex wants."

"I know. And to be honest, I'd be with him if I weren't with Falio."

"You like him like that?"

"I do."

Just then, Falio called. She excused herself to speak with him. When she returned, Angelica told them Falio would be in Charlotte in a few days.

"Can I be honest with you?" Thad asked her.

"Sure."

Thad addressed Falio first. He knew she loved him but wasn't sure his lifestyle fit into her new one. Angelica was making big moves. She not only had her dream job and owned two homes, but she was also becoming an entrepreneur with the Tennessee project and perfume line. She wasn't the same young lady struggling and pushing herself to have better. He felt her loyalty was out of obligation because Falio helped her family. Thad believed that Falio and Angelica might've worked out had they stayed together after college. But with Angelica's exposure to the finer things, Thad felt it would be difficult for her to return to the way things were. Angelica was used to having Falio and whoever else she wanted because Falio was unavailable. Thad wondered if she was ready to completely change her ways to be with him again and endure his street life.

Next, he talked about Chad. Chad was enamored with Angelica because she was bold, brave and did things her way unapologetically. And he was attracted to that. However, Thad also felt Chad always got his way and controlled women with his charisma and money. So, he warned her to be careful even though Chad could catapult her to the next level. Thad felt Angelica was a project with sexual benefits. She was green regarding business and hadn't experienced his quality of life. Angelica was more of a student, and Chad could teach her a thing or two.

Last but not least was Alex. He was the perfect guy for her. He was rich, handsome, not from the streets, about his business, always creating wealth, no kids, no drama and she could train him to her liking. She'd have all of him and have the kind of life she wanted.

"That's true, sis."

"I know. Thad has a point."

"And I don't think it's going to last," said Thad.

"Who?"

"Alex and Kelly."

"Me either," said Asila.

Angelica rocked his world, and there was no turning back.

Asila and Angelica set the table as Thad brought out the food. Angelica changed the subject as they sat down to eat.

"How are the wedding plans?" asked Angelica.

"We still don't have a venue, but Dana says not to worry," said Asila.

"How many people?"

Thad immediately screamed, "Two hundred!"

"And that's small?"

Asila wanted a small but beautiful event. However, Thad had to invite certain people, and so did she. They settled on two hundred.

"And who's planning everything?" asked Angelica.

"One of Dana's good friends."

"We actually have to go to Miami the weekend after Thanksgiving to meet her," said Thad.

"Do you need me to watch Nina while you go on your honeymoon?"

"No. We're not taking one until after the relaunch party. Austin is paying some serious dough to have everything look nice. I can't bail," said Asila.

"I understand. How's that coming along."

Asila didn't tell her much as there were several surprises.

"I am going to need help soon," said Asila.

"Hire someone."

"Thad said the same thing."

"Well, you could. You have the money from the truck sale and you're getting paid from Sportie Fans."

"I know, but I'm also trying to find office space with a warehouse for inventory and a showroom floor."

"How exciting."

"I know, but it's scary, too."

"You'll do great."

Thad brought up Zeke buying his condo, which could help Asila, the expedited adoption process and Thanksgiving.

"My mom hosts it annually and would like it if all of our families could be together," said Thad.

"Well, we usually spend it with our parents," said Asila.

"We'll just have to invite them here," said Angelica.

"Papi has been talking about coming back. He enjoyed hanging out with Steve."

"My dad likes him too," said Thad.

Angelica excused herself to take a call from the private investigator. After a few minutes, she yelled, "That fucking bitch!" She said a few more choice words and then returned. Asila pointed to Nina.

"I'm sorry, Nina. Titi got upset."

"What happened?" asked Asila.

Angelica just found out that Angelo and Ricky weren't Falio's kids.

"I'm gonna beat her down when I see her," said Angelica, referring to Ariana.

"Oh my God, Angelica! This whole time?" asked Asila.

"Yes!"

"Damn…she's fucked up."

Angelica went into another room and called Falio. But he already knew. He assured her they'd talk about it in person when he arrived.

When Angelica returned, Matt and Elise were there.

"Hey!" said Angelica, hugging them.

They stopped talking about Angelica's life and socialized.

Chapter 27
Secrets

Meanwhile, in Miami, Claudia hung up with Angelica and showered. She threw on a short mini-dress and went to Seth's place. She wanted to fuck him before going to dinner with Nico, who had something important to tell her.

Claudia knocked on Seth's door. When he answered, he was naked. He immediately kissed her.

"I missed you," he said.

"I missed you too."

"Did you think about me?"

"Of course."

"What did you think about?" he asked, removing her clothes.

"This," she said, grabbing his dick.

Seth backed her up against a nearby wall. He sucked on her breasts and slid his finger between her lips. Not only did he make her wet, but Claudia's hips moved like she was having sex the faster he rubbed.

"Baby…" she said, holding on. "I'm about to cum."

Seth bent down and intensely sucked on her clit, tasting her juices. Claudia let out a scream as she came. He quickly stood up and slid inside of her. Seth wanted to feel her pulsating. Claudia scratched him as she tried to hold on, but Seth didn't care. He fucked her hard, showing no mercy. Claudia loved it.

They moved to the sofa, where she straddled him. They kissed as she rocked back and forth. Seth held onto her waist as it felt so good. They enjoyed their sexual escapade.

"You were amazing," he whispered in her ear.

"You too."

"You do something to me."

"I understand."

"I can't stop thinking about you. It's like I crave you."

"That's a good thing, right?"

"You blow my mind, Claudia, and I have to have you."

"Seth…"

"Let's go to dinner."

"I can't. I already have dinner plans."

She knew she'd better choose her words wisely.

Seth felt it was with a man but didn't ask so she wouldn't lie.

"Are you coming back?" he asked.

"No."

"Why?"

"Because I hadn't planned on it."

"Well, I want you here no later than nine."

"I don't know if I…"

"I don't care. If you're not here, then I'll be at your place. But I will see you again tonight."

"Why?"

"I want to fuck you again," he said, kissing her.

"Just like that?"

"Yes! I like being inside of you."

Claudia didn't know how she'd swing it but agreed, fearing he'd show up at her house.

Claudia thought about Seth as she drove back to her place.

She got butterflies thinking about his sex game but wasn't sure what to think of him. He was confident, assertive and knew what he wanted. But there was something about him she wasn't sure about.

She made it home and jumped in the shower. As she washed Seth off, Nico walked in. He removed his clothing and showered with her. Claudia fucked Nico extra spicy, thinking about Seth.

They got dressed and smoked on the way to Kuba in Bayside. Claudia was craving Vaca Frita and empanadas.

Claudia saw her bartender friend when they walked in. The ladies waved as the hostess immediately seated them. Minutes later, Claudia and Nico received a fishbowl mojito to share.

"My parents are in town," she told him.

He just made a face.

"Don't be like that. They came to drop off my dad's new boat."

"Another one?"

"You know how he is about his toys."

"What kind did he get?"

"I don't know."

Nico thought her dad was cool. It was her mom who was very opinionated and judgmental.

"I heard Falio is going to see Angelica," said Claudia.

"Yeah…he told me."

"I'm happy for them. They finally get to be together."

"Yeah."

"Why did you say it like that?"

"I have something to tell you, but you can't tell Ange."

"Why?"

"Falio is going to tell her."

"What is it, Nico?"

"Claudia, you can't say anything."

"What is it?" she sternly asked.

Two women were claiming to be pregnant by Falio.

"Is it possible?"

"Yes and no."

Claudia looked at him in silence as the waitress came to take their order. She couldn't believe what was happening.

"Who are they, Nico?"

Nico wasn't worried about the first woman because Falio never had sex with her. But there was a woman Falio had been seeing off and on. The woman always knew they wouldn't be anything because of Angelica. However, Nico assumed she got pregnant deliberately to keep Falio in her life and to keep the money flowing.

"Angelica is gonna be mad as fuck," said Claudia.

"I know. Falio is devastated about the whole situation."

"As he should be."

Claudia couldn't understand how Falio allowed this to happen when he'd been planning his great escape from Ariana for Angelica.

"He didn't mean for it to happen," said Nico.

"He knew that girl had feelings for him."

"He can't control that."

"Like he can control this?"

"That's not fair, Claude. And you know it."

"All I know is that this was supposed to be their time. And now…it may very well be over."

"But that's not fair to him either. He cleaned up his shit after the divorce. Why do you think he took some time before asking Angelica to marry him? He didn't want nothing coming back to her."

"Well, look how that worked out."

"Claude…stop! This is Falio we're talking about."

"I know. I'm sorry. I'm just pissed. They deserve to be happy without other people interfering."

Falio and Angelica were the representation of love. No matter what the other was doing, love prevailed. They always got back together.

"There's something else," said Nico.

"What?!?"

"Ricky and Angelo aren't his kids."

"What!"

"Yeah...Ariana lied. They're Ricky's kids."

"Oh my God! How did you find out?"

"Falio told me. He had Ricky and the kids tested."

"Damn! That's fucked up. This whole time!"

Claudia was in shock.

Nico mentioned Falio removing his name from the birth certificates and replacing it with Ricky's.

"What did Ariana say when Falio confronted her?"

"She tried to lie but couldn't. Falio showed her the DNA results."

"She's so trifling. Those poor kids."

"Yeah, she's fucked up."

Claudia didn't like what was happening.

"Do you think Angelica will leave him?" asked Nico.

"Because of the baby?"

"Yeah."

"She might."

"He's afraid of that."

"But he can't control her actions."

"He knows that, but to finally have her back, and this happens...it's tough."

"True, but he better tell her, or I will."

"No, you won't."

"Yes, I will. She's my best friend and doesn't deserve this."

"Let Falio tell her."

"I am but it better be soon."

Nico changed the subject and talked about Sal and Jazmina.

"I like Jazmina for Sal," he said. "She's a positive influence."

"I agree. And she likes him a lot."

"All Sal talks about is modeling and building a future with her. He wants to do new headshots and find an agent."

"I'm sure Jazmina can help him with that."

"She is. They have this master plan."

"I think it's great. And I think Sal will do well."

"Me too, which is why I agreed to pay for whatever he needs."

"I guess we'll see where it goes."

"I think they'll be together. Neither one of them seems afraid to go all in."

She knew he was throwing punches. So, she looked at him and said, "Yeah…as long as he doesn't cheat on her with another woman."

Nico kept it neutral as Claudia threw a punch of her own.

"Yeah, he just helped her move into her new place."

"I heard."

"Now, he wants a house, too."

"That's good. Sal is dreaming big."

Nico warned Sal about Claudia's parents, though. Claudia understood. They weren't the easiest people to deal with.

After dinner, they headed back to Claudia's. Seth pulled up as they were walking up to her building. Claudia made a face.

"Who is that?" asked Nico.

She didn't let on that she was sleeping with Seth. Instead, she commented that her parents sent him.

Claudia played it cool as Seth got out of his car. He walked up to them and asked to speak to Claudia alone. Nico stared Seth

down, and Seth didn't budge. She got between them and walked
Seth to his car.

"I told you to be at my place at nine."

"And I told you I had dinner plans."

"I don't like waiting."

"I told you I didn't know when I'd be done."

"But you agreed to come back."

"I know but…"

"Ok…let's go."

"I'll meet you at your place."

"I'll tell him about us right now if you don't get in this car,"
said Seth, getting irritated.

"Don't do that."

"Then let's go. I told you I wasn't done with you. So, I'm not
leaving unless you get in my car."

She just looked at him and said, "Go fuck yourself."

"That's what I have you for."

Claudia tried to walk away, but Seth grabbed her arm. Nico
approached with guns blazing. Seth stood right there fearless,
staring into Nico's eyes.

"Stop! Nico put them away."

Claudia pulled Nico aside and told him she had to go. He was
angry because he assumed her mother was up to something.

"I'll call you later," said Claudia, getting into Seth's Lambo.

Seth looked at Nico as they drove away.

Chapter 28
New Beginnings

"What the fuck was that, Seth?"

"I told you you're mine."

"We're not dating! You're not my man!"

"Let's change that."

"Just like that?"

"What do you want me to say, Claudia? I want you! And I didn't like seeing his arm around you!"

They'd been going at it so hard that Claudia didn't realize they'd parked and were in front of his yacht.

"Take me home."

"Get on."

"No!"

Seth took her out of the car and carried her onto the yacht. They immediately left.

Claudia went to the top deck to get away from Seth. Unbeknownst to her, Seth had candles, roses and several gifts from his family's brand, Arman Alarie, waiting for her.

"Please have a seat," he said.

"Fuck you, Seth."

"You will," he said, smiling.

She gave him a dirty look.

Seth rolled a tray over with several shot glasses and numerous liquor bottles.

"I wanted you to try our new…"

"Are you seriously acting like you weren't an ass with me?" asked Claudia, fuming.

He leaned back and calmly said, "What are you talking about?"

Claudia got up and went down to the second level. She stood at the back of the boat, looking out into the darkness. He followed her.

"Why are you angry?" he asked.

"I don't like what you did."

"What did I do?"

"You showed up at my house and then embarrass me in front of…"

"In front of your drug-dealing boyfriend that pulls guns out on people."

"He was protecting me!"

"That's what protecting you looks like?"

"He loves me!"

Seth laughed and said, "No wonder you fall for these losers."

"Go to hell!"

She went back up to the top deck and poured herself a drink. She saw Seth's pipe and smoked. Claudia needed to calm her nerves. He showed up and sat down.

"I won't apologize for what I did or how I feel," he said.

"I know. You just want to sleep with me."

"I never lied to you. As a matter of fact, I told you I liked being inside of you and that I wanted to fuck you again. I also told you that I'd be at your house at nine if I didn't see you."

"But you just showed up demanding that I go with you!"

"But I told you what I would do."

"Seth, you can't do that!"

"Why, because you were gonna fuck him?"

"No!"

"It didn't look that way to me."

"How would you know? You didn't give me a chance to come back."

They both took a sip and smoked.

"Nico is none of your business. And the only reason you called him those things is because of what my mother told you."

"Claudia, what are you really upset about? The fact that you lied or that you got caught?"

"Why am I here if I lied?"

"Good point."

"And you didn't catch me doing shit. I went out to dinner, was gonna smoke and come see you."

"And you think he was going to let you leave?"

She laughed.

"What's funny?"

"You."

"What?"

"I can do whatever I want. I'm not with anyone. That means I can FUCK anyone I want."

"No, you can't!"

Claudia was done entertaining him. Now, she sat back watching him get angry at the truth. He got so angry that he left. After cooling down, he returned with two glasses of champagne.

"I have to apologize. I can get a little nasty when I feel like someone is trying to take what's mine."

"Now I'm yours?"

"Aren't you?"

"Not that I know of."

"Claudia…you don't get it."

"What exactly don't I get, Seth?"

"Why do you think it took me as long as it did to go out with you?"

"Because you're a hoe."

"No, Claudia. You were always my endgame. I knew that once we got together that was it. I was going to settle down, get married, have kids and do all the shit that people do. You are my forever."

"Bullshit!"

"It's not."

"How can you have forever with someone you don't trust? 'Cause I can't trust you."

"Why wouldn't you? I've never done anything for you to withhold it."

She stayed quiet.

"Claudia, how long have you known me?"

"Since high school."

"And have I ever tried anything with you?"

"No."

"Why do you think that is?"

"I just figured I wasn't your type."

"You're every man's type. You're beautiful, smart, head-strong," he said, laughing.

She nodded.

"We've known each other at least half of our lives. You know who my first girlfriend was. You know when I lost my virginity. You know when I joined the family business, when I was promoted, how much I make and what some of my interests are. Just like I know those same things about you. I also know how hard you worked in college and how proud your parents were when you graduated. I know you don't want to get into the family business like your siblings. And I know you're trying to figure out life your way."

"You're right."

"I make it a point to know everything about you. And now… it's my chance. I'm ready for you and the life we can have. And no one will get in my way."

She got up and sat on his lap. She looked into his eyes and then kissed him. Afterward, they discussed being in a relationship until they reached his island.

Seth escorted her to his closet. There were big and small gift boxes from all the top designers. Seth outdid himself.

"What is all of this?" she asked.

"It's yours."

"Why?"

"Because I want you to know how serious I am about you, Claudia," he said, wrapping his arms around her. "I want to share everything with you. I want to be with you exclusively. No other women, just us. And I don't want another man touching you."

"Seth…"

"No, Claudia. I want you to marry me, have my babies and share this home with me. I want you to have my last name."

Seth didn't let her speak. He showed her the handbags, luggage and shoes he'd gotten her from his family's new collection.

"You have wonderful taste."

"I know."

He led her into the other room where he stored his merchandise. There was a huge picture of her on the front of a magazine in the swimsuit she wore their first night together.

"What is this?"

"My ad."

"What ad? And why am I on the cover?"

"Why not? You're so beautiful."

"But I'm no model. And who took the picture?"

"My staff…and this picture tells a different story."

Claudia just stared at herself in disbelief. She was no model. Jazmina was the model in the family.

"I have this whole campaign I want you to do."

"Me?"

"Yes. Everyone will be here tomorrow. We will model the men's and women's swim wear and some accessories I plan to launch."

After a few minutes, she said, "Sure…why not?"

He swung her around with joy.

"Be my business partner," he said, taking off his clothes.

"What?"

"You're going to be my wife. Be my business partner."

Seth removed her clothes and pushed her onto the bed. His hot tongue tickled her spot. Claudia's body moved uncontrollably as he tasted her goodness. After she came, he slid inside of her. She jumped as he moved like a savage. He kept her moaning, groaning and gasping for air. Seth pulled Claudia's hair as they talked dirty and he got her to say she was his.

After an intense session, Seth escorted Claudia to the indoor pool. They played around and stood in each other's arms.

"Are you sure about us?" she asked.

"Do you question everything?"

"Yes."

"Haven't you ever been so sure of something that you just do it?"

"Yes."

"Ok."

"But this scares me, to be honest."

"Why?"

"It's too fast. Earlier, we were just fucking, and now we're getting married."

"Are you doubting me?"

"No."

"And I never said we were just fucking. You did."

Seth got out of the pool and put on his robe. He handed Claudia hers and went back to his room.

"Seth, stop! Why do you get so angry?"

"You're the first person I've ever said those words to in a while and you keep questioning my intentions. I've done nothing to make you doubt my words but yet you do."

Claudia felt like shit. He'd been honest even when she didn't want to hear it.

"I'm sorry," she said, hugging him. "It's me, not you."

"Claudia, I'm not into games. I want you so bad that it hurts when I'm not with you. But I'm prepared to let you go if I'm not who you want. I'm not the kind of man you want to cheat on."

"I understand and I agree. However, you have to do something for me."

"Name it."

"If your feelings ever change, tell me before you cheat and lie. Because like you, I'm not very forgiving."

Needless to say, their sex was passionate and hot the rest of the night.

Chapter 29
New Business

The next morning, Claudia jumped up when her phone alarm went off. She looked around, and Seth was gone. Then, she got up and called out of work. It was obvious she wasn't going to make it.

She decided to take a bath and ran the water. She felt like she'd been hit by a train. She drank, smoked and fucked too much.

"Good morning, Sweetheart. Drink this."

"Good morning. What is it?"

"Just drink it. It'll make you feel better."

So, she did.

As they sat in the tub relaxing, he rubbed her hair.

"You're not a morning person, are you?"

"Not right now. My boyfriend fucked the shit out of me last night and this morning."

He smiled and whispered, "I like the sound of that."

"Me too."

They talked for a while before getting out.

"I have a surprise for you," he told her.

He led her inside the closet. There was a key with a note

sitting next to a large floral arrangement on the center island. The card read, "Welcome home, Baby".

"Is this my key?"

"Yes."

She kissed him before heading downstairs to eat breakfast.

"Your house is beautiful."

"Our house and thank you."

When they got to the dining room, there was a spread on the table.

"Claudia…this is Marie. Marie…this is Claudia."

"Nice to meet you," said Claudia.

"Whatever you need, she can help you," said Seth.

"Thank you."

Seth had a full day planned. First was the tour of Alarie Island. This 57-acre island was quite the place. The main house resided on the northeast and spanned over 30,000 square feet on six acres. It had all the bells and whistles of luxurious island living. Seth designed his 3-story home to be habitable and entertaining, which included an arcade, bowling alley, pool tables and an indoor basketball court. He even had a 30-seat movie theater, a wine and cigar room and a spa. Seth also dedicated land for staff housing, farming and a small warehouse for all island receivables. However, half of the island wasn't developed.

After their eventful morning, they showered and got ready for their photo shoot with Octavio Farrelli. He was one of the hottest and most desired Italian photographer in the industry. Octavio made a name for himself taking photos for most of the prominent fashion houses. He currently worked for the Alarie family brand but was doing Seth a favor.

Seth built a 5,000 square-foot loft next to the main house as his workspace. Being in the fashion industry, it came equipped with a photo shoot area, space for hair and make-up and lots of storage.

There were also clothing racks for inventory and mannequins to use as displays.

The glam squad arrived and started on their hair and make-up. Soon after, the infamous Octavio arrived.

"Octavio…glad to see you," said Seth, giving him a bro hug.

"Of course," he said with an Italian accent.

"Claudia…this is…" Seth started to say.

"Octavio Farrelli," she said, listing a few of his accomplishments.

"The pleasure is all mine," said Octavio, kissing her hand.

Seth showed Octavio the rack of swimsuits. He and his assistants began photographing them as Seth and Claudia continued getting ready. Once they finished, they met Octavio by the pool.

Claudia came out in a golden yellow bikini with gold mesh detail and chain straps. She accessorized in gold chains and ankle bracelets with the signature logo. Seth wore the matching golden yellow shorts with the brand name and logo around the waistband.

Next was the red ensemble. Claudia wore a red bikini with a triangle top, clear straps and cheeky bottoms. She wore several gold bracelets and diamond earrings to accessorize. Seth wore red swim shorts with a front tie.

They went through several wardrobe changes. Claudia modeled different pieces to show the diversity, including a white one-piece with a plunging neckline and wrap-around waist tie with rhinestones, a 2-piece bikini with thong bottoms and charm detail, and a 3-piece set with a monogrammed pattern. Seth wore matching shorts to each swimsuit.

Last, they modeled the sleek black and gold collection. In this collection, Seth used textures, florals and jeweled details on the swimsuits. As for the men's shorts, he used monogrammed patterns, minor jeweled detail and different fabrics.

Once they finished, they got a sneak peek of the proofs. Octavio captured lust, romance and sex appeal. He and Seth were pleased with the images. Claudia couldn't believe it was her.

"Wow! You look amazing," Octavio told her.

"You did it."

"It's easy with a model like you."

"Thank you, but I'm no model."

"I can't tell by these photos."

"That's because you're amazing."

"I can say the same to you."

Seth interrupted the complimentary session.

"Thanks, Octavio. I appreciate your help with this."

"No problem."

Seth handed him a check. They shook hands, and Octavio and his crew left.

"Wow. You were amazing today!" said Seth excitedly.

"Thank you. I've never done that before."

"You're a natural."

"Look who's talking."

Seth excitedly talked about his plans. He discussed other collections, more accessories and different fabrics. She excitedly threw out some ideas of her own the more they talked.

"Fuck me," he told her, taking off his swim shorts.

Claudia sat on top of him and fuck the shit out of him.

It was a long day, and they hadn't eaten since breakfast. Seth and Claudia were famished. So, they got dressed and went downstairs to the dining room.

"Will you be my business partner?" he asked her.

"How much do I need to invest?"

"Nothing."

"You're just giving me half of your company?"

"It will be our company once we're married and there's still plenty to do."

They discussed changing the name of the company and the logo. They also discussed branding, merchandising and models for their campaign.

"Do you have a website?" she asked.

"We need that too."

Claudia understood that Seth needed more than money. He needed a partner to handle day-to-day tasks. She agreed to be his business partner.

"I'll have the paperwork drawn up right away," he said.

"Ok. I'll have my attorney look at it."

"Great! What about your job? You'll need to quit."

"Quit?"

"Yes. I want this project up and running by early next year. I need your undivided attention."

"Well, I'm not quitting just yet."

"Why?"

"I need time to get my affairs in order."

"Well, we leave for Italy at 5 a.m. We need to meet with vendors, discuss distribution, look for real estate to open shop and look for new fabrics."

"We're opening the store in Italy…not here?

"It's a better market."

"When were you going to tell me?"

"I just did."

Claudia shook her head and grabbed her phone. She texted her manager, however, he already knew she'd be out the rest of the week.

"You texted my boss?"

"Yes."

"Don't ever do that again."

"Why?"

"Because…"

"Wouldn't your husband text your boss if something happened?"

"Yes, but nothing happened and we're not married."

"But your boss doesn't know that."

"Seth!"

"In my mind, you're already my wife and I'm your husband. It's just a matter of when we actually to do it."

She didn't say a word. She wasn't sure how to feel. It felt like she was on a roller coaster ride and couldn't get off. Things were moving too fast. Seth was a lot to handle but knew what he wanted. Claudia, on the other hand, hadn't quite wrapped her mind around being in a serious relationship yet. She still thought of them as dating while he was making long-term commitment moves. And she didn't know why she was afraid since she wasn't committed to Bronson and wasn't sure where she stood with Nico. She needed to change her way of thinking. But she knew Nico would be hurt.

"And I'm not waiting a year to marry you," he said. "By Spring, we'll be married."

Claudia finally understood Angelica's statement about a man being dangerous for her. Chad was Angelica's and Seth was Claudia's.

The last order of business was Nico. Seth wanted her to tell Nico about them. He didn't want any more mishaps or run-ins at her building. Claudia wasn't prepared to do that right then but had no choice if it was really going to work between her and Seth.

Chapter 30
Busy Tuesday

Angelica had a full day scheduled. Falio was coming to town Thursday, so everything had to be done before then. She was also leaving for Paris on Sunday.

When Angelica became Sr VP of HR, she revised the regions and split up the map accordingly: northwest, southwest, central north, central south, northeast and southeast. Zeke was in charge of the northeast, Damian had the southeast and Cherry had central north. The other three directors were Chris Lewis in the central south, Paul Lindsay in the northwest and Selena Fuentes in the southwest.

Angelica started her day with a staff meeting with her Senior Regional Directors. She conference called Chris, Paul and Selena. First, they discussed problems and issues as a whole team. Then, they discussed Paris. She needed to know who would be able to go as their assistance was needed. Paul and Selena could make it. Chris was dealing with some legal issues and couldn't leave town. Last, they went through company travel plans, holiday schedules and year-end vacation requests. She reminded them of the Christmas party and hoped everyone would attend.

"When do you think you'll have Heather's position filled?"

Angelica asked Damian.

"I have interviews today and tomorrow."

"Perfect. Let me know."

"I will."

"I'd like to get the person on board by the time we get back."

"Ok."

After the meeting, Angelica asked Cherry to stay.

"I didn't get a chance to talk to you yesterday," said Angelica.

"What happened?"

She told her about Chad calling, all of the gifts, Alex stopping by to take her to lunch and her conversation with Thad.

"Thad has a point," said Cherry.

"I know."

"What are you going to do about Chad?"

"Nothing. I blocked him."

"Why?"

"I can't deal with Chad right now. He fuels me emotionally and I'm with Falio."

Cherry just gave her a look.

"Are you going to invite Q to Paris?"

"No. He has something going on with his music."

"Ok."

"I do have news."

"Do tell."

Cherry told her about Q moving to Charlotte after the new year.

"Are you ready for that?" asked Angelica.

"Yes, I think so."

"Girl, you better know. You can't kick him out after he's here."

"Why would I do that?"

"I'm just saying. What if he makes you mad?"

"We will discuss the matter like adults."

"You know…that might actually work for you."

"It doesn't for you?"

Angelica just laughed.

She asked her about school. Cherry graduated in a few weeks. Angelica hugged her and signed her paperwork for her increase.

"Don't you have to wait until I graduate?"

"Are you graduating?"

"Yes."

"Then, I'm turning it in."

Cherry smiled.

"I do have a question, though," said Cherry.

"Sure."

"I have to study for finals. Would it be rude if I didn't hang out as much in Paris? I need to be prepared."

"That's fine as long as you eat dinner with everyone. After, you can lock yourself in your room."

Cherry agreed as she was not going to turn down free food.

Matt knocked on Angelica's door.

"Angelica…"

"Hey, Matt. Come in."

Cherry left as Matt walked in and closed the door.

"Is everything ok?" she asked.

"Yes, thank you. I actually have a favor to ask you."

"Ok."

"Elise just told me that you guys are heading to Paris for the grand opening of our flagship store."

"Yes, we are. We'll be gone next week."

"I wanted to know if I could go with you guys. I want to propose to her, and what better place than Paris?"

Angelica silently screamed and hugged him tightly.

"Of course! I'll approve your travel right now and let Austin know you'll be assisting. How exciting!"

"I don't need any more time. I'm ready."

"That's awesome!"

"Yeah, I want what my siblings have."

"Nothing wrong with that. Please let me know if I can help."

"Actually…"

Matt told her some of his ideas. They came up with a game plan, and Angelica excitedly gave him another hug before he left.

Just as she sat down, Alex called.

"Hey, Handsome."

"Hey, Beautiful."

Alex sounded upset. He and Kelly had just broken up. She'd met someone and wanted to give the relationship a try. He didn't care but was mad that he listened to everyone about giving her another chance. He knew it was never going to work out, especially after Angelica.

"I'm sorry to hear that," she told him.

"Thanks, but it was bound to happen."

"Alex…"

"Angelica…"

"Don't say that. You could've made it work."

"I didn't want to. I know what I want, and it's the last time I go against myself."

"Are you upset about the other guy?"

"No. Oddly enough…I'm relieved. I knew I couldn't hold up my end of the deal."

She hated to rush him off the phone but had a meeting to attend. Before she hung up, she mentioned Falio coming to town in case she wasn't available. Alex didn't like it but understood.

After her meeting, Angelica returned to her office and thought about Alex. She wanted to do something nice for him. So, she sent him flowers, balloons, a gigantic teddy bear and chocolates in hopes of making him smile.

As she was packing up for the day, Thad came into her office.

"Come with me."

He dragged her down the elevator and next door to the Distribution Center. Thad led her down a hall and into a small room.

"Thad, what…"

He immediately covered her mouth as she heard sexual noises.

"Who?" she whispered.

"Shana."

The blinds were open in an office where Shana and some guy were seriously fucking.

"Do you see who that is?" whispered Thad.

"No."

Angelica tried to see who it was but couldn't. She did catch a glimpse of his penis and smiled. Thad realized Angelica was checking out his package and they left.

"You're nasty," said Thad.

"What?" asked Angelica, laughing.

"I saw you smile when you saw his dick."

"Well…he was packing."

"You seriously didn't recognize the guy?"

"No!"

Thad made her post up in the lobby with him. To their surprise, security was on serious crowd control outside. There were cameras, reporters and fans inching towards the front doors.

"Damn…who are they waiting for?" asked Angelica. "They're acting like there's a celebrity in the building."

"You'll see."

"And how did you know what Shana was doing?" Angelica asked Thad.

"The cameras. No one knows they were installed. Austin thinks someone is stealing merchandise and asked me to install cameras with 24-hour surveillance."

"Damn…I didn't know."

"And you still don't. You better not say anything."

"I won't. I can't. I'm HR."

As they discussed work, a beautiful, caramel-skinned man with captivating hazel-green eyes, a groomed beard and an alluring smile walked through the front door. This Dominican/Cuban man stood 6'3", had short dark brown hair and was impeccably dressed. He walked with confidence and was desired by many.

"Oh my God," whispered Angelica. "That's Leland Hernandez."

"Only the greatest outfielder in baseball today."

"He just signed a crazy contract with LA for some ridiculous amount."

"Three hundred and twenty-five million for seven years."

"Damn! And he's fine as hell."

Leland walked towards the reception desk, where they were standing.

"Excuse me," he said to Angelica.

"Yes."

"May I speak to you for a moment in private?"

"Certainly."

Thad excused himself while they stepped to the side.

"How can I help you?" asked Angelica.

Leland Hernandez was currently the "it" man in baseball. Women loved him, the media loved talking about him and he had endorsement deals from just about everyone.   He was a pillar in his community and often got in trouble with the ladies as the most desired playboy. Angelica couldn't think of a reason he'd need her help.

A few minutes later, Shana walked by. Then, Angelica saw this bronze-skinned man with deep brown eyes, a low fade and well-groomed goatee turn the corner. He walked with confidence as well and was wearing the hell out of a custom-tailored suit.

"Freddie Jimenez?" she said out loud.

Leland looked and said, "Yep…that's Freddie."

Freddie approached them. Leland asked for a favor. Angelica obliged and walked them to the other side of the building.

When Angelica returned to her office, she was smiling.

"What do you think you're doing?" asked Shana. "And aren't you engaged?"

"It's called working. And yes…I do believe that's what this ring on my finger indicates. Do you need something?"

"Why were you talking to Leland and Freddie?"

"It's none of your business."

"He is my business. I'm carrying…"

"Oh…you mean Freddie and his wife's baby?"

"Forget I said anything," said Shana, heading for the door.

"Yeah…I suggest you stop talking if you don't want to get sued. I know you signed a Non-Disclosure Agreement."

"Shut up, Angelica! Just stay the fuck out of it."

Shana told Angelica to keep her mouth shut. She couldn't afford that scandal. Besides, Freddie planned on taking care of Shana after the baby was born. She didn't want to mess that up.

Before closing her door, Shana said, "You can have Leland. You're both deserving of one another."

"What does that mean."

"You're both whores."

Shana smiled and closed the door.

Angelica called Thad to gossip about what they saw.

Chapter 31
Falio in Charlotte

Falio arrived in Charlotte around noon. Angelica picked him up in General Aviation. As soon as she saw him, she ran to him.

"Hi, Baby," she said, kissing him.

"Mi Angel."

Falio looked out of the window as she drove towards her Ballantyne home.

"There's a lot of trees here. So much greenery."

"Yes, there is."

"It's nice."

Falio commented on everything he saw.

"Are you hungry?" she asked.

"Yes."

"Ok."

Angelica detoured and stopped at Bentley's restaurant. He was pleasantly surprised.

"This is nice," he told her.

"Glad you like."

The hostess seated them in a booth. Their waitress immediately took their drink and appetizer order.

"They're nice here," said Falio.

"Yes, they are. It's different from Miami."

They made small talk until their appetizers came. Then, they ordered their entrees. Falio ordered king crab legs with a steak and lobster tail. Angelica ordered salmon.

"How's Nico?" she asked.

"In bad shape."

"I'm sorry he's going through this."

"Yeah…me too."

Falio didn't like what Claudia did to Nico or how she did it. She could've had the decency to tell him in person and not over the phone with Seth talking in the background.

"Nico had big plans for them."

"What do you mean?"

"He bought the house that Anthony just sold…where they had their engagement party."

"He was the buyer?"

"Yep. He knew Claudia loved that house. And since she and Anthony never actually lived it, he was willing to make it their own."

"Damn! Does she know?"

"No. Nico was going to surprise her. He bought tickets to Hawaii for this coming weekend. He was going to propose and everything. Look at her ring."

Falio showed Angelica the picture of Claudia's ring that Nico bought for her.

"Oh my God…that's nice as hell! I feel so bad for Nico."

"Me too. He traded the other ring he bought her for this one. But she'll regret her decision."

"Why do you say that?"

"Because Nico is making big moves."

Nico started a real estate company selling luxury homes. His company was focused on the Orlando and Tampa market at the moment. He was also buying abandoned buildings, renovating them and using them as entertainment facilities for weddings, birthday parties or other special occasions. He stood to make millions. Angelica didn't realize Nico was doing so much to change for Claudia. She could only imagine his pain.

"Why didn't Nico ever ask her to be exclusive?"

"He assumed they were."

"So, he never said…let's be together? Let's date? Be my girl?"

"Not in those words, but Claudia knew she was the only one. He told her that."

"And they've been there before and he cheated. So, she didn't know how serious he was."

Angelica explained Claudia's view of her relationship with Nico. Falio understood but didn't like it.

"My team and I fly out on Sunday morning," said Angelica, changing the subject.

"Where to?"

"Paris."

"How's that going?"

"Good."

"Has your boss tried anything?"

"No. And you know I won't allow it."

"Just checking."

He asked lots of questions about Paris.

"We'll have to go one day," she told him

"Ok."

When the bill came, Falio dropped seven hundred dollars in cash. The waitress was very grateful. Afterward, they headed to Asila's. He wanted to see how she was living. He also wanted to talk with Thad.

When they pulled into the driveway, Falio couldn't believe

how well Asila was doing.

"This is nice," said Falio.

"Wait until you see the inside."

Asila ran to Falio and hugged him. He appreciated the love.
Thad hugged Falio as well and invited him in.

"Wow, Asila! This is nice," said Falio.

"Thanks."

"I'm extremely proud of you."

"Thank you."

Thad showed Falio around while the ladies talked. Falio handed Thad a bag of cash with twenty thousand dollars inside. Falio
told him to consider it a wedding gift. Thad thanked him.

"How does it feel having him here?" asked Asila.

"Good. We just had lunch."

"Which house are you staying at?"

"The one down here."

"Does he know you have two houses?"

"Yes."

They stayed for about an hour and then drove a short distance
to Angelica's Ballantyne home.

"This is your house?"

"Yes. Why do you sound surprised?"

"Mi Angel…this is nice. Who bought it?"

"It was an investment."

"Victor?"

"Yes."

Falio just made a face.

"You're still dealing with him?"

"Falio…he's just my business partner. That's it!"

"What kind of business? And when did that happen?"

Angelica couldn't tell him the truth about their arrangement
with the property management company. So, she told Falio that

Victor had been teaching her how to create wealth by investing in real estate, which wasn't a total lie. Victor was supposed to sell the Ballantyne house, but she fell in love with it. So, she decided to keep it. Angelica was buying Victor out, according to her story.

"How much do you need?" he asked.

"Nothing. We just sold another property and my profit covers what I needed. "

Falio couldn't believe how cheap real estate was in Charlotte compared to Miami.

Then, she told him about the Tennessee project and Victor's land surrounding hers.

"I plan to buy sections of his land and develop it until it's all mine," she said.

Again, she couldn't tell him the truth.

"How much do you need to buy all his land?" asked Falio.

"I don't know what he'd sell for."

"Ask. I'll give you the money."

Angelica didn't want him to because of his new business endeavors. Besides, she had the money in her account but couldn't tell him. So, Angelica agreed to find out. She didn't want to explain how she got the money.

Just then, Sasha called. Matt told her about Paris and how Angelica was helping.

"You should come to the BBQ this weekend. Nicole hosts one every Saturday as a pregame ritual," said Sasha.

"Well, Falio came to visit me and…"

"Bring him. You know he's welcome to come."

"Are you sure we won't be imposing?"

"Girl, stop. Thad, Asila, Matt and Elise are coming."

"But they're family."

"And so are you. See you Saturday."

"Ok. Can I bring a friend?"

"Sure."

"Thanks."

After she hung up, she told Falio about Saturday. He couldn't believe they were going to hang out with the Atlanta football team. Then, she texted Cherry and told her about Saturday.

"How do you know her?" he asked.

"You're not going to believe it, but she's Thad's sister. And she's married to Devin Williams."

"The Devin Williams?"

"Yes! And she's best friends with Nicole, who is married to Lucas Franco."

"The Lucas Franco?"

"Yes!"

"He's one of the best linebackers out there."

"Yes, he is. And he's cool."

"And you just hang out with those kinds of people?"

"What kind of people are they?" asked Angelica, confused. "And they're family. Asila is marrying Thad."

He apologized for sounding offensive. He just realized that Angelica wasn't the same girl he knew in Miami. She was living in a million-dollar home, flying to Paris on business and hanging with professional athletes and their wives.

Falio prolonged the talk for as long as he could. He rolled a blunt and smoked with her.

"Mi Angel...come here."

He sat her on his lap.

"I have something to tell you, but I'm scared."

"What? Tell me."

Falio hesitated and then said, "Melissa is supposedly pregnant by me."

Angelica tried to get off of him, but he wouldn't let her up. He explained when it supposedly happened.

"It happened before we got back together! I've never cheated on you!"

"And what am I supposed to do with this information, Falio?"

"It doesn't change anything."

"It changes everything!"

"Why?"

"Are you serious right now?"

"Baby, please…don't say that."

"Falio let me up!"

She went out back and he followed her.

"I knew you were fucking other women, but I always thought you were careful," she calmly said, hitting the blunt.

"I was careful."

"How is she pregnant then?"

"I fucked up."

Falio simply fucked up. She was his "go-to" person when Angelica wasn't around. He never thought this would happen. And Angelica didn't know what to say. He pleaded with her to be patient and let him fix it.

"How do you fix it, Falio? You could be having a baby with another woman."

"It's not mine, though. The dates don't line up."

Falio hadn't been with her since he got divorced. He'd been cleaning house and getting his affairs in order to be with Angelica. Melissa claimed to be seven weeks, but it was longer than that since Falio was with her.

"Why would you tell me if it's impossible?" she asked.

"Just in case you hear anything. Melissa is playing games about how far along she is."

Angelica didn't want anything to do with his mess. She looked at her ring and took it off. She gave it back to him.

"This shit needs to be fixed by the time I get back from Paris.

If not, it's staying off."

"Just like that…you not gonna wear the ring?"

"You have unresolved shit to deal with!"

"So, if it's mine, you're not gonna be with me?"

"Truthfully, I don't want to deal with baby momma drama. You just got rid of your fucking wife and now a baby? What if I was pregnant with someone else's baby?"

"Don't even play like that!"

They went back and forth arguing about the situation. Failo didn't like her reaction but understood. He hoped for a different outcome. However, he knew he had to fix it. He couldn't lose Angelica again.

After they calmed down, they talked about Angelo and Lil Ricky. He made Ricky take a DNA test. She was surprised when she heard the news.

"I'm fucking her up when I see her."

"Angelica…"

"Watch."

They discussed their relationship for several more hours until they both made peace with their decisions. Angelica didn't want to argue or be mad at him the entire visit. He was only there a couple of days, and she wanted to enjoy him.

They went to her bedroom, where she gave him all his birthday gifts. He couldn't believe how much stuff he had. She bought him casual and business attire, jewelry and shoes.

Angelica spent the following day showing him around Charlotte. They went to the mall to get some suitcases, tried a couple of new restaurants and rode around checking out the different neighborhoods. He finally understood how she was able to obtain her house.

Chapter 32
Nicole's House

Angelica and Falio woke up and made breakfast. Then, she took Falio to her other house.

"This is nice?" he said.

"Thanks."

When he looked around, he knew that Angelica primarily lived there.

"Why did we stay at the other house if you live here?"

"Because I'm transitioning to that house. And I wanted my first nights in that house to be with you. It's our home."

Falio went up behind her and kissed her neck while rubbing on her nipples.

"I love you, Mi Angel, and wherever we are together is our home."

"You better get your shit together."

He softly bit the side of her neck.

Angelica went and grabbed her can of weed so they could smoke before the trip.

They met up with Thad, Asila, Matt, Elise and Cherry at the airport around 1 p.m. Hugs were passed around before boarding the private jet. Once seated, Falio just looked at Angelica interacting with the others. He knew he had to step his game up. She moved away and got better. She was making boss moves with her plans to develop the Tennessee property. That meant he had to make even bigger moves than the bank and a few investments.

Before takeoff, Angelica received a text from Tom. He wired her 4.5 million dollars. She let out a quiet scream and then showed Falio the message. Falio inquired about it and she told him how she made the money. Again, Falio's concerns were warranted.

They made it to DeKalb-Peachtree Airport about an hour later. When they landed, two SUVs were waiting for them.

Falio looked out of the window as they drove to Nicole's. The driver turned onto her property and stopped at a double gate. He punched in a code and drove past the island of green shrubbery. They rode around the fountain and stopped in front of a beautiful traditional estate with a Colonial entrance.

"This is beautiful," said Angelica.

"You've never been here?" asked Falio.

"No."

The twenty-foot-tall entryway resembled the White House with four Roman columns evenly spaced apart. Inside was even more luxurious with a cathedral ceiling in the foyer, a see-through glass dome roof and decorative Italian marble flooring. Everything in her house was big, expensive and designer name brands. They even had a double-island kitchen, an indoor and outdoor pool, a hair salon, bowling alley and a large tennis court next to the 2-story, 5-bedroom guest house.

Nicole welcomed everyone as they walked in. Then, she rushed to the kitchen to check on the caterers, but not before grabbing Asila. She wanted to talk business and introduce her to some people. The others went to find Sasha and Devin.

Angelica found Sasha, who was with Devin and a few other

guys from the team. The ladies hugged and introductions were made. Then, Devin took Thad, Matt and Falio and showed them around. Elise saw one of the wives, who was a long-time friend and went to catch up while the other ladies talked.

"Damn, girl…he's fine," said Sasha.

"Thanks."

"Alex is here. I know. He texted me last night."

"You guys still talk?"

"Yes."

Nicole and Asila joined the ladies. Nicole wanted to know about Alex and their time in New York. Angelica told them the short version.

"That's why he can't shut up about you," said Nicole.

"We had fun."

"I still think he's perfect for you."

"I know, and I am forever grateful you introduced us."

She asked about Falio. Angelica summed up their whirlwind romance.

"Damn, that's fucked up. I understand now," said Nicole.

"Yeah…so now we have a chance."

"I would do everything I could, too," said Sasha.

Asila looked at her hand and asked, "Where's your ring?"

"Falio has it."

Asila just made a face.

"Stop, Asila."

"Angelica, what's going on?" asked Nicole.

"I don't want to talk about it."

"Just tell us. We're family at this point," said Sasha.

"Yeah, 'cause you're not getting rid of me either," said Nicole.

"Are you guys together?" asked Cherry.

"Let's just say we're on a break after he leaves tonight."

Angelica told them about the Melinda situation. There were

mixed comments. A couple of the ladies felt she shouldn't leave no matter what. They weren't together when it happened. Others felt she did right by giving him time to fix it.

Nicole changed the subject and talked about Kelly. It turned out that Nicole had been watching her like a hawk. She had two private investigators on her. Nicole found out that Kelly was seeing someone else. So, she called Kelly and told her to tell Alex or she would. The crazy part was that she didn't deny it. That was how Alex found out about her extracurricular activities.

"Why did she give him an ultimatum if she wasn't interested?" Angelica asked Nicole.

"Because she thought he was just going to walk away, which he should've done. Instead, he listened to his parents."

"I'm sure they meant well."

"Yes, but he never really liked her in a long-term way. I know it sounds weird."

"I get it."

"He liked her at first, but she became overbearing and needy. She always had to be the center of attention and he's not like that."

"I know."

"Then, you came along and knocked his socks off."

Alex walked up and heard that.

"That's true," he said.

When Angelica saw him, she bit her bottom lip. He looked so damn good. But she collected herself as she hugged him. Nicole saw their chemistry and was secretly determined to get them together.

"I bet you guys end up together," said Nicole.

"Nicole!" said Angelica.

"What!"

"Stop, please!"

"Ok…ok!"

Nicole thought Falio was cool but was obsessed with Alex and Angelica being together. But she left it alone out of respect for Angelica.

The ladies headed out back to join the madness. Nicole's husband, Lucas, was grilling with a couple of his teammates. They had different meats and veggies cooking. Plenty of people were drinking and snacking. And everyone was having a great time with the music blaring in the background.

Angelica saw Falio and Austin talking of all people.

"What do you think they're talking about?" Cherry asked Angelica.

"Me."

"Are you nervous?"

"No. I don't care."

"And did you see Austin's new girl, Lauren?"

"Yes."

"She reminds me of someone."

"Oh, hush."

The ladies laughed, and then Cherry said, "I saw how Alex looked at you."

"I know. Me too. And he looks delicious."

"Angelica…stop," she said, laughing.

To Cherry's surprise, she saw her one-night stand from Frank's party.

"Cherry?"

"Liam…how are you?" she asked, hugging him.

"Great, now that I see you."

Cherry had the biggest smile as she went to talk to him privately.

Falio saw Angelica and asked to speak to her alone. She agreed and they walked towards the tennis court.

"How was it?" she asked, referring to his conversation with Austin.

"It was cool. He's actually not a bad dude."

"You were making sure nothing was going on with us, weren't you?"

"That too."

She laughed.

Falio talked about how laid back and chill everything was. Everyone embraced him and showed love.

"I understand your change now," he said.

"What do you mean?"

"I mean these types of people you're hanging out with."

"Again with that?"

"Hear me out."

Falio didn't mean it negatively. He was simply pointing out how she'd surrounded herself with people that could elevate her life. She was talking the talk and walking the walk. Angelica was living out her dreams with multiple opportunities for financial growth. Falio admitted that moving was the best thing for her personal and professional development.

"I have to be better for you," he told her.

"But you have to also want it for yourself. If you aren't good, I'm not good."

He hugged her. They smoked as they talked about new dreams.

As evening fell, Falio looked at his watch. It was time for him to head out. Nicole called to have the jet fueled and insisted he use it to fly home. He thanked her for everything and hugged her. As he went to say goodbye to everyone, Angelica went to use the restroom. When she came out, Alex was standing right there.

"I need to talk to you."

"I can't right now, Alex."

"Are you leaving too?"

"No."

"Where's your ring?"

"Long story."

"Stay with me."

"Alex!"

"Drop him off and come back."

"Ok, but I'm not coming back here. Everyone saw me with Falio."

"Meet me at my house."

"Ok."

Angelica found Falio and left for the airport.

Before getting on the plane, he said, "I love you, Mi Angel. Thank you for this experience."

"You're welcome, and I love you too."

"Give Paris hell and see you when you get back."

"You better be ready for me, too."

He hugged and kissed her a little longer before boarding the jet.

Chapter 33
Another Rendezvous

Angelica texted Alex when she was on her way. Alex was standing outside upon her arrival. He opened the car door.

"Hi," he said, kissing her.

"Hi."

He held her hand as they went inside.

Alex opened a bottle of wine and joined Angelia in the living room. They sat on an oversized chair near the fireplace to talk.

"Who's going first?" asked Angelica.

"I'll go first."

Alex started with the Friday after she left. He tried to get mentally prepared for his conversation with Kelly but was distracted by Angelica's stuff.

"I kept imagining you lived here."

"Did Kelly see my stuff?"

"Yes."

"What did she say?"

"She asked whose stuff was in my closet."

"What did you say?"

"Nothing. I didn't answer."

She shook her head.

Just before Kelly arrived, Alex called his sister, Val. He didn't want to try with Kelly. Alex wanted Angelica. However, Val told him to be sure he didn't have any unresolved feelings for Kelly before moving on. He understood.

"When she got here, I was nervous. I wasn't sure how I'd feel about her after being with you."

"How was it?"

"It was a little weird."

"Did you sleep with her?"

"Wow. Ok. You really want to know?"

"Yes, and expect the truth."

"I did."

"How was it?"

"She said it was amazing. Better than before."

"And you?"

"I threw up afterward."

"Literally?"

"Yes. I told her I must've eaten something that didn't sit well with my stomach."

"I'm sorry."

"I felt disgusted like I was cheating."

It was the last time he slept with her. All he could do was think about Angelica. He didn't want to be touched by anyone else.

"Only one other woman has ever made me feel like you do."

"Who?"

"Nicole."

"I knew something was up with her!"

"She means well, I promise. And we are strictly just friends."

"I see that, but she's insanely invested in you. I knew something was up."

"And she will fight for our friendship. Her and Lucas."

"Do tell."

Alex and Nicole met in college. They dated a few months before she met Lucas. She thought Alex was cute but wasn't as interested in him as Alex was in her. They slept together once to see if it would change anything, but it didn't. Nicole left him for Lucas, but they remained friends. Eventually, the trio grew close and stayed protective of one another.

"That's crazy!"

"I know."

"You never became jealous of Lucas?"

"I did, but we talked."

"I admire you."

"Why?"

"You were mature about it at an early age."

"I struggled with my feelings but got over it. I couldn't stay mad at someone because they didn't want me. So, I threw myself into school and my work."

"Ahhh."

"The thing is that I've been looking for that feeling ever since."

"Which is?"

"That feeling where you think about a person and get giddy on the inside?"

"I know what you mean."

"And I mean think about that person all day. Think about that spark…and that fire. And as a Cuban man, I know that I'm a sexual person. I wanted someone who could keep up."

Angelica rubbed his dick.

"Don't start nothing, young lady."

"I can finish it."

"I know you can," he said, kissing her.

Alex talked about believing in love and described his version in detail.

"I get it. That's why you were mad at yourself. You knew Kelly didn't have what you were looking for."

"Correct. Yet I went against it anyway."

Alex got up and grabbed another bottle of wine. It was time for Angelica to spill the tea about Falio.

"Now tell me what happened?" he asked.

Angelica told him about Melissa possibly being pregnant by Falio, her calling things off and his time limit to fix it.

"Wow. That's crazy."

"It is. After everything we went through with my sister, now this."

"I don't think he purposely did this, though."

"I don't either, but I don't want to deal with bullshit right now. I have too much on my plate."

"And you shouldn't have to," he said.

"Thanks."

"One week, huh?"

"Yes."

"You know it won't be resolved in that time frame."

"Why do you say that?"

"The results from a paternity test take at least forty-eight hours and that's if he can get her to take one."

"How do you know?"

"My sister and I had to take one."

"What!"

"Yes, but mine took at least four days to get the results."

Angelica wanted to ask why he took one, but she didn't.

Angelica changed the subject and talked about work. She reminded him that she was off to Paris the following day. He was also leaving for Japan. His latest project was all the buzz, and he was looking at a 9-figure deal.

"Nice! Congrats."

"Thanks."

She got on top of him and kissed him. Alex held her tight. Then, she took off her top and pressed his head into her breasts. Her head went back as his tongue tickled her nipples. Angelica took slow, deep breaths as her body tingled.

"I missed you," he told her.

"Take those off."

They removed their clothing and sat back down. Angelica played with him as he did her. They each became so aroused that Alex couldn't take it anymore. He slid inside of her.

"Fuck," yelled Angelica.

He held her waist as they moved slowly and in sync. Their lips stayed locked as they were immersed in one another. There was lots of hair pulling, sex talk and high emotions.

After their lovemaking, they sat in the chair, savoring the moment.

"You're amazing," he said.

"I know."

He laughed.

"You're ecstasy," she said, rubbing his nipple.

Alex let her do whatever she wanted.

A few minutes later, she asked about food. She was hungry. She didn't eat much earlier.

"Let's sneak over to Nicole's and grab some food. I know they have plenty of leftovers," said Angelica.

"Ok."

She put on one of his dress shirts, sweatpants and her long coat. He put on sweatpants, a long-sleeved T-shirt and his hat.

When they arrived at Nicole's, most of the cars were gone. He opened the side door to the kitchen and escorted Angelica in. All eyes were on them after they walked inside. Nicole, Lucas, Asila,

Thad, Matt, Elise, Sasha, Devin, Austin and Lauren just looked at them. Cherry left with Liam to check out his new Buckhead condo.

"Hi," they both said at the same time.

"So that's where you ended up," said Asila.

Nicole just winked.

"Soooo…we were wondering if we could have some food to go," said Angelica.

"Come in," said Lucas, showing them where everything was.

Angelica looked at Austin and saw a confused look on his face. She left it alone.

Before leaving, Angelica reminded everyone about their afternoon flight to Paris.

"Everyone can hitch a ride to Charlotte with me around seven in the morning," said Austin.

"Ok," they all said.

Angelica texted Cherry the flight details. Austin and Lauren said their goodbyes as they headed to his place. Sasha was hosting her siblings and their soon-to-be spouses. They left as well. Angelica grabbed a couple more plates of food, thanked Nicole and left.

"Why was he looking at you funny?" asked Alex as they drove back to his place.

"Who?"

"Austin."

"He knows about Falio."

Angelica told Alex the truth about her previous relationship with Austin.

"Wow," said Alex. "Wasn't expecting that. And you can still work for the guy?"

"Yes, without a grudge."

"How can you do that?"

Angelica realized he was better in the friend zone. In this case, they were not only friends but colleagues.

"I love my job and want to help him build his company. It's a great business structure, and he notably cares about the people. And I love being a part of that."

"I understand."

"Austin apologized, and I accepted. It's over. He knows he doesn't have a chance in hell with me romantically. Once I'm done, I'm done. However, I stand by him in business. He's a smart businessman."

"I admire you."

"Why?"

"You do the right thing even when you're hurting."

"I had to. I couldn't blow up my life."

"But it couldn't have been easy."

"Honestly, not at first. But we talked. I understood why it happened. Just regretted that it did."

"Well, I'm not," he said, laughing.

"Funny story...do you remember that night you tried to call me at my brother-in-law's party? I was at the hotel, and I couldn't hear you?"

"Yes!"

"That's when I found out."

She told him what happened.

"Damn! So, I'm the reason you found out?"

"Yep."

"It wasn't meant to be."

She laughed.

They got back to his place and practically stayed up all night having sex.

Chapter 34
Paris Bound

The Charlotte crew arrived in Paris Monday around 6 a.m. They waited around for Paul and Selena, who were scheduled to arrive by 6:18 a.m.

"Hi!" said Angelica, greeting her west coast staff.

Everyone hugged and introduced themselves. Then, they all went to baggage claim and met transportation out front after.

"It's so nice to see everyone in person," said Paul.

"Yes, it is," said Angelica. "Is this your first time in Paris?"

"Yes, and my wife was jealous," he said, chuckling.

"Mine too, but no husband," said Selena.

"Well, definitely not your last. I'm putting my staff on a rotation schedule to come here and London to check on things."

Everyone was excited about the news.

Paul Lindsay was a gorgeous white man who stood six-two with blue eyes, brown hair and well-groomed goatee.

Selena Fuentes was a beautiful Mexican woman that stood five-six with brown eyes, long black hair and curvy in all of the right places.

Paris was chilly. It was still a little dark as the sun hadn't risen yet.

They drove to the Bella Flor Hotel and went to the registration counter. Everyone got their own suite except Matt and Elise shared one. And of course, Angelica upgraded to the Royalty Suite.

"Ok...get settled in and meet me back here by nine. We'll grab breakfast, have a quick meeting and then head over to the store," said Angelica.

Everyone agreed and went to their rooms.

Angelica sent Alex a message that she made it to Paris. He called her.

"Hey, Beautiful."

"Hey, Handsome."

"You made it to Paris?"

"Yes. How's your flight?"

"I should be there soon."

Alex was still en route to Japan. He still had a couple more hours before landing.

"How do you feel about the meetings?" she asked.

"Good. I think the in-person meetings are just formalities."

"You're gonna kill it."

"Thank you. I appreciate that."

"Of course."

They talked until it was time for her to go.

By 8:30 a.m., Angelica was dressed and headed downstairs. Some were already eating while others were trickling in.

"Couldn't wait?" Angelica asked Cherry and Paul.

"Nope," said Cherry, stuffing her face.

Everyone finally made it and ate from the buffet. Afterward, they went into a small conference room Angelica reserved. They went over the game plan for the entire week, and then she gave them their assignments for the day.

"I've scheduled meetings with potential PR firms at the first store," said Elise.

"And I'm hitching a ride to check out the merchandise and inventory," said Destiny.

"Ok. I'll join you, ladies."

They nodded.

"Last but not least…I made reservations to dine here in the hotel's most exclusive restaurant. Our reservation is at eight. Formal attire."

Everyone was excited.

Their day was busy. They unloaded merchandise, hung up clothing, arranged the furniture, staged the store and unpacked bar glasses. Everyone pitched in and helped, including the employees hired to work there. The flagship store included more merchandise than the other stores and had a sports bar that doubled in size.

Angelica left Damian in charge while she rode with Elise and Destiny to the other stores.

Elise scheduled back-to-back meetings with three PR firms starting at two o'clock. She listened to their ideas and reviewed their marketing plans to make the company a household name. Meanwhile, Destiny and Angelica walked the store as Destiny wrote down all of the necessary inventory. They brainstormed and created a plan to make the store look livelier. After, Destiny and Angelica went to the other two stores and did the same. They came back for Elise and returned to the flagship store.

By seven o'clock, everyone made it back to the hotel. They showered and changed for dinner. The team looked amazing. The ladies wore evening gowns, while the men wore suits.

As the group was escorted to their table, a sophisticated, dark-haired French man eyed Angelica as she walked by wearing a black, one-shouldered dress with ruffled detail and a high split on the side. He watched with such admiration.

"Girl, do you see him staring at you?" Cherry asked Angelica.

"Yes. And he's cute."

They sat down and ordered a round of cocktails. Minutes later, quite a few a la carte items came out with the drinks.

"We didn't order these," said Angelica.

"Compliments of the chef."

As they looked at their menus, the waiter kindly explained Parisian cuisine. Meanwhile, another waiter brought over a bottle of champagne.

"This is from the gentleman at the bar," the waiter told Angelica.

Angelica looked and saw who it was. She raised her glass and nodded. He raised his and did the same.

"Oh Lord," said Cherry.

"Stop it," said Angelica.

"So, men just buy you expensive bottles of champagne just like that?" asked Damian.

She winked at him.

"You have no idea," said Cherry.

"Well, I'm for it," said Selena.

Then another bottle was delivered, but this time to Selena. She thanked the man who sent it, and the conversation turned to her. She didn't care. She was enjoying the attention.

Their dining experience was marvelous. Everyone tried new food, there was plenty of cocktails and the desserts were to die for. The kitchen even sent out extra food they didn't ask for, but Angelica didn't mind. They were having a good time.

Angelica discreetly asked for the bill.

"It has been taken care of, ma'am," said the waiter.

"By whom?"

"I'm not at liberty to say, ma'am."

"Please let me give you a tip, at least."

"No, ma'am. Thank you."

They couldn't believe Angelica got them a free dinner. Hell, she couldn't believe it. She didn't know who to thank as the gentleman from earlier was nowhere to be seen.

As they got up to leave, Angelica glanced over at the bar. Through the crowd, she thought she saw a six-foot tall man with sandy blonde hair and Chad's physique. However, when she looked harder, it wasn't Chad.

They reconvened in the lobby.

"Well, thank you, everyone, for today. We have another busy day tomorrow. I hope you enjoyed your food."

"It was delicious," said Cherry.

Everyone commented.

"Please be safe out there for those of you getting ready to explore the city."

Angelica headed to her room. Matt and Elise hung out with Destiny and Damian at the bar. Selena and her admirer stayed at the bar but sat separately. Cherry decided to explore Paris with Paul since they were both in relationships, and he wanted to check out the nightlife.

Angelica went onto the balcony to smoke. She took a few hits to relax and unwind. She got undressed and took a hot steaming shower. She wrapped a towel around her head and slipped into one of the luxurious robes hanging on the door.

She sat on the bed and thought about Falio. Then, she thought about Alex. She decided to stop thinking about men and get some work done. She grabbed her laptop and a few folders out of her bag. She began reviewing them when there was a knock at her door.

"Who is it?"

"Room service."

She tightened her robe and opened the door. A man was holding a large vase of flowers.

"Hi. I didn't order anything," said Angelica.

"Complements of the hotel, ma'am."

"Ok."

She stood by the door and let him in. Unbeknownst to her, there was another one behind him with another beautiful floral arrangement. Then another. And another. There was a total of ten men who brought in several floral arrangements. Soon after, a cart full of desserts, fruits, chocolate, whipped cream and champagne entered the room.

"Have a good evening, ma'am," said the last attendant.

"Wait. May I tip you?"

"No, ma'am. It's been taken care of. Thank you."

"No, thank you."

She closed the door and went straight for the cart. She dipped a strawberry in the whipped cream when there was another knock at the door. She opened it.

"You couldn't have forgotten any…"

The man walked into her room and closed the door.

"What are you doing here?" she asked.

He walked up to her and bit her strawberry. He untied her robe and opened it. She was in her birthday suit.

"Just the way I want you," he whispered in her ear.

"You can't have shit."

He smiled.

Angelica went to close her robe when he snatched it off. He took the towel off her head and grabbed her hair. He pulled her close and kissed her. It didn't take long before she gave in, especially since his tongue was magic in her mouth and his finger worked her clit. Once he felt her wetness, he went down on her. Angelica could barely stand as he sucked and twirled his tongue, making her cum.

He removed his clothes and kissed her until they reached the bed. He threw her on the bed and got on top of her. She let out a loud moan while grabbing the sheets as he fucked Angelica just the way she liked it. He was in total control and dicking her down. They both came hard.

As they lay in bed, she asked. "What are you doing here?"

"Fucking you."

"I mean Paris, Smart Ass."

"This is my hotel."

"So, you took care of our bill this evening?"

"Yes."

"I thought I saw you."

It was Chad.

"How did you know I'd be here? Are you following me?"

"No. It was a beautiful surprise."

Angelica got up and put on her robe. She poured herself a glass of champagne and sat on the couch that faced Paris' extraordinary skyline. He wrapped himself in a towel and joined her. They smoked as they talked.

"It's not a real marriage, Angelica. It's a business merger."

"Is that what we're calling it?"

"That's the truth."

"Ok."

"What about you? You said you were engaged before you hung up."

"Do you see a ring on this finger?"

"No."

"Ok then."

"I was bothered by that statement. I thought it was true."

"Why?"

"Because I don't want you to be with anyone, let alone get married."

"Selfish much?"

"Very when it comes to you."

He kissed her and blew smoke in her mouth. Angelica wasn't going to tell him the truth just yet.

"Did you like your gifts?" he asked.

"They were all beautiful. Why did you do all of that?"

"Because I knew you were mad. I fucked up!"

"You could've told me."

"How would that have gone, Angelica? Thanks for a magical night…oh and by the way, I'm getting married."

"I could've handled it."

"You say that now."

"But I asked you if you were married."

"I'm not."

"But you knew you were getting engaged."

"Yes, but how was I supposed to tell you that when I asked you to be my girlfriend?"

"You weren't supposed to ask me that."

"But I want you for myself."

"I knew something was up with you. It was the way you asked."

They sat there in silence, smoking.

"I was prepared not to talk to you anymore."

"I know. I hated not being able to talk to you."

"I'm still not talking to you."

"I know," he said, pulling her on top of him.

He took off her robe and sucked on her breasts. She removed his towel and played with his dick. He slid back inside of her.

"You need to unblock me."

"No."

Chad punished her by making her his sex slave for the night. She didn't mind the punishment.

Chapter 35
Proposal

Angelica looked at Chad while he slept, wondering why she was so attracted to this man. She knew she'd fallen again.

Then, he said, "It's not nice to stare at people when they're asleep."

"How would you know if you're sleeping?"

"I can feel your eyes looking at me."

He hugged Angelica from behind and asked what were her plans for the day. She told him about work, shopping and the proposal.

"Do you want to come?" she asked.

"Sure."

"Good. You can pay for dinner," she said, giggling. "You're still working your way out of the doghouse."

"No problem."

Then, Angelica thought about something.

"When did you first see me?" she asked.

"Around seven in the hotel lobby."

"We were just getting back from the store."

"I checked with registration and saw your name for the dinner reservation and hotel room."

"So, you were sending us that food?"

"Yes. I wanted you to try some of our favorites."

"It was good. Compliments to the chef."

"After, I arranged for the flowers and a cart full of goodies."

"And who's the guy after Selena?"

"One of my managers."

"And who was the guy that sent the champagne?"

"Another one of my managers."

They continued the conversation in the shower.

"Don't worry about the room. It's on me," he told her, getting dressed.

"I know."

Before Chad left, he handed Angelica a blue card with just his name on the front.

"Go to Triangle d'Or and show this card in any store. Everything is on me."

"Thank you, Sweetheart. And don't forget to meet me back here at six," said Angelica.

"What time will you be back to get ready?"

"Around five."

"Can I get dressed with you?"

"Yes," she said, kissing him.

"Ok."

He pinched her nipple, winked and left.

Everyone went to work, but it was a short day. They finished around noon to go shopping for the big proposal that Elise knew nothing about. Angelica and the other ladies went in one direction while the fellas went in another.

Triangle d'Or was the area around Avenue Montaigne, Avenue George V and Rue Francois 1er in the 8th arrondissement. It was where the finest Haute Couture could be found. Angelica started their shopping excursion on Avenue Montaigne. She used Chad's card in just about every store she visited. She received the royal treatment every time and free delivery service to the hotel.

Angelica made it back to her suite around five. She found all of her purchases, including Chad, naked with a blunt in his hand.

"How was your day, Dear?" he asked, winking.

"Yassss," she said, snapping her fingers three times.

"Thought you might like this."

"Absolutely."

She took off her clothes and kissed him. They had a quickie before showering.

As the water rained down on them, Chad asked, "Am I forgiven?"

"No."

"Not even after your shopping spree?"

"No. That was just because."

"Just because what?"

"I said so."

Chad smiled while staring into her eyes.

"I know we don't have time to fuck again."

"No, we don't."

"But later…I'm going to fuck you until you forgive me."

"You might be a while."

"I don't mind," he said, kissing her.

As they got dressed, he looked at her with admiration.

"You look beautiful."

"Thank you."

Angelica wore a floor-length black and gold sequin dress with long sleeves and a low V-cut neckline that hugged her in all the right places.

"I have a surprise for you after the proposal," he told her in the elevator.

"What is it?"

"It will definitely get me out of the doghouse."

"We'll see."

Everyone met in the lobby, looking like a million bucks. Matt and Elise looked especially nice. Matt wore Sebastian Cruz from head to toe with black pants, a vanilla shirt and a black vest and bow tie. His beautiful vanilla and black paisley dinner jacket completed his look. Elise wore a floral embroidered lace gown by Oscar de la Renta. It had long sleeves with a beautiful scalloped low V-neckline.

Angelica introduced Chad to everyone as a business associate. Then they went out front to await their transportation. Matt rented a Rolls Royce Phantom for him and Elise while Chad and Angelica rode in his white-on-white Maybach S580. Everyone else rode in the limo Angelica rented. Cherry looked at Angelica with a confused look on her face. Angelica smiled.

They met up at Madame Brasserie. It was an elegant and cozy restaurant in the Eiffel Tower. It had the most romantic view of Paris blended into the night sky.

"This is beautiful," said Destiny.

"I agree," said Elise.

Damian pulled out Destiny's chair and sat next to her. Angelica looked at Cherry. Cherry gave her a look in return.

Chad immediately told them to order whatever they wanted. It was on him. They thanked him and started with cocktails. Then, Chad ordered an array of appetizers and entrees.

Angelica was surprised to see Chad enjoying himself. He talked and laughed as though he belonged.

Cherry tapped Angelica on the shoulder and asked for an explanation. She needed to know how Chad ended up back in the picture. Angelica told her the short version. Cherry knew she was a goner although she understood after hearing him interact with the group. He was well-educated, spoke intelligently and was fine as hell.

Matt received a text and then gave Angelica the look. That meant it was time. Angelica told Chad what was happening and then asked to speak to Elise alone. She made it seem like it was a work emergency. When the ladies returned, the table was empty and Chad was standing by the door with their stuff.

"Where did everyone go?" asked Elise.

"Our time limit expired. So, I paid the bill and we're meeting up with them," said Chad, partially lying.

"Ok."

They exited the Eiffel Tower and crossed over the bridge. They made a right on Av. des Nations Unies. They followed the street around until they stopped at Trocadéro Square.

"What are we doing here?" asked Elise.

"We're meeting everyone here."

Just then, Cherry appeared waving.

They walked up the steps to the platform and headed toward the Eiffel Tower. When Elise saw the scene, she covered her mouth. Her eyes quickly watered.

It was breathtaking. There were large floral letters that spelled out "MARRY ME" with tons of red roses on each side. There were also lots of balloons and the Eiffel Tower in the background was the perfect symbol of love and romance. The beautiful red carpet had red rose petals and different-sized candles on each side, creating the aisle. It was well-lit and so romantic. And Matt was standing in the center of it all.

The photographer and videographer captured Elise walking toward Matt with tears rolling down her cheek. As she stood in front of him, he gently wiped her tears and grabbed her hands.

"Elise, I've known you my whole life. Since we were little, I've wanted to spend the rest of my life with you. Through our name-calling, play fighting and me pulling your hair...I knew you were the one."

She laughed and whispered, "I remember."

"I used to tell my mom I was doing those things because I liked you. My mom, of course, had to teach me that those weren't signs of love but torture."

Everyone laughed.

"I've watched you become this beautiful, extraordinary woman. And I'll admit I messed up in high school when you finally gave me a chance. I acted like an ass. I was young and dumb, but I assure you I won't ever make that mistake again."

Matt pulled out a ring box and kneeled on one knee.

"Elise Raquel Ellington…will you marry me?"

"Yes!!!!"

He slid a 7-carat Princess-cut diamond ring on her finger. She kissed him as everyone cheered. There wasn't a dry eye in the crowd. Their family back home yelled, screamed and congratulated them as they were on video watching.

"That was so beautiful," said Angelica, tearing up.

Chad looked at her and wiped her tears. He couldn't believe how sentimental she was.

Everyone congratulated them and toasted with a glass of champagne. Afterward, everyone bid them farewell as they had more photos to take, and Matt had his own plans.

Chapter 36
Her Surprise

When they got into Chad's car, Angelica fixed her make-up.

"I didn't take you for a romantic," he told her.

"I'm a huge fan of love."

"You?"

"Yes. Don't sound so surprised."

"I didn't know."

"Love is the goodness in people."

"Oh…and you're optimistic."

She explained her version of falling in love.

"Do you ever want to get married?" he asked her.

"Yes! I want a husband, kids, the house…the whole American dream."

"You seem like you'll be a great mom."

"Thank you."

"And he'll be a lucky man."

"Thank you. I appreciate that."

Angelica talked about her dream wedding and the princess experience she wanted for the day.

"A princess?" he asked, laughing.

"Yes," she said, hitting him in the arm.

Her wedding would be like royalty. For one day, she'd be catered to and pampered with all the glitz and glam. She wanted the big dress with several wardrobe changes, lots of diamonds and an over-the-top event. She loved the idea of her bridesmaids getting dolled up, all of the decorations and family sharing in her special moment as she married her Prince Charming.

"My wedding will be a fairytale with fancy cars, beautiful wedding dresses, all of my bling and celebrating love," she said.

"Sounds nice."

"Don't you believe in love?"

Chad took a deep breath and said, "Yes, I believe in it. I just don't think I've experienced it with much transparency."

"Have you ever shown anyone your true self?"

Chad thought about it and said, "One person."

He shared a little of what happened between him and the woman.

"After she left, I immediately shut down. I dated here and there but always knew when a woman wasn't being genuine," he said. "And once the money came rolling in, I entertained women to get what I want."

"I understand that."

"Besides, I think I'm a good judge of character."

"Well, I don't know about that," she laughed.

They stopped at one of the office buildings outside the La Defense area.

"I know we're not about to conduct business?" she said, giving him a look.

"Of course not," he said, winking.

Chad helped Angelica out of the car and inside the mirrored tower named Equinox. They rode the elevator to the twenty-seventh floor.

"Chad Matthews," he said, walking up to reception.

Immediately, a French woman with long black hair, blue eyes and fashionably dressed greeted them.

"Celia Monroe…nice to meet you."

Introductions were made as Celia escorted them upstairs. They walked into a large, open room with racks of clothing.

"Please look around. I'll be back," said Celia.

Angelica glanced at some of the tags and couldn't believe it. She was looking at designer collections that hadn't been available in years.

"Pick everything you want. I'll be back. I need to speak with Celia," he whispered in her ear.

Then, a young woman, also fashionably dressed, approached Angelica.

"Hi. I'm Dominique. I'll be your assistant."

Dominique grabbed a clothing rack and followed Angelica around as she selected items. Dominique scanned each item and then hung it up on the rack. Each time a rack got full, a new one came out.

Next, Dominique came out with a large bin. Angelica followed her to the next room to select accessories. Angelica was able to take whatever she wanted. Again, as the bins got full, new ones came out.

Chad returned and heard Angelica speaking French with Dominique. He hugged Angelica and whispered, "I didn't know you spoke French."

She whispered back, "You don't know a lot of things about me."

He laughed as he took her by the hand and led her to the twenty-ninth floor.

They walked past reception and into another large, open room with multitudes of tables. Each table had a cosmetic or skin care product on it, separated by category. None of the products had labels on the bottles but listed the ingredients.

"I need your help with something," Chad told Angelica.

"Ok."

"Select the products you like and place them in the basket on each table. Then, tell me why you made your selections."

"Ok."

Angelica started with eye shadows. She picked up a palette with fall colors and gold glitter. Angelica also selected a palette with earth tones and natural colors. She liked the natural look with a hint of sparkle. Last, she picked a palette of thirty small sample colors. It provided a variety of colors for that extra pop.

Next, she went to the lipstick table. She selected one lipstick and one lip gloss separately but paired them together. For example, she picked up one red lipstick with a clear, shiny gloss. Then, she selected one cocoa brown lipstick with a nude gloss.

"Smart," said Chad.

"I like a little shine with my color."

Angelica went to each table, selecting cosmetics and skin care products, like facial cleansers, mascaras, eyeliners and creams.

Next, Chad invited her to change the formula of the cosmetics and beauty products she selected. For example, Angelica looked at the eye shadows. One set needed more pigmentation for vibrancy. She also wanted a more matte finish on another set. The glitter eye shadows needed more glitter. And Angelica wanted a creamy, pigmented eye shadow for a rich smoothness with bold colors.

Chad looked at the chief engineer, Luke, and asked if he could make the changes. Luke was sure of it.

Luke and Angelica mixed ingredients to test the colors and consistency she wanted. They did this for all of the products she selected.

"Great job," Chad told Angelica, winking.

Angelica winked back.

Each basket was placed on a large cart and carted to the next room. There were multitudes of containers and packaging materials for cosmetics and beauty care products.

"Now, I'd like you to select the containers and packaging for each item selected," said Chad.

She started with her first basket. She picked up a few small, square metal containers for each eye shadow color and then selected a case to put them in. She did this for every product as instructed.

"How would you market these products?" Chad asked her.

She looked at all of the products and said, "Me personally…I'd sell them as sets."

"What do you mean?"

Angelica paired items together as sets. For example, she labeled one lipstick, lip gloss and lip pencil as a lip set. Or an eye palette, eyeliner and mascara as an eye set. Last, she mixed one eyeliner, foundation powder and lipstick and called it a minimal set. It could be used as a quick refresher when going out.

"Make at least ten sets with what you have," he told her.

Dominique handed her a basket for each set she made. She made fifteen sets and gave each one a name.

The last stop in the building was an exclusive room with one-of-a-kind dresses and accessories on the thirty-second floor. When Chad opened the doors, he thought Angelica stopped breathing.

"Are you ok?"

"Don't tell me I can have whatever I want," she said, covering her mouth.

"You can have whatever you want," he whispered in her ear.

Angelica touched the fabrics, looked at the details and selected quite a few things.

"Are you happy?" he asked Angelica, hugging her from behind.

"This is princess status."

"I got to princess status?"

"You did."

She turned around and kissed him passionately.

As they rode down the street, Angelica sat back and held onto Chad's arm. She was on cloud nine, thinking about her clothes and accessories.

"Am I out of the doghouse?"

She smiled and said, "Can I show you something?"

"Sure."

She gave the driver an address.

"Where are we going?" he asked.

"You'll see."

They talked about the Equinox experience until they arrived. Angelica got out of the car and helped Chad out. He laughed as she took his hand and led him inside her home. He looked around and nodded.

"This is nice. Who lives here?" he asked.

"Me."

"You?"

"Yes."

"How did you manage this?"

"Let's just say a deal that paid off."

"I'd say. May I?"

Chad toured every floor. They started on the first floor. He touched the cream-colored walls as the room featured gold gilding and beautiful chandeliers.

"This is beautiful," he said.

"Thank you."

They went to all the other floors except the third floor. Angelica saved it for last.

"Wow…impressive."

"Thanks."

It was her bedroom. This master suite had white marble floors with gold spider veins, the same cream-colored walls throughout the house and Louis XVI intricate baroque paneling on the walls. Her king bed was like royalty with a crystal-button tufted head-board and footboard. It had extravagant carvings and raised floral ribbon moldings on the wood frame. Behind the bed was a center tufted wall with curtains on each side, matching night tables with gold lamps and a matching dresser and mirror. She decorated in pale pinks, creams and gold.

Chad removed his jacket while walking towards Angelica. She felt his eyes piercing through her. She couldn't move. He un-buttoned his shirt and took it off. He walked up to her and stared while unzipping her dress. She was paralyzed, anticipating his next move. He slowly removed her dress off her shoulders and let it fall to the floor.

"You are beautiful," he said, kissing her neck.

"So are you."

He laid her on the bed and slowly slid her panties off. He passionately and intensely pleasured her as his tongue played with her pearl. He tightly wrapped his arms around her thighs as he devoured her. Angelica quivered and uncontrollably shook as she came. It was euphoric. Chad meant what he said earlier.

He got naked and went to get on top of her, but she wouldn't let him. Instead, it was Chad's turn. Angelica decided to show a little appreciation for her surprise.

She laid him on his back and got on top. She licked his nipples and continued downward. His moans got louder and his stomach sank in the closer she got to his dick. She watched him grab the sheets as she tasted him. More noises escaped his mouth as she slowly sucked up and down. Chad grabbed her hair and gyrated his hips as she pleasured him. Angelica eventually had Chad talking nasty, gasping for air and curling his toes as she went beast mode. She sucked until he came.

After convulsing, he lay there still. He couldn't do anything. He just looked at her and softly swept her hair away from her face.

"You're dangerous for me," she told him.

"What does that mean?"

"You make me want to love you and I can't do that."

He didn't say anything.

"You're such an amazing man.

"Thank you."

"I'm serious. You're a beautiful man with so much to offer. I know you'd be a great husband if you'd allow yourself to love."

He stayed quiet. So, she lay there quietly next to him.

After a while, Chad was ready for action. He got on top of her and cupped her shoulders. He was ready for their slow, hard, rough, deep sex.

Chapter 37
Princess Magic

The week was coming to an end. Angelica and the staff had been working to open the store by Friday.

"I'm sad we leave tomorrow," said Selena.

"I know. This has been quite an experience," said Paul.

"And to think…you will be back next year," smiled Angelica.

"Well, this trip was certainly memorable," said Elise.

"Were you surprised?" asked Angelica.

"Yes. I had no clue what Matt was up to."

Angelica and Matt slapped their hands. They pulled it off without her knowing.

Because they worked so late the night before, everyone was required to leave at noon. European labor laws were different than U.S. labor laws.

"What are you about to do?" Angelica asked Cherry.

"Study since I've hung out with Paul this week."

"And, how is he?"

"He seems nice."

"And have you seen Damian and Destiny?"

"Yes!"

They went back and forth, sharing stories.

"I'll talk to them."

"You know they're getting it on," giggled Cherry.

Angelica just laughed.

Everyone left except Angelica. She stayed behind to finish up a few more things. As she was leaving, she received a text from Chad. When she walked outside, Chad's car awaited with a dozen white roses, champagne and a note that read "Princess Magic." She wasn't sure what he was up to but was off to a great start. So, Angelica sat back and enjoyed the champagne.

A short distance later, the driver pulled up to her house. Chad was standing in front of the door.

"What are you doing here?"

"Hi," he said, kissing her.

"Hi."

"Are you ready?"

"For?"

When Chad opened the door, there was a full production happening. She saw cameras, lights, backdrops and glass pedestals with beauty products on top of them.

"What is all of this?" she asked.

"I'll explain later. Right now, you're needed in hair and make-up on the second floor."

Angelica went upstairs and saw a beautiful chaos. The second level was like a huge closet. The clothes from Equinox were separated by designer, color and style. There were also mock photos of the cosmetics and beauty products she created. Several ladies worked feverishly, pairing clothing, shoes and jewelry to each product photo.

Then, she saw the make-up station and walked over. Make-up artists and hair stylists began working on her immediately.

An hour later, she came out in her first ensemble.

"You are breathtaking," he told her.

"Thank you."

She wore a purple A-line, asymmetrical dress made of organ-za. It had a one-shouldered ruffled sleeve, short in the front and a full ruffled back. She stood in front of an eye shadow kit and took several pictures.

Over the next five hours, photographers told her where to stand, how to pose and which products to hold. Her background matched each wardrobe change. And she'd taken pictures on four levels of her house, including the grand staircase. She felt like a model at a photo shoot. Chad even stood in a few of the photos.

When they arrived at the fifth level, she recognized the prod-uct.

"Is this my perfume collection?"

"Yes."

"Oh my God…it looks great!" she said excitedly.

"They did a fantastic job."

Angelica picked up Amoré and sprayed it into the air. She closed her eyes to embrace the smell. The photographer captured those images as Angelica fanned the scent towards her nostrils. She loved it. Angelica did the same thing with Dulcé and Re-beldé. She also sampled the matching lotion.

As clean-up began, Chad had one more surprise for Angelica. They went to her bedroom, where the glam squad was waiting to change her hair and make-up for the last time.

Angelica arose from the seat with straight hair slicked back, and her make-up was subtle but glamorous. She had a natural look with bold eyes, a hint of silver glitter, medium-length lashes and bright red lipstick.

"Your final wardrobe change for our dinner reservation, Mad-am," said Chad, leading her to the bed.

"Oh my God!"

Angelica's grand finale was a beautiful silver sequin and rhinestone dress. It had a sweetheart neckline with one long sleeve off the shoulder, a thigh-high split with fanned rouging and a chapel train. And next to it was a pair of rhinestone-detailed stilettos.

"Baby…"

"Let me help you."

She changed into the dress, and Chad zipped her up. When she turned around, he was in awe.

"You did good," nodded Angelica.

"Thank you, but one more thing."

Chad showed her a beautiful diamond necklace set. The necklace was made of cushion-cut diamonds and had a twenty-carat teardrop pendant. It had a matching bracelet and droplet earrings.

"This is gorgeous," she said, touching it.

He draped her with diamonds.

Everyone in her house stopped and watched Chad and Angelica walk down the stairs. They made comments as they got into his Maybach.

"Did you just Pretty Woman me?" she asked.

He winked at her.

Angelica felt glamorous. She felt like royalty. And she had Chad to thank for that.

"Are you going to tell me what all that was about?" she asked.

"Yes, but right now, I need to warn you."

He told her where they were going and why. He also warned her about the sea of flashing lights coming her way.

Their first stop was the Musée d'Orsay. Chad had a private gala to attend, and Angelica was his plus one.

They got out of the car and walked the red carpet. Cameras photographed their every step. They stopped several times before making it inside.

"That was a lot," she said.

"You better get used to it."

More pictures were taken of them inside, along with Chad and other important businessmen.

Just as the cameras stopped following them, a Frenchman approached Chad and asked to speak with him privately.

"Do you mind…"

"Go ahead."

Angelica preoccupied herself with the art. She stood looking at a very famous painting when a handsome, average-sized man approached her.

"You are extremely beautiful. I hope I am not being too forward."

"No…and thank you."

She turned to look.

"Hi. My name is Simeon…"

"Wilcox," said Angelica, finishing his introduction.

"Wow. I'm impressed. You know my name, and I don't know yours."

"Angelica Zambrano," she said, shaking his hand.

"Angelica…are you an art lover?"

She excitedly but calmly talked about the museum, its art and her love for it. She even talked about when he became in charge and all the changes made. Angelica complimented Simeon several times and gave him an idea for a fundraising event.

"Angelica, it's been a pleasure."

"Likewise."

He handed Angelica his card and told her to use it. She thanked him and hugged him.

"I can't leave you alone for one second, can I?" asked Chad.

"Wasn't that exciting?" she whispered.

He smiled and said, "You do know who that was?"

"Yes!"

"And he gave you his card?"

"Yes!"

She told him the idea she gave him for a fundraising event.

"You should've negotiated a commission."

"Sometimes it's best to have one in the pocket."

Chad nodded in agreement.

"You ready?" he asked.

"Yes."

Angelica talked about Simeon as they rode to their next destination.

They stopped in front of a tan brick building on Rue de Rivoli and walked inside. The lobby was dim, with a glimpse of light coming from underneath a set of double doors. A tall Frenchman greeted them and opened the doors.

"This is beautiful," she told him, looking around.

"I'm glad you like it. It's all for you."

The large Versailles-inspired dining room was a romantic fairytale with tons of floral bouquets everywhere, multitudes of candles lit and a romantic table for two. Soft music played in the background, and a photographer was there taking pictures.

Chad pulled out her chair and then sat down. The waiter came and poured them a glass of champagne. They raised their glasses and toasted. The photographer took many pictures to capture the ambiance for ads Chad wanted to run.

"What business are you conducting now?"

"I may purchase this hotel."

"Will you add it to your chain?"

"I'm not sure yet. I was thinking of a more high-end, exclusive chateau."

They discussed his business options over dinner. The entire dining experience was magical. The food was incomparable, the wines were exquisite and the desserts were orgasmic.

They went back to his penthouse after dinner.

"The entire floor?" asked Angelica.

"Yes."

Chad's penthouse at the hotel occupied the entire top floor of the building.

"Can I get you anything?" he asked her.

"Are we in for the evening?"

"Yes."

"Great. Can you please unzip me?"

"With pleasure."

After changing into something a little more comfortable, Chad took out his weed paraphernalia. He handed Angelica a pipe and smoked.

"Did I succeed?" he asked her.

"At?"

"Making you feel like a princess."

"You did."

"As I recall, there had to be fancy cars, lots of diamonds, wardrobe changes and a glamorous event."

"You nailed it. Thank you."

He raised his pipe and said, "To princess magic."

"To princess magic."

They toasted with the pipes and laughed. Angelica went over all of her favorite parts of the evening. They talked, laughed and had a great time for hours. It ended with another night of amazing sex.

Chapter 38
Grand Opening

It was their last day in Paris. Angelica met everyone in the hotel's cafe for breakfast. She was tired and needed a pick-me-up, so she ordered an espresso.

"Rough night?" Cherry asked Angelica.

"Yes. And you?"

"Yes. We were out late,"

"But it was so much fun," said Paul.

"My gentleman friend got us into the hottest club and bought us drinks all night," said Selena.

"Sounds like fun," said Angelica.

"Is this why you're tired?" asked Damian, showing everyone pictures of her and Chad at the museum.

"Yes. It was a work event."

"Mmm hmm. You guys are all over social media."

Angelica downplayed the news, telling them about the meeting with the museum director and the charity event Sportie Fans would participate in. However, they still teased her.

Everyone made it to the store around ten. Destiny double-checked inventory while Elise was with the new PR team, taking photos and flooding social media. Angelica did one last walk through before opening.

"Wow…look at the line," said Damian.

Angelica opened the doors at eleven. Staff greeted customers as the first hundred received a free gift. The bar also filled quickly because of the drink specials and discounted appetizers.

Chad walked in and congratulated everyone on a job well done. He stayed and offered to help. Angelica put him to work.

By 2 p.m., Angelica and her crew headed to the hotel. They had to collect their things to catch their 7 p.m. flight back to The States.

"May I speak to you?" asked Chad in the hotel lobby.

Everyone went up while she stayed behind to talk to Chad.

"Stay with me," he whispered.

"What do you mean?"

"Stay the weekend with me. I want to show you something."

"Ok."

Angelica went to her suite and packed her things. She took a bag and the rest went to Chad's penthouse.

Angelica wanted to check on everyone and let them know she was staying. Her first stop was Matt and Elise.

"You guys ready to go?" she asked.

"Actually, we decided to stay the weekend," said Matt.

"Yeah. We want to do some shopping for the wedding and do a little sightseeing," said Elise.

"Ok. Where are you staying?" asked Angelica.

"Here. We just extended the reservation," said Matt.

"Ok…well, it's on me."

"Thanks."

"And you have your return tickets already?"

"Yes. We're squared away."

"Ok, good. And I'm staying too but not sure if I'll see you. So have fun."

"He's really into you...ya know," said Elise.

"Who?"

"Chad."

"It's just business."

"Well, he wants more than that," laughed Matt.

"Hush."

She left and went to speak to Destiny and Damian in Damian's room.

"Hello," said Angelica with a stern look on her face.

"What's wrong?" asked Destiny.

"I need to know what's going on with you two."

They were quiet, and then Damian said, "I like her and want to date her."

"I like you too," said Destiny, kissing him.

Angelica cleared her throat and hugged both of them.

"I'm happy for you!"

"Thank you," said Damian. "You scared me for a minute."

"There is the matter of work."

Angelica needed them to sign paperwork disclosing their relationship and review the workplace policies.

"We'll sign the disclosure statement when we get back," said Destiny.

"Ok."

Angelica informed them she was staying and asked to speak to Damian alone in the hallway.

"Are you sure about this?" she asked.

"Yes. Destiny is a wonderful woman. She's been dealt a bad hand like me."

"I understand. I'm just making sure."

"Yes, I'm sure."

"And does she know about us?"

"No! I'm not telling anyone."

"Ok…thank you."

"I want this to work, so I'm keeping the past in the past. Besides, I don't think it will go over well, considering you and I were together when you were with her brother."

"Right!"

"How is that by the way?"

"It's cordial. I don't hold any resentment. I'm focusing on my job."

"Gotcha. And this Chad person?"

"It's business."

"Is he the reason you're staying?"

"Yes."

"Business, huh?"

"Yes."

"Mmmm hmmm."

"Shut up."

She gave him a big hug. Angelica was happy for him.

Cherry, Paul and Selena walked out of their rooms and saw Angelica and Damian in the hallway. Angelica wished them all safe travels as she was not joining them. Cherry gave her a look and pulled her aside.

"What's going on?" asked Cherry.

"Chad."

"You're staying with him?"

"Yes."

"How long?"

"The weekend."

"Be careful."

"I will."

Everyone hugged before leaving for the airport.

Just then, Katrina called Angelica.

"Hey, girl."

"Victor is at it again. I need you to come to New York."

"This is quick."

"Yes, he wasted no time."

The new woman was named Susan. She reminded Katrina of another woman he dated named Colleen. Colleen was rude, obnoxious and used sex to get what she wanted. That was the same vibe she got when she met her.

"Susan doesn't let him come up for air. She's using sex to work her way into his life."

"Ok. How long do I have?"

"At least a couple of weeks before he starts. We need contracts signed."

"Make him sign everything now, and I'll be there as soon as I can."

"Ok."

"And make sure there aren't any pending contracts or deals we don't know about. I don't want a repeat of what happened with Lyness."

"Ok."

Angelica couldn't believe Victor was at it again.

Angelica met Chad in the lobby.

"So, where are you taking me?" Angelica asked Chad.

"You'll see."

They went to the airport and boarded a private jet to Ibiza. The flight time was approximately two hours.

Chapter 39
Private Island

"It's all yours," said Chad right after take-off.

"What?"

"Princess Magic."

"What do you mean?"

Chad was in Paris for two reasons: to purchase Equinox and start a marketing campaign for Angelica's perfume collection. He hoped the grand gesture would change her mind about talking to him. However, as Fate would have it, she was in Paris.

"You thought pushing my products would make me talk to you?" she asked.

"I was hoping."

"It wouldn't have just to let you know."

"Why?"

"Because you can't buy me. I was extremely bothered by the news of your engagement. You should've told me you were getting married."

They went back and forth until he apologized.

"So, what's all mine?" she asked.

Equinox was the largest cosmetics and beauty manufacturer and distributor in the world. It had at least fifty well-known brands under its umbrella and was adding another one with Angelica's line.

"You're going to make a shit ton of money," he said.

"Wait… you just bought the company and gave me my own beauty line?"

"Yes. You're both good investments."

"Why?"

"You sold me."

He heard the passion in her voice as she went around selecting products. She knew about colors, scents, textures and what went well together. He paid attention to her body language and her smile. She knew what she liked and how to enhance it. He also watched everyone else's facial expressions as she spoke. The enthusiasm was evident throughout the room. And she came up with the best marketing idea for selling the products.

"And what name did you use?"

"Angelica."

"Why?"

"It goes with the perfume collection. You want your brand to match collectively so people know who you are. Besides, who better to sell the brand than the creator?"

"Is this really happening?"

"Yes," he said, laughing.

"That's why you had me pick out all that stuff?"

"Yes."

"So, how much do you get because I know it's not for free?" she asked.

"You're right."

As the manufacturer, there were costs for production and distribution, but she stood to make plenty of money if she sold it as a high-end exclusive brand.

Chad handed her the preliminary market research report his

team conducted. It had different price points for selling the products and what she stood to gain. It also showed which demographics would sell out first. Angelica's eyes got big when she saw the numbers. It would catapult her into multi-millionairess status.

"We're going to get the buzz started next week. I have an elaborate plan to get us rich," said Chad.

"You're already rich."

"Richer."

"And how did you get the products finished so quickly? It usually takes years of research, testing and product sampling."

"Honestly, a client backed out of the project right before it was finished."

"What do you mean?"

Equinox had been working with a celebrity client for just over four years. They tweaked product formulas to a specific recipe, made special containers and changed the packaging a million times. Just as the project was finishing, the client backed out. She didn't want to put any more money into it. However, one of the stipulations for purchasing the company was that they had to find another client to take over the project.

"So you thought of me?" she asked.

After Chad saw her with the perfume collection, he knew she'd be perfect for the project. He knew Angelica would add her spin on it and change the formula, packaging and containers. This prevented any laws from being broken since the original client forfeited the contract and the original formula was altered.

"So, someone just walked away from their creations?" she asked.

"Yes."

"I couldn't do that."

"Good to know."

Chad had people working 24/7 to finish Angelica's changes. They'd already spent so much time developing the products that it was time to get them out. Chad needed cash flow for this project.

"I want to be your business partner."

"What do you mean?"

Chad presented her with a two-year contract. He'd handle setting up the office, marketing and money side of the business while she handled the creative side. She'd be required to create products and collections that yielded high-profit margins. In return, he'd own a percentage of her company. After the two years, they'd re-evaluate their partnership and decide if they'd continue working together or dissolve the partnership. Chad agreed to sell his shares to her for the initial investment if dissolved.

"You'll receive monthly financial statements to see where your money is going," he said.

Angelica jumped on top of him and kissed him. She couldn't believe what he'd just done.

They arrived in Ibiza around eight. They took a helicopter to his private island and landed on a well-lit helipad next to a mega-mansion.

"Don't tell me this is yours."

"Yes."

Angelica just shook her head. She wasn't sure why she was surprised.

"We're going to a friend's club," he told her.

"Ok."

Before they left, Chad introduced her to a strain of marijuana called sex weed.

"Why do you call it that?"

"You'll see."

They arrived at the club and went around back. Security greeted Chad and escorted them up the side stairs to the second floor. Chad had his own VIP area with a high-back, half-circle booth, a chaise lounge chair, blackout windows and bottle service.

"This is nice," she told him.

"Thank you."

They ordered drinks and then headed to the dance floor. Several guys stared at Angelica as she wore a sexy yellow mini dress that was tight fitting with a lace corset bodice. It made Chad keep her close while dancing.

Chad was high and feeling good when they returned to VIP. He began rubbing on Angelica's leg.

"I want to fuck you."

"Right here?" she asked, teasing him.

"Yes."

"Right now?" she asked, licking his lips.

"Yes."

He unbuttoned his pants and pulled out his dick.

"Sit on him."

She got naked and sat on him. He sucked on her breasts as she moved her hips. The more she moved, the more aggressive Chad became.

"Get up," he told her.

Chad took off his clothes and turned her around. He sexed her from behind.

"Yes…fuck me!"

They were like two wild beasts in a jungle. Chad pulled her hair as she fucked him back hard. Angelica came several times.

Chad wasn't stopping any time soon. The sex weed gave him a long-lasting erection. That meant he could stop to drink and dance and go right back to it. And that's exactly what they did the next few hours.

By 1:00 a.m., he was ready to go. The helicopter ride back to his house was fifteen minutes. Angelica experienced a whole new side of Chad.

While they showered, Chad kept kissing her.

"Are you happy?" he asked her.

"Yes."

"Why?"

"Because I'm here with you."

"I make you happy?"

"Yes, when you're not being an asshole."

"Why aren't you afraid of me?"

"Why should I be?"

"Because most people are."

"I'm not most people."

"I know," he said, kissing her.

"Are you happy?"

"Yes, when I'm with you."

"Awww…that's sweet."

"It's true. You bring out the goodness in me."

They got out of the shower and threw on a couple of robes. They went downstairs to the kitchen. Chad took out all kinds of food from the fridge.

"Who cooked all of this?"

"My chef."

"When?"

"Earlier. I told him I'd be in late so he whipped up all this food."

Chad had a buffet on the island. There were mini beef tourtieres, honey-mint lamb skewers, shrimp tartlets, a fruit and cheese board, chicken pot stickers, Caprese salad kabobs, chicken puffs, stuffed asiago-basil mushrooms and grilled zucchini with teriyaki chicken.

"We can't eat all of this food," she said.

"Yes, we can."

Chad became very chatty. The marriage was a business proposal. He and Delilah had to stay married for at least six months
for him to earn upwards of ten billion dollars. If he didn't, it'd be
forfeiting and he'd have to pay around fifteen billion. Or if she
didn't marry Chad, she'd have to pay the fifteen billion.

"When's the wedding?" she asked.

"After the new year."

"Well…six months isn't a long time."

"Yes, it is."

"But you're going to do it anyway."

"Of course, but it means staying away from extracurricular
activities for that time. The press would have a field day if they
caught either of us. So, she can't see Tom, and I can't see you."

"Tom? Your business partner, Tom?"

"Yes."

Angelica finally understood his behavior in Tennessee.

"To be honest, I'll probably be married."

She told him everything about Falio and what her sister did.

"Wow, that's fucked up."

"I know."

"And now he's coming for you?"

"Yes."

"I don't blame him. I'd marry you right now if I could."

She just looked at him and said, "What?"

"Nothing."

Chad was unbothered by Falio. He wasn't changing his plans
for Angelica. Instead, he talked about his family, how he grew up
and always knew he didn't want to be poor.

"My father instilled in me that money equated to freedom."

"Do you believe that?"

"I do."

"Any regrets because of it?"

"A few."

"Like what?"

"Like I've made enemies I wish I hadn't. Also, maybe I would've been married with a family by now."

"Is that what you really want?"

"Sometimes. But my life is very hectic. I don't know when I'd spend time with them."

"You make time."

"It's easier said than done."

"You made time for me."

"I did."

"That means you do what you want to do."

Angelica talked about her family and how she grew up. Her parents did their best with four girls, but she knew she wanted more. She mentioned all of her accolades in college, how she'd changed and how attaining financial freedom would help her family.

"Wow. You're impressive."

"Thanks."

"I admire you even more."

"Thank you. I appreciate that."

"Be sure you're ready for this life. It can tear you down and spit you out if you're not."

"I know, but I have a strong support system."

"That means you're ready?"

"I think so."

"You think so?"

"I mean…I feel like I can handle it, but I keep asking myself if this little girl from Miami can have it all. Love, money, family…"

"Let me stop you. Since I've known you, you're this beautiful chameleon. You adapt to your environment and blend in. You're professional, knowledgeable and get shit done. You light up rooms when you walk through doors. You handle yourself with respect and grace. Those qualities alone will get you into any room you want."

"Thank you."

"No…I'm serious. You're a force to be reckoned with, but you have to believe that."

"I understand."

"Not yet, but you will."

After their bellies were full, they went to lie down. Chad held Angelica close as they cuddled.

"You're the closest I've come to experiencing love," he said.

"Lucky me."

"I'm serious."

"Me too."

"It's like you get me, and I don't have to wear a mask with you."

"I hope not."

Chad held Angelica as she fell asleep. Then, he whispered, "I love you."

Chapter 40
Sweet Moments

Chad woke up and looked around. Angelica was nowhere to be found. He got up to look for her. The closer Chad got to the kitchen, the more food he smelled. He stood outside the kitchen watching Angelica prance around making pancakes.

"Hi," he said, walking in.

"Good morning, Honey. I hope you're hungry."

He looked at the table and saw more food.

"You cooked all of this?"

"Yes. I got a burst of energy this morning."

"I know where that energy came from, Honey," laughed Chad. She did, too.

"So, we're "Honey" kind of people now?" he asked.

"Would you prefer "Sweety"?"

Chad hugged her from behind and kissed her neck.

"Can I help?"

"Yes. Can you make the orange juice?"

"I can do that."

Chad cut and juiced the oranges to make freshly squeezed orange juice.

"Is this what normal married couples do?" he asked.

"Yes."

They sat down to have breakfast. They talked about the club, the sex and what Chad had planned for the day.

"Ok... now we clear off the table," she said.

"Why? I have people for that."

Angelica made him help bring all the leftovers into the kitchen. Then, they went to change.

"That was nice," he said.

"What?"

"Breakfast...conversation...you...clearing off the table."

"You're acting like you've never done it before."

Chad stayed quiet.

"Chad!"

"What?"

"Never?"

"Never had to."

She just shook her head.

It was a bit chilly outside. The high was sixty degrees, and they planned on being on the yacht all day. So, they packed accordingly.

They boarded his mega-yacht with ten cabins, large entertaining areas, a theater, a gym and a massage room. He led Angelica to the flybridge on the top level. There was an oversized lounge sofa that looked out onto the water. He turned on the heat lamps and grabbed a blanket. They snuggled as they departed.

"Is this what married life looks like with you?" he asked.

"Yes. Why do you keep talking about marriage?"

"I don't think my marriage will ever look like this."

"Well...it does for today."

"What do you mean?"

"I'm Mrs. Matthews today."

"Ok."

"Ok."

Chad kissed her and talked about the movie Pretty Woman. He told her all of the references he'd made, including her shopping with his blue card and him naked when she arrived back at the hotel. She laughed at herself for not catching it.

"I can't believe you watched it," she told him.

"I did."

Their first stop was a short ride to the farmer's market just off the southeastern coast of Ibiza. The yacht docked near the outer port while Chad, Angelica and the chef boarded the speedboat that took them to land. There was an SUV waiting for them at the port.

"Oh my God. Look at all this freshness," said Angelica, walking into the farmer's market.

"I know."

The trio went up and down the aisles, selecting fresh fruits and vegetables for Chad's special dinner. Next, the chef went next door to the butcher to grab what was needed while Chad selected several cases of vintage wine. Last, Angelica got all kinds of goodies, including baked goods, candy and nuts. They filled the truck, and the chef headed back.

Chad and Angelica stayed in town to do some shopping and sightseeing. They stopped at an outdoor marketplace across from the farmer's market. They stopped at a stand that sold tote and beach bags. Chad bought each of them two huge tote bags for her knick-knacks.

"Once we fill these, we'll rent scooters and check out the town," he said.

"Ok."

Their first stop was a vendor selling rings made of different materials. Chad saw a tray of beautiful ivory bands in rare shapes.

"Pick one," he told her.

"No, you pick."

Chad picked a wavy ring for her, and she chose the matching one for him. They each slid a ring on the other's finger. They were officially married for the day.

"Perfect," she said.

Chad spent forty dollars on their wedding rings.

They continued shopping as she bought straw hats, summer dresses, sarongs, jeweled purses in different fabrics, distinctive necklaces and a few pipes.

"Señor Chad," said a little boy pulling a wagon.

"Hi, Pablito. This is my wife, Angelica."

"Hi," said Angelica, shaking his hand.

"Bonita," said Pablito, raising his eyebrows up and down.

They laughed.

Pablito walked around with them as Angelica got more clothes, towels, sunglasses, jewelry, little musical instruments and paintings.

"Come on," she told Chad when she saw a caricature artist.

Angelica sat on Chad's lap while the artist drew them. Chad kept tickling her, making her laugh. He also frequently kissed her, making her smile. The artist drew Chad as a superhero rescuing Angelica. It was cute.

The driver texted Chad that he was back. Chad paid Pablito to take their stuff to the truck. They not only filled up the four bags they had but filled up another eight bags.

"Ready to go sightseeing?" he asked.

"Yes."

They walked around the corner to a scooter shop and rented two scooters. The truck followed behind them as they rode around.

Angelica saw a gelato shop and stopped. She got a mango, pistachio and Dulce de Leche gelato topped with pretzels, crushed nuts and sprinkles. He got a basil mint, passion fruit and Italian creme gelato topped with crushed cookies.

Next, they went to a nearby clothing store. They had beautiful linen dresses and 2-piece swimsuits. Angelica went crazy shopping. She got over twenty dresses, fifteen tops, ten skirts and ten swimsuits. She even got Nina a few 2-piece ruffled linen skirt sets.

They continued going in and out of stores. The truck filled quickly with all of their purchases. Angelica bought over twenty pairs of shoes from one shop. Then, she stocked up on crochet maxi dresses from another shop. Chad bought some clothing and accessories as well. As for food, they tried things like açaí bowls, sushi and tapas.

Around 7 p.m., they headed back to the yacht to smoke and change. Chad invited her to an island party. Angelica changed into a long, white boho maxi dress with a deep V-neck, high side split and a wrap-around tie waist. He wore a white Italian linen outfit. It was loungewear and perfect for attending the outdoor event.

They heard music near the port as the speedboat approached. They got off and walked to the main street adjacent to the port.

Angelica was surprised. Everyone knew Chad as this regular guy wearing comfortable clothing, sandals and having a great time. He drank beer out of a bottle and was carefree. It was a humbling moment for Angelica. She enjoyed watching him.

"Señor Chad…" they heard as they entered the crowd.

"Hi, Pablito."

"Tienes que bailar con tu esposa."

"Esta bien. I'll dance with my wife."

Chad led Angelica to the streets to dance with the locals. There was closeness and turns with lots of kissing. Chad was caught up in the moment. Even as it began to drizzle, it didn't stop the party. Everyone was out there still dancing like out of a movie. Chad didn't care, either. The feeling was euphoric.

"I love you too," whispered Angelica in his ear.

He just looked at her and smiled.

As it came down harder, everyone found cover. Chad pulled Angelica under an awning on the side of an apartment building.

"Thank you for today, Mrs. Matthews."

"You're welcome, Mr. Matthews."

"It felt amazing being your husband."

Just as Chad was going for Angelica's breasts, Pablito called him. His mother wanted to see him.

"Saved by the bell," whispered Chad.

Pablito's mom hugged Chad and thanked him for the party. Next, she hugged Angelica and told her a few things about Chad in Spanish. Chad reached into his pocket and handed her an envelope filled with money.

Around ten, the younger crowd filled the streets. Chad said his goodbyes and they headed back to the yacht. They changed out of their wet clothes and sat at the dinner table.

"This is beautiful," said Angelica.

"Glad you like it."

The exquisite black marble table had two place settings with candles and flowers, creating a romantic ambiance.

While Chad talked about Pablito and his family, the chef poured the wine and served their food. Pabilto's mom kept Chad's house in order while he was away. And the money he paid her was her salary and monthly expenses.

"Did you pay for the party?" she asked.

"Yes. They're good kids."

"You're an amazing man."

"Thank you."

"Thank you for letting me see this side of you."

"Thank you for allowing me to trust you."

"You're welcome."

Chad was all smiles referring to Ibiza as his humbling place. He had an amazing life, but it got very stressful. So, he visited every few months to de-stress and disconnect from the world.

Then, he looked at his ring.

"I know today was a fantasy, but I loved it," he said.

"I agree."

"I can see myself married to you."

"Me too. You're not as bad as I thought."

"Ouch."

"You have a strong personality."

"I'm still that person."

"Well, I can never see you the same."

He rubbed her hair while staring at her.

After dinner, they went into the lounge area and talked some more. Angelica and Chad really got to know one another. They smoked more sex weed and ended their night making sweet and passionate love with tender touches, kissing and admission of feelings.

The next day, they got up early and flew to Milan. They spent the morning sightseeing, shopping and eating. By afternoon, they were conducting business at Chad's place near the Indro Montanelli Gardens. Chad met with designers for his private boutique in New York. Angelica reaped the benefits from those meetings as well. They headed back to the States that night. They pretended to be married the entire day.

Chapter 41
Short Week

Angelica was exhausted walking into work Monday morning. She'd just returned from Milan and had a full schedule. It was Thanksgiving week, and they only worked Monday and Tuesday. Austin gave corporate three days off for Thanksgiving.

Just as Angelica entered the building, Falio called.

"Mi Angel…good morning."

"Good morning, Mi Amor."

Falio didn't have good news for Angelica regarding Melissa. She wouldn't take the DNA test. She didn't want to let Falio off the hook. Angelica was upset and disappointed.

"What are you going to do?" she asked.

"I'll figure that out."

Falio mentioned the pictures of her and Chad at the museum and how beautiful she looked. She thanked him and explained it was a work event. Then, Angelica asked if he was flying up for the holidays. Falio declined as he had to work.

"Good morning, Elizabeth."

"Good morning, Miss Angelica."

Elizabeth followed Angelica into her office. Angelica ordered breakfast and discussed her calendar. Afterward, she hurried to meet with Austin.

"Knock knock."

"Come in, Angelica."

When she walked in, she found Damian and the new hire in his office.

"Good morning," said Angelica.

"Good morning, Angelica," said Damian. "This is Whitney Allen…my replacement."

"Nice to meet you," she said, shaking her hand.

"Likewise," said Whitney.

"Well, we'll leave you two to it," said Damian.

"Please stop by my office this afternoon," Angelica told Whitney.

"Ok."

Whitney was a living, breathing Barbie doll. She had long blond hair, blue eyes, pouty lips and a small frame. Angelica tried not to stare.

Angelica updated Austin on all of the developments with the Paris stores. He congratulated the team on a job well done. They discussed London, the Christmas Party and the pay increases.

"I'm sending Jerry and a few others to Paris and London next week."

Jerry was the COO of the company. He and a few of his key staff were checking out Paris and meeting with vendors for London.

"That's a great idea. How long will everyone stay?"

"Probably a week and a half."

She asked that Jerry keep her updated from an HR perspective.

"I know you want a team in London the first of the year. Who should plan to go?" asked Angelica.

"Take whoever you need, but definitely Destiny and Elise. Mandy is going to London tomorrow to sign the contracts for three buildings."

"Ok."

Angelica smiled at the mention of Mandy's name.

Austin reserved five possible locations for stores in London. Mandy would select three of the five buildings and lock them down. Austin wanted Angelica and her team to start the hiring process, Destiny needed to order all the merchandise, and Elise had to hire a PR team in that region. There were a lot of moving pieces, and he wanted the stores open early next year.

"Have you decided which city will be our international headquarters?"

"Yes…Paris."

"Great choice."

After discussing work, Angelica brought up the pictures trending on social media of her and Chad in Paris.

"I have something to tell you," she said.

"Does it have anything to do with these?" he asked, showing her pictures from news feeds and tabloids.

"Yes."

"You looked beautiful."

"Thank you."

Angelica shared how nervous she was walking towards the museum. There were so many cameras flashing in her face. She didn't know how Austin did it all those years. He admitted it was difficult at first, but got used to it, considering his profession at the time. He gave her a few tips for the next time.

"Next time? I'm not sure about that," she said.

"There will be a next time. Now, the world wants to know who you are."

"I don't see why."

"Do you even know who was at that event? Do you understand the room you were invited into? People would've paid to be in your place. But you…you not only got invited but showed up looking glamorous and shined. There was no scandal or drama. That means you were a success. And…with Chad Matthews. There will be a next time."

"Why did you say Chad's name like that?"

"You really don't know who he is, do you?"

Austin showed Angelica his company and how much Chad was worth. There were a lot of zeros.

"There's a rumor that he just purchased this beauty company for a ridiculous amount," said Austin.

"Really?"

"Yes. I can only imagine how much he'll make on that deal."

Angelica didn't say a word. She wasn't confirming anything, especially with her new business ventures. So, she changed the subject.

"I have news."

Angelica talked about the charity event she recommended to Simeon Wilcox. She wanted to give five thousand dollars in merchandise to charity to gain exposure and boost sales.

"I love that idea but donate ten thousand dollars of merchandise. Maybe we can get an athlete or two to promote us," said Austin, signing a blank invoice.

"I agree."

"You're always working, aren't you?"

"I am. You have a financial goal, and I'm here to help."

"Thank you."

"You're welcome."

Angelica headed for the door but stopped.

"Austin…"

"Yes."

"I know I don't owe you an explanation for what you saw last weekend."

"It's none of my business."

"I know, but…"

She explained what happened with Falio and the ultimatum she gave him. Austin couldn't believe he'd be that dumb after his pursuits for her. Then, she made it sound like she met Alex in New York for the first time through a mutual acquaintance. Angelica couldn't tell him she met Alex at the mansion party in Atlanta while she was with Austin.

"Alex is a nice guy."

"He seems like it, but why entertain him if you're going back to Falio?"

"I don't know that I am."

Austin couldn't believe the words that came out of her mouth.

She went back to her office with a to-do list. However, when she got there, Shana was waiting.

"Shana."

"Angelica."

"How can I help you?"

"Don't try to act all righteous with me."

"What now, Shana?"

"You're a conniving, manipulative bitch that preys on men with money."

Angelica just laughed and said, "I'm on to you." Then said, "Shana, what do you want?"

Shana showed Angelica the pictures trending of Angelica with Chad.

"So?"

"So, you're engaged and out with other men. And you talk about me."

"Not that it's any of your business, but I was working."

Angelica showed Shana the blank invoice from Austin and Simeon's card. Sportie Fans would be participating in a charity event hosted by the museum. Shana had nothing to say.

Before Shana left, Elizabeth brought in a bouquet of roses.

"Thank you," said Angelica.

Shana glanced at the card. They were from Leland.

"You were saying," said Shana, walking off.

That afternoon, Angelica was busy with meetings. First, she met with Damian and Destiny to sign the necessary paperwork acknowledging their relationship. Immediately after, she met with Zeke.

"Hey."

"Come in."

Zeke discussed everything that happened in New York. He resolved most of the issues except one.

"Great job!"

"Thanks."

Angelica saw that he was a bit tense.

"What's wrong?"

"I need to ask you something but am afraid of what you might say."

"Ask."

Zeke wanted to move to Atlanta. He was opening his restaurant and wanted to be close.

"I don't have a problem with that, but for how long?"

"How long what?"

"How long will you give me before you quit?"

"I don't plan to."

"Zeke, it's just a matter of time. You can't do both."

"I plan to hire a manager."

"You'll eventually have to choose."

"Well, I want to see how I do the first three months."

"Ok. I'll give you that."

"Thanks."

"What about Thad's condo?"

"He's not selling it anymore, which works out. I'll buy a place in Atlanta."

"I wonder why Thad's not selling?"

"He didn't say."

"Did you get your money from Diyani?

"Yes, ma'am."

"Are you excited? And I'm happy for you."

"Thank you. I'm just concentrating on work and the restaurant right now."

"I understand."

Angelica asked him to stay and called Damian and Cherry into her office. Then, she conference-called the other directors. She needed to know who was available after the first of the year for the London trip. They discussed a few dates and agreed on the second week in January. Zeke, Selena, Chris and Damian were available. Cherry and Paul couldn't make it. Angelica suggested Whitney go. Damian agreed and would reach out.

After the meeting, Elizabeth brought in Angelica's lunch.

"Thank you," said Angelica.

"You're welcome."

As Angelica ate, she thought about Chad. She realized she never looked him up. She had no clue who she was dealing with. She knew he had money by the way he moved. But after hearing Austin, she knew Chad was someone bigger than she thought. But Angelica wasn't phased by it. To her, he was just Chad.

Then, she thought about the holidays and decided to invite Alex over.

"Hey, Handsome."

"Hey, Beautiful."

"How's your day going?"

"Good, and yours?"

"Good."

"So, what's up?

"I was wondering what you were doing for Thanksgiving."

"My parents are flying in from Cali."

"You should come to Charlotte and bring them too. It'll be a good time."

"Thank you. I'll let you know."

"Cool."

Alex talked about the photos of her and Chad in Paris. She looked beautiful and he congratulated her.

Before Angelica left for the day, she called Leland. She thanked him for the flowers but asked him not to send her any more gifts.

"I was simply showing my appreciation for what you did for me and Freddie," he said.

"You thanked me already."

"Not properly."

"Thanking me was good enough."

Leland asked Angelica to help them out of the building without being seen. She took them to the opposite side of the building, where no one would see them leaving.

"Are you in love?" he asked.

"Yes."

Leland wanted to hear Angelica's story and convinced her to go to dinner with him. It was purely platonic, but she had a great time.

Chapter 42
Another Bet

That evening, Angelica called Claudia to talk in-depth about Nico and Seth. Angelica knew what happened, but they'd been so busy that Angelica didn't know all the details.

"So, you and Seth? What happened?" asked Angelica. "You were so against him."

"Ange…he just got to me."

"Don't leave out any details."

First, Claudia talked about the last dinner with Nico and how Seth drove up when they were outside her place.

"What did Nico say?"

"He was pissed."

"I bet."

"Especially after I left with Seth."

Since that night, Claudia had been with Seth on his island and traveling in Europe.

"Ange…this is some different shit."

"What do you mean?"

Seth was very confident about their relationship. He wouldn't allow Claudia to doubt his intentions. Seth made her feel secure and loved. He desired her and constantly reassured her that he wanted forever with her. Seth wanted Claudia's love and devotion in return.

"He wants me to quit my job," said Claudia.

"Why?"

"To go into business together and have a family. He wants us to get married?"

"Married?"

"I know! It seems fast, but it makes sense."

"How?"

"We've known each other practically our whole lives, our families are good friends and we've been catching up over the past couple of weeks."

"Claude…"

"Don't say it, Ange."

"No, we're going to talk about this. If it were me, you'd be all over me."

Claudia knew what Angelica was going to say. Claudia was moving too fast. And why was Seth reassuring her of things? It was clear that Claudia had her doubts and was trying to work through them. But Angelica wanted her to be honest with herself and answer all of Angelica's questions, which she did.

"It does seem like the next step would be marriage, but it's fast," said Angelica.

"I know. It's crazy because I get scared of all the plans but never of him if that makes sense."

"It does. Are you happy?"

"Yes! Extremely."

"That's all that matters. Tell me about your business."

Claudia described the swimsuits and accessories she wanted to add to the line. She even sent some of the pictures from the photo shoot they did.

"Wow! You look beautiful, Claude."

"Thanks."

"What's the name?"

"Not sure yet. Seth told me to pick."

They went through a few names, but nothing sounded right.

"How much money do you have to contribute?"

"Nothing. Seth is fronting all of it."

"How will you own half, then?"

"He's just adding me to the paperwork as fifty percent owner since we're getting married."

"I think there's more to it than that. Talk to your dad and see what he says."

"I plan to."

Claudia's dad was a beast when it came to business and she trusted him. However, Claudia sought legal counsel from her attorney, Bronson. She hired him to review the business contracts.

"Bronson knows about Seth?" asked Angelica.

"He thinks he's my business partner."

"I'm sure he doesn't believe that."

"Well, we're going with it for now."

"How are you going to keep them from colliding?"

"I don't know."

"Well, you guys should come for the holidays so I can meet Seth."

"Ok. I'll see if he's planned something already."

"I'm not taking no for an answer."

"Ok."

Claudia changed the subject and asked Angelica about the men in her life.

She started with Falio. Angelica wasn't sure what to do because Melissa wasn't cooperating.

"I feel bad," said Angelica.

"Why?"

"Because I want to be with him but not like this."

"I don't blame you. You've gone through too much shit with him already."

"I know, but I feel like I should be standing by his side. Not pushing him away."

Claudia understood but didn't want Angelica to get caught up in those feelings. She'd been through enough shit with Falio. Nonetheless, Angelica told her about his visit, showing him around Charlotte and going to Atlanta.

Then, she talked about Alex. Angelica dropped Falio off at the airport and went to see Alex. She gave details of their last rendezvous and mentioned how she felt.

"You know...I like him, Claude, but I feel like he's holding back."

"What do you mean?"

"Sex is phenomenal...don't get me wrong. But Alex is a hot-blooded Latin man with confidence, passion and fire. I see it in his professional life. I want that from him on a personal level."

She wanted Falio's passion and desire while craving Chad's aggressiveness and sweetness. She also wanted sexting and dick pics.

"But if Alex fully opens up to you, what will happen to him if Falio gets his shit together?"

"True. He's probably protecting himself."

"Exactly! It's not like you've reassured the man that he's the one."

"But I do like him, Claude."

"Maybe, but you can't settle down with everyone."

"I know...I know. But I did invite Alex to come for Thanksgiving."

"Well, that answers my question."

"What?"

"If Falio was going for Thanksgiving?"

"No. He said he's working."

"That's bullshit! He can go for one day. Hell, everything is closed."

"Honestly, I was ok with it."

"I know but still. Falio can't want you by his side with this Melissa BS, yet can't visit you during the holidays."

Angelica knew Claudia was fired up.

Last, Angelica told her about Paris and seeing Chad.

"Claude…that man is amazing."

"How did that happen? And I saw you at the museum. It was all over social media."

"Surprisingly, my staff and I stayed at his hotel. Chad saw me when we went to dinner."

"He owns hotels, too?"

"Girl…"

Angelica raved about the five-star restaurant in the hotel and all the delicious food. She talked about her flowers and cart full of goodies. Last, Angelica mentioned Chad attending Matt and Elise's proposal event and helping with the grand opening of the store.

"We went to his private island off the coast of Ibiza and spent the weekend together. I saw a different side of him."

"What happens now?"

"Nothing. We knew what it was."

"Ange…I'm sorry. I know you like him."

"I do, but oddly enough, I'm ok. I think because we talked and I understand his situation now. And I told him about Falio."

"What did he say?"

"That Ariana was messed up, and he didn't care about my rela-tionship with Falio. He was still coming for me."

"Wow! You guys just had this picture-perfect weekend, and

that's it?"

"Well, I'll still see him."

She mentioned the ads for the restaurant and sent her pictures. But she didn't mention the perfume or beauty line. She hadn't signed the paperwork yet.

"You two look amazing."

"Thanks."

"Does Falio or Alex know about the ads?"

"No! No one does yet. Everyone just knows about the museum. But I'll tell Alex this weekend."

Angelica circled back to Nico.

"Have you spoken to him since your last dinner date?"

"Girl, he isn't speaking to me."

"Claude, do you blame him?"

"No, but I didn't think he'd be this mad."

"Why not? He loves you. He had plans for the both of you."

"I guess because he didn't get that mad about Anthony."

"Yeah, but you guys weren't really talking because of that girl he cheated with."

"I know, but still."

"And look how that turned out. You were still with him."

"I know."

"This time, he was doing it right."

"Well…he blocked me."

"What!!!!"

"Yes!!!"

"Falio said he was mad."

"What did he say?"

Angelica told her what Falio said about Nico changing his life for Claudia.

"Falio said Nico was going legit. Like he's been working on it for a while. He was going to surprise you."

"With what?"

"I don't know, but he knew how important your family meant to you and wasn't going to make you choose. He was changing for you."

"Oh my God...I feel bad."

Claudia talked about Nico and some behaviors she saw before she left him. She thought he was trying to change but didn't know on what scale.

"Ange, it wasn't easy for me to do that to him. You know that, right?"

"I know, Claude."

Claudia cried on the phone. She was extremely hurt about it. Claudia wasn't sure about Nico until she had to leave him. It'd been extremely hard going through that process.

"And what about Bronson? I haven't heard you talk about him."

"He has major drama right now."

Chasity was claiming that Bronson was stealing from his family's company. She leaked a travel expense report claiming they took a personal vacation on the company's dime.

"That's fucked up," said Angelica.

"Hell yeah! But you know what she's after."

"Shit...she wants that money money."

"Yes, she does, but Bronson's family is not going for it."

"I like him for you."

"I like him too. He's nothing like what the tabloids describe him to be."

"I still think he's your Mr. Right."

"Don't say that. I'm with Seth."

"So! Things can change."

"You don't like him, do you?"

"I don't know him yet. I'm going based on the chemistry that

I've seen between you and Bronson."

"Yes, he is amazing."

"And even your voice changes when you talk about him."

"How?"

"I don't know. It's like a giddy schoolgirl."

"I don't know about that."

Angelica wanted her and Claudia to finally be happy and have the lives they'd dreamt of having. So, she said what they always say.

"Let's bet."

"Oh no, Angelica! I'm happy where I am."

"Bullshit! You still have feelings for Bronson. That's why you told him that Seth was your business partner."

"Ok…fine! But if I'm going to end up with Bronson, then you'll end with Alex."

"That's cool."

"And no more Falio. Nothing! Like me and Nico."

"That's tough."

"I know."

The ladies made the bet. However, there were rules. They had six months to be in a loving, stable relationship with their designated partner. If either one married someone other than Alex or Bronson, then she'd lose the bet. But if either one married their person, she'd win the bet. The point of the bet was for them to finally settle down. And the prize was the other's dream wedding dress, no matter the price.

"May the best bride win," said Angelica.

"I can't believe I just bet you and I'm with Seth."

"If he's meant for you, then you have nothing to worry about."

Claudia wasn't sure how to feel but knew she hadn't told Bronson the truth about Seth for a reason.

Chapter 43
Angelica meets Seth

Angelica had been staging the house in Ballantyne since Monday. She wanted it perfect for Claudia and Seth, who'd just landed. Her parents, Alina and Colin were already in town and staying with Asila and Thad. And Alex and his entire family had arrived and were over at his aunt's house. She couldn't wait for everyone to meet and enjoy a fun, family-filled holiday.

Angelica called Asila to check on her Spanish celebration. Even though they were having dinner at the Vaughns', Angelica was having her own kind of Thanksgiving at her house later that evening. Everyone was invited.

"Asila!"

"Angelica!"

"Did you find a caterer for tomorrow?"

"Yes."

"And did you…"

"Angelica…trust me. I got it."

"Ok…thanks, sis."

"You're welcome."

"What's mom and dad doing?"

"Dad is with Steve at the golf course, and mom is here helping me decide what we're having for dinner."

"Well, I'll be by after Claudia and Seth get here."

"Ok."

"Love you."

"Love you."

Just as she hung up with Asila, Alex called.

"Hey, Beautiful."

"Hey, Handsome. Where are you?"

"I'm ten minutes out. I dropped off my parents and sister."

"Ok."

When Alex saw Angelica, he picked her up and kissed her. He held her tight.

"I missed you," she said.

"Me too."

Angelica led him upstairs to her bedroom.

"Fuck me," she whispered in his ear.

So, Alex did. They got a quickie in before Claudia's arrival.

"Damn…I missed that," he said.

"Me too."

Angelica missed him but wanted what she told Claudia.

"Your house is beautiful," he said, taking a quick tour.

"Thank you."

"They must pay you well at your job."

"They do, but I actually won this house from a bet."

"What!"

"Yep."

Angelica didn't give specifics but implied how she won it from Victor.

"I didn't think he'd actually give me the house, but he did."

"Wow. That's honorable."

Angelica couldn't tell him the truth.

Claudia texted that she and Seth had arrived. Angelica

grabbed Alex's hand and went to the front door. When the ladies saw one another, they screamed and hugged.

"Angelica, Alex…this is Seth. Seth…this is my best friend, Angelica and her boyfriend, Alex."

"Nice to meet you," said Seth, shaking Alex's hand. Angelica hugged him.

"Hi, Claudia," said Alex, hugging her, but Seth didn't like that.

Angelica showed them inside and took them to their room.

"Please make yourselves comfortable. We'll be downstairs," said Angelica.

Angelica and Alex sat on the couch in the living room.

"Claudia looks happy," said Alex.

"She does, doesn't she?"

"Yes, but did you see his face when I hugged her?"

"No."

"He gave me a dirty look."

"Seth?"

"Yes."

"That's dumb."

It gave Angelica controlling vibes.

Angelica was kissing Alex when Claudia and Seth interrupted.

"What's on the agenda?" asked Claudia.

"Smoke?"

"Hell yeah!"

They went out back by the outdoor kitchen that overlooked the Olympic-sized pool. They talked about their first impression of Charlotte, Alex's family that lived in Charlotte and work.

"Claudia is joining me on my next venture," said Seth.

"I heard. Congrats!" said Angelica.

"Our luxe swimwear line should be out next year."

He showed her some images from their photo shoot. They were different from the ones Claudia showed her.

"Wow! You look so beautiful, Claude."

"Thanks."

"You make me want to buy a swimsuit."

Claudia laughed and then said, "It was fun. I didn't think it would feel like that."

"She's a natural," said Seth.

"You guys look great," said Alex.

"What did your parents say?" asked Angelica.

"They don't know yet."

Claudia still hadn't signed the contract. Bronson was still reviewing them. He wanted to be sure adding her name as co-owner would be beneficial. Besides, Seth and Claudia had plenty to do, like create a new business structure, hire models and design an attractive website. Claudia was excited about the project.

Then, Claudia looked at Angelica a certain way. It was the perfect opportunity for Angelica to tell Alex about the ads she'd done with Chad.

"I guess we're both modeling these days," said Claudia, chuckling.

Angelica gave her a look, but Alex asked, "What are you talking about?"

Angelica showed them a few pictures.

"Wow! You're so beautiful," said Alex.

"Thanks."

"You know…it's not a competition," said Seth.

"No, it's not," said Claudia. "And why would you think that?"

"Well, you talked about your project, and then she talked about hers."

Claudia pulled him aside and explained she pushed Angelica to tell Alex about her project. Angelica wasn't trying to compete with her. They didn't do that. Seth apologized when they returned.

"It's good to know you have her back," said Angelica.

"I do."

"Ok…let's go," Angelica told Seth.

"Where?"

"Please follow me."

They stepped to the side and leaned against the round balustrade balcony.

"First, I'd like to say thank you for coming. Claudia didn't want to come without you."

"You're welcome."

"So, I'm curious. What was that back there?"

"I've seen friends do the tit-for-tat thing amongst themselves."

"But we're not like that. We've always celebrated and supported one another's accomplishments."

"Good to know."

"We've done that for one another since college."

"Well, I'm here now, and I have plans for her…for us."

"What does that mean?"

"It means you aren't the only person looking out for her anymore."

"And that's fine as long as your intentions are pure."

"I do love her. And I finally have my chance to be with her. I'm not letting anyone come between that."

"Are you implying something?" asked Angelica, getting pissed.

"Look…maybe we got off on the wrong foot. Shall we try this again?"

"I'd like that."

Seth talked about marrying Claudia and having a family. He wanted them to have financial wealth outside of their family's businesses, which was why he wanted Claudia as an equal partner in his company. He wanted something they could call their own.

Angelica asked some financial questions, and it sounded like Claudia would have to invest money.

Angelica heard lots of red flags. Even though he spoke with intensity and passion, she felt something was off about him.

"Early next year, she'll be my wife, and we'll be unstoppable."

"When do you plan to propose?"

"Christmas."

"Isn't that kind of fast?"

"No. Why waste time when she's the perfect woman for me."

"She does seem happy."

"I plan to make her the happiest woman alive."

"Let me know if you need my help."

"Thanks, but I've been planning this since she left for Colorado with you."

"That's sweet."

Meanwhile, Claudia talked to Alex.

"Is that her way of checking him out to see if he's good enough for you?" asked Alex.

"Yes. You know…the hotel in New York."

"Yes, I do."

"We do that for one another."

They talked about his feelings for Angelica, Angelica and Falio and what he'd do if he had the chance to be with her. Alex was also glad Angelica was meeting his parents.

"You really like her, don't you?" asked Claudia.

"Yes."

"Why are you holding back?"

"Because of the Falio situation."

"You feel like she's not going to choose you?"

"Yes. So, nothing I do matters."

"Yes, it does."

"How?"

Claudia compared it to his work. Angelica always told her how passionate, headstrong and aggressive Alex was about his work. He expected nothing less than perfection and always went after what he wanted. Alex was determined when it came to business, which was why he was so successful. He agreed. Claudia advised him to take that same approach with Angelica. She required a certain level of passion and intensity in her love life.

"She feels like you're holding back," said Claudia.

"Can I be honest with you?"

"Yes, please."

"She's addicting, and I'm afraid of that."

"Why?"

"I've never felt like this, and I'm the one who'll get hurt if she chooses Falio."

"But you already believe she will, and you're still here."

He didn't know how to let go. He fell hard for Angelica.

"Look…I'll be honest with you. The baby news threw everyone off. And yes, she would've been with Falio if that didn't happen. But it did, and you're here for a reason. Besides, Angelica is not the same person she was when they were together long ago."

"What does that mean?"

"That means get that Cuban passion flowing and talk dirty to her or send her some dick pics. Be bold. Be daring. Get in her face. Show her what you want."

Alex laughed. He wasn't into that stuff but could give it a try.

"And you know you're already in too deep," said Claudia, laughing.

"So, she knows something is off with me?"

"Yes."

"Did she say something?"

Claudia just looked at him.

"Please tell me," he said.

She reminded him of his assertiveness the night of the masquerade ball when he thought it was the last night. But somewhere, it changed, and he became too careful rather than just going for what he wanted. He agreed and thanked Claudia for the great advice.

"Make her choose you. Do crazy things. Don't treat her like she's fragile. Fuck like porn stars whenever you want. Just be a little more assertive but in a flirty and sexy kind of way."

Alex thought about that statement and said, "Damn! She's very observant."

"Because she's into you. Besides...you're a Leo. You better use your freakiness," laughed Claudia.

Alex just laughed.

Angelica and Seth re-joined them. Claudia looked at her, and Angelica gave her a look of approval. She was not going to ruin her friend's happiness. Angelica was going to carefully investigate on the side. Something was not sitting right with her about Seth.

They all gathered their things and headed to Asila's. Angelica invited Alex's family over so everyone could meet.

Angelica pulled Alex to the side when they got there.

"I'm worried about Claudia."

"Why?"

"Something about him isn't right."

"Let me know what I can do."

Alex saw genuine concern on her face.

Chapter 44
Thanksgiving Day

It was Thanksgiving Day, and the Vaughns hosted this year's celebration. It was larger than usual, but Dana enjoyed planning this grand event. She was expecting about fifty people, including Asila's family, Angelica's friends, Alex's family, Elise's family, friends and each of their own siblings with their families.

Dana chose to host the dinner on the lower level, transforming the space by replacing the furniture and game tables with dining tables and chairs. The room was adorned in autumn hues, with rustic orange linens, gold tableware and elegant name tags marking each guest's place. She also added a thoughtful touch by purchasing charming little gifts for everyone.

Angelica and her crew arrived around one o'clock.

"Hi," said Angelica, hugging Dana.

Angelica introduced Alex, his family and her friends. Dana welcomed them graciously and left to check on the caterers.

Autumn was a season Dana cherished. Each year, she transformed the Vaughn home with vibrant ivy, garlands of colorful leaves, decorative pumpkins and elegant candlestick holders. Some garlands even twinkled with lights, casting a warm glow. The scent of cinnamon and pumpkin filled the air, while shades of fall graced nearly every room. Angelica adored it all.

Alex's mom, Estella, noticed Alicia chatting with Rania Ellington and a few other ladies in the living room, so she joined the
conversation. Meanwhile, Alex's dad, Humberto, spotted Alfredo
with Steve and Duke Ellington out on the patio smoking cigars
and decided to join them. Austin, Lauren, Damian, Destiny, and
Devin gathered with Thad and Matt to watch the game, while
Angelica, Claudia, and Val joined Sasha, Elise, and Asila on the
covered terrace just off the kitchen.

Cherry stopped to get something to drink in the kitchen.

"Cherry?"

"Sean?"

They hugged as they were surprised to see one another.

"What are you doing here?" he asked.

"My friend, Angelica, invited me and my boyfriend."

"Asila's sister?"

"Yes. What are you doing here?"

"This is my uncle Steve's house. Thad is my cousin."

"Oh…wow. Small world."

They talked about going back to school and getting their master's degrees. Sean was still in IT, and Cherry was in Human Resources. It turned out that they both graduated at the same time.

"Thad is trying to get me a job where he works," said Sean.

"Really? Then, I will see you every day. I work there, too."

"I really hope I get it now."

Sean smiled as he enjoyed their conversation.

Promptly at two o'clock, Dana invited everyone downstairs.
Everything looked scrumptious.

Dana spared no effort in preparing a feast for her guests. She
offered two types of turkey: one deep-fried and the other perfectly
roasted with herbs and butter. For variety, there was also roasted lamb with a pomegranate glaze and garlic parmesan eggplant

steak for the vegetarians. The spread included fresh herb stuffing with nuts and cranberries, buttery mashed potatoes, green bean casserole, creamy mac and cheese, sweet potato soufflé and skillet cornbread served with honey butter.

Dana received several compliments regarding the room decor and the food.

"So, I have news," said Sasha after everyone sat down.

"What is it, honey?" asked Dana.

Sasha looked at Devin, who nodded.

"We're having a baby!"

Cheers spread throughout the room. Dana immediately got up and hugged her daughter.

"Lots of plans," said Dana excitedly.

The Vaughns laughed because they knew Dana was about to go overboard.

After discussing the baby news, Dana brought up Thad and Asila's wedding.

"I have a bit of news myself," said Dana. She turned to Thad and Asila and said, "I got Vizcaya for your wedding site. However, it will be on Christmas Day, not New Year's Day."

Asila screamed and hugged Thad. Then, they hugged Dana tight. Dana thanked Asila for not giving up on her.

"Even better. I love Christmas!" said Asila excitedly. "But how did you swing that one? They've been booked for years."

"Well, I have a friend who has a friend who told him about a cancellation on Christmas."

"That's amazing."

"The event planner needs all of the designs by the end of next week."

"I want all my bridesmaids and maid of honor in red dresses. I want to wear red shoes. And I definitely want red and gold decorations."

"We can sit down and go through your vision," said Dana.

"Thanks, mom," said Thad.

"You're welcome, Dear." Then, Dana turned to Matt and Elise and asked, "Any plans for your wedding?"

"We're having a simple wedding with about a hundred people," said Matt.

"Yes, we're having an outdoor wedding at my parent's house in the Spring," said Elise.

"We'll talk later, Dana. We have a lot to plan," said Rana.

"Ok."

Dana was in heaven. She lit up like Christmas morning with all of the news. She was having another grandchild, her sons were getting married and she was planning Asila's bridal shower. Dana also rejoiced for the upcoming events, including Sasha's baby shower, Elise's bridal shower and Nina's next birthday.

"Speaking of Nina…" said Thad. "She is officially my daughter. She is officially a Vaughn."

Everyone clapped and cheered for them. Alicia got emotional. The Zambranos knew it was because of what she'd been through and knew Thad was a good man.

Alicia brought up another wedding. Alina and Colin were getting married next summer. They reserved the Alfred I. Dupont building for their June wedding. Alina was working with Angelica's close friend to plan the event.

"Who might that be, Dear?" asked Dana.

"Marina Gonzalez," said Angelica.

"I haven't heard of her."

"She's amazing."

After Angelica gave Marina rave reviews, she turned to Alina and whispered, "Why didn't you tell me you were starting to plan the wedding?"

"We just decided last week."

"So. You still should've told me."

"I'm sorry."

Angelica hugged her sister and insisted on paying for some of the wedding expenses.

"So, the last bit of news we have is about my soon-to-be wife," said Thad.

"I officially registered my business, A. Vaughn Events," said Asila.

"That's wonderful, mija," said Alfredo.

"Smart woman," said Dana and winked at her.

It truly was a joyous occasion with all of the news.

After dinner, the younger fellas watched football while the older gentlemen relaxed out back with cigars and whiskey.

"So, Sean, huh?" Angelica asked Cherry.

"He's a friend. We went to college together."

"He hasn't stopped smiling at you."

Cherry pulled Angelica aside and whispered, "We kissed once."

Angelica laughed at Cherry's attempt to be incognito. So, she kept her voice down when questioning Cherry.

"Does that mean you like him?"

"I did, but I'm with Q now."

"But you didn't say no."

"I have a strong admiration for him."

"His girlfriend noticed you two as well. She's very clingy all of a sudden."

"I saw that," said Cherry making a face.

Since Sean talked to Cherry, his girlfriend hasn't let him out of her sight. She followed him around everywhere he went.

"He's trying to get a job at Sportie Fans," said Cherry.

"Really?"

"Yes. Sean works in IT like Thad. So, Thad is trying to get

him a job."

"Then, let's make it happen."

"Angelica…"

"What? I see you smiling when he looks at you. There's something there."

"But I won't entertain him because I'm with someone. Besides, I'm no home wrecker," said Cherry, giggling.

Angelica was going to help Sean get a job at Sportie Fans. Angelica liked Q, but she liked Sean better.

Alex approached Angelica from behind and quietly asked to speak with her alone. As Cherry excused herself to find Q, Alex took Angelica's hand and led her upstairs to one of the bathrooms.

"What are you do…"

Alex unzipped Angelica's dress and it fell to the floor. Alex kneeled and kissed her lips. Angelica held onto the counter as he indulged. She couldn't believe what he was doing. After she came, Alex turned her around and fucked her from behind. He whispered things that turned Angelica on. Then, he came.

"What got into you?" she asked.

"You."

"What did I do?"

Before he could answer, they heard a male voice nearing the bathroom. They stayed quiet to avoid getting caught.

Angelica recognized the voice, especially after hearing things like "Claudia has no idea" and "She doesn't suspect a thing". It was Seth. Angelica started to say something, but Alex covered her mouth. The last things they heard were "I told you I'm on it" and "Come by Monday. I'll have the money."

Angelica peeked out the door after hearing footsteps fade. He was gone.

"I don't like this," Angelica told Alex.

"I know. It didn't sound good."

Angelica's mind ran through many scenarios. Alex tried calming her down. He suggested that she let it play out. If Seth was cheating, Claudia would know soon enough. But Angelica wasn't having it. She texted the P.I. and wanted him in Miami on Monday to see what Seth was up to.

Chapter 45
Spanish Celebration

Everyone left the Vaughns' home around five. Angelica's family, Alex's family and all their friends headed to Angelica's to celebrate the traditional Cuban Thanksgiving with all the fixings. Sasha, Devin, Matt and Elise also attended the festivities.

Angelica turned on Spanish music while the wait staff began serving appetizers and the bartender began making drinks.

"Thanks, sis. Everything looks great," Angelica told Asila.

"You're welcome."

Angelica saw the younger Vaughn clan arrive, including Sean and his siblings. She showed them where everything was and went to look for Cherry. However, Val saw her and stopped her.

"Angelica, can I speak to you?" asked Val.

"Sure."

Valentina Duarte was a Cuban bombshell. She stood 5'6" with had long black hair, sensual brown eyes and a cute shape.

They walked to the indoor pool area.

"Your house is beautiful," said Val.

"Thanks."

Val wanted to talk to Angelica about the situation with Falio and Alex. Angelica explained Falio using Val's husband, Marco, as an example. Val understood but didn't like it.

"Alex really cares for you. He talks about building this life with you. He's trying to be optimistic."

"I know. And I've imagined a life with him."

"I think we…"

"We who?"

"My parents and I want to see you two together. You've helped him open up again."

Angelica never felt like Alex was closed off. From the very beginning, he'd been open and honest. Angelica hadn't experienced that person she was talking about.

"Alex isn't very trusting," said Val. "So, letting you in…that's a big deal."

"I understand."

"I'm sure he'll tell you one day, but honesty is very important to him."

"I understand. It is for me, too. That's why I've never lied to him."

"That's good."

Val implied that something made Alex close himself off to people, but it wasn't her place to say what happened. But since Alex had been hanging out with Angelica, he was back to his fun loving self.

"We love who he is with you. You add that spark to his life. We haven't seen him like this in a long time."

"That's sweet."

"It's the truth."

"You should know I'm thinking about cooling things off with Alex."

"Why?"

"I don't want him in the middle of my mess. I need to figure out things with Falio first."

Val hugged her. She knew Angelica was looking out for her brother.

"You should know the entire family is encouraging him to fight for you."

"You shouldn't do that."

"Too late," said Val

Val grabbed Angelica's arm and headed back to the celebration.

There were some new faces when Angelica returned. Estella's sister, Matty, arrived with her husband, Mark, and their two children, Joesph and Lisette. Alicia invited them over to partake in the festivities.

Alex saw Angelica and wrapped his arms around her.

"What did my sister say?"

"None of your business."

"I hope she wasn't mean."

"She was just protecting you."

"From what?"

"From getting hurt."

"She can't predict that."

"No, but she can see where my head and heart are to know if I'm playing games with you."

"Are you?"

"No. I wouldn't do that."

"Then, we're good."

"Alex…"

He picked her up and kissed her. However, Alex spotted his parents approaching and quickly warned Angelica.

Estella Mendoza was a striking woman with bronzed skin, shoulder-length red hair, and captivating light brown eyes. Her full lips and subtle curves added to her allure. Always impeccably dressed, she had a flair for fashion, donning designer clothes, shoes, and accessories that reflected her sophisticated style.

Humberto Mendoza was exceptionally handsome for an older man. His salt-and-pepper hair, slicked back, framed his slanted brown eyes and strong jawline, while his glowing smile added to his charm. Standing at six-two, he was still in excellent shape, aging gracefully with an undeniable presence.

Estella and Humberto wanted to have a private conversation with Alex and Angelica to get a sense of who Angelica really was. Angelica opened up and told them the truth about everything happening. His parents appreciated her honesty. They all hugged and then went to the dance floor.

Everyone danced when a Bad Bunny song came on. Angelica grabbed Cherry, pulling her to dance with her and Alex. Sean rushed over after spotting Cherry alone. Soon after, Claudia and Seth joined in. When 'Eres Mía' by Romeo Santos started playing, Alex pulled Angelica close, swaying with her in a slow Bachata. She gazed into his eyes, smiling, as they danced. Everyone around them watched in awe, captivated by how in love they looked. Their parents exchanged smiles, feeling that Alex and Angelica were perfect for each other.

Moments later, Angelica saw Cherry and pulled her to the side.

"Where'd you learn to dance like that?"

"In college."

"Clubbing?"

"No. I took dance classes at a dance studio."

"Of course you did," laughed Angelica.

Cherry gave her a look.

"I see someone is pissed about you dancing with Sean."

"He'll be ok. It was just a dance."

"He knows it's more than that."

"No, it isn't."

"He's not blind. Everyone can see Sean flirting with you."

Cherry changed the subject and asked, "What's going on with you and Alex? I saw his sister and parents talking to you."

"Yeah, they just want to know what's up with our situation."

"What did you tell them?"

"The truth."

"What'd they say."

"They appreciated my honesty, but they still want us together."

"But was about Falio?"

"I know. That's why I'm thinking about leaving Alex alone until I figure things out with Falio."

"And Chad."

Angelica talked about what happened on his island.

"Wow! It sounds like he showed you a different side of him."

"He did."

"I knew there was more to Chad."

Angelica told her what Thad said. Cherry agreed. Chad was the fantasy, Falio was the bad boy and Alex was the dream.

Thirty minutes later, Falio called. Angelica excused herself to speak with him. She went up to her bedroom, where they argued and then talked. After they hung up, Angelica paced, thinking about her life. She knew she had to do something. A few minutes later, Alex knocked on the door.

"Are you ok?" he asked.

"No."

"What's wrong?"

Angelica explained everything to him, deciding that she would no longer drag him into her problems. He didn't deserve to be caught in the middle anymore

"Let me decide that."

"No, Alex. You deserve all of me. I would expect nothing less from you."

"You're just leaving me?"

"I have to. It's not fair…to me or you."

"Stand up."

She stood up.

He hugged her and whispered, "I already love you. You can't leave me."

"No, you don't. It hasn't been that long."

"I don't need more time to decide how I feel."

"I already love you too."

"I'm going to fight for us."

"You shouldn't. Not right now."

"Too late."

She kissed him.

They went back downstairs and played games, danced and drank.

Around 9 p.m., the food was ready, and the spread was stunning. It featured lechon (roasted pig), white rice, yellow rice with vegetables, black beans, red beans with ham, yucca in ajo, sweet plantains, tostones, green salad and potato salad. Angelica added a few more of her favorites: mac and cheese, ropa veja and lobster and crab enchilado.

Alina and Angelica talked about her wedding. Alina made her promise to be there when she picked out her wedding dress. Then, she mentioned taking the bar exam the following week. Angelica was excited for her.

After a fun-filled family event, Alex and Angelica went upstairs to shower.

"I love you," he said, kissing her.

"I love you, too."

As the water rained down on them, they kissed. He touched her body as she did his. Then, she did something he wasn't expecting. Angelica went down on him. She started slowly sliding back and forth. He guided her head as she pleasured him. He got excited and grabbed her hair as he talked dirty to her.

"Oh my God," he said.

They finished their shower and went to the bedroom. Alex popped her clit out and sucked. Angelica jumped so high that her body rose and fell back down. Alex wasn't playing games. He licked and sucked that pussy until she came. Then, he slid deep inside, making her scream. He stroked fast and slow, making Angelica cum multiple times.

Alex wasn't finished. He flipped her over so she could ride him. And that she did. Alex's toes curled when she leaned forward and bounced. He rose up, trying not to cum. However, Angelica wasn't having it and bounced harder. He came.

"I'm not done with you," he told Angelica, trying to catch his breath.

"I know."

They passed out.

Chapter 46
Black Friday

All the ladies met at Angelica's for Black Friday shopping around 5 a.m. Angelica hired the same chef to prepare a hearty breakfast before their excursion.

"Wow! This is a lot of food," said Matty.

"I want everyone to be nice and full because we aren't stopping until noon for lunch," said Angelica.

"She always loved getting up early and shopping since she was a little girl," said Alicia.

"Val, too," laughed Estella.

Alex, Seth and Colin joined them in the kitchen.

"What are you guys doing today?" asked Angelica.

"Thad has this whole thing planned," said Asila.

"Well, have fun."

Falio texted Angelica, knowing she was getting ready to leave. He told her to have fun and spend as much as she wanted on his card. She thanked him and promised to call him later.

Angelica stood by the front door, looking through her purse when Alex approached her.

"Do you need money?" he whispered.

"No, thank you. I was looking for my bank card to give to my mom. I want her to buy whatever she wants."

"Well…here," he said, handing her a black card.

"No…I'm ok. Thanks."

"No. Take it."

He showed her the card. It had her name on it.

"Alex…why did you do this?"

"I've had it since you left for Colorado."

"Why?"

"I fell for you then and wanted to make a grand gesture. I just never gave it to you out of fear. But after last night, I meant what I said…I'm going to fight like hell for you, I promise."

"But Alex…"

"Don't tell me not to. And if things don't work out, it won't be because I didn't try. So, do your worst with the card. I need to know how my future wife likes to shop."

Angelica jumped on him and kissed him.

"Thank you."

"You're welcome."

It was a mad rush when the doors opened at South Park Mall. Hundreds of people lined up to be the first in their favorite stores. The ladies weren't too worried as they were sure to find something.

"Here, mom. Take my card and buy whatever you want. It doesn't matter the cost," said Angelica.

"But mija…"

"You're the queen today, mom. Buy whatever you want and as much as you want. I promise I have the money."

Alicia hugged her and kissed her on the forehead. Then, she asked, "Can I buy Papa some stuff too?"

"You can do whatever you want. You have a million-dollar budget."

Alicia laughed as Angelica winked. Alicia didn't know she

was telling the truth.

"That was sweet," said Alina.

"She deserves it and more."

The ladies split up as they went in and out of different stores. They took several trips to the car and snacked at the food kiosks.

Chad called Angelica while she was in Burberry.

"Hi, Honey ."

"Hey, Baby."

"How are you?"

"I'm good, and you?"

"I miss you, Angelica."

"I miss you, too."

First, they discussed his restaurant in the chateau he purchased in Paris.

"I named it."

"What is it called?"

"Saveur Amoré"

"I love the name."

He told her about the chef he hired, all the reservations confirmed and how far out they were booked.

"Wow! That's amazing," she said.

"Thank you for all of your help."

"You're welcome. I can't wait to go back."

"When? I'll meet you there."

"Not sure, but soon. I was thinking about taking my sisters to visit."

Angelica wanted to take Alina and Asila to Paris for some quality time together. She was eager for her sisters to see her home and especially excited to help Alina pick out her wedding dress. She also planned to take them shopping around the city and dine at his restaurant. Chad reassured her that the house would be finished in a few weeks.

"I love you," she said.

"I love you. How's the shopping going?"

"Good."

She told him about giving her mom her bank card to shop with while Angelica used her credit card to spoil her sisters.

"I'm coming to see you."

"When?"

"I'll let you know."

"Ok."

While they were on the phone, she heard a ding. It was a bank notification. Chad sent her $500K.

"Why did you do that?"

"I want you to have a nice time with your folks. Besides, call it a bonus for the work you've done."

"Thank you, but you didn't have to."

"You're welcome."

Angelica bought everything Asila, Alina, and Cherry wanted, plus a little extra, using Falio's card. She wanted to maintain her usual Black Friday spending to avoid raising any suspicion. At the same time, she had to use Alex's card so he could get a first-hand look at her shopping habits.

While Claudia was shopping, Bronson called. He remembered she got up early to Black Friday shop with her best friend. So, he felt it was a good time to call and chat.

"I miss you," he told her.

"I miss you, too."

Claudia admitted she was seeing Seth. He figured from the contacts.

"I need to see you before you sign this contract."

"What's wrong?"

"Just come to New York."

"Ok."

Claudia asked about Chasity. She was causing more drama by posting Bronson coming out of a hotel with another woman on social media. It was a lie. He didn't know who the woman was.

"I'm so sorry," said Claudia.

"Thanks. My dad is pissed. He has every lawyer on the team handling this, especially since she called the IRS."

"What!"

"Yeah. She told them we weren't paying taxes. My dad had to agree to an audit."

"Wow! She's causing a lot of problems."

"Yes, she is."

They conversed for a few more minutes before hanging up. Then, Claudia looked for Angelica.

"Ange! Come here!"

"What's up, Claude?"

"I just spoke to Bronson."

"How is he?"

"Good, but he needs to see me about the business contract."

"When are you going to see your husband?"

"Angelica!"

"What?!?"

"What am I going to tell Seth?"

"The truth. You're going to see your attorney to review the contract."

"Yeah…and I can see him wanting to come with me."

"No bueno…not good."

Claudia just gave her a look.

Angelica laughed and told her about the money Chad sent.

"Bitch! You really put it on him."

"Shut up!"

"That's some mojo between your legs."

"Hush, Claude. He said it was for the photo shoot at the

restaurant."

"Mmm hmm."

Around noon, everyone met up at the country club. Steve and Duke were members and reserved a banquet room for their family and friends. Dana arrived with Rana after shopping at different high-end boutiques. Dana was uninterested in the mall madness.

All of the ladies hugged their men. Then, Seth asked to speak to Claudia privately.

They ducked into one of the business rooms.

"So, what's the…"

Seth kissed her and felt her up. He wanted to fuck her badly.

"Seth…what are…"

He took off her jacket and shirt. Then, he leaned her against the desk and pulled her pants down. He smelled her pussy.

"What are you doing?"

"Making sure you didn't fuck no one else."

"I didn't! I've been…"

He stuck his tongue between her legs and ate her until she came. Then, he turned her around and dropped his pants. He grabbed her hair while fucking her from behind.

"You're mine. Do you understand that?" Seth asked.

"Yes."

"No one fucks you but me. Do you understand that?"

"Yes."

Claudia could barely talk as Seth was giving it to her good. He was a little rough but reminded her of what she had.

"I missed you," he told her.

"I missed you too."

"You know you're mine, right?"

"I know, Seth, but what was that about?"

"I don't like that your friend talks to your ex."

"Too bad."

"I can tell you to stop hanging out with her."

"You can try," she said, pushing him away.

"I'm not going to share you."

"You're not."

"Claudia, I'm not into games."

"Where is all of this coming from?"

"I don't want to lose you. You're my girl," he said, sticking his tongue down her throat.

She pushed him off and said, "Don't try to control me. You'll lose."

He got in her face and said, "I love you, and I don't know how to control these emotions. I want you all the time. I get scared that someone else will come along and take you from me."

"I love you too, but you will not control me!"

"Ok…I'm sorry," said Seth, hugging her.

Behind her back, he smirked. It was the beginning of his plan.

After lunch, everyone dispersed and did their own thing. Cherry went home; the older women went to Matty's house; Val, Alex and Lisette went to handle some business; and Claudia and Seth rode around sightseeing. So, Asila, Alina and Angelica continued shopping. Thad took care of Nina at his dad's house with the older gentleman, Colin and his family.

"I miss you guys," said Alina.

"We miss you, too," said Asila.

Asila told Alina about her business endeavors.

"Dana asked me to do Sasha's baby shower," said Asila.

"That's great," said Angelica.

"I'm proud of you, sis. I thought you were going to be a statistic," said Alina.

"Wow! That's not nice," said Angelica.

"But it's true. She was going down the wrong path."

"But don't judge her for it. She had to find her way."

"I'm just glad you found Thad."

"Thanks," said Asila.

"And what about you and this nonsense of Falio when you have a billionaire sitting right next to you?" Alina asked Angelica.

Angelica explained everything that was going on with Falio. She also shared what Alex had said about fighting for her, even though she didn't want him to. She needed to sort things out with Falio first.

"I wouldn't let him go," said Alina.

"I know."

"You know mom and dad like him, right?"

"I know."

"And his parents love you. I overheard them talking. They practically have you two walking down the aisle."

"I can only imagine," laughed Angelica.

"What are you going to do, sis? You can't play with both of them. And now our families are involved," said Asila.

"I know...I know."

Angelica took her sisters to the high-end boutiques Dana recommended to shop. Angelica invited them to Paris early next year to shop for Alina's wedding dress. Then, she sent a mass text message, inviting everyone back to her house. There were plenty of leftovers, plus Angelica had the chef fry fish and shrimp.

Chapter 47
New Owner

Austin had the building decorated over the holiday weekend. The exterior was grand with colorful lights, garland and two tall Christmas trees, one on each side of the entrance doors. The lobby had more lights, garlands and an enormous red and gold-themed Christmas tree with fake presents underneath.

"Good morning, Ms. Angelica."

"Good morning, Elizabeth. How was your Thanksgiving?"

"It was wonderful. Got to see the grandbabies."

"Sounds nice."

Angelica walked into her office and was in awe. It was Christmas overload.

"Isn't it beautiful and festive?" asked Elizabeth.

"It is."

Angelica walked into a Candyland-themed office. There was a fully decorated pink tree with candy all over, garland with ornaments and candy hanging from the windows, ceiling decorations and presents under the tree. She knew who was behind it and called him.

"Hey, Handsome."

"Hey, Beautiful."

"Thank you for my office. That was very thoughtful of you."

"I'm glad you like it."

"I love it."

Alex had placed real gifts under the tree and wanted Angelica to open one each day. She couldn't help but wonder how he managed to get into the building to set it all up. Alex explained that he had spoken with Austin on Thanksgiving, who gave his designer permission to enter over the holiday weekend. Grateful, she thanked him for everything.

Angelica called Elizabeth back into her office. She asked Elizabeth for a double espresso as she was exhausted. Claudia and Seth returned to Miami Saturday morning. Angelica's family returned Saturday evening. Alex's family flew back to L.A. on Saturday as well. And Alex stayed with Angelica until late Sunday night. They fucked almost all day Sunday, but she finally told him about her business endeavors with the perfume, cosmetics and beauty lines. He was proud of her.

Austin called an emergency meeting in the conference room. Angelica walked in like a Tiffany model. She wore a baby blue long-sleeved jumpsuit with flared sleeves and a belt. Her shoes were baby blue Manolos, she accessorized in gold, and her hair was in a messy bun with sweeping bangs.

Austin was pleased to announce record sales in Paris, with weekend numbers just shy of seven figures. He congratulated the team for their hard work. Then, he addressed a robbery that had occurred at one of their stores in San Jose, California over the weekend. Fortunately, the thieves didn't get away with much since the cash was secured in a safe. However, Austin emphasized the need to increase security at all stores nationwide. Lastly, he reminded everyone to submit their RSVPs for the Christmas party.

"Angelica…please follow me to my office," said Austin.

"Ok."

Austin closed the door behind them.

"You look very nice."

"Thank you."

"It was good seeing your parents."

"They said the same about you."

Austin needed a team in Paris the following week. He wanted everything up to par when he arrived for Christmas.

"I'm spending the holidays out there with Lauren," said Austin. "I want to be sure everything looks good when I get there."

"That sounds nice."

"Yeah…Destiny and Damian are coming as well."

"How do you feel about that?"

"I'm fine with it. She deserves a good guy."

"True. And how's it going between you two?"

"Good. Lauren is an amazing woman."

"She seems nice."

"She is. Thanks."

Angelica suggested Zeke, Selena and Chris go this time since Damian and Destiny were going with Austin in a few weeks. He agreed.

"If things continue like this, we can repay the investment company faster."

"That's great!"

"Yes, it is. And we'll be ahead of schedule paying off our debt. Thank you for all of your help."

"You're welcome," she said, hugging him.

Austin hugged her tight and discreetly smelled her before letting her go.

"And don't forget London the second week in January," he said.

"I know."

Angelica got back to her office and stared out of the window.

It was pouring rain outside, but it seemed to relax her.

Cherry knocked on the door. Angelica invited her in.

"I need to talk to you," said Cherry.

"What's wrong?"

Cherry and Q had a slight disagreement because of Sean. Q felt that Sean wanted Cherry, but she downplayed his concerns as being Sean's personality. Angelica agreed with Q. Sean was very interested in Cherry still.

"Where's Q now?"

"He went back to Miami."

"Is he upset?"

"We're fine."

Cherry didn't want to talk about it, so Angelica left it alone.

"I get a bad vibe about Seth," said Angelica.

"Did he do something?"

Angelica mentioned the conversation with Seth at her house and what she overheard while in the bathroom at Dana's house. Cherry giggled because she knew what Angelica and Alex were doing.

"It does sound a little suspicious."

"I think so, too."

They talked for a few more minutes before Cherry left for a meeting.

Angelica was about to call Elizabeth when she strolled in with a large manilla envelope.

"I was just about to call you."

"How can I help?" asked Elizabeth, handing her the envelope.

"Can you please ask Zeke to come see me?"

"Yes, ma'am."

Angelica opened the envelope and pulled out the documents. "What!"

She immediately called Victor. He didn't know anything about the documents she received. He asked her to fax over copies for Arnold to authenticate. In the meantime, she basked in the glory.

"I can't believe it. I'm the sole owner of Victor's land in Tennessee," she said out loud.

Just then, Zeke knocked on the door.

"Come in," she said, waving her hand.

She conferenced Selena and Chris to deliver the news about Paris. They were all pleased to be going.

After her meeting, Angelica looked at the documents again. She carefully reviewed them and noticed an additional three thousand acres.

"What the hell?" she said out loud.

Angelica felt like it was a joke. Who would just give her that much land?

That afternoon, she received an email from Equinox with the photos from the shoot.

"Wow...they're beautiful," she said surprised.

Angelica looked gorgeous. She had to select the photos she wanted to use for the perfume, cosmetics and skincare campaign. There were so many good ones. She called Chad.

"Hey."

"Hey, yourself."

"Did you see the pics from the photo shoot?"

"I did."

"What did you think?"

"You're beautiful."

"Chad! I'm being serious."

"Me too."

They discussed marketing campaign ideas and the photos that corresponded. Then, Chad told her how much Tom recovered from her tip. She'd be receiving a transfer for $6.25M by the end of the day. She was surprised.

"I told my mom about you," she told him.

"Uh oh."

"She thinks you're the fantasy guy."

"What does that mean?"

"The kind of guy that doesn't want to live in reality. You want a fantasy with me."

"What's wrong with that?"

"Nothing…if that's what you're into."

Alicia felt he was a good guy in an unfortunate situation. She felt like Chad never really experienced love the way Angelica sees it. So, he liked looking at love through Angelica's eyes. Chad agreed.

Angelica hung up with Chad and stared out of the window.

"Angelica!"

She turned around and said, "Thad!"

"I could scream right now."

"Why?"

Thad made small investments with John, and one hit big. He just made $800K.

"Wow! That's great," she said, hugging him.

"Thanks. I'm so excited."

"You should be."

"But that's not why I came in here."

"What's up?"

"I need your help."

"I know. What do you need to get Sean on board?"

"He already has an interview with my manager. Wait! You know about that?"

"Yes. Cherry told me."

"How does she know?"

Angelica spilled the tea. Thad had no idea about them.

Thad told her the real reason he went to see her. He wanted

to surprise Asila with her wedding jewelry and needed Angelica's help finding the perfect set. She agreed to help.

"Thad…before you go."

"What's up?"

"I trust you."

"I know."

She locked her office door and showed him the deeds for the different land parcels in Tennessee.

"This is amazing! You got it back."

"Yes, with additional acres, but Victor said he didn't buy it for me."

"Damn, girl! You put it on someone."

"Shut up!"

"Who do you think did this?"

"Victor or Falio, but Victor has his attorney looking into it as we speak."

"Where's your attorney?"

"I need to get one."

Thad reached into his wallet and handed her his attorney's card.

"Call them. They're good."

"Ok."

Thad sounded like Alex.

"Well…congrats. I know you have big plans for it."

"Thanks."

"Does Shana know what she started when she betted her land?"

"No clue."

They laughed as she discussed her and Chad's ideas for the land.

"Stop with Chad," he said.

"What do you mean?"

"This is yours, Angelica. All of it! You decide what you want. You tell them what to do. They work for you."

"I know, but I've never done this before, and he has."

"Yes, but he's helping you for selfish reasons."

Thad called his friend, who was an architect, and asked if he could see Angelica privately that evening.

"My friend, Cody, will see you tonight at seven. He'll tell you what you can and can't do. I trust him."

"Thank you." Then she asked, "You don't like Chad very much, do you?

"I don't like him for you."

"Why?"

"I know his type. I've been surrounded by people with money my whole life. I know how conniving they can be. They will sweet-talk you out of your underwear. In the end, it's always about money! And him wining and dining you while he's engaged, it's a cop-out. He wants his cake and eat it too."

Angelica saw Thad's frustration.

"You say you want to have what Asila and I have. Well, Alex is that person. I see how he looks at you when you're together. It's the same way I look at Asila. And all he talked about was loving you and wanting the best for you."

"I know. He's a great guy."

Thad points out a few more things before leaving.

That evening, Angelica was on her way to Ballantyne to meet Cody when Victor called her back. Arnold had confirmed everything—it was true. She was now the sole owner of all the land, including the additional acreage. He also discovered that the purchase was made through Chesapeake Bank. Knowing Victor had business ties with the bank, Angelica decided to keep up the charade until she uncovered the full truth.

Angelica arrived at Cody's gym just off Park Road. As she

exited her car, she saw this cute white boy with spiky black hair, gray-blue eyes, a rugged goatee and a very chiseled body used as a canvas for all his tattoos. He walked out with no shirt on.

"Hi…Angelica?"

"Yes. Cody?"

"Yes. Nice to meet you."

"You as well."

"Sorry about meeting me at the gym. I don't usually meet clients outside of my office."

"It's ok. I love the view."

They laughed as he put on a sweatshirt.

"You must be really important for Thad to call me."

"I am. I'm his fiancé's sister."

"Oh…ok. I think Asila is great."

"Thank you.

They walked to the nearby coffee shop and discussed business over coffee and croissants.

As Angelica drove home after the meeting, it hit her. She could keep the money she was going to use to purchase the land back.

"I'm rich," said Angelica, laughing at herself.

She had over twenty million in her bank account, including Tom's deposit.

Chapter 48
Call It Quits

Falio called Angelica on her way to work.

"Good morning, Mi Angel."

"Good morning, Baby."

"I need you here."

"What's wrong?"

"We need to talk."

He was tired of them being at a standstill. They were going to talk and straighten things out once and for all.

"Ok. I'll be there tomorrow."

"Ok. Love you."

"Love you."

It was time to face the music. Angelica couldn't hold Falio off any longer. She called Alex.

"Hey, Handsome…do you have a minute?"

"Anything for you, Beautiful."

"I need to talk to you."

"Right now?"

"Yes, but in person."

"Ok. Come over tonight. We'll have dinner."

"Ok."

"What do you want to eat?"

"Soul food."

"The plane will be waiting for you."

"Ok. Thank you."

"You're welcome."

Angelica's work day was busy. She had several meetings about Paris, London and the paperwork for everyone's bonuses. She met with Austin to tell him about leaving early and traveling to Miami. And Cherry was off all week taking finals.

Angelica called Val and asked for a favor. She wanted to surprise Alex, and it was the perfect time since he was leaving work early. Val gladly called his assistant, who called Angelica to arrange everything.

Just before landing, the private investigator texted Angelica about Seth. Seth's meeting was with a private jewelry dealer. He purchased an engagement ring. There were pictures attached.

Angelica made it to Atlanta by 4 p.m. Alex was there waiting with a smile. Angelica stepped off the plane looking like a boss, wearing black leather pants, a red lace-ruffled shirt and red knee-high boots. She wore gold accessories, a red Birkin handbag and a red mink coat.

"Damn, Baby...you look amazing."

"I can say the same about you," she said, biting her bottom lip.

Alex wore a dark gray 3-piece Kiton suit with a white shirt and black tie. He had on a black trench coat.

"I missed you," she said.

"Me too."

She felt him up as he hugged and kissed her. Alex started getting hard when she rubbed on his dick.

They got into the car and headed towards his house. Angelica leaned over and pleasured him until he was stretched to capacity. When she saw they were close, she climbed into the back seat and began removing her clothes. He watched her through the rearview mirror. By the time he pulled into the driveway, she was naked with her legs open, ready to fuck. Alex closed the garage door, removed his clothes and climbed into the back seat. It was a hot and steamy session fueled by passion as Alex held nothing back.

"Damn, Baby," he said, breathing hard.

"That shit was fucking ridiculous."

"What got into you?"

"You. You look too damn good."

"Thank you."

Alex opened the door to stretch his legs before he caught a cramp. Just then, the doorbell rang. It was their food. Alex put on his pants and went to the door.

"Babe! Come eat," he said, calling for Angelica.

When she saw the dining room, she covered her mouth.

"Is this for me?"

"Yes."

Alex had the most romantic setting with large bouquets of red roses everywhere, lots of candles and wine chilling.

"This is beautiful…thank you."

"I wanted to show you how special you are to me."

She felt guilty because of what she was about to do.

They both showered and came back down to enjoy the deliciousness. He got some of Angelica's favorites: fried fish with shrimp and lobster mac and cheese, collard greens and candied yams. He also got smothered cube steak with white rice, creamed corn and potato salad. And he didn't forget slices of caramel cake, peach cobbler and banana pudding.

They sat by the fireplace and smoked.

"Thank you for dinner."

"You're welcome."

She kissed him and said, "Delicious."

"Same."

Angelica quietly lay in his arms. She wanted to remember that moment before she blew it up.

"So, what did you want to talk to me about?" he asked.

"You're not gonna like what I have to say."

"Ok."

She was going to Miami to have a serious conversation with Falio. He was tired of her indecisiveness about their future.

"When are you going?" he asked.

"Tomorrow morning."

"Are you going back to him?"

"Probably."

"Why?"

"You know why?"

"No, I don't!"

Alex got up and went onto the covered patio. He watched as the rain began to come down hard. So many thoughts ran through his mind. Angelica came up behind him and hugged him. They stood there silently for a few minutes.

"I don't understand how you love me and want to go back to him."

"You have every right to feel like that."

"I need more than that, Angelica."

"What do you want me to say, Alex?"

"That you'll stay with me. You'll choose me."

"I do want you, but you know it's not that simple."

"Are you doing it out of obligation?"

"Maybe a little, but I do love him. I'm not gonna lie to you to make you feel better."

Alex sat on the lounge sofa, and Angelica sat on him.

"Do I even have a chance?"

"I don't know, but I need to see this through."

"Marriage?"

"Possibly."

Alex grabbed a blunt. As they smoked, she talked about Falio and how they went to college together, grew up together, looked out for one another and planned a future together. He was her first everything, has always been nurturing and protective and has never left her, no matter what.

"And what about his lifestyle?"

"I can't say anything about it. It took care of us when we didn't have anything. He always made a way."

Angelica started tearing up as she remembered how hard it was for her parents to raise four girls. Falio was the only one there.

"Even if things don't work out between us, he'll always be in my life."

"Why?"

"Because he's family."

Alex was starting to understand her love for him.

"You know Claudia told me I needed to step my game up. Now, I understand why."

"What!"

"Yeah…we talked when she came to visit with Seth. She told me some things I needed to improve on, including our sex life."

"But there's nothing wrong with our sex life."

"No, but there's so much I've wanted to do to you but didn't."

"Is that why you've been in beast mode?"

"Yes."

Alex was afraid of coming on too strong, however, Angelica turned him on in a way he'd never experienced before. They were both like sex addicts with high sex drives. He'd never met a woman like that.

"Since our first encounter, I've wanted you by my side."

"That's sweet, even though I had to chase you."

"What are you talking about?"

"You know."

They laughed, and then he said, "That was embarrassing."

"Still…you could've answered my phone calls."

"Nah…I thought that was it, honestly. I didn't think you'd show up wearing what you had on…oh my God."

"I knew you had potential, Alex Mendoza."

"Yeah, I fucked you good that night."

She laughed at how he said it. Then said, "And every time after."

"You stretch him to the limit."

Angelica kissed Alex.

Alex looked at her and said, "I just want you, Angelica."

"I know, but I have to do this."

"I get it. I just don't like it."

Alex sat quietly for a moment.

"You know…my only regret now is holding back. There's so much more to me. I guess I thought I had time," said Alex.

"You went at your pace. There's nothing wrong with that. I've enjoyed getting to know you. I don't want you to be some-one you're not."

"Yeah, but I feel like I'm out of time."

"Alex, we both had situations when we started this. You know that. It's just Kelly left, and Falio didn't."

"I know, but now I want a family with you. I want to go to work and come home to you…fuck you every day."

"Every day?"

"Yes. Why? You can't handle that?"

"I can handle anything you give me."

"Oh yeah…"

"Yeah."

Alex laid her on the outdoor kitchen table and scooted her to the edge. Alex sat in front of her and dove in like dinner time. His soft, fluttering motion made her back arch as he tickled her. The harder he sucked, the more her hips moved like waves in an ocean. Alex grabbed her and didn't let go. He continued pleasuring her until she came.

He pulled down his pants and flipped her over. He slid inside and held her close. They fucked intensely and passionately.

"Damn!" she said, trying to catch her breath.

"I second that."

Alex smiled as they put their clothes back on.

"This could be our life," said Alex, smoking again. "Fucking outside to the sound of the rain."

She laughed and said, "I know, but I've been running from that one I have. I've enjoyed this one too much."

"You should stay."

She got quiet.

"Well, do me a favor."

"Anything."

"When you guys talk, pay attention to what he says."

"What do you mean?"

Alex wanted her to pay attention to his words, demeanor, actions and life plans. He wanted her to listen to what Falio wanted versus what she wanted. Alex pointed out her business endeavors and wondered if Falio's life lined up with hers. Were they going in the same direction? Was he going to be supportive? And most importantly, what did their life look like even in five years?

"I know what our life looks like in five years…four years… hell, next year," he said.

"Oh yeah…what?"

They'd get married at St. Patrick's Cathedral Church in New York like she wanted next year. The following year, they'd have their first child. Meanwhile, the project in Tennessee will be ongoing and residual income will flow in. She'd have several perfume and beauty collections making millions. They'd own plenty of real estate all over the world. And he wanted her to be the face of his latest fashion app.

"Sounds nice," said Angelica.

"We'll be the "it" power couple."

Angelica laughed at him doing the quote marks. It was cute.

"Thank you for being concerned about Falio, but I know he supports me. And I didn't tell you yet, but I own the Tennessee property."

"The one that Victor's ex sold?"

"Yes."

"Congrats! How did that happen?"

"Thanks. I think Falio purchased it."

"Why would you think that?"

"Because he was adamant about helping me buy Victor's land."

"Did you ask him about it?"

"Not yet. I will when I see him."

Alex got quiet.

"What's wrong?" she asked

"I've lost you, haven't I?"

She didn't answer. Instead, she told Alex about Seth and the ring. After, she told him about hiring an architect. Alex listened but mostly was in his own thoughts. He could never say goodbye to her, especially after all of the sex they just had. Alex felt alive with Angelica and believed her heart belonged to him. So, he decided they'd be together and played Eres Mía by Romeo Santos. They danced, gazing into each other's eyes.

Chapter 49
Miami Bound

Angelica flew back to Charlotte early the next morning. She thought about Alex and their wonderful evening. Then, she thought about Falio and wondered if she could give up Alex and Chad.

Angelica ran a bath as soon as she got home. She smoked while soaking in the tub with Epsom salt. She tried to ease some of the soreness from all the fucking she'd done with Alex. Especially since she knew she'd be at it again when she got to Miami.

She packed a suitcase and texted Claudia. Then, she called for a car. Angelica stopped by work before heading to the airport.

"Good morning, Elizabeth."

"Good morning, Ms. Angelica."

Elizabeth followed Angelica into her office and went over Angelica's schedule. Then, she called Zeke to discuss last-minute details for the Paris trip. Last, she met with Damian, leaving him in charge in her absence even though she'd still be working.

On her way to the airport, Alex called.

"Good morning, Beautiful."

"Good morning, Handsome."

"Thank you."

"For what?"

Angelica knew what it was for and asked for pictures.

"Do you love it?"

"Yes."

"And you like the theme?"

"Love it!"

Angelica had his office decorated in the Nutcracker theme. She remembered him talking about the statues at Christmas time and how it was his favorite.

As Angelica entered the airport, Cody called. He had some preliminary designs ready for her to review but needed to reschedule their meeting for the following week—he was heading to Miami on business. Coincidentally, she was also headed to Miami and invited him to join her. Cody agreed, and she picked him up at the terminal before they headed to the general aviation terminal.

When they landed, Falio was waiting. Moments later, a motorcycle pulled up. After disembarking, Cody shook Falio's hand and then left with the woman on the motorcycle.

"Mi Angel," he said, kissing her.

"Hi, Baby."

He hugged her tight as he swung her around.

They drove towards her parents' house with Bad Bunny blasting through the speakers. Angelica danced while smoking. She was in her hometown and felt alive. The air was different. The vibe was wild. And she was with the person who always took care of her no matter what. She quickly snapped back into Falio mode.

Falio passed her parents' street, S Northlake Dr. He drove five minutes south to a corner house on S Southlake Dr. It was just on the other side of the lake.

"Who lives here?" she asked.

"It's mine."

"You brought me to a drug…"

"No! And stop being loud."

She thought it was a drug house.

He drove into the garage on the side of the house. When they walked inside, it was enormous. It had elevated ceilings, upscale furnishings, a gourmet kitchen, marble flooring, floor-to-ceiling windows facing the pool and lake, and it was a smart home. The house exuded elegance.

"This is…"

Angelica couldn't finish as his tongue was down her throat. She jumped up on him. He carried her to the kitchen island.

"I missed you."

"I missed you too, Papi."

Falio removed her blouse and sucked on her breasts. Angelica's head rolled back as he felt so good.

"Take those off."

Falio removed his clothes as she took off her pants. He sat in the chair in front of her and tasted her juices. He went crazy pleasuring her. She moved uncontrollably. Once she came, he let her up.

Angelica slid down and sat on him. Falio let out a loud moan. He started pulling her hair and talking really nasty. That turned her on. She tried to bounce but was afraid the chair would break. So, they went to the nearest sofa, where she sat on him. His head sunk into the back of the couch as she bounced hard. Falio tried to control his breathing as she fucked him real good. She went savage on him, and he loved it.

Falio flipped her over. She held onto the back of the sofa as Falio dug deep. She shook her ass as he fucked her until he came.

"Fuck!"

"What?"

"I didn't want to cum yet. My pussy is so good."

"My dick gets her like that."

Falio never disappointed. Their sex was always wild and delicious.

They showered and attempted to get dressed to leave. However, Angelica didn't let it happen. She laid him on the bed and tasted him. Falio got excited as she did tricks with her tongue, making him grow. Falio was not a short-timer the second time around.

They finally made it to her parents' house. Alina and Colin had just arrived. Alina took the first part of the bar exam. Angelica hugged Alina and congratulated her.

"I go back tomorrow for the second part," said Alina.

"You got this," said Angelica.

They were in the middle of a conversation when Ariana and Ricky walked in. Ariana hugged her mom and Alina, then greeted Angelica and Falio. Without a word, Angelica lunged at her, unleashing a squall of punches to Ariana's face and body. Ariana grabbed Angelica's hair, struggling to push her off. Alicia screamed for them to stop, while Falio and Ricky tried to pull them apart. But Angelica, relentless like a pitbull, kept attacking her sister.

"Bitch, you ruined my fucking life!!" yelled Angelica.

"Get off me!" Ariana yelled back.

"NO! Sorry ass bitch!"

"Angelica!" yelled their mother.

Angelica wasn't letting up. Colin helped Falio get Angelica.

"You're a dirty bitch! How could you do that to those kids?" yelled Angelica, trying to catch her breath.

Alicia and Alina had no clue what was happening, so Angelica told them about Ricky and Angelo not being Falio's kids. They were Ricky's kids, who she'd been fucking the whole time. They couldn't believe it.

Angelica stopped for a moment. She was winded and needed to catch her breath. However, once she got her second wind,
Angelica attacked Ariana again. She snatched Ariana from behind
and drug her. Ariana tripped Angelica, but she fell on Ariana.
That was the perfect opportunity for Angelica to punch her in the
face. Falio grabbed Angelica and pinned her hands.

"Angelica! Enough!" yelled Falio.

Falio told Alicia he would take her home and let her cool off.
She agreed.

They got in his car and took off. Falio knew she was upset but
didn't know how much rage she carried.

"Mi Angel...are you ok?"

"Yes, I'm fine!"

Angelica started crying. Falio pulled over and got out of the
car. He hugged Angelica as she cried. She fussed, cussed and
expressed her anger. He saw that one of her hands was swollen
and painful when touched. She was able to move her hand, so it
wasn't broken.

"I'm good. Let's go," she said after a while.

They got back in the car and went to her condo. She let out a
sigh of relief. It felt good to be home. Claudia heard the door and
immediately went over. When she saw Angelica, she asked what
the hell happened. Failo told her about the fight.

"Ange...oh my God," said Claudia, hugging her.

Angelica cried again.

"I'll leave you guys alone for an hour. I'll be back, Baby,"
said Falio, handing her a bag of weed. "Put ice on it."

"I will."

"Love you."

"Love you too."

Chapter 50
Heart to Heart

Claudia grabbed ice for Angelica's hand and cleaned her up.

"Claude…I lost it when I saw her. I couldn't help it."

"Did she say something to you?"

"No."

"You just attacked her?"

"Yes."

"Angelica!"

"I know, but I couldn't help it."

Claudia knew it was years of dealing with Ariana's bullshit. Angelica held everything inside even when Ariana came for her and talked shit about Falio. Then for things to turn out the way they did…Angelica was done. Ariana manipulated their lives, lied about the kids being Falio's and was sleeping with his brother the whole time. Angelica had had enough. She just let it all go.

"Do you feel better?" asked Claudia.

"No. She's my sister."

"I'm sorry, Ange."

Claudia lit a blunt and passed it to Angelica. She listened as her friend talked.

Angelica told her about Alex and their conversation. Then, she admitted she was overly sore from being with Alex and Falio.

"Why did you fuck Falio a second time?" asked Claudia.

"He would've known something was up."

"Then that's what you get, Biatch," said Claudia, trying to make her laugh.

Angelica cracked a smile and got quiet.

"I think I'm different now, Claude."

"Of course, you're different, Ange. I saw it when we were up there."

"Is that a bad thing?"

"No. It's just different."

She teared up, admitting she didn't know if Falio was her future husband. She saw herself with Alex. It was easy with him. No street life. He could afford her. They could teach each other new things and mold one another. It was just a different vibe. He was loyal and could be trusted.

"He told me about your conversation," said Angelica, chuckling.

"Good."

"Girl, he is non-stop now, like the Energizer bunny."

They laughed as Angelica told her about the Sunday after everyone left.

"Am I with Falio out of obligation, Claude?"

"No, I don't think so."

"I don't know how not to have Falio in my life. You know how long we've been doing this?"

"Yes, I do. But what have you really been doing, Ange? Fucking, smoking, hanging out, getting money, him supporting you. You haven't been in a relationship with Falio in years. He's been there like Nico was for me."

"But I do love him. We were planning to get married."

"I know. And you'll always love him, but you're in a different place now, Ange. You've grown."

"But seeing him brings back all the feelings like I never left."

"Then, I don't know what you're going to do because your heart is torn between him and Alex, and Falio is not having that."

"The truth is that I was so angry with Ariana at first because she took my "could have been." But now, I'm faced with the reality of "what is" between Falio and I."

"And what does that look like now?"

"Don't know. I've used Ariana as an excuse for so long."

When Falio and Angelica broke up, it was difficult for Angelica. She never imagined a world where Falio wasn't in it. But once she started dating and men paid attention to her, she was exposed to different worlds. Her new world consisted of fancy dinners, weekend getaways, shopping sprees at high-end boutiques and sexual escapades. And when she wanted to smoke weed, go clubbing and be around someone familiar, she'd entertain Falio. She had the best of both worlds.

"I'll admit I used him when I didn't want to be in a relationship with someone. Austin was the first guy I was going to leave him for."

"But he fucked that up."

"Right!"

"So, let me ask you. Why do you love Falio?"

Angelica spoke with tenderness and admiration, describing her love for him.

"Then, what's the problem, Ange?"

"It's more of an observation. I like dressing up to attend fancy events and football games, walking around museums, jet-setting to different countries whenever I want and hanging out with professional athletes. I like the idea of social events, galas and starting new businesses to create wealth."

"And you don't think Falio will be on board?"

"I don't know, but I wouldn't have to worry about Alex every time he walked out the door."

"You know I understand."

Claudia advised her to talk to Falio and see where his head was. She also agreed with Alex. Angelica needed to pay attention to his plans for their future. If he wasn't thinking as big as she was, then it would never work. Angelica finally told her everything she was doing with Chad…the perfume, the cosmetics and beauty lines and the Tennessee project. She told her about Tom sending her money for a consultant's fee and how she negotiated the price. Angelica even mentioned her house in Paris that Chad was renovating. Claudia was surprised but loved it for her friend. Angelica was getting everything she deserved. However, she warned her about being reliant on Chad. It sounded like he was investing a lot.

"I see why you're infatuated with Chad," said Claudia. "Just be careful. I don't want you to piss him off, and he takes everything from you."

"I understand, but the Tennessee land is mine. If he pulls out, I'll find someone else to develop it."

"Ok."

"And we have contracts for the other businesses," said Angelica, even though they weren't signed yet.

"Smart."

"But it's not just that, Claude. I love him."

"Ange…"

"Not in a complicated way. We both have someone and understand that. But he's just bold, royal and rich. He commands what he wants and is aggressive about getting it. It's hard not to be attracted to that."

"Does he know about Falio?"

"Yes."

"And?"

"He doesn't care. He only cares about me, our business and my showing up. He won't tolerate anything that gets in the way of making money. He's business first and everything else second."

"Good, you need that. You get caught up with men and lose sight of what you want until you're mad and pissed off."

"Damn, Claude. You don't have to say it like that."

"I don't mean it in a bad way, Ange. I just meant that you've had to keep starting over with developing a business mindset, yet Chad won't let you out of it. Business first."

"It's true. He pushes me all the time. And when I get pissed, it's a lesson he's teaching me. I'm finally getting that entrepreneurial mindset and stepping my game up."

"Are you telling Falio about all of your projects?"

"We'll see how the conversation goes."

"I don't know, Ange…you're blowing up. I don't know if you two can survive, especially in different cities."

"I know."

"And to be honest, I like Alex for you. He has the heart you need."

"I know."

Claudia wasn't sure who Angelica would end up with, but she had to decide where Falio was concerned.

"I have to tell you something and no judgment," said Claudia.

"Ok. No judgment."

Claudia had some concerns about Seth. Angelica asked all the important questions, but Claudia wasn't sure how to answer them. Angelica wanted to know if she should be concerned, but Claudia told her no. She just needed a confidante to talk to. Claudia was, however, excited about their business venture. She finally named the brand.

"What is it?" asked Angelica.

"Body Me."

"I like it."

"Thanks."

Claudia had Bronson doing the name search to register the business. Angelica gave her advice about Seth before Falio knocked on the door.

Chapter 51
Serious Talk

Falio walked in with several bags. Claudia hugged her friend as she left them alone. Falio hugged Claudia and thanked her for being there.

"I got some stuff for your hand."

"Thank you."

Angelica stared at Falio as he wrapped her hand. He was gentle and caring.

"Thank you," she said, kissing him.

"For what?"

"Always taking care of me."

"Always!"

He finished and cleaned up his mess.

"You good?" he asked.

"Yes, but it hurts."

"Let's go, Rocky."

She chuckled as Falio grabbed her things.

Falio drove across the MacArthur Causeway and exited on Star Island.

"Who lives here?"

"Nico."

"Really?"

"Yes. I told you he was making moves."

"Ok, Nico."

They parked beneath one of the carports adjacent to the garage. When they stepped inside, Angelica was awestruck. Nico lived in a sprawling 14,000-square-foot estate, boasting nine bedrooms and nine bathrooms. Marble floors stretched throughout, while floor-to-ceiling windows offered sweeping views of the infinity pool and ocean. The minimalist décor featured oversized furniture and striking paintings, creating an atmosphere of grandeur and simplicity.

"Nico!" yelled Falio.

"Yeah…out back!"

Angelica hugged Nico as best as she could. Then, she greeted the two beautiful blonde-haired, green-eyed women standing beside him.

"What the hell happened to you?" he asked.

"Ariana."

He shook his head and made the introductions.

"Isabella…this is Angelica. Angelica…Isabella."

"Nice to meet you," said Angelica, waving.

Isabella was bad. She had butt-length wavy blonde hair with green eyes, beautiful make-up and a badass shape. She had tits, ass and a small waist, wearing the hell out of her bikini.

Then, Falio introduced the other.

"Baby, this is Mila. Mila…this Angelica."

"Nice to finally meet you," said Mila.

"Likewise."

Mila looked like Isabella except she had straight blonde hair down to the middle of her back, and the shape of her face was more oval, whereas Isabella's was rounder.

Falio stepped to the side to speak with Mila. Angelica saw

familiarity between Falio and Mila as they talked. They smiled at each other, and there was lots of playful touching. She even caught Mila gazing at him.

"Come here, Baby," Falio told Angelica.

Angelica walked up to him and hugged him. Mila showed her some documents that required her signature.

"Just call me Falio, and I'll file them for you," said Mila.

"Ok."

"It was a pleasure meeting you, Angelica."

"Likewise."

Falio kissed Angelica before walking Mila out. Angelica watched them.

Nico saw her and said, "She's ready to ride if you fuck up."

"Damn, Nico. That's rude."

"That's honest."

"Fuck you, Nico."

He shrugged his shoulders and said, "So, what happened?"

She told him about the fight between her and Ariana.

Falio came back in, grabbed the envelope Mila left and said goodbye. He led Angelica to the dock, where they boarded a speed boat. It was a short ride to his private island just off Fisher Island.

"Wow! This is beautiful."

"Thank you."

Beyond the wall of towering trees and lush shrubbery stood Falio's secluded, three-story, eight-bedroom French chateau. Spanning over 20,000 square feet, the estate featured soaring vaulted ceilings and elegant Italian marble floors. A grand double-stair foyer, a chef's kitchen and an elevator added to its luxury. What made the home truly unique was its location on a freshwater lake—an island within an island.

"Who lives here?" she asked.

"I do."

"Since when?"

"I moved in over Thanksgiving weekend."

"You staying here?"

"Yes. It's mine. In my name."

"Damn…ok."

"I told you I'm making moves."

"I see."

Angelica greeted the chef while they went poolside to smoke.

Angelica told him what Nico said.

"Don't pay him any attention."

"No, he said it for a reason. Don't play with me, Lilo."

"She's one of my attorneys. So, I wouldn't fuck her because I need her. But Nico thinks she likes me."

"Nico wants you with someone else?"

"Not that. He feels like you're playing games. You should've been by my side figuring out this Melinda bullshit."

"Is that how you feel?"

"Yes."

"So, you're mad?"

"Yes. I've done everything I can for you and still…it seems like it's not enough. So what do you want?"

"Falio, that's not true!"

"That's how it feels."

Angelica didn't say anything.

"I asked you to marry me and you gave me my ring back at the first sign of trouble. I was surprised."

"How was that fair to me?"

"No, I didn't say…"

"No! First, I had to deal with years of my sister's bullshit to now dealing with some bitch saying she's pregnant by you!"

"I get it, but…"

"But nothing! If the tables were turned, you wouldn't have even fucked with me."

"Hell nah!"

"Why?"

"Cause some other dude got you preg…"

He didn't finish his statement because he realized what he was about to say.

"How do you think I felt, Falio? It was finally us and here you come with more bullshit?"

"I get it. But it hurt when you gave the ring back. I've wanted to give it to you for so long."

"I get that, but you needed to figure this shit out!"

"Well, it ain't mine."

"How do you know?"

"She did the paternity test."

"That's why you wanted me here?"

"Damn right! I got you the results. Now you need to decide."

Falio led her to the bedroom and reached into the top drawer of his dresser. He took out the ring box and opened it.

"Will you marry me and not take it off…ever?"

She stuck her hand out. Falio slid the ring back on her finger and kissed her. Then, he took her into the closet. She had clothes hanging up, shoes on shelves and accessories on racks. He opened a chest that was inside the closet. It was literally stacked with cash.

"Take whatever you want."

"Only you," she told him.

As she was changing, he grabbed her. They had more sex.

They lay in bed afterward.

"When do you want to get married?" she asked.

"Today."

She laughed.

Falio got up to get the documents Mila gave him.

"Why did you go off to the side to talk to Mila?"

"Because I wanted to make sure she listed everything as I instructed. And I didn't want you to know what I was doing yet."

"What do you mean?"

He got back in bed and asked her to read everything aloud. Falio listed her as the sole heir of his estate if something happened to him. It mentioned the bank shares, his real estate properties, cars and accounts with undisclosed amounts.

"Really?" she asked.

"Yeah. Who else?"

"Falio…this is everything you have."

"Not everything. Keep reading."

Falio had gotten serious about his investment endeavors. He owned a trucking company that he bailed out, purchased two car lots and was doing business with Nico, including opening a club. They were buying million-dollar homes and turning them into entertainment centers. People paid top dollar to use mansions for special events, like weddings and bachelor parties.

"Damn. That's actually pretty smart," said Angelica.

"I know. Nico's new girl has him on another level and John has been helping me with good investments."

"I was going to ask you about her. She's bad as fuck."

"Yeah, she's nice. Nico is moving slowly, but he likes her."

"I'm happy for him."

"Me too. He's reaching new heights. Isa came in at the right time to help him organize everything."

"Where did they meet?"

"She owns Luxington Realty."

"Damn! I've heard of them. They sell luxury real estate nationwide."

"Yep. Nico called her when he was going to sell the house

he bought for Claudia. However, Isa convinced him not to. She proposed different options for the home and they hit it off. She knows about Claudia and what she did to him."

"That's what's up. He deserves to be happy."

"Yeah…he does. So don't run and tell your friend."

"I'm not. I know how much to say. Besides, I don't want to talk to her about Nico."

"How is it going with the new guy?"

"Honestly, I think he's planning to ask her to marry him soon."

"Will she?"

"Yeah."

"That's so fucked up."

"But I think something is off with him."

"Like what?"

"I don't know. He just kept talking about their new business and money…"

"You spoke to him?"

"Yes."

"When?"

"When they came up for Thanksgiving."

Falio made a face and said, "Well, she better be careful."

"I know, but I can't say anything."

"Why?"

"Because I promised."

"But that's your friend. I wouldn't give a fuck. I'd tell Nico everything I was feeling."

"I did, but she didn't like some of it. So, she'll figure it out on her own."

"True."

"Besides, I have my investigator on him."

Falio laughed because he knew she wouldn't just sit by and do nothing.

Then, she asked about Thanksgiving. She wanted to know the real reason he didn't go. He was moving into his new place and spent it with Paula and John.

Angelica changed the subject and told him about her new business ventures. He knew about Tennessee but not the perfume, cosmetics and beauty lines. Falio was surprised to hear that she had that much going on. She also asked questions, trying to see if he purchased the land for her. It didn't sound like it.

"I'm proud of you. Do you need anything from me?"

"No, Sweetheart. Thank you."

She talked about Cody's ridiculous plans he designed for her Tennessee project. She couldn't wait to start and show off his work. He was a brilliant architect who was about to catapult to the next level.

Falio thought about the financial aspect of her projects and decided to get her a business account. The bank needed more cash flow to attract new business. She agreed.

Chad called Angelica from the perfume shop. He had everything rushed and needed her in New York Friday to finalize her first collection, including scents, packaging and ad photos before heading to production. She agreed but told him she was in Miami. He knew what it meant and would send the jet for her anyway. She thanked him and hung up.

"What was that about?"

"My first perfume collection. I have to go to New York Friday to finalize…"

"Finalize? I thought you were just getting started on your "new" business endeavors."

"I am…sort of."

"How long have you had these businesses that you're already in the final stages?" asked Falio, irritated.

"Not long."

"What's not long, Angelica?"

"About a month."

"What!"

"Babe!"

"That's a long time, Angelica. Who's been helping you?"

"Do you really want to know?"

"Let me guess…Victor?"

Since Falio didn't like Victor, Angelica deliberately threw him under the bus. She didn't want Falio to know that Chad was the real mastermind behind her new business ventures, so she made it appear as though Victor and his associates were responsible for her success.

Falio got out of bed and went back poolside to smoke a blunt. Angelica followed and tried to explain. She downplayed how it came about.

"It started with one of those create-it-yourself scent shops. The shop manager liked what I created and suggested I sell it to the masses. Victor talked to him and now I'm launching my first perfume collection."

"Why did you keep this from me? You know I would've supported you."

"Honestly, I didn't know what this was. I picked out ingredients, bottles and packaging. I threw out some names and joked about what I would call it. Then, I get back from Paris and I have a collection. I haven't been that involved."

Falio sat there quietly. He looked at Angelica as they smoked in silence.

"Do you trust me?"

"Falio…seriously?"

"Answer me."

"Yes, of course."

"Then, tell me everything."

Angelica had already shared the details of the perfume collection with him. So, she moved on to the Tennessee project, referring to Chad as Victor's associate while outlining the plans. Then, she mentioned another one of Victor's associates approaching her in Paris with a business deal for a cosmetics and beauty line, which she was still finalizing. As Falio listened, he began to grasp why she'd been so busy. She then revealed the potential financial impact of her ventures, and the amount that would flow through the bank left him overjoyed.

"Your life is about to change."

"I know."

"That means your face will be plastered everywhere."

"I know! I'm scared but excited at the same time."

The chef came out and invited them to the dining room. The table was set with plenty of food, including steak, shrimp and crab legs.

Angelica talked about Thad officially adopting Nina, Thad and Asila's wedding on Christmas Day, Alina's graduation party and Alina's summer nuptials. Falio was happy with all of the news. He also shared that his mom had a new boyfriend. He thought the guy was cool but applied a little pressure so he wouldn't break his mom's heart. They talked about Ariana and Ricky, Angelica's parents possibly moving to Charlotte and Sal and Jazmina.

"I heard she's introducing him to the parents," said Falio.

"Really? It must be serious."

Falio told her what he knew.

Chapter 52
A Breakfast Surprise

Claudia was nestled under Seth as they lay in bed.

"Good morning."

"Good morning."

Seth rubbed her stomach.

"I can't wait to have a family with you," he said.

"Me too."

"I'm going to be the best dad."

"How many do you want?"

"I want four."

"Four!?!"

"Yeah," he said, laughing.

"I don't know about that."

Seth laid on her and said, "You'll have as many as I want."

"I don't think…"

She quickly got quiet as he sucked her nipple.

"You were saying."

"I don't…"

Seth began playing with her clit. Claudia lost her concentration as Seth did this for a few more minutes. Then, he took off his pajama pants, and they had passionate morning sex.

"I want this every morning," he said.

"Me too, Sweetheart."

"I love you, Claudia."

"I love you, Seth."

Seth was very sweet to Claudia. He washed her body as the water rained down on them in the shower. He dressed her and gave her more flowers and jewelry. He loaded her up with gifts from his family's line. Seth had been apologetic about his actions in Charlotte and wanted her to know how much he loved her. Claudia was overwhelmed with it all, yet a great sport.

They got up and went to eat breakfast. Seth pulled out her chair and poured her a glass of orange juice.

"Thank you."

"You're welcome."

He served her some eggs, fruit and croissant. Then, the chef brought Claudia a stack of strawberry swirl pancakes with whipped cream, caramel drizzle and the words "Will you marry me?" in strawberry icing. Claudia screamed as she covered her mouth and looked at Seth. He got on one knee and pulled out a ring box.

"I don't want to wait until Christmas. I know what I have now and want the world to know it, too. Will you marry me?" he asked, opening the box.

"Yes!"

She immediately stuck her hand out as he slid a 13-carat diamond ring on her finger. The 12-carat Cushion solitaire sat on a single band of micro-pave diamonds.

She jumped on him and kissed him. The staff congratulated them.

"I love you," she said.

"I love you too.

"It's beautiful."

"I'm glad you like it."

After the initial excitement, Claudia grabbed her phone and snapped a picture. She texted Angelica with a caption that said, "I'm engaged!" Angelica congratulated her and sent a photo of her ring finger with a message that said, "Double wedding!"

"Oh my God!"

"What?"

"Angelica is engaged again, too," she said, showing him the picture.

"What do you mean engaged again? And we will not be having a double wedding."

Claudia told him about Falio and asked him not to mention Alex. It was over between them.

"She has a lot going on," said Seth.

"Not anymore. She's getting married."

"And what happened to Alex? She just dumped him like that? They looked so in love."

"Well, it wasn't like…"

"He was her boyfriend? So, you lied?"

"It's complicated."

Seth was starting not to like Angelica's games and felt her behavior could rub off on Claudia. He was going to find a way to distance them.

"I want us to get married on Valentine's Day," said Seth.

"What! That soon?"

"Yes."

Claudia sat there quietly.

"You don't want to marry me?"

"Yes, but I thought I'd have time to plan."

"You'll have everything you want."

Claudia wanted a huge wedding. It had to be the event of the year. She wanted several dress changes, white doves and Angelica standing by her side. She wanted simple but elegant decor, beautiful floral arrangements and lots of pictures.

"Where do you want to get married?" he asked.

"I haven't figured it out yet, but it has to be big enough to hold at least two hundred and fifty people."

"That's a lot of people."

"I figured between both our families…"

"I'm not inviting everyone to the wedding."

Claudia got quiet. He knew she was upset. So, he rectified his statement.

"You can have whatever you want, Sweetheart. I just thought it'd be more romantic if it were me and you, with a couple of friends and immediate family. We could fly to Italy, get married on a beach, have a wedding reception and then fly to our remote island somewhere."

"Our island?"

"Yes. I plan to buy us an island."

Claudia kissed him and went to call Angelica.

Claudia invited Angelica to go shopping. Seth overheard their conversation and where they were going.

"Take my AmEx, Baby," said Seth.

"Thanks, Babe. Where is it?"

"It's in my wallet. Get it. I'll call the credit card company now and add you."

She found it on the center island in the bedroom closet. Opening the wallet, she pulled out the card, and a small folded piece of paper fell to the floor. Unfolding it, she saw a list of numbers next to bank names, which she assumed were account numbers. Letters beside each set of numbers looked like initials, though it was unclear. An email address at the bottom caught her eye. She quickly took a photo of the paper, then folded it back and made sure everything looked untouched.

As she was leaving, he said, "Behave."

"What's that supposed to mean?"

"I know who you're going with."

"So."

"Nothing, Babe," he said, hugging her. "Just be careful and call me if you need anything."

"Ok."

Claudia met up with Angelica in Bal Harbour. They screamed and hugged as they showed each other their ring.

"I thought he was proposing on Christmas," said Angelica.

"He didn't want to wait."

"Damn, girl."

"And what about you…what happened?" asked Claudia. "I thought you weren't feeling him."

"I didn't think so either, but we talked. He's changed a lot. He's not running the streets as much."

She told Claudia about his house registered in his name.

"Like uses it as his address?" asked Claudia

"Like it's legit his house in his legal name. I saw all of the paperwork."

"Wow."

"I know…right? He is different. And you know he takes care of me; our sex is off the Richter scale and look…"

She showed her the cash in her purse.

"Just like old times," said Angelica.

"He hasn't stopped selling drugs completely, has he?"

"Not yet, but he doesn't spend as much time out there. We were together all day yesterday. He didn't leave once to make a run. If anything, he was on the phone with his attorney going over business ventures."

"What!"

"Yes! But I think his female attorney likes him."

Angelica told her about Mila and mentioned Nico and Isabella. "Is he happy?"

"I think he's adjusting but doing it well. I can't lie…she's bad as fuck. I'd fuck with her if I swung that way."

"Well…as long as he's happy."

Angelica saw Claudia's face and apologized. Her statement obviously bothered Claudia.

"I'm sorry, Claude. I didn't mean to throw salt in the wound."

"It's ok. I knew it was going to happen."

"Ok, enough about him. Tell me…how did he propose?"

Claudia smiled as she told her everything he'd done that morning.

"That was sweet," said Angelica.

Then, Claudia told her about the piece of paper she found. She showed her the picture.

"What do you think it means?"

"Well, it looks like account numbers for those banks, but I don't know what the letters mean."

"Maybe initials?"

"Could be."

"And the email address on the bottom."

"Did you try sending a message?"

"No."

"Why not?"

"I don't know who it is yet?"

Angelica logged into her anonymous email account. She sent a simple email that said, "Hello."

"What are you doing? Why did you do that?" asked Claudia.

"You want to know, don't you?"

"Yes, but…"

Just then, a reply appeared. Angelica clicked on it. It said, "How are things going?"

Claudia took her phone and replied, "Good."

"How much do you need?" appeared in the email.

"I don't know. What should I say?" Claudia asked Angelica.

Angelica took the phone back and typed, "5".

"What is that?" asked Claudia.

"A number."

They sat there waiting for a response.

"Do you think we spooked the person?" asked Claudia.

"I don't know."

Shortly after, a response popped up.

"I just sent you 5 last week. What do you need it for? The job isn't finished yet."

"Job?"

"I don't know, Claude."

Claudia replied, "Well, I need it for expenses."

All communications stopped. After a few minutes, Claudia tried to send another email. It came back as "undeliverable".

"Oh, Shit! He's gonna know I sent the message," said Claudia.

"So what! He's your fiancé."

"But how did I get the email if I wasn't looking through his wallet?"

"You can look through whatever you want. He's yours! Why do you sound nervous?"

"You're right. If Seth says something, I'll admit to it. But I'm not volunteering that I did that shit."

Angelica laughed.

"Besides, it fell out of his wallet when I went to get the card."

"Exactly!"

They left Bal Habour and went to Dolphin Mall. They ate at Texas de Brazil and continued spending money.

Chapter 53
NYC Bound

Early Friday morning, Angelica was headed to New York to meet with Chad about her perfume collection. Claudia decided to join Angelica to see Bronson. However, Claudia made Seth believe it was a girl's trip to shop for wedding dresses.

Falio drove Angelica to the airport. They parked near the plane and waited for Claudia, who was minutes out.

"Here," said Falio, handing Angelica a black pouch.

"What's this?"

"Open it."

Inside were Angelica's new business and personal checking accounts with his bank. She looked at her balances. The business account had $250K, while the personal account had $100K.

"Start using the business account. We need the cash flow."

"Ok. I'll transfer money into it this weekend."

"Cool."

"And why the personal account?"

"To send you money."

"Thank you, Papi."

"You're welcome."

Just then, Falio received a text from Mila. She insisted that

Falio stop by the office.

"Who was that?" asked Angelica.

"Mila."

Angelica just made a face.

"She needs to see me about more paperwork. I'm investing in a yacht rental company."

Angelica was happy for Falio but didn't like Mila. She felt like something was up with them.

Falio pulled Angelica onto his lap.

"You know you're always going to be good, right?"

"I know."

"You know I got you no matter what?"

"I know."

"It's always me and you, Mi Angel."

"What's wrong, Falio?"

"I just want you to know that."

"I do."

"Give me a kiss."

They kissed and fooled around until Claudia arrived. Then, Falio got out and grabbed Angelica's bag. Angelica grabbed the black pouch and put it in her purse. He also handed her a Gucci backpack. When she looked inside, it was full of cash.

"Buy your wedding dress too."

"Thank you, Baby."

"You know I wasn't gonna let you go without getting one."

She said her goodbyes and headed towards the plane. Seth grabbed Claudia's bag and kissed her before she boarded. Falio and Seth caught a glimpse of one another before Falio drove off.

The ladies arrived in New York City by eleven o'clock. Chad had a car waiting to take them to their hotel. He also had a special package in the back for Angelica. When she opened it, it was edibles. But they didn't need any as they were already high as a kite.

New York was absolutely beautiful in December. Not only was it the best time of the year to visit, but the city twinkled and came alive as the holiday season was in full effect.

Rockefeller Center was iconic in New York during this time of year, with its towering hundred-foot tree and bustling ice-skating rink drawing thousands from around the world. The famous Saks Fifth Avenue light show and the Rockettes' performances at Radio City Music Hall added to the holiday magic. Landmarks like Cartier, wrapped like a gift with its bright red bow, and the New York Stock Exchange, glowing in festive green and red, captivated audiences. Elaborate window displays at Bergdorf Goodman, Macy's, and Bloomingdale's enchanted onlookers, while The Nutcracker Ballet and horse-drawn carriage rides through Central Park were holiday musts. Other seasonal highlights included the train show at the Botanical Garden, the world's largest gingerbread village on GingerBread Lane and FAO Schwartz's 'Big Piano,' made famous in movies. With endless holiday shopping, packed restaurants, parades and light shows, New York was a truly enchanting winter wonderland.

Chad reserved the Royal Suite at the Ritz Carlton Hotel at Central Park for Angelica and Claudia. Like many hotels in the city, the lobby was grand and opulent, featuring an enormous Christmas tree adorned with twinkling lights and ornaments. Wreaths, garlands and festive lights were elegantly displayed throughout the space. As Angelica glanced around, a smile spread across her face—she was in New York, and the holiday magic was undeniable.

After they settled into their room, Angelica called Falio while Claudia called Seth. Then, Angelica called Katrina, followed by Chad. Claudia called Bronson.

"What are you about to do?" Angelica asked Claudia.

"Have lunch with Bronson. We need to talk about Seth.

You?"

"I have to go see Katrina and then meet up with Chad."

"What do you think he's going to say about your ring?"

"I don't care. He's getting married soon anyway."

"Ok…well let me know how that goes."

"I will."

"And no fucking!"

"I'm not!"

Angelica wanted to entice Chad a little, even though he was off-limits. So, she changed into a pair of fitted black pants, a camel turtleneck, her Burberry scarf, over-the-knee boots and a wool Burberry coat. Angelica couldn't forget the Burberry hand-bag. She wore her hair down and bundled up as it was thirty-one degrees outside.

She made it to Victor's office and immediately met with Ka-trina.

"How is he?" asked Angelica.

"He's still in his right mind but losing it every day."

"Did he sign the paperwork?"

"Yes, but he wanted to talk to you."

"Ok."

Angelica knocked on his door and walked in.

"Hi."

"Angelica," said Victor, hugging her.

"How are you?"

"Fantastic."

"I see. What's her name?"

"Why do you always assume it's a woman?"

"Isn't it?"

"Yes," he said, laughing. "Her name is Susan."

"And what does Susan do for a living?"

"She's an artist."

"What kind?"

"The painting kind."

Angelica laughed because he had no clue what Susan did.

She called Arnold to be certain there weren't any outstanding business deals that weren't included in the contract. Victor included everything this time. Angelica signed, and Katrina witnessed. It was then sent to Arnold.

"Saw the lists of properties you purchased. They're nice."

"Thank you."

Victor purchased three clusters of properties. One list was on the West Coast, the second was in the Quebec region of Canada and the third one was along the East Coast. Angelica quickly glanced at the West Coast list of properties.

"I want the one in Seattle on Shoreline Drive."

"I knew it. I picked it for you," said Victor.

"You know me well."

Angelica still had to select homes from the remaining two lists.

"I have one more list to give you. These homes are in the Caribbean," Katrina told Angelica before she left.

"Ok."

Angelica left and went to Chad's place. When she got off the elevator, he greeted her with one red rose.

"Hi."

"Hi."

"May I take your coat?"

"Yes, thank you."

When Angelica took off her coat, Chad stared. He wrapped his arms around her waist, but she pulled away. She showed him her ring finger. He didn't care. He wrapped his arms around her waist again and got close to her face.

"I just want a hug," he said.

She hugged him.

"You're really doing it?" he asked.

"Yes."

"Ok."

Chad didn't press the issue anymore. Instead, he was going to make Angelica want to sleep with him and knew just how to do it.

"I have a surprise for you," he said.

"Ok."

He led her into his bedroom closet, where her perfume sat on the center island. It was the exact specifications she wanted and was ready to go if she approved.

"Oh my God! It's beautiful."

"Try it on."

Angelica sprayed her neck area.

"May I?" asked Chad.

"Yes."

Chad leaned in and inhaled the scent of her neck. She closed her eyes, tilting her head from side to side, letting him savor the fragrance. Her hand rested on the nape of his neck as she felt his breath warm against her skin. He was so close. However, she quickly backed away when his lips kissed her neck.

"What do you think?" she asked.

"It smells good."

"I think so, too."

Chad pinched her nipples as they were hard and poking out.

"Don't do that."

He just laughed.

Chad handed her a checklist. Angelica needed to mark down what she liked and didn't like about the perfume. They had a meeting in thirty minutes to either start production or re-do the sample.

"Do you want to smoke?" he asked.

"Sure."

"Grab the silver box in my top drawer. And hurry up with the checklist. We need to get out of here."

"Don't rush me! You just gave it to me."

Angelica opened the drawer and saw the box. There were also multiple packages of unopened sex toys inside. She opened the mini bullet and turned it on, knowing he'd hear it.

"Which one?" asked Chad.

"None of them," she said quickly returning the item and closing the drawer.

When she turned around, he was standing there naked, holding two sweaters.

"I know what you're doing," she said.

"Yes…trying to get dressed. Now which one?"

She pointed to the one she liked.

"And those aren't for you. They're for my girlfriends."

Angelica made a face as she followed Chad into the closet.

He slipped into a pair of jeans and asked, "Which one do you like?"

Chad picked up each of the three cologne bottles sitting on his island and sprayed into the air. Once Angelica picked her favorite, he sprayed it on his neck and chest.

"What do you think?" he asked.

Angelica leaned in and took a whiff. Chad tilted his head back the closer she got to his neck. She inhaled the fragrance on each side of his neck. Chad was getting hard as she purposely pressed her breasts against him.

"You smell delicious," she whispered in his ear.

"Thank you."

Angelica tried to be funny and kissed his neck before moving away. However, Chad felt he was entitled to a kiss since she got one. He pulled her in and stuck his tongue down her throat. At first, she resisted. But then, she went with the flow.

"I didn't kiss you like that."

"You chose your kind of kiss…I chose mine."

Angelica quietly repeated Falio's name. Chad drew her in, but she had a fiancé.

Chad got dressed, and they headed out. They finished her checklist in the car.

Chapter 54
New Business Prospects

Roshi greeted Chad and Angelica as they walked in. While Chad spoke with the manager, Angelica followed Roshi, excitedly discussing minor changes. Chad watched as the two chatted enthusiastically.

"You inspired someone," Roshi told her.

"What do you mean?"

"Those three fragrances he had you smell…"

"Yes."

"Well, he's giving you the one you chose for your first collection."

"What!"

"Yes. Chad wanted you to have his and hers in your first collection."

Angelica knew better. It wasn't for free since he was manufacturing it.

A few minutes later, Chad joined them. They discussed the pros and cons of the men's cologne. Angelica wanted to make changes to the shape of the bottle while Chad felt the packaging needed work. Angelica suggested a few more design changes and requested to keep the other two men's fragrances for future collections. Chad agreed.

"What are you going to call it?" asked Chad.

Angelica thought about the names in her collection and said, "Seduce."

"I like it!" exclaimed Roshi.

Chad nodded.

Afterward, they went to have lunch at a nearby restaurant that wasn't open to the public yet. The renovations were almost completed and Angelica could tell it would be upscale and expensive.

"Yours?" she asked him.

"Yes."

"Of course, it is."

"I wanted you to try some of our dishes and get your thoughts."

"Ok."

They were seated in an upper-level booth and handed menus.

"What looks good?" Chad asked her.

Angelica named quite a few items. Chad nodded as the waitress wrote them all down. He ordered drinks as well.

"When is the wedding?" he asked her.

"I don't know yet."

"Aren't you supposed to be busy planning your grand event?"

"I will…next year. Right now, I'm busy making my millions."

"Billions."

"Right…making my billions."

"Did you get an assistant yet?"

"No, but I have something to tell you."

Angelica decided to use Falio's bank for all business transactions. Chad didn't think it was a good idea. He didn't think she should mix business with personal. Angelica didn't see it that way. She was adamant that all business transactions go through Falio's bank.

"You're very trusting," he said.

"Yes, I am."

"Why is that?"

"I've known him a long time. He won't hurt me."

"Don't be so sure."

"That's your life…not trusting people. Not mine."

"It is until it isn't."

She just looked at him.

Angelica changed the subject and talked about the architect she hired for the Tennessee project. He couldn't understand why when their development company handled that. She wanted someone outside of their company with fresh ideas. She admitted she didn't want everything tied to them.

"May I ask why?"

"I can't put all of my eggs in one basket. Anything can go wrong."

"You were listening."

"Of course, I listen when you speak."

"What about residential sales and commercial leasing?"

"I will hire people."

"What if you owned it all and kept the money in-house?"

"Ok."

Chad felt his suggestion flew over Angelica's head. It could've been because she was high and ready to eat. Nonetheless, he knew she'd figure it out.

Angelica asked Chad for his boutique services. She wanted to shop for wedding dresses with Claudia. He agreed to set it up. Angelica hugged and thanked him.

"Are you going to try one on?" he asked.

"No."

"Why?"

"Because we're here for her."

"But you're getting married, too."

"I know but…"

"No buts. You're trying one on, too."

She just smiled.

Chad's next order of business was The Westchester House in Chelsea. He invited her to tour some condos, mentioning his interest in acquiring investment properties. In reality, Chad already owned the building and wanted to conduct a personal inspection. The property had undergone renovations and was now in its final stages of completion.

"Did you see anything you like?" Chad asked Angelica.

"I want the townhouse."

"Ok."

Chad planned to write it off as a business expense.

This elite building featured twenty-seven floors with only forty-five units, ranging from two-bedroom apartments to a luxurious triplex penthouse. Residents would soon enjoy amenities such as a gym, garden, game room and spa. Each unit was outfitted with high-end finishes, including marble floors, oversized windows for ample natural light and kitchens equipped with Gaggenau and Thermador appliances. Chad owned the largest real estate in the building, a two-story Royal penthouse occupying the top two floors.

"I'm keeping the Royal penthouse for myself," said Chad.

"Why?"

"I need somewhere to bring my sex partners."

"But I thought you couldn't…"

"I'm gonna do what I want. I just can't get caught."

Angelica got irritated by his comment but knew she couldn't do nothing about it.

While Chad conferred with his realtor, Angelica checked the remaining two listings from Katrina. She chose a six-acre waterfront estate in Quebec and Woodland Hills manor in Atlanta. Angelica also chose a luxurious villa in Dominican Republic from the Caribbean listing.

"Where to next?" asked Angelica.

"My office."

Chad and Angelica were headed to his new Equinox office building in Tribeca when Angelica spotted a Starbucks on the corner of Broadway and Reade Street. Without hesitation, they hopped out of the car at the red light. Angelica needed a coffee pick-me-up since she was feeling sluggish from lunch.

While waiting for the car to circle back, Angelica strolled down Reade Street, with Chad casually following her. She suddenly stopped in front of a seven-story building displaying a "For Sale" sign in the window. Angelica was instantly captivated by its striking stone facade and elegant cast-iron columns.

"This is it!"

"What is it?" he asked startled.

"This building! I must have it!"

"Let's go look inside."

The seven-story building was a mixed-use property, with each floor spanning approximately 4,300 square feet.

The first floor was an open, fully renovated space, originally designed for an upscale clothing boutique. However, Angelica imagined her perfume collection and beauty line taking center stage instead of clothing. She pointed out the perfect spot for the perfume display, envisioning large posters from her Paris photo shoot adorning the walls. On the opposite side, she imagined her cosmetics and beauty products showcased, with a photo of Chad featured by the men's line. There would be custom boxes for customers to mix and match items, along with a dedicated section for curated boxed sets.

"The boutique is nice, but why do you need this building?"

asked Chad.

"It could be Angelica, Inc headquarters."

"Your products will be mass-produced and sold in all major retail stores. You don't think it's too small?"

"No…or maybe a showroom."

Angelica's mind started racing with more beauty products to add, like makeup remover wipes, brush sets and makeup bags.

"I've seen the building for your corporate office," said Chad.

"But I want this building."

Chad laughed because she had no real reason for owning the property.

After finishing a conversation with another couple, the real estate agent approached Chad and Angelica. She invited them to take a look around but hinted that there was already a serious offer on the table. Chad asked a few questions, but the agent's responses were curt. Chad turned around, called his own realtor and gave him the building's address. Then, he and Angelica took the elevator to explore each floor.

The second floor was a spacious area lined with shelving units, seemingly set up for storage or inventory.

The third floor featured two residential units, each roughly 2,150 square feet, with soaring ceilings, oversized windows, remodeled kitchens and electric fireplaces. The elevator opened on both sides, and just outside each front door was a small storage space for items like bicycles or carts. The fourth floor mirrored the third but had not yet been renovated.

The fifth and sixth floors were a bit different, with three units on each floor instead of two. On one side were two smaller units, each about 1,075 square feet, while the other side housed a larger 2,150-square-foot unit. All of these units required renovation.

"These units need a lot of updating," said Angelica.

"I agree."

They made it to the seventh-floor penthouse.

"This is gorgeous," she said, touching the marble countertops in the kitchen.

"You still need some upgrades."

The penthouse had been freshly updated with new paint, white oak flooring featuring custom heirloom finishes, modern chandelier light fixtures and a completely renovated kitchen. The grand living room flowed seamlessly into the dining area, boasting oversized windows, coffered ceilings, crystal chandeliers and an electric fireplace. The kitchen was a chef's dream, equipped with a 36-inch gas range, dual sinks, marble countertops and paneled appliances, including a refrigerator, dishwasher and built-in wine cooler. However, the rest of the space didn't have the same level of luxury.

Maybe it was the coffee, but Angelica was pumped. She had so many ideas for the building and wanted it badly.

"Thank you," she told him.

"For?"

"Everything."

"You're welcome."

The agent tried to get Chad's attention when they got back downstairs, but he took Angelica by the hand and walked out without saying a word.

Angelica was ready to smoke, but knew they couldn't walk into his office smelling like weed. So, Chad offered her a chocolate edible instead. He warned her that the THC levels were slightly higher and it was mixed with sex weed. She wasn't concerned because no weed would make her fuck him.

Upon arriving at his office, they immediately inspected her sample products. Angelica tested the color, ingredients and texture of each one, carefully evaluating them. She quickly determined which products she'd keep and which needed revisions.

Chad asked Angelica to do a quick photoshoot with him for the men's cologne. She didn't mind and was escorted to the photography area.

"Why did you do that? Why did you give me your fragrance?" she asked.

He got really close to her and whispered, "It's the only thing I'll ever give away."

"But why?"

"Because I love…me."

She just smiled. She knew what he meant.

Angelica changed into a tube top while Chad simply took off his shirt. They were photographed up close to capture the sensual allure of the fragrance while suggesting nudity. In one shot, Angelica leaned in to inhale the scent from Chad's neck. In another, she teasingly grazed his earlobe with her lips. But the most captivating moment was when she straddled his lap, facing him. Their proximity created an intense, intimate vibe. Angelica was holding on by a thread as images of them having sex flashed in her mind. And it didn't help that his dick was getting hard. The effects of the chocolate were starting to make her feel frisky.

They made it back to Chad's place. He poured them a glass of wine and discussed the cologne ad. Just as she mentioned the storefront on Reade Street, he received a text. Chad cut their conversation short.

"Sorry, but I have to get ready for my date. We can finish our discussion tomorrow," he said.

"Ok."

"I'll have my car take you to your hotel."

"Ok."

They hugged and then he asked her to see herself out. Angelica knew she should've left but didn't. Instead, she waited until she heard the shower and walked into his bedroom.

She quietly stood at the door, staring at his nakedness. Chad was aware of her presence and decided to entice Angelica. He lathered soap on his body, gently massaging his penis. Angelica grew extremely aroused and joined him. She knew she was making a big mistake but didn't care. She wanted his dick inside her.

As they intensely kissed, he grabbed her hair and said, "Don't you ever tell me you're not fucking me."

"I'll say whatever I want."

Chad turned off the water and went into the bedroom. He gently threw her on the bed and dove between her legs. He pleasured her until she quivered when she came. Angelica did the same, but Chad backed away before he popped. He went to the drawer and grabbed some toys. They fucked like two wild beasts in a jungle. It was a fun night.

Chapter 55
Dress Shopping

Angelica woke up nestled under Chad. She smiled until she realized where she was. Angelica immediately jumped up.

"I have to go," she said.

"Wait…" Chad softly said while gently holding her hand.

"Chad…stop! I can't! I feel horrible."

"Guilt won't change what we did."

"I know that."

Seeing that Angelica was upset, Chad left her alone. However, once she began blaming herself for their wild and passionate night, he asked her to leave. He was not interested in watching or engaging in her pity party.

"What about the dress shop?" she asked before leaving.

"It's already set up. Be there by three. And Claudia will need her credit card."

"Ok. Thanks."

He didn't reply.

"Will you be there?"

He said nothing. Instead, he held the elevator door open. Chad was now pissed at her.

Claudia was mid-conversation with Seth when Angelica

walked in. One look at Angelica's facial expression, and she told Seth, "I'll call you back later." Angelica hugged Claudia as tears rolled down her face. Claudia knew she cheated on Falio.

"Ange…what happened?"

"I fucked up, Claude."

"How did it happen?"

Angelica talked about everything, including the chocolate that started it all.

"I need some of that," said Claudia jokingly, but apologized as it wasn't the right time.

Angelica didn't know what to do. She felt awful, especially after listening to a cute voicemail message Falio left on her phone.

"Listen…go take a shower, change and come have lunch with me at Bronson's."

"What's up with you two?"

"Nothing. Just hanging out and going over the contract."

"I thought you handled that yesterday."

"We never got around to it."

Angelica nodded, and said, "Oh, and we have a dress appointment at three."

"No. Kleinfeld is tomorrow at 11."

"No, this isn't Kleinfeld. But you'll like it."

"Ok."

Angelica went to her room and called Falio. It was time to face the music.

"Hi, Baby."

"Mi Angel."

"What are you doing?"

"Nothing."

Falio sounded weird. So, Angelica hung up and called him on video. She asked questions, trying to figure out what he was hiding. The more he spoke, the more she was convinced something was wrong.

Then, Angelica heard, "Babe! You like what I'm wearing?"

Mila walked up to Falio wearing lingerie. Angelica just hung up. Falio called back several times, but she didn't answer.

"Claude! Claude!" yelled Angelica frantically.

Claudia came running. Angelica told her what she witnessed. Claudia couldn't believe he'd cheated on Angelica.

"Call him back," said Claudia.

Angelica went to call Falio, but he called back. So, she put the phone on speaker and answered.

"Hello…hello," said Angelica, but he didn't respond.

Instead, Angelica and Claudia overheard Falio and Mila arguing. He apparently butt-dialed Angelica.

"Why did you do that?" Falio asked Mila.

"I didn't know she was on the phone. I thought it was Nico."

"Well, it wasn't!"

"I'm sorry. What can I do to fix it?"

"Nothing! You can't fix this. I fucked up! Last night was a mistake. You were a mistake."

"Mistake? You chased me these past couple of weeks! Not the other way around. You've been the one flirting, buying me nice things and taking me to dinner. So, don't fucking call me a mistake, Asshole!"

"I'm sorry. I didn't mean it. It's just…yes, I'm attracted to you, but Angelica…she's my life. I'm never leaving her. You know that."

"Well, she deserves someone better than you!"

Then, there was silence. Falio must've seen the phone because then they heard "Hello…hello." Angelica hung up.

"I'm so sorry, Ange."

"That Mother fucker!!!"

"Ange…"

"Don't, Claudia! There's nothing you can say to fix this."

Claudia didn't even try.

Angelica was irritated. On one hand, she was pissed that Falio got upset that she didn't want to deal with the pregnancy bullshit, yet he was wining and dining his attorney, bringing more drama to their relationship. And on the other hand, she was relieved because she messed up, too. And the truth was that she wanted to have sex with Chad over and over again.

Claudia made Angelica get up and join her for lunch. Before leaving, Angelica took her ring off and put it in her suitcase.

On the way to Bronson's, Angelica texted Chad and apologized. Acknowledging that she'd been inconsiderate, she wanted to make it up to him and asked if he was free that evening. Angelica also asked if he could have some of that "special" chocolate delivered to the dress shop. But Chad made it clear that he was fucking someone else and was unavailable.

They arrived at Bronson's Fifty-Seventh Avenue penthouse around one. He hugged them as they entered. Angelica was impressed with his place but not surprised since he was a Wells. And she loved how festive his place looked with all the Christmas decorations.

"I love your place," said Angelica.

"Thanks."

"And it smells good in here."

"Thank you. It's my famous Chicken Alfredo."

"Smell delicious."

He turned on some music, poured them a glass of wine and lit a blunt. Then, there was a knock at the door. It was his older brother, Blaine and little sister, Bethany.

"Well, hello, Gorgeous," said Angelica under her breath.

Claudia heard her and laughed.

Bronson made the introductions. When Blaine saw Angelica,

he stopped in his tracks.

"Well, hello, Gorgeous," he told her.

"Hello."

"She literally just said that," said Claudia, telling on her.

Blaine was slightly older but strikingly handsome. He was tall, athletic and fit with sandy blonde hair, sparkling blue eyes, a well-groomed goatee and a beautiful smile. He stayed for lunch.

"Oh no. He's at it again," Bethany said out loud.

"Don't worry...my girl can handle him," said Claudia.

"I don't think so. I've seen Blaine in action. Women fall at his feet."

"Not Angelica."

"Care to make a wager?"

"Let's bet."

Bethany was 5'8" with long, silky brown hair, sultry brown eyes and thin with C-cup-sized breasts. Claudia felt her bathing suits would look fabulous on Bethany. So, Claudia proposed that if she won, Bethany would be the face of her new swimwear line. And since Bethany wanted to be a fashion designer, she'd get the needed exposure. Bethany agreed and proposed that if she won, Claudia had to go away for a weekend with Bronson and have sex. They shook on it and agreed not to tell Blaine or Angelica about the bet. Claudia made the bet, knowing she wouldn't lose.

"What do you do, Blaine?" asked Angelica.

"He's a corporate attorney for the Wells Corporation and makes a lot of money," said Bronson and Bethany, mocking him.

"Shut up, both of you!" laughed Blaine.

Blaine was one of the family's attorneys. His siblings teased him because he used that line to get women.

"Can I speak to you in private?" asked Angelica.

"Sure."

"And it begins," said Claudia under her breath.

They went out onto the balcony.

"Do you take on private clients?" asked Angelica.

"Occasionally. Why…what did you have in mind?"

Angelica couldn't quite explain it, but she got a good feeling about Blaine. So, she gave him a brief overview of her business ventures, sharing everything she had in the works. She needed an attorney that was ruthless yet practical and willing to go the extra mile to safeguard her and her assets.

"I can help you, but I'm not cheap."

"So, you say," she said, laughing.

As they talked, it hit her what Chad meant by "Own it all and keep the money." So, she asked Blaine about owning different businesses under one name. Angelica not only wanted to build the houses in Tennessee but also sell them and provide home loans if needed.

"I recommend that you use different business names and keep them separate. There are different rules for each business. And if one is in trouble, you'll have the others to fall back on," said Blaine.

"So, I'll have three businesses? One to sell the homes, one for commercial leasing and Angelica, Inc for my perfume and beauty lines?"

"Yes."

"And I know the bank I want to use for the home loans."

"You're pretty ambitious."

"Yes, I am."

She referenced some of the laws Victor had taught her but admitted she needed assistance navigating them legally. Blaine was impressed by her intelligence and depth of knowledge.

Angelica negotiated a retainer's fee along with a generous monthly stipend for his services. She knew how hard he'd have to work, but he wasn't sure if he'd do it. They exchanged numbers anyway.

Around 2:15 p.m., they headed to the shop. Bronson and Bethany asked if they could tag along. Blaine, however, had other plans but hoped they'd join him for dinner, especially Angelica. She agreed and the four of them left.

They stopped in front of a light brown brick building on Broadway near Spring Street. This location specialized in bridal wear and tuxedos. When they walked inside, a blonde-haired woman asked for Claudia and took her to the back for measurements. The other three went upstairs to the second floor, where they were handed champagne and waited for the bride-to-be.

"Angelica Zambrano?" asked a young lady who worked there.

"Yes."

She handed Angelica a box with four pieces of chocolate inside. She smiled as she sipped her champagne. She sent Chad a thank you text.

Claudia tried on several dresses but never had that "love" feeling. But Angelica thought she looked beautiful in every one. Claudia tried on a few more until she found "the" dress.

Claudia chose a simple yet elegant white dress. It was fit and flare and had symmetrical off-the-shoulder straps, a sexy V-neckline and a chapel train. A dramatic veil completed the look.

"Ange...I love this dress!"

"Then get it, girl."

"You look beautiful," said Bronson with sparkling eyes.

"Thank you."

Bethany wanted to see what she'd look like getting married. So, she convinced Bronson to change into a tux and stand next to Claudia as though they were at the altar. They faced each other while reciting vows. Angelica watched them in awe. Bronson was hard not to watch as he was very sweet staring into Claudia's eyes. It was evident that he really liked her. Claudia was caught up in the moment as well. Angelica knew she liked him.

Bethany got a phone call and left. The same young lady that worked there handed Angelica a bag. It had a dress, shoes and accessories. The note inside read, "Work event. Be ready by nine. A car will pick you up." She smiled. Then, the young lady told Angelica to pick whatever she wanted. It was already paid for. Angelica chose a beautiful gown.

On the car ride back to Bronson's, Angelica offered Bronson and Claudia a piece of chocolate. She warned them about the effects before they ate it. Bronson and Claudia thought she was crazy and ate them anyway. Then, Angelica apologized for skipping out on dinner but had a work event to attend.

"Are you coming back?" Bronson asked Claudia.

"If you want me to."

"Yes, I'd like that."

"Ok. I'll just go change and come back."

"Great. I'll whip up another one of my famous dishes."

"I'd like that."

Angelica smiled as she knew Claudia would be fucking him tonight. Then, she ate one to prepare for her evening with Chad.

Chapter 56
A Night at the Gala

"Girl, I see why you like him," said Claudia.

"Who?"

"Chad."

Angelica nodded.

"I could get used to that lifestyle, too."

"Right!"

Angelica showed Claudia the note about the mysterious work dinner and wondered if it was Chad's way of being romantic. Or was it really another door he was opening for her to walk through?

"I don't know what tonight is about, but I'm gonna fuck him until he's happy," laughed Angelica.

"Did you text Blaine about dinner?"

"No! I forgot."

Angelica texted Blaine, apologizing for skipping out on dinner and asked for a rain check.

"And what about Falio?"

"He's been texting me, but I told him I heard everything and needed time. I asked him for the weekend."

"What did he say?"

"Ok."

"Wow! I'm still surprised."

"I am…a little. But I understand it."

At 9 p.m., Angelica stepped into the car Chad had sent, and Claudia left for Bronson's. Minutes later, Angelica arrived at The Pierre Hotel and made her way inside.

"May I check your coat?" a young man asked Angelica.

"Yes, thank you."

She took off her full-length black mink and handed it to the attendant. He gave her a ticket and she was escorted to the main ballroom.

The interior was beautifully adorned in festive holiday colors. In one corner stood a grand white Christmas tree, elegantly decorated with gold and red ornaments. Bar tables were draped in crisp red linens, white lights twinkled throughout and every detail shimmered with touches of gold.

Angelica commanded attention as she entered the room, turning heads in a black, form-fitting lace and sequin gown. The dress featured long sleeves, a mermaid skirt with a sweeping train and an open back. Her hair was styled in a messy bun, with loose strands framing her face and her makeup was impeccable. She completed the look with stunning onyx and diamond droplet earrings.

A waiter approached Angelica, carrying a tray of champagne glasses. As she reached for one, she saw Chad hugging a middle-aged white woman. Her first reaction was to leave. How dare he invite her to this event and be with another woman. But before she reacted, she took a step back and sipped on her champagne while staring at Chad. She contemplated leaving until a handsome, older white gentleman approached her. She was pleasant as he flirted and discussed business. It turned out that the gentleman was a well-known shipping magnate who ran his 60-year-old family-owned business. His company owned the largest shipyard on the East Coast with hundreds of cargo ships. Angelica quickly realized what kind of people were in the room and played her part as Victor showed her.

Angelica mingled but kept her eyes on Chad. She thought they'd be there together, side by side. Instead, he was very flirty and stood close to the woman he was with. Angelica had to put her feelings aside and work the room. If the older gentleman was any indication of who was there, it was show time.

While standing near the entrance, a young Latino man approached her. He was the son of South America's communications conglomerate. They spoke in Spanish and laughed at a few inside jokes. She cozied up to him and exchanged numbers.

Angelica made her way to the bar and ordered a glass of wine. Suddenly, the room seemed to hush as a tall, gorgeous man entered, exuding effortless charm in a perfectly tailored Italian suit. She overheard people calling his name as he moved through the crowd, shaking hands with ease. His suave demeanor, charismatic smile and unmistakable confidence captivated the room. Women flocked to him, but he remained unfazed. For a fleeting moment, Chad was the last thing on her mind.

This mystery man was headed her way. Angelica suddenly felt nervous but didn't know why. It wasn't like she was interested in this beautiful stranger. As he approached, the bartender handed the man a drink without him asking.

"Thank you," he said, leaving a generous tip.

The man turned and looked at Angelica. She smiled as she sipped her wine.

"You're a new face."

"I am."

"A beautiful one, I might add."

"Thank you. I can say the same about you."

"Sebastian Morrone," he said, smiling while extending his

hand.

"Angelica Zambrano."

They shook hands as he stared at her. It was a bit creepy. However, he broke up the awkwardness by asking her a question.

"Where are you from, Angelica?"

"I'm Cuban. What about you?"

"Italian."

"It makes sense."

"What does?"

"You."

He moved closer to Angelica and asked, "Is that a bad thing?"

"Not for me to say. I don't know you, but it was a compliment."

"Thank you."

"You're welcome."

They moved to the side, exchanging playful banter. Sebastian was generous with his compliments, and Angelica understood why women were drawn to him. His deep brown eyes, smooth olive complexion and impeccable grooming made him irresistible. He smelled divine, and the way his pouty, kissable lips moved when he spoke had a way of holding attention. And while flattered by his interest, Angelica grew bored with his transparent attempts to seduce her. With a polite smile, she excused herself.

Angelica was standing near the Christmas tree when Chad walked up to her. He kissed her on the cheek and held her by the waist. That was the rich and subtle way of marking his territory.

"You look beautiful," he whispered in her ear.

"Get the fuck away from me," she whispered back, smiling.

She tried to walk away, but he took her around the room and introduced her to some political figures, tech geniuses and fashion designers. Then, she saw Blaine and hugged him.

"Blaine."

"Chad."

"How are you these days?"

"Well, and yourself?"

"In good company."

"Ok…you two obviously know one another," said Angelica.

"Yes, we do. How do you know Blaine?" Chad asked Angelica.

"He's my attorney?" she stated but asked.

"I see."

"Not yet, but you will," said Blaine, winking at Chad and then asked to speak to Angelica alone.

Blaine decided to represent Angelica after finding out that Chad's company was developing her Tennessee property.

When she returned, Chad told her, "Don't you ever walk away from me with him."

"What are you talking about?"

Chad walked away from Angelica and caressed another woman. Angelica was over his bullshit. Two could play at his game. So, she went looking for Blaine when Sebastian found her.

"May I speak to you for a moment?" he asked.

She smiled and said, "Sure."

He rested a hand on the small of her back as he guided her toward the rear of the room. They settled comfortably on one of the sofas and ordered drinks. He confessed he was surprised she had walked away from his flirting. Most women wouldn't have. She admitted she didn't appreciate his forwardness to bed her. He apologized for his approach, and from there, they shared a genuinely enjoyable conversation.

Angelica appreciated her time with Sebastian but was ready to go. So, he escorted her to the coat closet to retrieve her coat.

"It was a pleasure, Angelica."

"Likewise, Sebastian."

He kissed her hand and gave her his number. She promised to use it.

"Well…it seems you made an impression on someone," said Blaine.

"He's cool."

"You really are something else. Do you know who that was?"

"A flirtatious man."

Blaine chuckled at how she downplayed his importance.

Blaine invited her to dinner, but Chad intervened, saying there was someone he wanted Angelica to meet. Blaine offered to meet with her the next day instead. She accepted.

Chad escorted her into one of the offices and locked the door. He stuck his tongue down her throat while removing her coat.

"What the hell was that?" asked Chad, trying to talk and kiss at the same time. "And you're not going to meet with him."

"You can't tell me what to do."

"Yes, I can."

Angelica pushed him off and asked, "Why are we here? I thought you were fucking someone tonight. You weren't available for me, remember?"

Chad stopped and looked at her. Then, he slowly removed his suit jacket and began unbuttoning his shirt.

"Take your hair down," he demanded.

Angelica started to say something sarcastic but saw the look on his face. So, she took her hair down.

Next, Chad removed his shirt and unbuttoned his pants.

"Take off your dress," he told her, watching her slowly slide it off her shoulders.

When her dress fell to the floor, she wasn't wearing underwear. Chad made a face as he came out of his clothes and sat on the sofa. Angelica followed and straddled him. He licked his fingers and rubbed between her lips.

"Who were you trying to fuck tonight?" he asked, pulling her hair while making her wet.

"You."

"Better be."

Chad licked her nipples as he played with her. Angelica got goosebumps as she was being tickled. She played with his dick, showing him the same enthusiasm. They were hot and heavy, talking nasty when she came. Chad immediately slid inside of her, feeling a pulsating sensation. Angelica's head fell backward as she screamed. The movement of his hips while pulsating was euphoric.

They fucked for about thirty minutes letting out all of their aggression. Afterward, Chad called for his driver, who took them to the pier for their helicopter ride.

"Where are we going?" asked Angelica.

"Get in."

Chapter 57
The Hamptons

Twenty minutes later, they landed on a large patch of grass on his waterfront estate in The Hamptons. Stanley, the caretaker, awaited their arrival near the rear of the house. Chad introduced Angelica to Stanley as they went inside.

Chad's Water Mill estate was one of a kind. He owned the largest parcel of land on Burnett Creek with over twenty-one acres in total. His primary residence was a sprawling Contemporary mansion with fifteen bedrooms, seventeen bathrooms and more than 30,000 square feet of living space. The property boasted every luxury imaginable, including a two-story guest house by the pool and a private dock with direct access to Mecox Bay.

A second estate, just as stunning, spanned over 25,000 square feet and boasted some of the same luxuries as the main estate. Both homes sat on the same parcel of land and Chad used the second estate an exclusive guest house.

Chad led her to his spacious master bedroom, which featured lots of windows, an electric fireplace, a relaxing sitting area and a television the size of the wall.

"I think you need a bigger TV," giggled Angelica.

Chad, on the other hand, striped down and climbed into bed

with Angelica. They finished their sex session the way he wanted.

"I bought you something. It's in the closet," he said afterward.

"How did you know I'd be here?"

"When you texted about the chocolate."

"You just assumed…"

"You weren't going home with no one else," he said, kissing her.

They got up and put on sweatpants and oversized sweatshirts. Angelica followed Chad into the kitchen where Stanley had food and snacks sitting on the counter. They placed all of their goodies on a tray and settled in the family room. Chad turned on the two fireplaces and big-screen TV for a little background noise.

"Why do people think you're this mean guy?" she asked.

"Because of my actions. I take what I want."

"And you don't take no for an answer."

"Correct."

"But that can be perceived as persistent. Why mean?"

"Because I'm a shrewd, no-nonsense businessman. I had to be to get where I am. That's why I tell you certain things because it was tough for me. I can only imagine how tough it'll be for you."

"Why…because I'm a woman?"

"Especially because you're a woman."

Chad poured them a drink and lit his weed pipe as he told her some ugly truths about the rich. They loved money, didn't want to share it and always looked for ways to have more of it. They railroaded anybody who got in their way, and some men didn't look at women as their equals, no matter how much money they had. He told her a few of his own horror stories and when he decided to change.

"Is that why the deal between you and Delilah is so important?"

"Yes."

"I understand."

"She moved up the wedding date."

"When is it?"

"In two weeks.

"What!"

"It's not real, so it doesn't matter."

"But still…"

He pulled Angelica on top of him and hugged her.

"What's the deal with you and Blaine?"

"I got the girl."

"It's always a woman."

Chad was dating a woman named Frances. Frances never told Blaine about Chad and cheated on him. Blaine, however, wanted to date her, but she wasn't leaving Chad for him. Chad wound up leaving her after he found out she cheated with Blaine.

"I know why she didn't want to leave," laughed Angelica.

He laughed and said, "And I wasn't even as good as I am now."

"I don't believe you."

He hugged and kissed her.

"Where did you meet Blaine?"

"He's Bronson's brother."

"Yes, I'm aware."

"Well, my friend, Claudia, is friends with Bronson."

"Isn't she the one getting married?"

"Yes."

"Why are they friends?"

"Well, he's actually her attorney now, but they met the same night we did…at the masquerade ball."

"Oh…the night you wanted to fuck me."

"Shut up!" laughed Angelica, hitting him in the arm.

Angelica talked about Bronson and Claudia hanging out and

getting to know one another. Claudia even met his sister.

"He doesn't have those kinds of friends."

"Well, Claudia says he's not the way people perceive him to be."

Angelica showed Chad the video of Bronson and Claudia pretending to be at the altar. Chad agreed that Bronson was genuinely enamored with Claudia.

"I shared my chocolate with them," said Angelica.

"They ate the chocolate?"

"Yes, why?"

"Your friend is fucking him tonight."

"No, she's not."

Chad just looked at her.

"Shut up!"

Angelica secretly wanted Claudia and Bronson to have sex.

Angelica tried to get off Chad, but he held her. He asked what happened with Falio. She told him what she saw.

"Why are men such assholes?"

They talked about it and Chad explained the male perspective. She didn't like it, but he made sense. Then, he took the opportunity to express how upset he was about the way she made him feel after their amazing night. Angelica left his place like he did something to her. It really bothered him.

"I'm sorry. I didn't mean to make you feel that way," she said.

"Thank you."

"But I didn't think you had feelings."

"Of course, I have feelings. I just don't show them."

"Why me?"

"I really like you, Angelica."

"Well, I sure as hell don't understand you. You're hot one minute and all about me. Then, cold the next and hugged up on other women."

"Those women were business. You're all pleasure."

"You're avoiding what happened tonight, but it's ok."

"That's one of the reasons right there. You always call me out on my bullshit. You speak up and aren't afraid to say what's on your mind. And I can take you anywhere, and you fit in."

"I thought you were going to say something sexual."

"That goes without saying."

Chad admitted he did extra with those women to get a rise out of her. He even wanted payback for what she'd done. He wanted to see if she was really bothered by his actions.

"Wow. You're fucked up."

"I could say the same about you."

"You were that bothered by my actions this morning?"

"Does that mean you were bothered by mine this evening?"

"Hell yes! You come to me, kiss me and put your arm around me. Then, two seconds later, you're all over another woman? I looked like a fool."

Chad remained quiet as he looked at her. She finally understood.

"I get it…and again I'm sorry. It wasn't fair to you."

"I love you, Angelica, and I think about you all the time. You challenge me."

"Well, you certainly challenge the hell out of me!"

"Because I want you to be better than the best and never depend on anyone financially. I challenge your entrepreneurial side, but you challenge my humanity."

"Chad…"

"No, you don't get it. I've never done this for anyone. No one! I'm not pretending with you. Princess magic, the businesses, what's to come…it's real for me. I genuinely want to see you elevated."

"I didn't know that. I thought you did this kind of thing all the time."

"What gave you that idea?"

"Because you just did those things without any hesitation."

"Precisely my point. You're everything I want in a woman— beautiful, smart, business savvy and you fuck me like I fuck you."

"Well, I like fucking you," she said, looking into his eyes. "It's like I can't say no to you."

"I don't care who we end up with. You'll always be my princess. I'll always come for you."

"Don't say that. You can't keep that promise."

"Yes, I can."

"That's not true, but we can pretend."

"We're business partners, and you're making money off me."

"You're making money off me!"

"And not even charging you the premium rate," laughed Chad.

After they laughed, she said, "Thank you for trusting me."

"Thank you for reminding me I'm human."

"I have to be honest…"

"Ok."

"I feel the same way you do."

"How's that?"

"That you're mine, and I don't want to share you. I realized that tonight. I don't want you doing those things for other women. I don't want them feeling the way I do. And I don't want my dick in them either," she said, rubbing on him.

Chad was done talking. They returned to the bedroom where they removed their clothes and Angelica got into bed. Chad went into the closet.

"I'm sending you three million tomorrow."

"Why?"

"It's the last payment from Tom plus a little extra."

"Ok."

Chad came out holding a small black bag. He climbed into bed and held her in his arms.

"Ms. Matthews…"

"Yes, Dear."

"You forgot to put your ring on this evening. Let me help you with that."

Chad pulled a black velvet ring box from the bag. As he opened it and revealed the ring, Angelica let out a scream. He then slid it onto her finger.

"I cannot believe you bought it!" she said, overly excited.

"I saw how you looked at it when Jean Luke took it out of the case."

"But isn't it gorgeous?" she asked, holding out her hand.

"It's beautiful like you."

During their trip to Milan to meet with vendors at Chad's home, Angelica spotted the ring and immediately fell in love. It was a stunning 25-carat diamond engagement ring featuring an 18-carat princess cut solitaire set on two rows of baguette diamonds, all encased in micro pavé diamonds along the band.

"Mr. Matthews, where is your ring?"

"Right here."

Chad pulled out the second ring box from the bag and opened it. Angelica took it out and slid it on his finger. Chad's band matched her ring.

"I love your wedding dress, by the way," he told her, sucking on her breasts.

"Thank you."

Chad was emotionally driven and vulnerable. He pretended Angelica was his wife and kept saying it throughout their lovemaking. And everything he said pierced her soul. Once again, princess magic.

Chapter 58
Sundae Charm

Meanwhile, Claudia arrived at Bronson's and knocked on the door.

"Come in!" he yelled.

When she walked in, she was pleasantly surprised. There were lots more Christmas decorations, along with bouquets of roses everywhere.

"Who did all of this?"

"Bethany."

"Is that why she left?"

"Yes."

Claudia smiled. Then, she walked into the kitchen and said, "Smells good."

"Thanks."

Bronson was near the stove grilling their steaks when Claudia walked up behind him and hugged him. Once he finished, he turned around and hugged her.

"Wow! You look gorgeous."

"Thank you."

Claudia dressed comfortably but freshened up her makeup and curled her hair.

He kissed her on the lips and said, "I hope you're hungry."

Claudia instantly felt butterflies in her stomach from the kiss. She wasn't sure what was happening, but the softness of his lips got her tingly inside.

"So, what's on the menu?" she asked, trying to calm down.

He whipped up some Bourbon-flavored steaks, a veggie stir-fry and a salad.

"Dinner should be ready in ten minutes," he said, handing her a glass of wine.

"Ok."

He placed the steaks in the oven and set the timer. Then, they moved to the living room, where a romantic Christmas atmosphere awaited them. A stunning red and gold sparkling Christmas tree stood in the corner, surrounded by garlands and ornaments hanging from the walls, alongside enormous Nutcracker figures and stockings by the fireplace. Bouquets of red roses adorned every surface, candles flickered softly, and the fireplaces blazed warmly. The curtains were drawn open, allowing the city lights to cast a magical glow through the wall of windows.

"This is amazing!" she told him.

"I'm glad you like it."

"All of this for me?"

"Yes."

Bronson handed her a single red rose.

"Thank you."

"You're welcome."

They sat on the sofa and talked about the bridal shop.

"You looked beautiful in your wedding gown."

"Thank you, Sweetheart."

"He's a lucky guy."

"He is."

"And what did you think of my vows?"

"You said some nice things for fake nuptials."

"It's funny because I could never imagine the woman I'd marry until today."

"Really?"

"Yes. I can see myself marrying you."

"Standing there next to me changed your mind?"

"Yes, but it wasn't just that. It was your smile, the way you looked at me…us holding hands. It felt right and made sense."

"How did I look at you?"

Bronson made funny, googly eyes, making them laugh.

"You know…I don't think I've ever been this open and honest with a woman."

"What do you mean?"

"I let myself be vulnerable with you, which I don't understand."

"Well, I think it's a good thing."

"It is. But I guess it's because you don't have an ulterior motive."

"Yes, I do."

"Oh…you do?"

"Yes."

"And what is that?"

"To get to know you…the real you and not that guy with a bad boy reputation that the world loves to talk about."

"It's easier being that guy than explaining that women just want me for my money."

"Maybe…but maybe that's why women flock to you to begin with. And how do you get away from that stigma when you do meet your wife?"

"She'll know who I really am and trust me. And together, we'll change the world's mind."

"That's a tall order. You're expecting a lot from her."

"She can handle it. I know she can."

"You speak as though you know who she is."

"I do, and I won't stop coming for her until she has my ring on her finger."

The look in his eyes gave Claudia butterflies again.

"How will you propose?" she asked for giggles.

Bronson got on his knees and crawled between her legs. He tore a piece of a magazine page sitting on the table. He folded it into a wedding band and said some kind words. Then, Bronson asked and Claudia said, "Yes!" He slid the paper band on her finger and kissed her. She didn't stop him either. After a few minutes, she stopped him.

"I can't," she whispered.

"I know. I'm sorry."

"Me too."

They got up and fixed themselves. Claudia saw his dick print through his shorts and craved him. He was the total package… height, body and dick. Bronson, on the other hand, excused himself to grab more wine. The truth was that he had to step away to calm down. He was so aroused by just her presence. He didn't want to come across as too eager.

He returned with a glass of wine. However, it spilled all over her when he went to hand it to her.

"Oh my God! I'm sorry," he said.

"It's ok. That was my fault. I wasn't paying attention."

Bronson took her into his bedroom.

"Take those off. I'll wash them."

"Ok."

Bronson went into the bathroom and got her a towel. When he returned, he stared at her body. Her tits looked scrumptious and her ass was tight.

"Quit staring," she said, laughing.

"Can't help it. You are fucking beautiful."

Bronson threw the towel on the bed and laid her down. Her legs were securely wrapped around his torso as they kissed intensely. Her nipples were hard and pushing through her bra. So, he removed her bra and sucked on them. She moaned and groaned as her hips fiercely gyrated. This made Bronson play with her clit. As she got louder, he rubbed faster.

"Bronson, we have to stop."

"Ok."

He continued rubbing her spot.

"I'm about to cum."

"Give it to me, Baby."

"Babe…"

He made her cum.

After, he tasted her and said, "Sweet."

He left her on the bed and went to serve dinner. Claudia came out in one of his T-shirts. They adjourned to the dining room table for dinner.

"Bronson…"

"I know. It can't happen again. You're getting married. You have a fiancé. Did I cover everything?"

"Yes."

"We're good."

Claudia changed the subject and asked about Chasity.

"Now, she's posting that I beat her up."

"What!"

"Yes. She's saying that I cheated on her and she found out. That's why I beat her up."

"That's fucked up. I'm sorry this is happening to you."

He grabbed her hand and thanked her. He appreciated her support.

"So, how about dessert?" he asked.

"What do you have?"

He cleared the table and invited her into the kitchen. She sat on the island as he brought out three different flavored ice creams and plenty of toppings.

"Which one would you like?" he asked.

"Butter Pecan, please. It's my favorite."

"I know. I remember from our first conversation."

She smiled.

"Would you like a sundae?"

"A small one."

As he made her a sundae, he kept putting the cold ice cream scooper on her thigh. Each time, it made her jump. So, she picked up a few sprinkles and tossed them at him. He grabbed some chopped nuts and threw them at her. She grabbed the chocolate syrup and pointed it at his shirt. She threatened to squeeze if he did it again. He made sure he had a big scoop of ice cream and rubbed it on her legs. So, she squirted him with chocolate syrup.

"Oh…you're gonna pay for that," he told her, taking off his shirt.

His body was perfectly sculpted with hard abs and a well-defined V.

She took off running as he chased her with caramel syrup. She didn't think he'd squeeze it, but he did. She took off her shirt and ran around in her bra and panties. She grabbed the strawberry syrup and whipped cream and shot it at him. They ran around the kitchen squirting syrup and whipped cream at one another. That was until he trapped her against the wall.

"You give up?" he asked close to her face.

"Never."

"I can keep…"

She leaned in and kissed him.

In their moment of passion, he picked her up and carried her to the bedroom. As he got naked, Claudia's eyes got big when she saw him hard and at full attention. This time, he wasn't playing games.

"Can I have you?" he whispered as he lay on her.

"Bronson…"

He kissed her before she could answer the question. Bronson unsnapped her bra and kissed her neck. She pressed his head in as her head moved from side to side. He slid down and sucked on her breasts. Her hips moved as his tongue tickled her nipples. He threw caution to the wind and did what he wanted, sliding his tongue down her body until he reached her sweet spot. He ripped off her panties and held onto her as he dove in. Claudia let out a loud sigh as she moaned and groaned. As soon as her breathing got heavy, Bronson sucked harder, making her cum. He tasted all of her sweetness.

He got up and settled between her legs. He positioned his dick to go inside the second she said yes.

"Can I have you?" he whispered, breathing heavily.

"Babe…"

His head slightly slid inside, and he asked again, "Can I have you?"

"Bronson…"

Stay tuned for what happens next in...

The Betting Game 4

www.ingramcontent.com/pod-product-compliance
Lightning Source LLC
Chambersburg PA
CBHW070158120726
47909CB00001B/165